MIM L

MUNDIS VERIDIS
and the end of the world

ink
books

SYDNEY | AUCKLAND

Ink Books
PO Box 1321, Mona Vale NSW 1660
Australia
Telephone: +61 2 9007 5376
PO Box 47212, Ponsonby, Auckland
New Zealand
Telephone: +64 9 416 8400
www.arkhousepress.com
Ink Books is a division of Ark House Press, a division of Media Incorp.

Cataloguing in Publication Data:
Author: Lennon, Mim.
Title: Mundis Veridis and the end of the world / Mim Lennon.
ISBN: 9781921589492 (pbk.)
Dewey Number: A823.4

Printed and bound in Australia
Cover design and layout by Media Incorp
www.mediaincorp.com

Endorsements

Multitudes of books have been written on this vast subject, but as far as I am aware, this book is unique. I remember hearing a speaker say "if you want to know what is important to God, look and see what the Devil is worried about". This anthology of books looks at the past, present and future of the nation of Israel, from the perspective of the one who has the most to lose.

David Silver, Out of Zion Ministries

Mim Lennon's Trilogy, Mundis Veridis and the end of the world, is a series of Christian apologetics novels written in captivating style in defence of the establishment of the Modern State of Israel. Those believing that the Bible teaches a future for Israel will welcome the author's thesis, and enjoy her insightful, racy, easy-to-read, **Lewisian 'Screwtape Letters'- type approach. Highly Recommended reading for all!"

Deane J. Woods, M.A., B.D. (Hons), Th. D. Pastor/Bible Teacher & Conference Speaker.

Dedicated To

He Who Cannot Be Mentioned

And

Is Best Left Alone

With Adoration,

Love And

Absolute Amazement…

Acknowledgements

I would like to thank the Institute of Jewish Studies for their excellent on line learning courses, without these, this book would never have been written.

I would also like to thank Andy for his encouragement and Deane and David for their endorsements and my wonderful husband, Tim for doing all the cooking whilst I researched and wrote this book.

I would also like to thank my darling friends Nettie, Colleen, Christine and Fiona for their sense of humour and input .

Contents

BOOK ONE

INTRODUCTION

"In the beginning God created the heavens and the earth."
Genesis 1:1

G od also created two different kinds of beings, Angels and Men. In the Bible, Angels are referred to as the Sons of God. In this story I will call them higher beings, or higher fallen beings… and in the case of the latter I shall often call them simply green beings.

Men in the Bible are sons of Man, but for this exercise I will call them lesser beings.

"What is man that You are mindful of him,
The son of Man, that You care for him?
You made him a little lower than the heavenly beings,
And crowned him with glory and honour."
Psalm 8:4-5

Angels, or Sons of God, are 'higher' in every sense of the word, spiritually, physically, and intellectually.

And that is why it was such a devastating thing when they turned against God and sinned. For when they sinned there was no chance of repentance; they could not turn back, they were locked in for all eternity.

These spectacular higher beings had been created into such a privileged environment that when they ('they' being a third of the angels) rebelled and followed Lucifer, exalted Music Master in Heaven, they lost their place for all eternity and were relegated to masquerading as 'angels of light or darkness' in the like of their revered and inestimable Boss SATAN…

Their whole purpose being to deceive mankind into following him.

In ages past these higher fallen beings also cohabited with lesser beings and produced children, super human beings who became the Nephilim of old.

It was this particular sin and the wickedness that ensued that caused GOD to send the flood in Noah's time, thus destroying the earth and preserving righteousness through Noah and his line.

Is God going to intervene again in human history? Is He again going to rescue a remnant from the flood of wickedness that threatens to engulf this earth?

"Do not let your hearts be troubled; trust in God, trust also in Me. In my Father's house are many rooms; if it were not so, I would have told you. I am going there to prepare a place for you. And if I go and prepare a place for you, I will come back and take you to be with Me; that you may also be where I am. You know the way to the place where I am going."
John 14:1-4

My story is one that is continuing to happen all around us. Indeed on the non-fiction side it is in every newspaper, on television and radio news broadcasts, internet blog spots and one of the principle discussion points at the United Nations.

It is the story of Israel… present day Israel.

And on the fictional side it is the story of how one little green being/fallen higher being called Mundis Veridis was sent back in time to get the names and numbers of those demons who 'with such lack of insight' allowed the Nation of Israel to be reborn.

Mundis travels from the time of the trial of Alfred Dreyfus in 1894 all the way up to the United Nations vote for the State of Israel in 1947 and the eventual Declaration of Independence in 1948.

In between he encounters Herzl, the Battle of Beersheba, the Balfour Declaration, the British Mandate in Palestine and World War II.

During his adventures he finds much to his amazement, that there is another Power at work.

For this story we will call this power, 'He who cannot be mentioned and is best left alone'.

As Mundis discerns this Power, he discovers that it is far greater than anything he has ever encountered before… at least within his 'selective memory' time frame.

And this Power, dear lesser being, promises in His word that one day He will send His Son back to the nation of Israel to rule and reign as King over the entire Earth and from His capital Jerusalem.

This day will not come until His chosen people the Jews are back in their land, Israel.

"On this day, His feet will stand on the Mount of Olives, east of Jerusalem, and the Mount of Olives will be split in two from east to west, forming a great valley, with half of the mountains moving north and half moving south."
Zechariah 14:4

So, dear lesser being, put aside any prejudice you may have with relation to Israel and look at it through Mundis' eyes, yellow, green and catlike…

Enjoy his escapades, relate to his somewhat marred character traits and rejoice in the fact that you as a lesser being, can indeed repent of such gross misdemeanours, and as a repentant and restored lesser being you can look forward to an eternity with God, whilst the higher fallen beings are destined for the Lake of Fire forever…

Not that Mundis is entirely sure of his destination - although he does have an aversion to flames and water…

The Boss on the other hand, has spent all history trying to escape the inevitable - his punishment for rebelling against 'He who cannot be mentioned and is best left alone' . Hence his fierce and bloody struggle against Israel and the Jewish people and his absolute horror that they are indeed back in the Land.

He knows his time is coming to an end…

Yours Faithfully,
Mim Lennon

PART ONE

"And when it came to pass, when men began to multiply on the face of the earth, and daughters were born unto them, That the sons of God saw the daughters of man that they were fair; and they took them wives of all which they chose. And the Lord said, My Spirit shall not always strive with man, for that he also is flesh: yet his days shall be an hundred and twenty years. There were giants in the earth in those days and also after that when the sons of God came in unto the daughters of men, and they bore children to them. The same became mighty men who were of old, men of renown."
Genesis 6:1-4

"But as the days of Noah were, so shall also the coming of the Son of Man be."
Matthew 24:3-7

"And He said unto them, 'I beheld Satan as Lightning fall from Heaven. Behold, I give unto you power to tread on serpents and scorpions, and over all the power of the enemy: and nothing by any means shall hurt you. Notwithstanding in this rejoice not, that the spirits are subject unto you, but rather rejoice because your names are written in heaven'."
Luke 10:18-20

1

It was a large, round light building set in a remote mountainous area of Australia, difficult to see as planes seldom flew that route and if they did pilots simply attributed the building to a space tracking station.

They were not far wrong.

Surrounded by a steep gorge on one side, dense bush, towering eucalyptus, deep icy cold ponds and beautiful wild flowers in spring, the area really deserved better tenants than it had.

In fact it had been there for eons, century after century, peopled, or rather unpeopled, by demonic beings that had fallen from grace so long ago that they could no longer remember a time when they were not the dreadful beings they had become.

And yet to look at some of them, they were quite lovely, ethereal looking, tall, blonde, magnificent physiques, an utterly beautiful people… at least these are the ones you would have seen had you been unfortunate enough to stumble across them.

There were others who worked far underground, small greenish beings who did the processing work, helped by reptilian-like creatures who were the dogsbody help around the place.

As you entered the building you were struck by an enormous florescent light work that boasted the different words attributed to the word 'light' - inscribed in Latin, Ancient Greek, Hebrew, Phoenician, Ancient Egyptian and other such languages, and in the left hand corner, as you looked at it was written the word 'Lucifer', Angel of Light.

Lucifer was the CEO of this organisation. Seldom seen but nevertheless eternally present and busy, he roamed from one end of the earth to the other, watching, acting and carrying out his Machiavellian purposes.

Sometimes he called in, but mostly he just used his iPhone to connect with Headquarters. An iPhone that was the latest in technology and yet had its conception many thousands of years ago.

The small greenish beings were busy today in the computer room, pulling up their latest piece of demonic file.

Mundis Veridis, the head librarian, was in a foul mood. His greenish skin giving off a horribly unpleasant odour, a regular occurrence when his latest demonic strategy had been discovered by those detestable beings called humans that had an understanding of 'He who cannot be mentioned and is best left alone' and His true purpose on earth.

"We thought we had this nailed," he screamed. "This was one of our last pitches, I'm not sure we are ready for the final throw."

"Oh, yes we are," came a horribly seductive voice through a loudspeaker system, every 's' a lingering hiss. "This pitch is ushering in our final one world plan."

"This plan entails all the church has stood for throughout the centuries, we got it all. Candles, icons, meditation, all-inclusive thinking, an abundance of wafers, tolerant strategies. Ah yes, my Emergent Church is my masterpiece, my *piece de resistance*, bringing together all that a mature, wide-thinking community will embrace, ah yes.

"We will incorporate it everywhere," the voice continued. "Places of worship, Disneyland, all fun parks, every television show, all movies. It is truly marvelous stuff, we will bring in every leader the world respects, everything will be touched...and as for those eternal nuisances who think they know everything, well, they won't be around for long, we don't need to worry about them."

Mundis Veridis shrugged and agreed - who was he to argue with Lucifer? Mundis was just a small greenish being who had fallen so long ago he had forgotten he had ever had another Master.

"Okay," he said, and uploaded a file called emergent church, which went immediately into the minds of every religious, agnostic and atheistic human being on the planet.

Except for those eternal nuisances who wore a ridiculous out of date armour covered by an aura that gave off a blood-like smell, repulsive and a repellent to any demon worth his salt.

These eternal nuisances also carried a sword that spewed forth words that had razor-like edges; these people were untouchable and unreachable. They were also utterly broken and completely humble; sure they messed up (some more than others) but they had this horrible habit called repentance - and 'He who cannot be mentioned and is best left alone' seemed to have an undying love for them, forgave them and restored them.

From somewhere in Mundis Veridis' deepest darkest place, a tiny sad sigh escaped.

Post Script

Mundis Veridis, when not in the computer room uploading files, was often sent on missions abroad, a part of the job he thoroughly enjoyed.

In fact his outings had increased dramatically in the last 150 years, so much so that he no longer sang that popular song *Don't get around much anymore,* instead whistling themes from well known movies and television shows.

Mundis' favourite visiting places were university grounds and college corridors, parking lots under tall city buildings, shopping malls, school playgrounds, Catholic and Anglican Churches - or any religious establishment really. He also had a penchant for all-night coffee lounges in large hospitals, where he loved to appear before highly educated doctors, and the rooms of lawyers and barristers and accountants offices in upmarket firms throughout the world's major capitals.

Ah yes, Mundis Veridis never sang, *Don't get around much anymore.*

2

The university town was quiet now; the summer break had started and most students had gone home. The beautiful college was resplendent in its emptiness, the flowers blooming in a profusion of vivid colour and the fountain in the centre playing for no one.

Except a small greenish being that strolled serenely along the outer pavement, whistling the tune from *Star Wars* and looking up at the windows above him.

He was dressed in green corduroy pants, a shirt with bow tie and sporting a pair of brown Oxford brogues of which he was very proud; every now and again he would stop and admire them and clean them on the back of his pants. He was also wearing an academic gown; in the back pocket of his pants he had some tobacco and in the top pocket of his shirt, a pipe.

"Mmm," mused Mundis, "he should be in, I know he has taken these rooms for the summer whilst his are being refurbished, I'll just surprise him with a visit…"

The little green figure disappeared through the walls of the building and ascended the stairs without his feet touching any of them. Coming to an old oak door he glided inside, helped himself to a gin and tonic and took up residence in a large comfortable leather chair, his short green legs sticking out in front of him.

Darlington Somerset the vicar of St Michaels, the Anglican church in the High Street, took the stairs two at a time. He'd had a dreadful morning arguing with the choirmaster and was sorely in need of a drink.

Bursting into the room and heading straight for the decanter, the vicar stopped short as he noted it was half-empty and devoid of stopper. Darlington turned to observe his visitor.

"Oh, it's you! Honestly, can't you at least put the stopper back in…and I was not aware that aliens drank, especially to the extent that you do. I hope you don't have to fly anywhere soon, I doubt you'd be able to see the controls…oh, and nice brogues - are they all the rage where you come from?"

No…but they certainly are where you come from, giggled Mundis to himself. He snorted; alcohol had no effect on him, it just served to make his disguise a little more plausible. He burped for effect, grinned and lifted his glass in salutation.

Darlington sank into the opposite chair and took a large swig of gin and tonic, smiling at his green friend. He settled in for a nice long chat; it had been many months since he had seen Mundis and he had missed him.

"Awful row with the choir master, totally uncooperative with the songs, refuses to delete any mention of blood, says it's pivotal to the Christian faith - absolute hogwash," Darlington said, exasperated.

"Honestly, I mean, how would he know, was he there? I mean was he there two thousand years ago? Personally old chap I am becoming more and more convinced that the Christ or whoever he says he was, really just fainted and was then revived and taken to India. I mean, I spent hours with this guru in Goa who has evidence that he, Jesus was there."

Mundis hiccupped and closed his eyes. "Absolutely ol' boy, couldn't agree more…anymore of that fabulous gin?"

Darlington sighed, poured him another drink and settled in to tell the rest of the story.

By the time Mundis left an hour later, Darlington's brain was so scrambled that the CEO personally congratulated Mundis on a job well done.

3

Matthew sat on the floor at the back of the church, his whole being exhausted and aching as a result of his argument with Darlington.

It was totally useless, what on earth was he doing here? The tension had been well nigh unbearable and the choir was definitely beginning to pick it up.

Matthew was crying - something he hadn't done in years - and praying softly. Matthew loved the Lord and obeyed Him in all things, but this assignment had taken almost all he had and he truly did not think he could go on any more.

"How much longer Lord, how much longer do I have to stay here and fight this out?"

Matthew smiled, for immediately into his mind came the words of a song that was popular years ago... *won't you staaay just a little bit longer... please please staaay just a little more*.

"Okay, you win, we have been here before Lord, and I know that it is no use going until you say so, but you are going to have to help me here, 'cos this vicar is wrong and he's leading his congregation completely astray."

Matthew smiled again as the last verse of Jonah sprang to mind. Matthew knew the Lord was telling him that he had many people in this church who truly loved Him and who needed protection; that He was concerned about them, and that at the right time He would move and all would be put right...but it would be in His time and not Matthew's.

Matthew picked himself up from the floor, flipped open his phone and called his grandmother.

"Gran, you doing anything, feel like a visit?"

Mundis, hanging upside down from the choir stalls, grimaced and hoped with every ounce of his horrible green smelly being that the CEO hadn't picked up *that* phone call.

4

Sometimes Mundis simply dispersed his ghastly green particles and reappeared on the other side of the world, but that involved calling headquarters and explaining where he needed to go. After his disappointment in the choir stalls he decided to keep quiet and hitch a ride.

Being prayed against was an exhausting experience.

Heathrow was teaming with travellers. Mundis threaded his way through the crowd and slipped past customs and into the first class lounge of a very new and smart airline, belonging to a people that seventy years ago would hardly have known what a plane was, let alone having flown in one.

Mundis waited for the boarding call, not because he had to, but because the power of Matt's granny's prayers were having such an effect on him that he could hardly put one foot in front of the other.

When the time eventually came he stumbled into first class, settled into a lounge chair and went straight to sleep. He did not even feel a very heavy gentleman sit on top of him.

Mundis slept the entire way to New York, only waking when the intercom system announced the approach and the seat belt sign went on, not that he needed to heed either.

Slightly refreshed by his sleep, he again slipped through customs and caught the roof of a taxi - he needed to feel the wind in his face as sitting underneath that enormous bottom on the plane had stifled him somewhat - to the United Nations building where he was to meet an important delegate from Headquarters.

The place was absolutely teeming with invisible extra-terrestrial life, each one waiting for their assigned human to arrive. Mundis' human was a woman new to her United Nations position, and quite overwhelmed by the whole experience.

Mundis positioned himself alongside her and managed to manoeuvre her next to a very nice elderly looking man from the

States who smiled, engaged her in conversation and then offered to buy her a coffee. With a nervous laugh, the woman accepted. *Good,* thought Mundis, *we certainly need to distract this one, her support of Israel is totally unacceptable and whatever she was going to say doesn't need to be said.*

Mundis and his fellow green being exchanged glances and excreted a fine smelling perfume just to add to the atmosphere.

What Mundis hadn't reckoned on was the absolute integrity of the woman and the work she did. Esther was the representative of a large international Charity and the CEO of her organisation. She was intelligent and kind and was no fool when it came to supporting Israel.

Whilst not a believer in 'Him who cannot be mentioned and is best left alone', Esther was the granddaughter of a Holocaust survivor who knew the Tannach and had bought his precious Esther up to know and love Yahweh.

The handsome elderly man from the States was soon thanked and left. Mundis and his counterpart drooped with disappointment, invisibly shrank and disappeared into a light fitting, turning off their mobiles as they did so; they wanted no unwelcome calls from their CEO.

So far Mundis was not having a successful assignment. The light fitting was warm and cosy and he certainly intended to stay there for the foreseeable future.

Matt and his granny and her cronies were still praying.

5

The place was dark, all meetings over. Mundis descended slowly from the ceiling, landed on his head, turned himself upright and padded toward the door. He slipped through and out into the night, the warm New York air blowing across his smooth green skin.

He was still wearing his university dress and his academic gown billowed out behind him, but he'd left the Oxford Brogues on the plane...drat and double drat.

If he had hair, that would have been blowing too, but the less said about this the better, he was very sensitive about his baldness.

He had that horrible sickening feeling in the pit of his stomach, he somehow just knew that Esther had spoken well and that his mission had been completely sabotaged. Turning his mobile on, he was not surprised to see at least 15 missed calls, all from Headquarters.

Mundis sighed and toyed with the idea of throwing the phone into the Hudson River, waste of time really, he would only be issued with another more updated one, possibly with a high speed tracking device and a web cam.

No, Mundis would hang on to his Nokia without the attachments.

The small green being wandered down the pavement looking for a coffee shop that was still open and a chance to relax and read the messages and listen to the voicemail - not that he wanted to. It was no easy feat being a small green being with evil intentions when there were larger beings with good intentions that delighted to serve and honour 'Him who cannot be mentioned and is absolutely best left alone'.

And having been curled up in a light fitting had left him with a crick in what used to be his neck.

Maybe he would slip into a movie house and watch a good Sci-Fi film; he had many friends who had been given bit parts in these and he was always amused and delighted with their success.

Just then his mobile rang. Mundis looked down and decided it was better to answer now than to keep putting it off.

The usual seductiveness of the voice was absent and a cold chill went through Mundis' being as the voice demanded to know where Mundis had been during the offensive meeting at the UN. Mundis mumbled something about light fittings and good views.

This was not met with approval.

Mundis was duly reprimanded and sentenced to three weeks in a Pentecostal church somewhere in a small coastal town in Australia.

Phaaaaaaa, thought Mundis, *small time evil, no challenge there.* He could see it now, an arrogant Pastor and his overdressed, well-intentioned bossy wife. They didn't need Mundis, they would be doing fine all by themselves.

Yep…there would be endless boring prayer meetings that revolved around the church, and 'Seeker Friendly Services' complete with coffee, fluff and a chance to meet the leadership team.

Mundis thoroughly enjoyed meeting leadership teams; in fact he loved them, especially if they didn't have a strong belief in the Boss and his followers. There was no end to the damage he could do if ignorance reigned, and happily for Mundis, ignorance often reigned.

In fact Mundis knew 'Ignorance' well. He was a despicable little light green fellow who ran around telling everybody what he didn't know but thought he did - not a great favourite with Mundis, but tolerated because he did a great job.

He was beginning to feel a little bit better already, not a lot but a little.

6

The town was small and built around a bay, the church on assignment a squat weatherboard building surrounded by a few wild lavender bushes and decorative rocks. There was a small car park to one side and an enclosed children's playground.

Mundis kicked one of the decorative rocks in anger as he walked past, but didn't feel anything as his feet were encased in a pair of very sturdy riding boots. He was also wearing a striped shirt and a pair of jeans and sporting a stockman's hat. He certainly looked Australian, well European Australian if one is to be politically correct.

Mundis walked straight through the wall and sat down by the pulpit where he struck a pose that looked very similar to Rodin's *Thinker,* a green Rodin's *Thinker,* except he didn't have a deep thoughtful expression, he had a very angry, rude, sulky one...nasty, spoilt little green being that he is.

Phew, he said again, *honestly, it wasn't that bad a disaster... she only quoted a few Scriptures that no one cared about and talked about the importance of daycare centres and women's refuges in Israel, so who cared, no one in that gathering. And that retort she made to that other Middle Eastern woman only raised a few interested eyebrows, and was lost on everyone else in the crowd.*

Mundis continued to sulk and to think about his strategy.

To be or not to be, this is the question - invisible demon or visible alien?

Mundis would have to observe the group and work out their movements. The leadership was always the focal point, no use aiming at a wannabe, they didn't hold any sway and were usually pretty lame ducks.

Yep, let's go for the jugular, any church is a bad church even if it is a terribly weak church. Mundis' assignment was to get rid of this one quickly, not really because it was a threat but just because it was there.

So he'd hang round, observing and plan his moves. Yep... observe, move and strike, all from behind this movable potted palm.

Arranging himself carefully behind the plant, Mundis stretched out and settled down to sleep. He was just drifting off when his eye caught something truly horrific.

Mundis sat bolt upright, eyes wide open and heart beating rapidly. A cold sweat broke out on his forehead and he began to turn a lighter shade of green.

It can't be, honestly perhaps I need contacts. Mundis peered again and got up and pattered over to the offensive banner.

It was what he thought it was, A BLUE STAR embroidered on a white background, an extremely blue and white STAR.

Mundis felt ill. He had underestimated this church, he was hoping for a quick close down, an affair between the Pastor and the worship leader, regardless of what sex they were - opposite, the same, no matter these days.

 (Mundis organised affairs well and usually had a one hundred percent success rate, I could tell you how he did it but that would be giving his game away, and I am just telling this story and I am meant to be discreet about some things.)

He certainly hadn't bargained on the Star of David, a disgusting display.

Utterly deflated, Mundis sank to the floor, and lay there with his arms over his head. *I am finished, vanquished before I have even started...*

He was a dramatic chap.

His mobile rang, and wearily he picked it up.

"Mundis Veridis speaking."

"And what is this assignment looking like?" came a powerful and accusatory voice.

Mundis swallowed hard. "I have it under control sir, just working out my strategy now."

"Good," said the voice, "do you need reinforcements?"

"Aaaaaahh, not at the moment sir, but I will call if I do."

"Good," said the voice, "keep in touch Mundis."

The line went dead.

Mundis was now almost white with horror. The Star meant more than just a banner; it meant truth, righteousness, and a high level of integrity, especially when seen in a church.

Mundis had better have a very good plan for bringing this place down.

Feeling utterly undone, Mundis crept back to the potted palm and went to sleep. When in doubt,

SLLLLLLEEEEEEEPPPPPPP.

7

Mundis was awoken two days later by a horrible noise. It was Saturday morning and the sound of the "Hatikva" was reverberating in his ears. He opened one eye and quickly closed it again.

It was bad, very bad.

The entire church was almost full and there was not one Star of David banner but at least twenty, plus other brightly coloured flags and worship banners. Hands were in the air and a group of young girls were doing Israeli dancing.

Truly the sight was abysmal.

Mundis sank down in shock. The Boss must be totally ignorant of this, for if he had known he would not have sent Mundis here alone.

Mundis was too proud to ask for help; he would have to fight it out.

Feebly he got to his feet, took a deep breath and surveyed the situation. There had to be a weak link somewhere.

Mundis scanned the crowd, realising he needed to see it from a higher perspective, so to speak. He floated up to the rafters and hanging by his riding boots from one of them, he could see the entire width and breadth of the congregation.

Repulsive, it looked like pure joy everywhere, phwew.

But wait; was there one disgruntled face in the crowd?

Ahh yes, down there by the loos, and there was another standing right next to her.

Okay, let's work with them.

The meeting ended and Mundis followed Edith and Graeme Dihard home.

8

Edith and Graeme Dihard were pillars of the church, or at least they had been. Unfortunately there had been some renovations and the pillars were no longer needed.

They could have been incorporated into the new structure but they were rather unbending pillars and not used to taking any place other than 'up front and noticed'.

Edith and Graeme were elders of the New Gospel Church. Edith and Graeme had been elders for a very long time, almost as long as Mundis had been an alien - well almost.

Something had happened at New Gospel, something so strange that Edith and Graeme and a dozen dissatisfied others were still spinning. Their trusted pastor and friend had been given a magazine called *ISRAEL, MY GLORY,* they had unfortunately read it, done the online courses and suddenly without warning had changed tack.

This stable predictable, sound man of God had become a fanatic for Israel and the Jewish people and for End Times Eschatology.

At least that is how it looked to the Dihards.

That did not mean he no longer saw the Church as fulfilling its role on Earth, he simply understood that God had a plan and a purpose for both Israel and the Church and that they were different but with the same eventual ending, reunited with Him.

This precious man of God studied history and discovered that many of the church fathers had been very anti-Semitic. He was surprised to read that the Council of Nicaea in 325 AD was the time when Easter was formally introduced and the Church no longer followed the Jewish Calendar. So therefore Easter and Passover were separated unless by chance they happened to fall on the same date. And unfortunately Easter was named after a pagan goddess 'Eostre' hardly an enlightening name to commemorate the sacrifice of God's Son on the cross, the Mighty God of Abraham, Isaac and Jacob.

He also read about the Jewish people under the Roman Emperor Theodosius 11, and how it was that during this time they as a race were legally condemned and formally set apart, all at the bequest of the young Church that ironically enough preached love for their fellow man, but only if their fellow man was exactly like it. A Jewish spiritual apartheid was begun that has successfully lasted throughout the ages.

Sad really when 'He who cannot be mentioned and is best left alone' had chosen the Jewish people to bring salvation to a lost and hurting world; indeed this is exactly how salvation entered our world...through the Jews and in a Manger.

This salvation was the fulfillment of prophetic words throughout the Old Testament, watched and waited for and recognised by some but not all.

His preaching reflected his understanding and his love for both the Church and Israel and the fact that 'He who cannot be mentioned and is best left alone' is faithful to His covenants, both old and new, and how we as redeemed lesser beings should rejoice in this.

This however did not register with the Dihards - they didn't like change or the Old Covenant, far too long and boring and that was all there was to it.

The Dihards also didn't really believe in the Boss and his tactics. All that red suited Devil stuff left them most unimpressed, and in not believing in him, they were a 'Boss send' to Mundis and his assignment.

There are none so blind as those who will not see or 'cannot see', as Mundis liked to point out, and of course it is indeed difficult to see when one has made one's mind up not to see...

Mundis smiled his pointy green-toothed smile and rubbed his nasty little green hands together.

Edith and Graeme and the dozen other dissatisfied people were flummoxed.

"I mean didn't the man read the papers, couldn't he see how the Israelis treated the Palestinians?"

Also didn't this poor deluded Pastor realise that Israel was finished and that the Church was the New Israel?

And didn't he know that we weren't going anywhere and the rapture was just a myth and the Second Coming of Christ was a nice thought but way off in the distance and really not worth thinking about, let alone talking about?

I mean honestly, didn't everyone know that?

And worse still, it made them feel very uncomfortable because it meant that they were possibly not in control of their own destinies… and that in itself was certainly not something they were going to put up with.

Horrified, they watched as church member after church member embraced this teaching. Stunned, they watched as their once grounded and solid Pastor organised a solidarity trip to Israel, taking with him half the church and the entire worship team.

Edith and Graeme were invited but chose to remain behind; the bowling final was on and they didn't want to miss it, well that was their excuse and they were sticking to it. Plus, they liked to be on hand to mind the grandchildren, feed the dog, clean the parrot's cage and water the roses.

A great weight fell from Mundis' shoulders. Phew, here were some members he could work with, here was some trouble he could stir, ah yes, here was a Church split waiting to happen.

Now if he could engineer that, then there was no need to tell the CEO about the Star of David and other things, he could just text 'Church split' and no one would be any the wiser. *Church split* wasn't as good as *Church fini* but it was attainment and not to be shirked at. Especially if the words, "Very unpleasant Church split" were sent.

Yes, definitely worth a mention at the annual green being Prize Giving. Mundis had won a number of awards and was really quite a well-known recipient at Prize Giving.

(He was certainly the best dressed; oh, but you should have seen what he wore last year, his fashionable attire assuring he had made it into both the *Daily Demonic* and *Devogue*.)

Yep, things were looking up, better and better; the scowl on Edith's face was positively radiant and the hard-done-by air that Graeme carried was truly marvelous, and all their disgruntled dozen had picked it up beautifully.

Here was a happy group of wingers if ever Mundis had seen a group.

All that was needed was a few demonic whispers in the right ear…

"He said…she said," all that sort of thing and there'd be a split, and Mundis would get to leave this demon-forsaken place and go home…

Just like ET.

9

On second thoughts, what about visible Alien? Mundis' yellow-green eyes had almost grown round with excitement.

Yes. He would message Headquarters, get them to send in a perfect circle of a spacecraft with extra large burner jets and then he would appear to the Dihards and friends and initiate them into alien craftology with all the frills.

Mundis knew he could nothing with the other crowd, they were lost to him, but the Dihard crowd were possibles… *yes, yes, easy prey.*

Mundis started to practice his moon walk, and to hum his favourite alien tune.

Edith and Graeme's house was surrounded by 149 acres of paddocks. There was nothing they loved more than to stroll through their land, check the dams and the creek and generally enjoy the great outdoors.

Mundis loved to stroll as well, check the dams and the creek and generally enjoy the great outdoors.

Mundis manouevred his craft to just north of the creek, making sure as he landed heavily with all gas burners going that the ground beneath was well and truly scorched. Once he was certain, he lifted off again and disappeared into thin air.

"Good heavens," exclaimed Edith as she climbed to the top of a small hill, "what on earth is that?"

"Blessed if I know," said Graeme, as he surveyed his burnt land; it was a perfect circle, about four metres in diameter.

Mundis watched from a hole in the gum tree. He was jammed up in a cockatoo's nest and the babies delighted in pecking at his skin. Mundis kicked hard and the babies bit harder; there was much pushing and shoving and eventually at just the right time, Mundis fell and ended up at Graeme and Edith's feet.

Stunned, the Dihards stared at Mundis as Mundis pretended

to stare back at them. He then rose to his feet, bowed and said majestically, "Mundis Veridis," then allowed a great big tear to roll down his green cheek.

He was looking particularly fetching in a skin-tight luminous green suit with added cape and hood plus a hologram of his head embroidered on the left hand side of the chest for identification purposes in case he was ever found 'dead'. He was also sporting a very nice pair of space boots with velcro fastenings... most authentic.

Edith and Graeme had seen *ET* when they were courting and could not believe their luck - just imagine it had happened to them! Although Mundis felt he was a little better dressed than *ET*.

After the initial introductions they were more than happy to take Mundis home for tea and cake. Mundis accepted with pleasure and accompanied them home over the hills, holding both their hands as they went; a most endearing picture.

Mission all but accomplished, without much more ado.

Mundis succeeded in completely brainwashing the Dihards and the Disgruntled Dozen.

Mundis put on a wonderful show. He sat on their best sofa drinking his tea and eating his lemon teacake, tidily, with his little legs not touching the ground. He even asked for more cake and said please very politely with a slight lisp, which had them in raptures for weeks afterwards.

The up-shot was that they all left the Church and Mundis got to return home, after sending a text that read, *Very unpleasant Church split*.

This was not completely true as to be honest the members of the New Gospel Church were very relieved to be rid of all the Dihards and the Disgruntled Dozen.

As for Mundis Veridis, he streaked across the evening sky in his small spacecraft whistling the tune *Imagine*.

'He who cannot be mentioned and is best left alone' smiled; another job well done and He had not had to use any of His Host to do it.

10

Home was in sight; Mundis could see it through the trees like an emerald glistening in the last rays of the sun. Mundis sighed with happiness; he enjoyed travelling but there was nothing better than coming home, especially when the boss was away and everything was relatively peaceful.

Mundis began his descent, skimming the tops of the gum trees now, the hangar was in sight and his very own reptile valet, Hornback, was waiting for him outside so he could park the craft.

Mundis could see him leaning up against the hangar door smoking a cigarette.

Mundis slowed down and came to a hover and hopped out.

"Evening sir," said Hornback, treading on the stub of his cigarette with his hard claw-like foot without even squeaking.

"Greetings Hornback, how goes it?" replied Mundis.

"Quiet sir, peace talks in the Middle East again, shall I hang the craft Sir?"

Mundis gave him the keys and Hornback squashed himself into the driver's seat, his tail standing up behind him, and flew off down to the garages. The craft would then be serviced, cleaned and generally gotten ready for the next batch of alien sightings.

Mundis wandered through the labyrinth that was his home, calling greetings to various green beings and reptiles. The latter were shedding and there was mess everywhere, scales, bits of claws and egg fragments.

It was also breeding season and the workers were slacking off.

Honestly, wouldn't happen if the Boss was home, mused Mundis.

He eventually found his way to his own apartment. Even though it was deep underground it still managed to have a ceiling-to-floor glass wall. Headquarters, whilst built in the mountains, was set into the side of a magnificent gorge, and the windows were deep-set and expansive.

Mundis smiled, here was his room with the last rays of the afternoon sun streaming in and turning the whole atmosphere yellow-gold, there were his books and paintings, there was his bunny rug all neatly folded over the back of his arm chair, there was his decanter of gin and his bottle of tonic, with his lemon sliced just the way he liked it.

There were his beautiful Persian rugs in wonderful intricate patterns, interwoven with Australian floral designs. Amazing sprigs of wattle, flannel flowers and gumnut blossoms all done in beautiful pinks and greens and yellows, the effect when you walked into the room was truly breathtaking and Mundis never tired of coming home.

Mundis had called ahead and Hornback had prepared his room.

"Bliss," sighed Mundis, and moon-walked over to the chair.

Just then, his phone rang and the strains of *We All Live in a Yellow Submarine* shattered the peace.

"Mundis speaking."

"Veridis," the voice was cold, tired and strained. "Veridis, I never admit defeat, and we are not defeated."

"No sir," stammered Mundis, "course not."

There was always much hissing when the Boss spoke and it was difficult to understand him. Mundis strained into the receiver, gripping the handset with both hands as the voice continued.

"I want to know Veridis how Israel ever managed to become a nation again. We wiped it off the face of the earth approximately 2000 years ago, wiped our hands clean, and moved on, yet the Jews continue to exist and we are faced with the problem again."

"Mmm," mumbled Mundis.

"We had even managed to change its name from Israel to Palestine, and *STILL* we are beset with the nuisance of it...."

"Tsk tsk," tsked Mundis.

"We strive and we strive to have done with it, and still it remains, for years it has blotted the face of my kingdom, for years we have battled."

"Honestly, it is a jolly nuisance," grumbled Mundis, not that he cared two hoots about Israel or what happened to it...but if anything could get the Boss' knickers in a knot it was that small country.

"There are demons out there Veridis who have not done their job, whose lack of insight and sensitivity has seriously hindered my plans. I want names and numbers, Veridis."

The voice became colder, and Mundis broke out into a sweat, the smell he exuded was most unpleasant. When the Boss' voice became cold, Mundis really began to listen.

"Check your data Veridis, tell me who is responsible for this debacle, *who Veridis, did not see Israel coming back and squash it when there was time?*

"Heads will roll Veridis, and yours is no exception."

"Yes sir," and the line went dead.

Mundis fingered his fat little green neck and poured himself a very strong gin and tonic, threw in a lemon and plenty of ice, and headed for his computer, his recent rendition of the moonwalk quickly forgotten.

Mundis sat down and grimaced, took a gulp of his drink and waited while his computer booted up and then Googled,

WHAT HIDEOUS AND EARTH SHATTERING EVENTS LED UP TO THE REBIRTH OF MODERN DAY ISRAEL?

It was a long Google but there is nothing that a demonically inspired computer Google cannot answer...

PART TWO

"What is man that you are mindful of him?
The son of man that you care for him?
You made him a little lower than the heavenly beings
And crowned him with glory and honour."
Psalm 8: 4-5.

"The LORD had said the Abram, Leave your country, your people
and your father's household and go to the Land that I will show
you. I will make you into a great nation and I will bless you: I will
make your name great, and you will be a blessing. I will bless those
who bless you and whoever curses you I will curse; and all the
peoples on earth will be blessed through you."
Genesis 12:1-3

"He shall cause them that come of Jacob to take root: Israel shall
blossom and bud, and fill the face of the world with fruit."
Isaiah 27:6

1

What came up surprised Mundis, it was a name he had never heard of.

Alfred Dreyfus, 1859-1935.
Religion: Jewish, *(well that was some clue)*
Incarcerated on Devils Island for treason, 1894 (wonderful place,
Devils Island, much sought-after leisure place for world-weary
Green Beings/aliens)
Exonerated in 1899.
Died in Paris in 1935 after being admitted back into the army.
Buried with full military honours.

So, thought Mundis, *What about him?*
The phone rang again.

"Veridis, if you think you are going to work out the whys and wherefores of Israel by just sitting there reading stuff and drinking then think again….go back Veridis, go back to Dreyfus' time and work out why he is a link, and what piece of a complete waste of time of a green being could have seen ahead and done a better job.

"And Veridis I do not need to tell you that you will be travelling under cover, this assignment is top secret, you are the only demon on this job. Apart from my Trusted Transfer Department I do not need others knowing my innermost thoughts, and having said that Mundis I do want you to know that you *are completely dispensable if this doesn't work out.*"

Mundis did a double sigh; going back was exhausting work, going back meant the Transfer Department and telling them about the assignment, although presumably they already knew.

"DRAT AND DOUBLE DRAT."

No, Mundis did not like the Transfer Department, load of good-for-nothing scaly, bumpy reptiles on cushy pay and no action. Mundis was also a very private being and he didn't like his assignments being known to any but himself and the Boss.

He liked to be to left to his own wicked devices and not told where to go and what to do. Yes, Mundis was a secretive character and one that moved with expert stealth and timing.

Mundis was truly poetry in motion.

Going back also meant reassembling his particles and transferring them to an earlier era and hoping they all arrived at the same time, a bit like travellers in airports with their luggage; it was hit and miss and therefore a jolly nuisance.

Mundis stood up, finished his drink and grimaced, left his comfortable library desk and went in search of the hated Transfer Department.

The Department was four floors down and along a spacious corridor accessible via a large air-conditioned lift. It was situated behind a waterfall; Mundis could see the water cascading down the side of the gorge through the huge panes of soundproof glass that made up the wall.

The room was well furnished with pale green sofas with loose fitting covers, magnificent yellow and green rugs, vases of purple and yellow irises and original Monet paintings of waterlilies.

A most beautiful sight.

A number of green beings were waiting for the doors to open in the various transfer booths, and were exchanging talk about where they were going, Mundis listened with envy - all were doing things more interesting than he, or so he felt.

As I have mentioned already, Mundis did not give two hoots about Israel, and why he had to work out the problem was totally beyond him, thank you very much.

Mundis stepped up to the desk and explained to the reptile in charge of his impending mission. Yep, it was as he had thought, they knew all about it and acted as though they had the upper hand already.

How Mundis loathed them.

He was told to take a seat and he would be called when his number was up.

As has already been stated, going back in time was quite a performance. Going forward was easier and simply transferring countries was a snack - just a matter of reassembling particles and moving them to the desired location…like moving house but easier and no cost involved, except of course if you had been discovered and were being prayed against. Now that was a real problem, slowed you up, exhausted you and generally made life very uncomfortable, like a gluten intolerant person having eaten wheat, all bloated and vague…

Mundis was gluten intolerant and generally prayer intolerant too.

Mundis waited, leafing through a magazine called *Extra Terrestrial Home and Garden,* which featured many photos of the stunning ethereal beings who had been sent out on assignment and were even now re-populating the world and generally causing a stir with regard to their extraordinary beauty. Mundis knew some of them personally; they were a snooty otty lot and thought they were a step above little green beings.

No matter, when they were in trouble they called pretty quickly.

"Veridis Mundis," called the reptile.

Mundis stepped up and gave his number and was pointed toward a booth, whose doors open automatically as he approached, and the sound of elevator music surrounded him.

Wagner's *The Ride of the Valkyries* bellowed forth and generally set the mood for transfer. A sort of a body and spirit shaking mood; Mundis didn't have a soul.

Mundis sat down on the heavily padded seat, strapped up and waited for the transformation to begin. There was plenty to look at while he waited; the walls were plastered with advertisements for upcoming *Opera Green Being Productions.*

2

Mundis arrived in Paris. It was 1894. He arrived head first and without his feet - they had arrived in Lille and were being sent directly by train.

Mundis sat by the river Seine and waited; as he was invisible he was not too embarrassed, although some rude green beings did walk by and snigger.

Mundis punched their names and numbers into his phone and vowed to report them later.

Mundis loved the Seine, such a pretty river, and from where he was sitting he could see Notre Dame, one of his favourite churches. The gargoyles depicted on the magnificent structure were favoured friends of Mundis and often joined him for drinks and canapés back home. Such good times, such good friends.

So where to now?

Mundis texted headquarters.

An email came through his iPhone. Mundis had had to upgrade his phone for this assignment so had left his favoured Nokia at home in his desk drawer and was just getting used to this advanced piece of equipment.

The reptile at the transfer desk had passed the details of his journey back to another librarian who was sending him details of the Dreyfus case as they became available. Mundis hated this sort of interference, middle men and such.

His new-fangled gadget beeped. Mundis read, *Proceed to court martial at Military headquarters, verdict of Dreyfus trail being given today.*

He was then issued with a detailed how-to-get-there email by googling whereisit.com.

Fortunately his legs arrived; they had walked all by themselves from Gare de Nord, arguing all the way, the right leg wanted to go sight-seeing whilst the left felt that getting back to Mundis was imperative. Happily the left leg won and Mundis was therefore able to set out directly.

Dressed in a top coat, stripey trousers and a bowler hat, Mundis looked a little like a green Toulouse-Lautrec, for he was about the same height, perhaps a little smaller...well, perhaps a lot smaller but as this was something he was very sensitive about, the less said the better.

Following the instructions, Mundis found himself in a room with French army personnel. There was a hushed atmosphere in the room and Mundis became aware of a tall, pale, upright young soldier dressed in full uniform standing in the dock. He was in his mid-thirties with dark circles under his red-rimmed eyes.

As well as the pale young man in the uniform and the other lesser beings also dressed in uniform, there were hundreds of Mundis' acquaintances present - green beings draped all over the room, hanging from the light fittings, seated next to officials, perched on the back of chairs and generally just lounging about. Mundis could see that they were doing a very good job; why the Boss would want their names and numbers was beyond him, the atmosphere positively spewed hate and venom.

Mundis did not have much of a heart, he was always very focused on his work and himself, but something stirred within him when he saw the young man, some half-forgotten memory of eons past. Maybe it had a name, maybe it was called 'pity'; Mundis couldn't quite remember, it was too long ago and the past for Mundis had always been a bit hazy.

The odds were against Dreyfus. The young man had no chance at all; there were some pretty influential green beings in this room, some of them quite senior and very close to the Top.

Mundis was overawed to be in such highly favoured company, although to be fair he was no light-weight himself, an expert in technology and languages and generally pretty well thought of and always a favourite with the Boss.

"Guilty," read the officer in charge. "Guilty of treason against France, guilty of handing artillery information to Germany, to be stripped of all military honours and sentenced to life imprisonment on Devils Island."

The young man gulped and swallowed, his hands clenched together, but he remained standing and upright, staring straight ahead, his eyes hardly blinking. Dreyfus had always been thought of as haughty; whilst not a virtue, it did in this case stand him in good stead, as he was able to control his emotions and appear as though he had all under control.

To some however it was a confirmation of his guilt.

In reality Dreyfus was only just coming to terms with the fierce spirit of anti-Semitism that was running rampant through France. Perplexed and amazed by it all, he was most of all saddened when he thought of the pain his parents had gone through in order to assimilate into French society.

What good had it done him or them? He was a disgrace to both his race and religion; who but his closest friends and relatives would believe that he was innocent?

The prisoner was then led away to a private room where he was left alone. On the table in front of him was a loaded revolver; Dreyfus did not flinch, whatever they thought of him he was not a coward. By killing himself he would be proclaiming his guilt, and that was something he would never do. He remained seated, his hands clenched and his eyes staring at an unseen point on the wall.

Mundis could only look on with some disgruntled respect; he knew what he would have done with the loaded revolver. He leaned forward with some interest to note the expression on the face of Dreyfus' personal demon but to his absolute amazement could not see him. The room was empty apart from Mundis and Dreyfus.

Mundis hung from the light fitting and continued to watch as an armed soldier escorted a tired looking young woman with sad eyes into the room. She was dressed in black and carried a satchel full of papers. He watched as the young couple who, were not allowed to touch, bade a sad and agonising farewell.

"Mon cheri," sobbed the woman, "my letter to you will arrive before you do. Take your quinine, it will help against the mosquitoes, and for my part I know you are innocent. We have friends, mon cheri, we have Emile Zola and others who are proclaiming your innocence to all France. Courage, mon cheri, courage."

She could say no more, her tears made talking impossible and Dreyfus was struck dumb with grief.

"Time," called another armed guard and with one agonising look back, Dreyfus left his sobbing wife behind.

3

Mundis followed him. Not that he wanted to. He wanted to visit Paris, see the sights, taste the wine, meet the other green beings.

Mundis had no interest in whether Dreyfus was guilty or not, nor could he care; his vague feeling of pity had long since dispersed.

Mundis boarded the ironclad battleship that would transport Dreyfus to Devils Island. He carried a baguette, a block of cheese and a bottle of wine in a little wicker basket with a checked cover over the top (a gift from a female green being admirer; he wasn't going to starve or die of thirst) and a very sulky expression.

Dreyfus was chained and put into solitary confinement. Mundis went in with him and sat hunched in the corner of the dank, hot and musty cabin.

The young man was given some gruel and water, and left alone. Mundis ate parts of his baguette and drank some of his wine, and nibbled at his cheese; don't ask how Dreyfus couldn't smell it…I don't know why, but he couldn't.

The creaking of the ship and the water lapping up against the side, added to the strange and eerie feel. Mundis longed for his apartment back in Headquarters and the attention of his personal reptile, Hornback.

Honestly couldn't someone else have been found for this dreary job?

Mundis could not understand where the other demon was, the one who should have been watching Dreyfus. No matter, he, Mundis, would wait it out, there was no other choice…and when he did turn up Mundis would let him have it.

YES! And just to emphasise the point he barred his nasty little green pointed teeth and clenched his horrible little hands.

Yes…he would blame the entire rise of Israel on this unfortunate culprit, and then heads would roll - the culprit's for a start.

And Mundis could go home! The very thought brought peace to his spirit.

Dreyfus sat and stared into space, occasionally muttering to himself and whispering the name Lucie. A twenty first century psychiatrist would have diagnosed traumatic stress, but this was the nineteenth century and Sigmund Freud was a long way away in Vienna and could be of no help to the embattled and wounded Dreyfus. Although he almost certainly would have heard about the case and wondered at the anti-Semitism that was raging through Europe.

Little would he have guessed at the state of Europe in a short forty-six years later, and how it would affect him and his family, and for that matter Dreyfus' as well.

For now Dreyfus would have to rely on his integrity and strength of character. He was totally unaware of a higher hand guiding his life - as such fanciful imaginings did not become a man of the military.

Fortunately his wife Lucie was an observant Jew who did pray and whose own strength of character would get her through more than just 'The Dreyfus Affair' as it was being called. Indeed it would see her through the horrors of the Second World War, when she again would be a mainstay of strength to her family.

The ship started to move. Mundis continued to sit hunched in the corner watching the young man. This was boring work, but this was his assignment and he was in no position to leave now; checking and re-checking his emails and texts and partaking sparingly of his bread, cheese and wine was all that he could do to distract him from the job at hand.

As Mundis' eyes became accustomed to the gloom, he could make out a being on the other side of the cabin, a being whose form became brighter and brighter as he watched. Amazing coloured shafts of light enveloped Dreyfus and moved continually around, above and beneath him as he sat upright on the bench, immovable in his grief and horror.

This being had a familiar feel to Mundis, an unpleasant feel that brought back more half-forgotten memories and an uneasy feeling of regret.

Dreyfus however began to relax and eventually dropped off to sleep, this could only be attributed to the presence of the light shaft, or complete and sheer exhaustion, depending on your perspective. Mundis was not going to tell Headquarters about the light shaft, so in lieu of anything better to do he too curled up and went to sleep, none too comfortably but nevertheless no one was going anywhere, so why stay awake.

The journey took days and Mundis was relieved to get 'there'. The continual movement of the ship, the cold and the dampness of the cabin had a negative effect on all who entered, and Mundis' presence was no help in this respect.

In fact he was fast cursing the Boss and this assignment, although cursing the Boss was a complete waste of time. Mundis was a cog in the wheel and orders were what he followed.

'There' turned out to be nothing wonderful; Mundis had read *Papillon* by Henri Charriere so he certainly was not expecting much.

The fact that many who met Mundis thought of him as just a small green being was an example of their own ignorance. The fact that many thought he was 'just like us' but maybe a bit more intelligent was another ridiculous misconception...

No alien is ever 'just like us'.

Mundis had an IQ that far exceeded the smartest human being on earth, and he spoke every known and unknown language fluently. He had passed the entrance exam for every major university in the world, Harvard, Yale, Oxford, Cambridge and every university in China and Europe, not once but at least once every couple of years. It was mandatory discipline for those who lived and worked in Headquarters and were Green.

However, like many incredibly smart human beings, Mundis lacked emotional intelligence and was horribly nàive when it came to judging character. He was therefore easily impressed with the wrong sort of created beings, Angels or lesser beings.

He may have picked up basic emotions but he had no idea what to do with them or how to reach out and help, nor had he any desire to do so; there was one being in Mundis' life and that was Mundis.

This of course had been his downfall, but he had, (as has been already mentioned,) fallen so long ago, that he could not remember doing it, falling that is, and he was so myopic that he could not see past himself to see his downfall.

4

No matter, small talk aside, for now we concentrate on Devils Island and we need to imagine the sounds and sights and smells that must have met Dreyfus as he stepped off the ship, his eyes smarting in the brightness of the midday sun and his entire body bowing to the relentless heat that would have swirled around him.

His uniform hung from him, its crispness long gone but the pride with which he had worn it remained.

Dreyfus was a man condemned to a living death but he was a man who knew he was innocent and in this he remained upright and unbowed.

Unceremoniously unloaded from the ironclad ship onto a small patrol boat and then taken to the prisoner offloading dock, Dreyfus' first glimpse of his 'forever' home would have been a glaring heat haze, blue water, tall elongated palm trees, piles of brown oyster-clad rocks, all beautiful in their own way but foreign and offensive to a sophisticated European soul.

One day it would be an Island Paradise, but that would be many years later, when cruise ships with rich western tourists would tramp the island for historical reasons. For now it was a penal colony with pinky coloured buildings dotting the landscape, palm trees and mosquitoes - a living hell for those unfortunate enough to be sent there.

Very few that were sent to Devils Island survived. A place that in nineteenth century reality was so dreadful that only those with the most enduring of characters would live to make it back to France - or anywhere for that matter - and they would pay for the experience for the rest of their lives.

Dreyfus was no exception. His health was ruined forever by this time of captivity, but his spirit was strengthened as 'He who cannot be mentioned and is best left alone' watched over him and guarded his precious life.

But for now it is the year 1894, and Dreyfus was being taken to his cell. After being incarcerated for many days he could hardly walk, so the bright shafts of light steadied his feet.

Mundis trotted behind them, glancing around and hoping to find a place that sold refreshments and food.

A pub, a Burger King, a Starbucks, anything! He was not fussy and he was very hungry as the baguette, cheese and wine had been consumed eons ago.

Mundis had forgotten he was back in time and the afore mention conveniences were yet to be invented, he had forgotten he was not in the twenty first century when everything was on tap for those who could afford to pay.

Mundis kicked a lesser being in frustration and again cursed the Boss and his infernal desire to get even with whoever or whatever had messed up his plans with respect to keeping Israel off the map.

Still handcuffed, Dreyfus entered the pink brick building. He and the Shaft of Light that accompanied him were led through the corridors and down sharp stairs to a cell with an iron door. Not that anyone could have said that the Shaft of Light could be led anywhere, it simply cascaded around Dreyfus and moved as he did. Beautiful showers of never-ending colours moving in every direction but never leaving Dreyfus.

The door was opened and Dreyfus was led inside. A window high up in the wall let in the only natural light and the bars that covered it were rusty with age and sea salt erosion. It was altogether a miserable sight and Mundis sincerely hoped it was one that he, Mundis, did not have to endure for too long. Mundis was not known for his ability to endure anything much.

Dreyfus was left alone with only the shaft of light and Mundis for company, although he could see neither. The young man put his hands to his head as best he could whilst sobbing softly and rocking backwards and forwards.

Mundis shook his head in wonder and for the hundredth time wondered, *What has Dreyfus to do with Israel?*

In desperation he sent a text asking the exact same question, the reply coming back almost immediately (iPhones transcended time and space with ease):

Updated information: Dreyfus there for four years, but will be exonerated and re-admitted to army, Israel connection with a Viennese Journalist called Theodore Herzl, responsible for covering the Dreyfus affair.

The text read on:

Herzl now calling for Jewish state as a result of anti-Semitic persecution re. Dreyfus. You are called to stalk this Herzl and find out what you can re; demons responsible for allowing him to continue…

We hear that suicide may have been an option for Dreyfus and if so what demon was there with Dreyfus and why had he not acted when Dreyfus was left with the loaded revolver?

Mundis texted back:

Shafts of light all around Dreyfus, no green being could get near him, couldn't see Shafts then but certainly can now.

Mundis did not like to add that he was feeling the presence of 'He who cannot be mentioned and is best left alone' and it was making him sick to his stomach and vaguely guilty as well as regretful - but guilty and regretful about what he could not remember.

There was no reply to that text. The Reptile at headquarters knew when to leave well enough alone.

Both the Reptile and Mundis hoped the Boss would not find out. The Boss was not good at coping with that sort of news, the sort that has anything to do with 'He who cannot be mentioned and is best left alone'.

This was the Boss's world and any interference from light shafts or any other strange phenomenon was always met with uncontrollable rage.

5

With the introduction of Theodore Herzl, Mundis' assignment with Dreyfus was over, and no one was more pleased than Mundis.

"I'm outta here," he yelled, disappearing through the solid stone walls and out into the midday sun without even a backward glance.

Phew, he was glad that was over; what a tedious job. Mundis was still none the wiser but apparently this Theodore Herzl was on the mark, and may lead him closer to the culprits responsible for the Israel debacle.

Mundis rested in the top of a large palm tree and waited to be transferred back to wherever this Herzl was. Transference across time within the same era was an easy business and all it took was one phone call back to Headquarters and a wait until your number came up and the rest was history, so to speak. Mundis made the call.

The selfish little demon had already lost interest in Dreyfus, not that he'd had much to begin with. The vague feeling of pity had evaporated some time ago and he couldn't have cared less about Dreyfus's four more years in prison.

Mundis was also glad to be out of ' He who cannot be mentioned and is best left alone's' presence and away from that infuriating Light Shaft; the never-ending blend of colours and the constant movement had given him a blinding headache. And now being out in the midday sun was really beginning to play havoc with his eyes.

Mundis wished he'd bought his Armani sunglasses and his hat, towel, swimmers and lotion. He did go such a lovely dark green colour when tanned.

No matter, his number would be called soon and he would hopefully end up somewhere more interesting and more productive so to speak, in relation to Israel, that is.

Not that he really cared two hoots about Israel.

"Israel be blowed and double blowed," was Mundis' attitude.

And who on earth put it where it was in any case, mighty silly place to put it, right in the middle of everything and just where everybody else wanted to be and a jolly nuisance to boot...

Mundis however had no wish to lose his head; growing another took time and effort and he liked the one he had, it had been with him for so long now he had forgotten he had ever had others.

So with respect to the above thoughts on Israel, he thought best to keep them to himself.

Just then his phone beeped. *Transfer in 60 seconds.*

Mundis braced for the jolt but when it came it was more like a soft pulling in a North Easterly direction with a forward slant, a slightly uncomfortable sensation but nothing like last time. He was aware of the change in climate, the tropics disappeared and the air, instead of being muggy and damp was clear, cool and pleasant.

It was August 1897.

6

Mundis found himself in Vienna. He arrived altogether this time to the smell of apple strudel and beer. He was just near St Stephens on a Friday night and the square around the Cathedral was busy. There was a wonderful sense of relief in the air, the week was now over and the two day holiday about to begin.

It was bliss, after the harshness of the tropics, bliss to be back in sophisticated civilization. Mundis rested in a plush little café, eating the apple strudel and drinking the beer and watching life pass by. The fashions were so elegant and the colours a feast to his gloom-accustomed eyes.

Mundis, whilst lacking in empathy was not lacking in sensitivity to atmosphere. He could sense any number of different moods and hone in on them to his advantage for his victim's demise or betrayal.

In this particular case he did sense he was in the wrong place even though it was immeasurably pleasant and so as to confirm exactly where he was meant to be, he texted headquarters.

No clear sense of direction here, where do I find Herzl?

The answer came back, *The Jewish quarter.*

Of course Herzl was Jewish, he would hardly be interested in the Dreyfus case had he not been.

Now to uncover the mischief that is Israel, to spur the lazy demon in charge of Herzl into action and to finish this tedious job and to get back to his gin and tonic. Too much time spent wallowing around in the past when there was so much fun to be had in the present.

He thought of the Dihards and fun he had enjoyed leading them a merry dance. Truly there is nothing that gives satisfaction like stupid humans, especially stupid religious ones…ah, more bliss!

Mundis' eyes had taken on a faraway gleam, and his apple strudel fork remained halfway to his mouth. Ah yes, the Dihards were deliciously stupid, Edith especially; she thought she knew everything and was the absolute leader in that household. He would text her soon just to remind her that he was still around and that what had happened was 'real'.

Edith would call a meeting about that text and forge her own religion, it would be called something along the lines of the 'Church for the Integration of Mundi Philosophy and the Bible' or CIMPB, shortened to IMP.

Mundis would suggest they set up a website and recruit international members; it was a good money spinner. In fact for the initial joining fee you would be sent your very own treckie suit, made to measure in the appropriate green colour complete with an embroidered monogram of Mundis' head, or perhaps a hologram for added effect.

How Mundis longed to see Edith and Graeme in their tight-fitting Treckie suits.

There would be a regular blog spot and the 'Word according to Mundis' would be a favourite, and 'Mundis' word for the day/month/ year' section would have pride of place, to be read like a horoscope.

There would be a place where you could **'Donate now'** thru Paypal and a Facebook-type set-up which would enable paid up members to chat and share stories, possibly even a singles site.

There would be '*ONLINE LEARNING*', fully accredited courses. Exactly what and with whom they were accredited with would remain one of those elusive type mysteries, bit like the course really...there and yet not really there.

Actually, a bit like Mundis.

And what you actually finished with was nobody's business... because nobody in their right mind could possibly work it out, and as Mundis planned that nobody who did the course would ever be in their right mind again ...then really everything was 'roses', as they say in the classics.

They would be run by people like Darlington Somerset, BA of Theology for Ministry, Cam. University & IMP. CERT - renowned vicar of noted English established Church and noted complete idiot.

Mundis began to giggle uncontrollably at this last thought.

At this point in time he realised what an amazing century the Twenty First was for deception, it was soooo easy and soooo much fun. Sure, the 1800's had their pros and cons but in the 'all and all' scheme of things the Twenty First was a corker.

Mundis would message Headquarters pronto and get them to assign personal demons to every paying and prospective member. Ah this was huge, there was no end to what he could organise…

Mundis got up from the table laughing and wandered outside. He was enjoying the thought of Edith's church and website so much that he did not see a horse and cart coming straight for him; it sent him scattering in a thousand different directions. It took quite awhile for him to pull himself together after that.

7

'Jewish quarter in Vienna' Mundis googled whereisit.com and punched in the required area. Fortunately it was just a pleasant stroll to the left of the Cathedral. Cobbled streets, soft lamplights, all were a feast to the senses.

Mundis so enjoyed the walk he wished he had some pleasant company to spend it with. He had not enjoyed a good chat for quite some time - in fact he had not really spoken to anyone since leaving Headquarters, no counting the silly middle reptile on the end of the phone.

The days spent in Dreyfus' cell had left him a little cramped and perhaps a little low in spirits. No mind, things were certainly looking up in Vienna.

When Mundis reached the Jewish quarter, all was quiet and the atmosphere was one of reverence. He had forgotten it was Shabbat, not that he cared; religious festivals meant nothing to him and if given half a chance he ruined any festival that he was fortunate enough to be involved in.

He arrived at the house and walked in, straight through the closed front door. To the left there was a room with another closed door; Mundis could hear voices, one deep and a second higher more melodious one. He listened and entered.

The room was a well furnished study complete with a marvelous array of leather bound books. Mundis eyed them greedily and planned to steal a few before returning to Headquarters (they would go beautifully in his private quarters and would be the envy of whoever came to visit). There was also a large mahogany desk, beautiful deep green velvet curtains and a small fire.

Mundis, as I have already mentioned elsewhere, had an aversion to fires. He did not know why, they just gave him an uncomfortable sort of close feeling - lakes had that effect on him too. Perhaps he would benefit from reading Freud - repression and all that stuff - no matter, he had a job to do and he would do it well.

Seated at the desk was a man in a dark suit with a very full beard. The woman standing next to him was older than he and was resting her arm upon his shoulder.

"Theodor, it is the Sabbath, do you not think you can finish out your writing and come join us for the Shabbat meal?"

"Mamma, I cannot, the first Zionist conference is to be held in Basel this coming week, I am to present my ideas to Jews all over the world! Mamma you saw for yourself the diabolical treatment of Dreyfus, and he still languishes in prison. We are not safe Mamma, my heart tells me we need our own homeland again, it is time, I have a burning within me Mamma and I cannot ignore it."

The woman patted his arm and agreed; she would support him, "Heaven knows Theodor's wife was no help, an uneven tempered woman who had terrible bouts of melancholy, no she was no help to Theodor at all."

Mundis felt sick, really sick. So this was where it really all began, this man was the reason for the Modern state of Israel. So where was his personal demon, what was the demon's excuse?

Mundis looked around, nothing and nobody to be seen. He checked the bookcases, behind the curtains, the woodpile, and the light fittings, always a favourite place of his own, but t'was all to no avail, the room was clean of all demonic activity.

Honestly, do I have to do everything myself, he sighed.

Mundis took a menacing step toward Herzl hands clenched teeth barred and *suddenly* fell backwards, knocking himself out on the arm of a very heavy chair.

8

When he came to the room was dark and empty and the fire dead - in fact it was not even smoking.

Mundis pulled himself up and went to find Herzl, dizzy and nauseous, but he had a job to do and do it he would.

His eyes and face took on a fierce warrior look; again he clenched his fists and gritted his sharp little teeth and strode forth with purpose and death in every step.

The bottom storey was deserted, the rooms cold and lifeless. Mundis floated up the stairs. He checked every room and found not one sign of Herzl, or anyone else for that matter. Mundis was alone in the house and he did not like the feeling.

Where is everyone, I could not have been out for that long. Mundis checked his iPhone and gasped; he had 'been out' for just under two days.

Mundis broke out in a cold sweat and hoped that headquarters was not aware that he had been unconscious for so long, there was to be no foul up in this assignment and no excuses.

Mundis's heart was beating wildly, he checked his iPhone, there were no calls and no texts…it was impossible, how was it that he was so lucky?

But where was Herzl? Mundis tried desperately to remember the last conversation he had heard…something about a conference in something beginning with B? What begins with B?

Mundis' head ached and his eyes swam. Feeling rather unsteady on his feet, he longed for his own room with the beautiful view and the careful attention of his own private Reptile, Hornback, and thought again for the umpteenth time how unfair it was that he was unable to travel with a valet.

Honestly, when the Boss travelled he took an entourage of hundreds, they milled around him like flies round a decaying corpse - not that Mundis would use that analogy within the Boss' hearing.

Mundis could not contact Headquarters and ask them for help. He did not want them to know where he had been for the last two days, so he would have to nut this one out himself.

B…B…B something to do with a herb - Mundis could smell it, in fact he liked it with pasta, but what was it? And where was it?

BBBBB. Mundis sank into a chair and put his head into his hands.

He could see that little restaurant in Venice, he could smell the pasta, he could taste the wine, he could see the delightful green being he was having dinner with, but where was the BBBBB.

"Basel," he screamed… "no, sounds like Basel."

Mundis checked his iPhone internet and googled in 'Basil, city in Europe' and it came back, *do you mean Basel*. The sweat was dropping from him and he gave a huge sigh of relief, the smell in the room was overpoweringly bad, but as he was alone it really didn't matter.

Not that Mundis cared when he wasn't alone.

Basel. Now how to get there; he could not call for a Transfer, he could not get a spacecraft, he would have to get there himself. And with this headache it was not going to be easy.

9

Mundis floated out the door and down the road, swaying a bit as he went. His head hurt something awful. The railway station, the only form of reliable transport, would be out dated and slow. Mundis longed for Heathrow or Charles de Gaulle or JFK; he longed for a first class lounge and a Pims with cucumber and ice in a long glass with a straw.

Ah, there was the station, ornate and overcrowded. No matter, he would go and his reward would be worth it, perhaps an all expenses paid trip to Hawaii or Tahiti. No, he was sick of the tropics, perhaps a skiing holiday in Verbier.

Mundis was an excellent skier and had recently taken up snow boarding. Ah, just the thought of that holiday kept him going…new ski gear, anti-fog goggles, hand warmers and toe warmers, what a dashing sight he would cut on the slopes. Perhaps that delightful little green creature he had not seen since Venice may like to join him?

Fantasies aside, there was a job to do. Gliding his way through the crowd to the departure board he read, "twenty four hours to Innsbruck and change there for Basel." Mundis groaned and floated on board. He found the first class carriage, a nice red velvet one with dark wood paneling, set his iPhone alarm for twenty three and a half hours, curled up in the luggage racks, closed his eyes and slept.

The alarm sounded and Mundis stirred and stretched. *Innsbruck, and now change to Basel.* Fortunately he travelled light; putting his back pack on he floated down from the racks and just missed a woman in a huge crinoline dress who was taking up most of the carriage.

Mundis moved past her and into the corridor, passing through the crowds like a little green knife through soft butter.

Mundis found the Innsbruck departure board and was deciphering the timetable when his phone rang.

He checked the caller and his heart sank; it was the Boss.

"Veridis, where are you?"

"Innsbruck, Sir."

"Innsbruck?" came the spine-chilling hiss. "Innsbruck!"

"Yes sir, I am tracking Herzl, and there was a miscommunication and a slight delay. I am on my way to Basel now sir, to deal with Herzl's personal demon, and if necessary sir, I will take over myself."

The line went dead. Mundis did not know it, but forward in the 21st century, Hezbollah had just attacked Israel and the Boss was needed in Southern Lebanon, masterminding tunnel patrol and weapon distribution.

Sometimes the Boss was very hands on indeed.

Mundis knew nothing about Hezbollah, but simply thanked his lucky stars that the connection had been lost, as he strongly doubted that the Boss would have believed the miscommunication story.

Innsbruck to Basel, another 24 hours. Mundis drooped, but being the essentially lazy little demon he was, he was looking forward to dinner and another sleep.

1Ø

The train arrived at six the next morning. Mundis did not enjoy early mornings; his eyes were all puffy and he was feeling decidedly de-hydrated after the bottle of wine he had drunk the night before.

In fact he had not slept well at all and was hoping to get some breakfast en route. Sadly the kitchen had closed and Mundis would have to find a café or restaurant that was open instead.

Mundis strolled along the pavement outside the station looking for somewhere to eat. Once his appetite was satisfied, he would then try and discover where Herzl might be. Again he dared not ask Headquarters, as he did not want them to know how far behind he was; he would just have to ferret it out himself.

Breakfast was consumed and now for eavesdropping and trying to piece some information together. Now where to go? Where did he visit last time he was in Vienna?

The Jewish quarter! Ah yes, the Jewish quarter in Basel.

Mundis sniffed it out - he didn't know how he found it, but he did - and when he got there it was just a matter of hanging round, literally, and picking up where Herzl would be meeting.

Mundis seated himself at the marketplace and waited. The place was not busy although there were a few women around. Mundis spotted one who had a 'look' about her; his heightened intelligence could piece together situations and people well. Ah yes, perhaps she was the local Rabbi's wife. Mundis followed her home.

Rachel was not the local Rabbi's wife, she was his daughter, and he, the Rabbi was sick and lying in bed. Mundis perched on the bed head and listened intently, stealing delicacies from the Rabbi's plate and generally making himself at home.

Mundis waited all day; the Rabbi was very sick and kept going to sleep. Mundis was very impatient and kept waking him.

"Papa, please eat something, the doctor will return tomorrow after the meeting and then we shall get more attention for you."

"Meeting, Rachel? I would not have my people involved in this meeting. Israel will not live in the land again until Messiah comes - and Rachel, in case you have not noticed, He is not here, and child I have no reason to believe He is coming soon. This is unnecessary fuss, what that this Herzl fellow wants everyone to pack up and move to Palestine! What would we do there, no strudel, no mountains, no snow…No Rachel, this is my home, I am an old sick man and I will not go to Palestine and I will not encourage my people to go either."

"Papa, please do not fuss, it will be over tonight and all will be normal again."

Tonight, Mundis felt ill, *tonight, tonight, sooooo where was this meeting?*

Mundis did not have to wait long for the answer, as the Rabbi continued, "Rachel, it is a disgrace that my people, or some of them, would be going to the Municipal Casino, what are they doing there?"

Mundis did not wait to hear the answer. He bolted right through the roof and floated as fast as he could to the main centre of town; surely he would be able to find a map or something that would help.

It was now late afternoon and Mundis had wasted a whole day. What if it was over, what if the damage was done, what if the demons, who were responsible, had all gone home and Mundis had missed the opportunity to harass and harangue them, get their numbers and send his report back to headquarters?

Mundis was now a pale shade of green and the smell he was exuding was horrific. He looked frantically around and his eyes fell on a local paper. He scanned the front page, nothing! He scanned the second and was rewarded for his diligence…

'Mr Theodore Herzl of Vienna will host tonight in the Concert Hall of the Basel Municipal Casino the last meeting to finalise the goals of Zionism.'

Mundis collapsed in an exhausted heap. *Tonight, it was tonight, I have not missed it completely, my head will not roll and I will not have to grow another and I will be snowboarding in Verbier this winter, ah bliss.*

Mundis picked himself up and whistled the first few lines of

Tonight Tonight won't be just any night and moon-walked in sheer relief.

Now where to find it, that would be easy, some grand looking place in the centre of town. *Shall I dress for it,* Mundis mused, *white tie and tails? No I won't bother, I will be invisible and who will care, 'tis hardly like I am back at Headquarters and it is the annual Demon and Alien dinner dance. No-one will know I am there apart from the unfortunates that I will be speaking with...*

11

Mundis relented and procured for himself formal attire. As well as being extremely intelligent and lazy he was also very vain and the thought of arriving underdressed was more than he could cope with. *I mean to say,* he thought, *this was Europe, not some island in the Atlantic that boasted absolutely no style at all - this was sophistication with all the stops pulled out.* Such elegance he had seen whilst procuring his outfit.

Mundis had discovered that Herzl was staying at the The Three Kings and had taken a room there himself. He shared it with some Jews from Germany who were disappointed that the Congress had not been held in Munich. The German Rabbis had complained and Basel was chosen instead. Of course the occupants of the room had no idea that Mundis was sharing with them, although one did complain of an awful smell in the bathroom.

Mundis could not do his formal tie up, and was getting most distressed…hence the awful smell.

Time to leave and Mundis and his fellow travellers hired a horse and cab to take them to the venue. Mundis sat between his hosts, his little legs sticking out in front. He admired the view, the mountains were beautiful and the air was warm…ah bliss, Mundis was enjoying this part of the job.

They arrived in plenty of time. Mundis got his iPhone ready to take down names and numbers so that the offending demons could be dealt with in the appropriate manner.

Mundis floated from the carriage and walked up the main staircase. There were some very elegant women in the party, and Mundis admired their dress, beautiful soft colours and gowns that floated from below the bust, princess gowns, oh most becoming.

Mundis entered the meeting room. He looked around,
he looked up and

he looked down,
he looked under the table,
behind the curtains,
in the light fittings,
in the public conveniences,
and back under the tables again.

Mundis Veridis was surprised to find that there was only one demon in the entire place...and that demon was Mundis himself.

Mundis sat down in shock. Where was everyone? Surely these people had resident demons that travelled with them. Surely they would have been on the job, but nothing and no one...again, how in the Boss's world was Mundis going to explain this – that there was no-one to blame.

Mundis looked again. He could see no light shafts, he could feel no presence of 'He who cannot be mentioned', he could feel nothing and no-one except his own beating heart.

Mundis went and helped himself to a glass of wine, in fact he had two very quickly, and then sat down again as his knees felt suddenly very unsteady.

The place was full of lesser beings and there were no higher beings of any description at all...Mundis was aghast.

At that moment Herzl rose to speak. Mundis could only listen in shock.

12

"Ladies and gentlemen, it has been an honour to present our ideas to you this week. We have tried to convey to you the importance of this project and we have not been disappointed with your reaction. You have embraced these ideas and ideals with enthusiasm, and for this we are so very grateful.

Let me go over again exactly what we have spoken about:

1. The promotion by appropriate means of the settlement in Eretz-Israel of Jewish farmers, artisans, and manufacturers.
2. The organisation and uniting of the whole of Jewry by means of appropriate institutions, both local and international, in accordance with the laws of each country.
3. The strengthening and fostering of Jewish national sentiment and national consciousness.
4. Preparatory steps toward obtaining the consent of governments, where necessary, in order to reach the goals of Zionism."

As Herzl spoke Mundis watched in amazement as the words he uttered became living seeds and floated from Herzl lips to the hearts and the minds of the people sitting in the room.

The words then, to Mundis' absolute horror, seemed to germinate! Mundis could see tendrils of small living plants sprouting in the hearts and minds of the people. These plants proceeded to grow and bear fruit.

Mundis soon found himself sitting in a veritable fruit orchard. Where there had been people a few moments ago there were now lemon trees, orange trees, pomegranates and the most amazing display of flowers he had ever seen.

The aroma permeated the entire room, in fact it was so strong Mundis could swear that it was indeed permeating the whole world.

There was a burst of applause and Herzl bowed, raised his glass and toasted the delegates.

Mundis did not raise his glass, he did not toast the delegates, and he certainly did not sing the Hatikva with the rest of the group. He sank lower in his chair and hoped the war in Lebanon went on longer, perhaps forever, and the Boss would never ring him again.

Mundis slunk out of the Casino and followed Herzl home. They were both exhausted.

Mundis curled around the back of Herzl's chair and watched as Herzl wrote in his diary before going to sleep...

"At Basel I founded the Jewish state. If I said this out loud today, I would be answered by universal laughter. Perhaps in five years and certainly in fifty everyone will know it."

Mundis knew he had written the truth, for somewhere in Mundis' selfish demon heart he could still discern truth.

He had seen the truth germinate before his eyes. Mundis knew that 'He who cannot be mentioned' was in charge here and there was no use denying it.

But what could he possibly say to the Boss? The Boss did not see truth, he saw exactly what he wanted to see and it was always his way and no other.

Postscript

'He who cannot be mentioned and is best left alone' smiled. It was the beginning, there was more to come but for now it was the beginning.

His children were coming home. It would not be an easy homecoming and for that His heart would break again and again and again, but they were on their way and no force in Hell or on Earth would stop them.

PART THREE

"And it came to pass, when Joshua was by Jericho, that he lifted up his eyes and looked, and behold, there stood a man over against him with his sword drawn in his hand: and Joshua went unto him, and said unto him, 'Art thou for us or for our adversaries?'

And he said, 'Nay; but as captain of the host of the Lord am I now come'. And Joshua fell on his face to the earth, and did worship, and said unto him, 'What saith my Lord unto his servant?'

And the captain of the Lord's host said unto Joshua, 'Loose thy shoe from thy foot; for the place whereon thou standest is holy'. And Joshua did so."
Joshua 5:13-15

1

Autumn in Switzerland, a wonderful nip in the air, perhaps the first flurries of snow, gluvine and schnapps, ah bliss.

A three hundred and sixty degree twirl,

a toss of his hat,

a little bit of moon walking and he was off.

Mundis, the lazy, vain, egocentric demon/alien felt it was time for a holiday. He had successfully lost Herzl, had last seen him off at the train station in Basel, and even waved a handkerchief as Herzl had left. Then in a rush of blood to the head he decided to take a train to Geneva and then another train up into the mountains to Verbier.

Mundis switched of his iPhone and safely deposited it in the bottom of his backpack. He wanted no Twenty First Century intrusions; in fact he was fast deciding that he wanted no Twenty First Century intrusions for the rest of his existence, which was, as far as he was concerned, forever.

How he was going to achieve this was beyond him, but he was just not going to think about it now; now was for his own enjoyment and he was determined to do just that…enjoy himself. Mundis was a being who lived for the moment.

Mundis was surrounded by spectacular scenery, the tops of the mountains capped in snow and the fir trees around him stretching their boughs toward him on each side of the path as he trudged along. The wild flowers were just finishing, the animals were getting ready for the long winter. Cattle would be housed under the farmhouses and the vibrant greens of the fading year would be replaced by a white blanket of snow that would remain well into next April.

Mundis as always, was dressed correctly for the occasion in lederhosen and a white shirt, and a short jacket complete with brass buttons with tiny flowers imprinted upon them. Add a felt hat and feather, sturdy walking boots and knee length socks and he made quite a picture if you could have seen him…

"I love to go a wandering, along the mountain track,

And as I go I love to sing, my knapsack on my back,

Valderi valdera, valderi valde ra-aa-aa-aa-aa-aah

Valderi valde rah,

With my knapsack on my back…"

Mundis had a good voice; he was a tenor, who had sung in many choirs and usually did a solo. He also had an amazing repertoire of songs; there was nothing he didn't know and couldn't sing. In fact, all in all he was really excellent company, a fun being, and as long as you were not fussy about where you were spending Eternity, then Mundis was definitely the being for you.

There was a marvelous little chalet about halfway up the mountain. Mundis had been there years ahead when he was the resident demon for a Church Camp that regularly used the place, and this was where he headed now.

Mundis' job then had been to disrupt worship, cause discord between the leadership and initiate wrong relationships between guests. Mundis excelled in all these activities.

The parties he had thrown there had included other green beings, disembodied spirits, ghouls and ghosts, and they had been legendary. In fact books had been written about them, so much so that the practice of taking groups there had been completely disbanded.

The premises had been sold to a developer who had paid next to nothing for it on account of it being haunted. The developer had since upgraded it and turned it into just another hotel, but this was all in the future; for now the place was just a beautiful little chalet in the late 1800's.

A marvelous find with wonderful wood paneling through out, complete with thick glass pained windows, it looked a bit like Snow White's cottage in the original Grimm Brothers version. It was also like a little musical house box that Mundis had on the mantelpiece back home at Headquarters. An unwelcome wave of homesickness washed over him. He pushed it to the back of his mind and moved on.

Mundis was generally good at moving on, he was definitely not a being who carried much baggage, emotional or physical.

In fact within no time at all Mundis was enjoying himself immensely, no work to do as the inn was empty. Mundis could sleep all day in the main guest room, bathe in the ensuite (after heating the water which was a real drag), certainly not like a twenty first century ensuite, no bidet, but nevertheless adequate.

He could also generally enjoy the views and walks. There was nothing like going back to a place where you had been very busy before and now you were free and could just holiday. Mundis was his own Being; he loved the sense of freedom and the lack of responsibility that went with it.

The food in the larder and the wine in the cellar were all usable; the village was also not far away and pilfering was something he was quite good at.

Mundis was an excellent cook and mostly reveled in his own company. There were many books to read, and if he were very lucky the Boss really would forget all about him and leave him here in the late 1800's. That would suit him fine; he would just hang round and work his way up to where he had been in the twenty first century and eventually get home that way.

He did miss home and his own personal reptile - there was nothing like home - but if this was his destiny then this would do fine.

And who was Mundis to mess with destiny, just a cog in the wheel,

Just a small green being,

No more,

No less,

No more important than any other small green being.

And he certainly wasn't going to volunteer any information to Headquarters re. Herzl. The entire escapade had been an absolute failure; he had not gotten one name or number because there was not one name or number to get except his own, and that would not do at all.

Mundis opened another bottle of red wine, poured a glass and proceeded to read *A Tale of Two Cities* by Charles Dickens. He was reading it in French, best to read it in French; it really created the right atmosphere.

Mundis had been part of the Revolution; part of his job had been to stir the mob against the Monarchy. He had regularly led stampedes around the Bastille and was considered an absolute must with respect to ferreting out the Aristocracy. In fact it had been Mundis and a group of his compatriots who had identified Louis XVI as he and the Royal Family tried to escape to Austria.

He had also been very well acquainted with Madame Defarge and indeed had since spoken to those who had visited her in her new residence where she was none too comfortable. A very cross, dissatisfied with life and after-life sort of person, she kept asking for more wool and needles, not that Mundis cared what she was about or what she wanted.

Mundis had frequently ridden in the tumbrels, although the jolting of the uneven wheels had given him a headache so he had taken to sitting behind the soldiers on horseback. He didn't like horses, they seemed to have an innate sense of judging character, and they did not like Mundis at all - twitching their tails, shying at all the wrong moments and generally making life an overall unbalanced experience.

The emotions involved in the whole revolution had left him unscathed. He was not interested in anything that did not touch him, and his head was safe. So why worry.

Back to Dickens, Mundis could not understand Sidney Carton's sacrifice.

"'Tis a far, far better thing I do than I have ever done,

'Tis a far, far better rest I go to than I have ever known..."

This was totally beyond Mundis. *And just where did Sidney think he was going, huh?*

Although it did stir something within his dark and misshapen spirit, something that made him feel slightly inadequate and perhaps less than what he had been called to be and maybe slightly uncomfortable about where he was perhaps going...

And where was he, Mundis going? Surely just back to headquarters, eventually.

And just what had he, Mundis, been called to do? This kept eluding him, like a half forgotten dream whose meaning had deep and significant importance but he just couldn't remember the full story in order to piece it together.

And when these more than half forgotten memories stirred again it made him reach for the wine bottle, although in reality alcohol did not deaden the feeling. Alcohol didn't touch him at all, he just liked the taste and the smell and the general feeling of achieving something.

Like drinking the whole bottle.

And then there was something else that was bothering Mundis; when he had been involved in other world-shattering events in ages past, there never seemed to be the extent of opposition that he had experienced with both Dreyfus and Herzl.

There were more than enough demons to go around with most earthly catastrophes. I would have thought Israel was an earth-shattering catastrophe... so where were the ground troops?

Mundis took another sip and pondered this question.

The brooding stillness of the night outside brought up the same feelings and had the same effect on Mundis as the atmosphere surrounding 'He who cannot be mentioned and was best left alone'.

Mundis grimaced and finished the bottle.

Outside the snow fell but inside the room was warm and cosy. Mundis had lit a small fire; he was going against the grain here, but his aversion to fires was overcome by his aversion to cold.....he was singing one of his favourite songs...

"The fire is slowly dying,

And my dear we're still goodbying,

But as long as you love me soooooo

Let it snow, let it snow, let it snow."

He was such a romantic, always falling in love, promising the world and then going off and doing his own thing.

He did have a bit of a reputation as a cad, but an extremely likeable one.

The weather was getting colder and perhaps he should travel south to a warmer climate...but where to?

Mundis put down Dickens and reached for his iPhone. He

googled up a map of the world and studied it.

Mmm, south of Verbier, perhaps it would be best to leave soon. Do I want to get snowed in? I do not, I have no skis, and the slopes here are not groomed.

Mundis didn't do powder, *he* was no powder hound.

No snow board or toboggan, and no really warm winter gear... mmm, but where to go...

He sat and stared at the ceiling, lost in his own thoughts and possible plans, his feet curled up under him and his head to the side, his wine glass empty in his hand as he twiddled the stem around his fingers.

The fire made flickering patterns on the walls and the soft light bathed him in an eerie beauty.

2

Using his phone however had been a mistake. It immediately alerted Headquarters to where he was. Munds had forgotten this small point.

"Drat...!"

If they had been singing anything in headquarters, and they were not renown for their singing, but if they had been singing it would have the Abba hit, "Ring, ring - why don't you give me a call... Ring, ring happiest sound of me all.."

Drat again, they had him...pinned him down, knew where he was and bingo...

Caught like the rat he was...in a trap.

Mundis grimaced and raised his eyes to the ceiling.

"Drat again, I say drat and double drat!"

The strains of "We all live in a yellow submarine" again shattered the peace of Mundis' mountain retreat.

Mundis groaned at his own stupidity; incredibly intelligent as he was, common sense he sometimes lacked. This is not uncommon in people with such superb giftings; they tend to think they have it all, where as in reality they are so myopic they cannot see past themselves and their own needs.

Mundis stood to answer - you didn't speak to the Boss with your feet curled under you and your thoughts all over the place.

"Veridis speaking."

"Ahh, Mundis ol' chap...how goes it? Verbier I see, well hope you have been havin' a restful time."

"Ahhh mmm, ahh yea...maybe Sir."

"Mundis, good news. This latest war against Israel was inconclusive. Can you believe it Mundis, we have not had an inconclusive war against Israel since the Romans sacked Jerusalem in 70AD. Indeed Mundis things are looking up."

"Ooh good sir, pleased to hear it."

"Now Mundis, I think it's time for a little more work... don't you?"

"Yes sir, right away sir."

"How about you google in the next big thing in the Israel story and see what comes up....and then...

"VERIDIS, you can hot tail it to where ever it is and get some names and numbers this time!!! One inconclusive war does not mean I ain't still working...this is my turf and I don't want anymore mess ups...

"Got it Veridis? Someone will pay for their lack of foresight and stupidity and as I have mentioned before Veridis, it may well be you!"

"Mmm, aah yep sir, I hear what you are saying...thank you sir..."

The line went dead and Mundis for all his intelligence went dead too, fell over backwards and lay there with his eyes closed for the best part of two minutes. The strain of dealing with the Boss was too much and Mundis, even having been in the game for centuries, was not up to the Boss's sarcasm.

But the adrenalin was pumping now and lying on the floor was a luxury that was not permitted. He needed to find out where to go next and whose name and number was to be punched in re. 'lack of insight and the Israel debacle'.

Mundis did not hold out much hope. He had not had much luck so far, and he really did feel that there was a bigger picture here and it did not include the Boss or him or anyone else he knew. For that matter, 'He who cannot be mentioned' was coming very strongly to his mind now.

Mundis kept seeing that amazing orchard growing in the Basel casino meeting as Herzl spoke about the aims of Zionism.

How to get it through to the Boss was not going to be easy...in fact put quite simply, it was just not going to *ever* happen...the Boss had one thing in mind and that was complete world domination and no one and nobody was getting in his way.

Mundis wished he was near a good café. What he really needed was a very strong mug of Jamaica Blue black, with no sugar.

He again lamented the fact that he was only a small green being and his intentions, plans, hopes and dreams were nothing when pitted against Larger Beings with other agendas.

Mundis did not have the luxury of even thinking like that, this was supposedly War and in War you just followed orders.

Drat, there was a cellar full of good red waiting to be drunk. Even if he had been thinking of leaving, it simply meant that now he had no chance to drink it. The decision had been taken out of his hands and Mundis did not appreciate that; he liked being his own boss and now he was back following orders again...

Drat and double drat and a whole lot of other bad and naughty words.

3

The dreaded Transfer Station called him before he had a chance to call them. Mundis could picture them lounging around drinking coffee and pushing buttons and giving orders, totally oblivious to their beautiful surroundings and incredibly cushy jobs.

They were a complete waste of space, how he loathed them and if he was honest, which he wasn't, how he envied them at this point in time.

"The Sinai, Veridis, you are going to the Sinai circa World War One, year 1915...

MISSION: locate the Nili group, major players being the Aaronsohn family, and sabotage their plans. They are the group responsible for bringing about the eventual Balfour Declaration, they helped the British with regard to spying against the Germans and the Turks in World War I, and the British in recognition of this and in hoping to further their own war efforts, formulated the Balfour Declaration. In short Veridis, they need to be stopped."

"Great," muttered Mundis, "I wanted warm, not intense heat, I don't like sand and I have absolutely nothing to wear."

"*Hard-to-Please* could have been your middle name Veridis, '*Mundis Hard-to-Please Veridis*'. Your wardrobe is of no importance to us, we will do our best to outfit you and you will arrive as well attired as we can manage. Now do us all a favour and get ready!"

Mundis braced himself for the journey, legs apart, eyes shut and hands clenched. Quick, one last look around the chalet, one last sigh and one last smile, and one last grab at Dickens - he needed something to read.

A sharp tug in a southerly and slightly east direction and a leaning-forward type stance.

The refreshing cold of Switzerland in autumn was left behind for the suffocating heat of the Sinai desert. Mundis could feel it on his green skin, and he could also feel that his legs were spinning out of control in an effort to keep up with him.

"Not again," he sighed.

True enough he landed on the back of a sand dune, totally legless, but fortunately dressed for the occasion. Mundis looked around and wondered if the Transfer Station had got it wrong and sent him to the moon.

Mundis had been to the moon many times. The Annual Demon and Alien Ball was often held there. It was a superb venue for the occasion and one that was keenly anticipated by all. No one ever opted for the sun; it was suggested, but it never passed the vote. Freud could have had a great deal to say about that.

Mundis looked down and was pleased to see that he was wearing a long flowing white outfit with a white veil-type head-dress complete with a band of material around his forehead. He looked like a green Lawrence of Arabia, but not as handsome (but we won't tell him that, being the vain creature that he is).

He waited impatiently for the remainder of his body to arrive, which of course it did, complete with some very sturdy looking Jesus sandals. He also had a bag over his shoulder containing a raw onion and a skin of water, his iPhone and Dickens' Little Dorrit.

"Honestly," he moaned, "do we have to be so authentic? Raw onion, indeed!"

Mundis threw himself down in a heap and proceeded to sulk and feel sorry for all he had left behind. This was one time when moving on wasn't his strongest point. This was a lot warmer place than he had intended moving to; it must be on earth because the moon is not this hot.

The sun was relentless and the heat unbearable. Mundis crawled to a rocky outcrop and positioned himself there until night fall. He was just settling in and even contemplating the raw onion when his phone beeped.

Mundis read the text.

You are in the wrong place Veridis.

Honestly, he muttered internally, *as if it is my fault that I am in the wrong place. I never said I wanted to come in the first place, you sent me here, make up your mind.*

Of course this was not spoken aloud, t'would not be wise. Being headless in the Sinai would be a very great disadvantage.

Change of plan, instead of getting names and numbers of Demons responsible re. Nili group, we have decided to concentrate directly on Balfour Declaration and Battle of Beersheba. Therefore Veridis we need you in two places at once. You are going to have to bring forth your alter ego Veridis; one of you we need in Palestine and the other in London.

We want names and numbers from both places Veridis, names and numbers, this as you know is a sensitive assignment, we need your skills... the 31st of October 1917 was a day when the upcoming re-establishment of Israel as a nation hit us from two directions at once.

Although I must say Veridis, your skills so far have been sadly lacking, the Australians are a tough bunch Veridisssss, very different character traits from the British, very unorthodox, took everyone by surprise really.

We need names and numbers Veridis, names and numbers of those responsible for not stopping one of the last cavalry charges in history and the names and numbers of those allowing the Balfour declaration to be passed.

Veridis, both have devastating results re. Israel, do you copy Veridis?

*Have we made this clear Veridis? **Names and numbers of the unfortunate culprits who with such devastating lack of insight allowed the Australians to push through the Turkish line at Beersheba and liberate Palestine, and the culprits who were not watching their assigned lesser beings in London re. the Balfour Declaration. Do you think, Veridis, that you may be able to do this? Mmm?"***

Mundis could have cried with relief. Their sarcasm was lost on him, he didn't care, although he was a little wary about the word 'cavalry'. Cavalry meant horses, and visions of the French revolution came flooding back.

The text read on.

Position yourself for split and transfer.

Happily, thought Mundis.

Mundis positioned himself, he sat up tall, put on a very soldier-like countenance, arranged his bag neatly in his lap, crossed his legs and waited.

The split was easy. Mundis could change into his alter ego whenever he felt like it; in fact he had more than one ego, he had many. He was actually a very fragmented demon, but for this assignment he only needed to be two Mundi,

so...

The second Mundi simply stepped out of the original Mundi, smiled, bowed and sat down next to himself.

For now we will call them both Mundis, Palestinian Mundis and British Mundis. However they are exactly the same Mundis - selfish, egocentric, highly intelligent, vain, lazy and exceedingly green.

Although they did have different quirks to their characters, and in being different one could bring up the old argument 'genetics or environment' and what is the greater influence?

We shall watch with interest.

Beep Beep. IMPENDING TRANSFER.

A quick adios, a slight bow and they were gone, leaving the desert a cleaner place without them, one Mundis straight to London, and the other to Palestine. However for the purpose of this book and because we cannot split in two, we will go with the Palestinian Mundi, and catch up with the British Mundi later.

Post script

They had two Dickens and two iPhones (best that way, no need for arguments), one water skin and the onion was tossed for.

4

THE ADVENTURES OF PALESTINIAN MUNDIS
c. October 31st, 1917

Again a slightly forward direction and a gentle sort of curve up the Mediterranean coast pointing northwards. Mundis could feel a sea breeze on his face and could almost taste the salt on his lips. He was travelling low down and at quite a gentle speed, and had time to survey the scenery and generally enjoy the experience.

But then to his disappointment, a sharp turn inland, the sea left behind and the heat and the desert returned.

His body was not too dispersed, he could see parts of it travelling alongside his head, limbs and torso twisting and turning and generally having a life outside of his control.

This was a new and interesting sensation.

Mundis did hope that his bag reminded upright; his Dickens was in it and he did not want to lose that, he had just begun *Little Dorrit*... the sweetness of that child would almost be his undoing, but not quite.

He didn't care about his iPhone.

He arrived all together, wearing army fatigues, heavy black boots and a slouch hat, he also had a small rifle slung over his shoulder, but no horse; he would have to borrow someone else's.

Thankfully the bag had arrived too, complete with iPhone, Dickens, water skin and onion. It didn't quite go with the outfit but Mundis would deal with this later.

Mundis had now decided that he really did hate horses. He could smell them from here, the manure, the sweat, the leather of the saddles. He could hear the flies buzzing and stamping of hooves and the swishing of tails as they vainly tried to keep their winged antagonists at bay. He could hear the snorting and the phwwwrrrrring sounds they made with their lips and various different types of whinnyings as well; all in all it made a fearful din and a most dismal picture.

The twang of flat Australian accents, after the relative softness of the different European tones was like a crashing on his eardrums. He shook his head and put his fingers in to block the sound.

Mundis was very sensitive to sound, a classical demon if ever there was one. A true connoisseur of the Arts, he was always in demand back at headquarters with regard to his feelings and opinions on form, style and taste.

In short Mundis was a snob, and felt that the Australians were a lower class bunch descended from convicts and ne'er-do-wells who couldn't make it back in the Old Country.

Silly Mundis, there is nothing as pathetic as a creature who is so puffed up with himself that he is unable to see and appreciate the finer qualities of other beings, wherever they hail from.

Indeed the qualities that caused a man or woman to leave Europe and travel to Australia in the 1800's and indeed the 1900's were not just consistent with ne'er-do-wells and convicts, and even if they had been of those varieties, the very harshness of the life in Australia caused the true characteristics of a person to rise to the fore and excel in areas he or she would never have had the chance to back home.

Indeed, the cream always rises to the top.

All in all the Australians were a tough rugged breed who did not suffer fools gladly and were just the right sort of men for the job in Palestine during World War I.

It was during this time in history that the Australians would begin to grow up and enter into Nationhood themselves; it wouldn't be overnight, but it would happen. The ties between her and Great Britain would eventually weaken and Australia would begin to shine forth in her own strength and in her own fiercely independent character traits.

The British would recognise that bravery of their Australian comrades, a poem penned by a British Officer during the Dardanelles campaign (1915) would speak for itself,

The skies that arched his lands were blue,
His bush born winds were warm and sweet,
And yet from earliest hours he knew,
The tides of victory and defeat;
From fierce floods thundering at his birth,
From red droughts ravening as he played,
He learned to fear no foes on earth –
"The bravest thing God ever made"

The bugles of the Motherland
Rang ceaselessly across the sea,
To call him and his lean brown band
To shape Imperial destiny;
He went by youth's grave purpose willed
The Goal unknown, the cost unweighed,
The promise of his blood fulfilled –
"The bravest thing God ever made"

We know - it is our deathless pride -
The splendour of his first fierce blow;
How, reckless, glorious, undenied,
He stormed those steel lined cliffs we know!
And none who saw him scale the height
Behind his reeking bayonet blade
Would rob him of his title right –
"The bravest thing God ever made"

Bravest where half a world of men
Are brave beyond all earth's rewards,
So stoutly none shall charge again
Till the last breaking of the sword.
Wounded or hale, won home from war,
Or yonder by the Lone Pine laid,
Give him his due for evermore –
"The bravest thing God ever made"

'He who cannot be mentioned and is best left alone' had hand-picked them especially for this occasion but Mundis was not to know this.

Having said this does not imply that the Australians were perfect; they were simply the right men for the job at the right time and place in history. Like all lesser beings they messed up, but unlike Higher Fallen Beings they had the chance to repent, and perhaps many would do just that after this war was over…but that is another story.

For now we concentrate on Mundis, who was standing forlornly on a small mound surveying the scene before him. Unbelievable was the only word he could think off.

Unbelievable!

Unbelievable because yet again Mundis was the only green being present. There was not one other that he could see, and his heart sank. Again he could not feel the presence of 'He who cannot be mentioned and is best left alone' and he could see no opposing forces that belonged to him.

Mundis was the only higher being present and he did not like the feel or the look of it at all.

He sank down into the sand on the edge of where the 4th Australian Light Horse Brigade was stationed and wearily put his head into his hands.

Should he text Headquarters; what would he tell them? No one to blame, there is no one here…

Forget it, they would then have him going back over old orders, and those responsible for not putting someone out here in 1917 would have to be hunted down - and then that could mean that Mundis would be hunting himself.

He wasn't sure what he had been doing then, but 'demon in charge of sending spies and scouts and general rabble rousers to Beersheba' had a familiar ring to it.

Mundis felt ill and sank lower into the sand. He was surrounded by the largest horses he had ever seen, 'Walers' they were called, because they came from the state of New South Wales. Mundis knew it well, great Opera House.

The horses were all stomping and pawing the ground, and making those infernal phwwwwrrring noises. They could sense battle and were preparing themselves for it. They could also smell water, and some of them had not drunk for more than fifty hours. This happened to be an added bonus as far as the storming of Beersheba was concerned - their desperation to reach the water was an undeniable factor in the victory, although as we shall see that there were other factors as well.

However when the time came only Mundis would see these added advantages.

Mundis did not know that the horses were thirsty, and what did he care if they were he didn't like 'em and he wasn't interested in 'em. He didn't like animals at all really; their welfare was of no concern to him. He thought of his reptile, Hornback, at home, did he like him? He was neither here nor there about him, besides, did one class an animal as a reptile? Or a reptile as an animal?

Either way it was confusing.

Mundis took a swig of his water and one of the huge brutes nudged his water skin out of his hands. They had no trouble seeing him, in fact they eyed him with decided suspicion and dislike.

Mundis scowled back.

5

Suddenly the scene changed and a lone voice shouted a command that was echoed throughout the group.

"Tighten up all your gear…in ten minutes we are going into Beersheba to water."

Mundis had ten minutes to decide what to do. Should I go with them, or should I stay and disappear into oblivion, lose the iPhone and somehow get back to Switzerland?

What to do?

WHAT TO DOOOO? He sounded like Katherine Hepburn in some movie that he'd watched somewhere.

However regardless of how he felt, the decision was, unfortunately for him, already made.

In his depressed and oppressed state, he had without realising it, placed himself next to someone's saddlebag and his foot had somehow become inadvertently entangled in the strap. As the young Australian tightened himself and his horse up, Mundis was hoisted into the air and attached to the saddle of the enormous brown Waler.

Fortunately he was quite good at hanging upside down and therefore didn't mind the initial sensation. Although he did eventually manage to right himself and sit astride the animal. Holding on to the belt of the soldier in front of him, he just had time to adjust his hat and straighten his seat before the call came through.

"MOVE OUT!" and the entire regiment in organised sections moved forward, gaining speed as they went and eventually pounding across the six kilometre empty space that lay between them and the Turkish line, their bayonets glinting in the setting sun and the dust and sand flying up before their faces.

They could just make out the dome of the mosque in the town and it was this they were heading for.

It was then that Mundis became aware that the Walers were not alone. Thundering along with them was a force that was far superior to the Australians, horses like Mundis had never seen before, huge animals with riders wearing the exact same apparel as the Australians but dressed in glowing white. The look of grim determination on their faces made Mundis' heart quake within him...

If Mundis had forgotten he had a heart, he knew now he did. The sight of these beings filled him with such terror that all he could do was cower behind his Digger, hold on and screw his eyes tight shut.

The relentless dust and machine gun noise and glare from the sun made him keep his eyes closed. The roar of the German planes overhead made him want to block his ears, but that was impossible because he had to hold on.

Mundis for the first time in eons was almost finished, in fact he knew no more until he was toppled off the back of the horse in the middle of the town of Beersheba. The horse was drinking and his soldier was fighting in hand to hand combat with a Turk.

No one needed to tell Mundis that Beersheba had fallen. He knew from being there and from the history books. He knew that this was the key battle that had liberated Palestine and paved the way for the modern day nation of Israel to be born. Of course there were other factors, any good Historian would tell you that, but this one was pivotal and Mundis knew it.

He also knew that 'He who cannot be mentioned' had sent His forces into battle and in knowing that...there was nothing else to say.

6

THE ADVENTURES OF BRITISH MUNDIS
c. October 31st, 1917

Not such an easy transition this time, Mundis hit some serious turbulence on the way to Britain and arrived with an upset tummy and a headache, still dressed as Lawrence of Arabia. Whilst Lawrence was a fascination for those in Britain at the time, it was not the correct dress for those average citizens in the street, at least not then anyway.

A quick text to Headquarters requesting the right outfit and a bit of a wait at the 'Green Toad in the Hole' pub on the corner of Bayswater Road and Park Lane whilst whiling away the time; this gave Mundis a good chance to sample the beverages and settle into the English way of life...again he surveyed the fashions.

Interesting, thought Mundis, *certainly different from Vienna in the 1890's*. There had been elegance and style in Vienna, but what an earth had happened here?

Mundis was amazed at how many men were wearing the same drab khaki grey, and how many were wounded and had a sad look about them. The women were even sadder, many of whom were nurses with red capes that could be seen hurrying into a hospital in Park Lane.

Mundis' pub was on the corner and he could see the hospital from his vantage point. What on earth were they doing? He watched as ambulances pulled up and carried men on stretchers to the door of the large elegant establishment. He could see family groups milling round in states of confused concern, happy that their men were home but unsure what the eventual outcome of their injuries would be.

For some poor souls it would be years and years in nursing homes leading to their eventual deaths, disfigured and sometimes forgotten by those who had loved them. Forced to relive a war that had taken their youth and their chances of happiness forever.

Honestly, what is the matter with these people, anyone would think there was war on, he grimaced. Mundis being the sort of creature he was, had forgotten that there was a war on. A war that had wiped out millions of young men and left millions of women and children and elderly parents without their husbands and fathers and sons.

Earthly concerns were nothing to do with Mundis, unless of course he had an assignment to intervene in, and then he just did his job and vamoosed.

He was not the slightest bit concerned about the world occupied by lesser beings; he had his own world, which was actually the same world as theirs but infinitely more interesting.

Mundis was able to do so much more than those poor lesser beings. He thought of his alien escapades, his disappearing tricks, his ability to read the future in glass balls and horoscopes, not to mention tarot cards… ahh, he had such fun and such powers.

Such mind stopping powers really.

In any case, one day the two worlds would join up and a New World Order would be established, and then the Boss would be unequivocally in charge, hidden but definitely in charge. There would be an upfront guy, a sidekick and a host of hangers on, and the Boss would be behind it all.

Who knows what exalted position Mundis would have to play, maybe something that involved a considerable amount of lying round by pools, skiing down marvelous slopes and generally enjoying himself…

aah bliss!!

But somehow Mundis didn't think it would pan out like that.

The Boss was very focused and he didn't seem to think much about enjoying himself. He was more into committees and meetings and generally boring people with his own ideas, and his temperament was not the light and breezy type that Mundis really enjoyed being with.

No matter, he was the Boss and Mundis did his best to fit in and keep out of his way.

The latter was his preferred option.

The day when the Boss would take charge was spoken of in hushed tones back in Headquarters and looked forward to with eager anticipation and perhaps just a little apprehension, a bit like Y2K, but definitely more of a certainty.

Rumour had it that it was very close, well back in real time it was close, that being the twenty-first century.

But for now we return to Mundis. Sitting with his short legs up on the table in front of him and wiping his greedy little mouth with the back of his green little hand, he made quite the picture of indolence. The scenes of sadness and misery did not affect him, for he was busy drinking and eating and thinking only of himself.

Fortunately he was invisible to lesser beings, and the higher beings (fallen higher beings) who saw him just smiled and waved and went their way. The other higher beings totally ignored him; he was beneath their attention.

Mundis ignored them too, they were beneath him.

He missed Switzerland but it was nice to be in society again, and definitely better than being in the Sinai. Perhaps he would pop into Harrods later and procure a hamper, a nice big wicker one. Christmas was coming up and did he so enjoy their Christmas fare. All the trimmings, the tree, the lights, perhaps this year he would go caroling with some friends…ahh bliss.

Yes Mundis did enjoy Christmas…it never occurred to him that perhaps others *this year* may not enjoy Christmas. No matter, he would still sing with the greatest of gusto, "Jingle bell, jingle bell, jingle bell rock…"

Thank Heavens I didn't get the Palestine stint. I do like a traditional Christmas in a traditional place, nothing traditional about Palestine, dreary place, yes thank heavens I got the London call - mistletoe, holly wreaths, girls with fur-lined hoods and muffs, skating and perhaps even some sledding…ahh double bliss.

Life *was* looking up.

Mundis' eyes had that faraway gleam in them again, and thoughts of losing the iPhone and disappearing into the middle distance were again taking shape. He really was not a creature to be trusted;

constancy was not his strong point.

Why the Boss had assigned him to the job is one of those mysteries that perhaps will never be solved.

Mundis' outfit had still not arrived and he was jolly well not going to find Members of Parliament dressed like this...even if he was invisible. The Members were sure to have their own personal demons and they were all sure to be stuck up little snobs who would invariably be dressed in the right attire.

Oh no, Mundis was not going to turn up like this, all white and flowing with a headdress on and Jesus sandals...phwefff to that, and he took another gulp of his drink, straight brandy.

7

Just then his outfit *did* arrive, and Mundis was horrified to see his legs that had previously been draped in white cotton flowing robes, suddenly become encased in the horrible drab khaki colour of the war uniform, and that his headgear had been replaced by a trench helmet.

The helmet didn't fit him properly and jiggled when he moved. He also had a gas mask and rifle - honestly did he have to be so authentic – and memories of his one onion came flooding back.

Mundis let out a huge sigh of disappointment, and was just about to send a protest text when Headquarters texted him.

Quit grumbling Veridis, we know you well. Your other half is wearing Australian Military apparel and you will do the same. Now proceed to the War Cabinet Rooms and take down the names and numbers of the demons who did not intercept the 'Balfour Declaration' and stop it being passed.

Those demons would have been assigned to each member of the Cabinet and indeed to Balfour himself, and he, Balfour should never have been able to pen the letter in the first place.

Mundis groaned. *So where are these Cabinet offices where these August gentlemen will be meeting? Honestly I s'pose I'll have to go... but why I don't know!*

It had suddenly occurred to him that this time may very well be like the previous times he'd been sent to track the offending demons down and they hadn't been there. It would be another wild goose chase with Mundis the Mug being the only green present...

Ahh, can I stand it? I mean so far we have had Dreyfus and his shafts of Light, Herzl and the Orchard and this won't be any better... there will be nobody green there, I know it.

I think the Boss is just going to have to accept that 'Israel happened' and that is that, the rest of the world is good enough. Surely, I mean if I were the Boss I would be happy with the rest of the world...

Mundis downed another brandy and sighed, "Jolly waste of time, but here goes."

Googling a map of London, he tried to work out the best way to get to 10 Downing Street.

Sounds familiar, have I been there before? Course I have, many times.

He had some time before the meeting was to begin so Mundis decided to walk. It wasn't that far from Park Lane to Westminster and on to Downing Street. Besides, Mundis loved London, and agreed with Samuel Johnson who said, "When a man is tired of London he is tired of life, for there is in London all that life can afford."

Mundis remembered Johnson well, a man of character and substance.

He and Mundis had nothing in common.

So with these thoughts in mind, Mundis set off for Downing Street and the War cabinet meeting, cursing his silly trench helmet as he went - totally unnecessary in London - but he didn't want to text headquarters about it, 'cause they may get really annoyed and send him to the Western front and Mundis hated unnecessary noise.

Best to leave well enough alone.

Mundis strolled along Park Lane, admiring the houses - pity so many of them would be turned into Hotels in the years to come. Life after this war would really be very different from what it had been, the whole Upstairs Downstairs way of Life with respect to social class and servants was about to change. Although no Lesser Being was really aware of it now; they were just living day to day and coping with the war and all it entailed.

Mundis was not a sentimental creature but he was a student of Sociology and he certainly preferred this sort of Sociology to any sort of tribe work in the back of beyond. That sort of Sociology did nothing for him; sitting cross-legged and watching corroborees and other ancient type traditional stuff left him very bored and usually very unimpressed. Just a big yawn really, honestly he was such an ignorant little demon in some respects.

Whereas the study of British society fascinated him. Oh yes, he could flit backwards and forwards for all eternity, in and out of different centuries, hob-knobbing with the aristocracy and generally enjoying all that life has to offer. Come to think of it, any European society appealed to him, as long as it was the very highest echelons and he was left pretty much to himself, to savour, enjoy and generally take it in his stride.

Buckingham Palace loomed up ahead; should he wander through the ground, did he have time? Not really, best to keep going, although he would love to have floated through the palace as well. Magnificent artwork…there was a very fine painting of Charles I by van Dyck.

Mundis remembered that unfortunate monarch well. He had not personally been involved in his demise, but he certainly knew those who had been. Mundis had never really decided if the whole Commonwealth exercise had been a good thing or not. The Boss was very opposed, and Mundis himself certainly didn't think much of their puritan way of life, very dreary, all those pudding bowl hair cuts and black suits, quite a relief when it all died a death and the monarchy came back. The monarchy was much easier to work with.

Mundis drifted on. His feet were tired now and the boots were heavy so he had taken to floating about a metre above the ground, although they did weigh him down a bit.

He wandered down Victoria Street and on to Westminster. A marvelous sight greeted him, the bastion of British government resplendent in the early afternoon sun. Mundis sighed in appreciation and made a mental note to book a time when Monet was painting the Houses of Parliament, he wanted a few tips, his easel was always up at home and he did like to dabble.

Now it was just a short stroll to Downing Street, number Ten.

There they were! The August gentlemen were just entering, and amazement upon amazement, they were accompanied by many small green beings all milling around them, talking and exchanging news and gossip!

Mundis was delighted, action at last.

"Whoopee!" He was so excited he leapt in the air (not very high, 'cause his boots were heavy) and his helmet fell off.

Mundis followed the group inside, tagging along at the rear end, like the last little duckling behind its mother.

The gentlemen took their seats in a very posh dining room adjoining a rather wonderful library. Mundis admired the décor, rich walnut table, huge and elegant, marvelous yellow velvet curtains with William Morris wallpaper.

Mundis loved William Morris wallpaper, he absolutely agreed with Morris's slant on life:

"Have nothing in your houses
That you do not know to be useful
Or believe to be beautiful."

Mundis' apartment back in Headquarters was truly beautiful and full of very useful things; his eyes clouded over just thinking of all the beautiful items he owned.

All were seated. Mundis and the other green beings took the chairs that were pushed up against the wall, their short legs not reaching the ground. They looked for all purposes like a bunch of naughty green children relegated to the back row.

Mundis got out his iPhone and got ready to punch in names and numbers. He stole a cursory glance at his cronies and his heart missed a beat.

Something terrible had happened to them. Just a moment ago they were chatting and gossiping happily together, exchanging rumors and telling lies; now they were bound head to foot in a sort of white gossamer. Their eyes were completely blindfolded and their mouths were taped. They seemed stupefied and almost dead, although Mundis knew that couldn't happen.

Mundis could not believe his eyes. There were no other higher beings in the room, especially of the sort belonging to 'He who cannot be mentioned'.

How on earth had this happened?

Somewhere, someone or others were praying and they may not even know what they are praying about, but whatever the prayer, it was extraordinarily effective, and the results were devastating with respect to Mundis' assignment.

Lord Alfred Milner stood up and presented the case for an

'establishment in Palestine for a national home for the Jewish people'.

There was an overwhelming vote in favour.

Mundis sat there in horror, his fellow green beings sat there zombie-like. The whole atmosphere was surreal.

Later the declaration would be formally made in a letter by Arthur James Balfour to Baron Rothschild and it would read as follows:

Foreign Office
November 2nd, 1917

Dear Lord Rothschild,

I have much pleasure in conveying to you, on behalf of His Majesty's Government, the following declaration of Sympathy with Jewish Zionist aspirations which has been submitted to, and approved by, the Cabinet.

"His Majesty's Government view will favour the establishment in Palestine of a national home for the Jewish people, and will use their best endeavours to facilitate the achievement of this object, it being clearly understood that nothing shall be done which may prejudice the civil and religious rights of existing non-Jewish communities in Palestine, or the rights and political status enjoyed by Jews in any other country."

I should be grateful if you would bring this declaration to the knowledge of the Zionist Federation.

Arthur Balfour.

There was nothing to do or say.

Mundis had been pipped at the post again, his entire assignment washed up and finished.

Post Script

'He who cannot be mentioned and is best left alone' smiled. The events of October 31st, 1917 were a red letter day in Heaven.

Two mighty victories on the same day.

His children were one step closer to coming home and His heart swelled in loving anticipation.

PART FOUR

"The king's heart is in the hand of the Lord;

He directs it like a watercourse wherever He pleases."

Proverbs 21:1

1

The meeting continued and Mundis' gossamer shrouded friends continued to sit there stupefied. Mundis was furious because he hadn't even had enough time to work out who they were so they could be reported, and now they were all so bound up he couldn't see 'em.

Mundis threw his iPhone down in disgust and bowed his head, folded his arms and sulked. Now he really did look like a spoilt naughty child.

And if the shoe fits wear it...I say!

What to do?

WHAT TO DOOOOO?

He sounded like Katherine Hepburn in a movie he had seen somewhere.

(How alike the Mundi were, they even used the same phrases, not surprising really, they were the same green beings.)

Mundis sulked for quite some time; he didn't hear a thing that was discussed, nor did he want to. Mundis had his assignment and it had been sabotaged; as far as he was concerned his part was over, so why bother listening to anything else.

Like if you are a doing a course at university and you get into the wrong lecture...are you going to bother taking notes? Course not, it's easier to sit there and pretend you are in the right place or that you are interested rather than embarrass yourself and get up and leave.

Mundis didn't care about embarrassing himself, no one could see him - he just stayed 'cause he didn't know where else to go.

The meeting dragged on and Mundis eventually fell asleep. He had climbed off the chair and slipped under the table, having removed his helmet and using his overcoat as a blanket and his arms as a pillow. He slept peacefully and solidly for hours.

He didn't hear the members of the War Cabinet leave and he

didn't hear the green beings go either. Although go they did, and in just the same way they arrived, chatting loudly and comparing notes and gossip.

They seemed totally unaware that they had been bound up and out of action, and that something momentous in the form of the Balfour Declaration had been passed and that they had missed it.

They had also missed their chance to better their cause and serve their Master.

They in short had no idea what had happened to them, nor did they care much, selfish little beings that they were. They all filed out and went straight to the nearest pub and enjoyed a hearty meal and a good ale, some of them slipping easily into lesser beings who were already the worse for wear.

Mundis on the other hand only woke up when he smelt the Welsh Rarebit that was being served and then he promptly got up, stretched and generally roused himself in order to partake.

2

Sitting himself at the other end of the grand table, he was able to eat quite a large portion of the delicious meal, and that was only because the Prime Minister Lloyd George was totally fascinated by the presence of a young and attractive woman who sat opposite him, otherwise he may have noticed the disappearing delicacies and the depleted wine decanter.

As Mundis worked his way through dinner, half listening to the conversation and half simply enjoying the fare, he became aware that he was not alone as far as higher beings were concerned.

Mundis was amazed. There hanging from the light fitting was his old friend Lust, and there coiled around the decanter of wine, and indeed half submerged in it was another old friend Lush, and lying half asleep upon the hearth rug were Flirtation, Infidelity and his absolute favourite friend of all time, Adultery!

Such age-long friends of Mundis' - he let out a squeal of joy and recognition, which made each demon jump to attention.

There was much hugging and swapping of gossip and exclaims of, "Glory! But what are you doing here?"

Mundis explained, taking care to point out that he was on a fact-finding mission and that it had not been going well at all, although he truly liked the feel of 10 Downing Street and was hoping he maybe able to swing himself a job here...you know, something along the lines of 'watering down the curse of the Balfour Declaration' and distracting the lesser beings from doing anymore damage re. the re-emergence of Israel.

This was met with stony silence and some muttered remarks along the lines of, *"Well what do you think we are doing here?"*

Mundis apologised for his tactlessness, although it was quite obvious that they were ignorant of the debacle in the War Cabinet room; they were simply affronted at the suggestion that they needed any help re. Downing Street, or anything else for that matter.

I mean excuse me, they had been doing this sort of work for as long as Mundis. They were all recruited at the same time, thank you very much.

So Mundis sort of coughed and looked suitably embarrassed and shuffled his feet a bit...well sort of.

In reality he couldn't have cared less. He just wanted out of Palestine forever. And he really did love London and wanted to do some shopping and some pilfering, see some Art Galleries, meet some friends for drinks and catch some shows...and if he could do it all from Number 10 then he really had arrived.

There was no better address - well, there was the Palace but that was something you sort of had forever if you were a higher being. I mean the demons that were in residence there had been there since the place was built, and even before then, in fact I think they arrived with the Romans in Slave Galleys or the Vikings in Long boats, either way it was an inherited position and one that you certainly could not engineer.

Mundis had again forgotten it was war. The chances of shows and shopping and general frivolities were not what they had been; no matter, he could certainly have stretched it into something.

Any case the moment passed and Mundis' heart sank as he realised he probably did not have a future at Number 10 and he would probably have to rejoin his other half in Palestine.

Drat and double drat. Worse still, he had not even passed on to the Boss the dreadful news about his gossamer-bound comrades.

What to do... what to dooooo.

He was beyond striking a Katherine Hepburn type pose - the disappointment was making his heart ache way too much.

Should he pre-emt this strike and text Headquarters before they called him?

"Good thinking Mundis ol' chap," said Mundis to himself. "Mmm, now how to word it?"

Let's see, how about... comrades in question were indeed present but was unable to get names or numbers because they were wearing disguises as per orders per you.

This of course was a lie, but as lies were part of Mundis' game… no matter.

No…that won't work…ahh, comrades were there, but very drunk and were wearing hats pulled down over faces.

Mmm no, alcohol has no real effect on us green guys.

Well, you can guess what happened next can't you.

Yes, you are right.

The strains of "We all live in a yellow submarine" broke the peace and sounded completely incongruous in the 1917 setting.

"Ahh Veridis, names and numbers Veridis, whose head will roll before the day is out? Yours perhaps, Mundis?"

Mundis felt the Welsh Rarebit threatening to return. There was no way out; the truth would have to be told and told it was….

Amazing really, the Boss was the Father of Lies and yet when it came to others and telling the truth, he was a real stickler, a being of very definite double standards.

The silence on the other end was deafening and the coldness palpable. Mundis stared ahead and tried to focus on the top of the wine decanter that was casting a brilliant glittering ball of light onto the ceiling.

"WELL VERIDIS… I expect you will have to rejoin your other half in Palestine; his story is similar, something about very large horses with very large Australians on them. Well no matter Veridis, up here in the twenty-first century we really have got the entire world against Israel and for all intents and purposes we have won… and I have good reason to believe that my time is just around the corner, well my official time for all eternity that is. It has always been my time really, would you not agree Veridis?"

"Oh very good sir," said a relieved and very smelly Mundis.

"But at the same time Veridis, I am not letting you off the hook, you will continue on with your Mission, getting the names and numbers of any demons you can… I do not believe that all assignments will be sabotaged and I do believe that I will have someone or others to blame, …and if not Veridis, well then, why not you? Something to look forward to, eh?"

Mundis swallowed hard. "Yes sir, right you are sir…"

The line went dead and so did Mundis. A pool of green vile-smelling liquid had gathered around his feet and the other demons in the room were standing in a huddle and shaking in fear, as well as holding their noses.

The Prime Minister and his pretty secretary were totally oblivious and were retiring upstairs to their shared bedroom. Lust, Infidelity and Adultery followed, still shaking and breathing with difficulty.

Flirtation and Lush stayed behind, relieved that they had done their job, and could legally rest.

The Prime Minister's wife was in Wales.

3

Life in the early years of the 1900s was, for the aristocracy, one of privilege and of discretion. Affairs between married men and women were quite commonplace and completely socially acceptable, mostly modeled on the behaviour of the late King Edward VII.

The Prime Minister Lloyd George, whilst from a humble background, certainly made good use of the social expectations of the day and was noted for his love of women and his many discreet affairs. He was reputed to have two wives, one, his official wife named Margaret and the other his secretary named Francis Stevenson.

Francis would be his mistress for thirty years and would later become his wife after Margaret had died. Therefore the woman who started her working life as a humble secretary ended it as a Countess, Lloyd George having been given a title just a few years before he died.

With all this in mind, (meaning the rather interesting domestic arrangements of Number 10) Mundis, feeling perfectly at home and having not yet heard from the Transfer Department, had decided to set up shop there.

He chose one of the extremely nice bedrooms for his own, the Red Boudoir, and he was more than happy to share it with his comrades, although he did insist on having the bed to himself. Why his comrades had been happy with light fittings and the tops of library shelves was beyond him...but then they were rather backgroundish fellows, whilst he, Mundis was the Boss' head librarian.

Mundis was able to forget the fear the Boss instilled in him whilst a long way away, and he tended to dine out on the 'Head Librarian' bit quite frequently. He also fervently hoped the Transfer Department and the Boss had forgotten him...well, just for a little while. Any longer was too much to hope for; he had been disappointed too many times.

The Red Room was beautiful, it was fully serviced every day by one of the maids, Sarah, who was puzzled as to why the bed looked rumpled, but preferring her place in service to a possible war job, she chose to keep quiet. Sarah was also well aware of the shenanigans that went on at Number 10.

There was a small library of good books, a very nice dressing room and some beautiful paintings donated by the National Portrait Gallery. Mundis as we know loved Art and felt very much at home. The rugs on the floor were pure Persian and the fireplace was satisfactory, mainly because it was unlit, although Winter was approaching and something would have to be done about that.

Mundis was also in the process of organising his wardrobe. He had managed to ditch his private's uniform and was now to be seen in the uniform of a British or German General or sometimes a Sea Admiral.

He did like the spike on the German's helmets, (they are called a Pickelhauben) and a small version of the Kaiser's uniform was his very favourite. The fact that he was living in the British Prime Minister's house did not concern him in the least.

Do not ask me how he came across these uniforms because I simply do not know, they just appeared.

Ahh, this was the life; breakfast at ten, lunch at twelve-thirty and dinner at eight or later depending on what was happening with the War Cabinet.

Mundis was in his element. He loved hobnobbing with society and had organised drinks, parties and dinners at Number Ten. The fallen higher beings in London had not been affected by the war at all; indeed they were having a glorious time, totally oblivious to any but their own needs and wants, and able to do as much mischief as they possibly could.

There were still shows on during the war and Mundis and his cronies were usually able to get front row seats in the dress circle. They would sit on the banister in front of the seats and dangle their legs over the side, and as they were invisible they certainly did not inconvenience any lesser being who wanted to see the show.

Their favourite show was 'Floradora' and they saw it over and over again, singing along with the chorus and sometimes joining in, much to the delight of the other green beings in the audience.

Green beings who were fortunate, they were able to stay in London; others who had fallen foul of the Boss or were working their way up the corporate ladder had to do a stint on the Western Front. Still there were certainly plenty around to keep Mundis and his other friends entertained and very busy.

4

The other sort of higher being, the unfallen type, were very busy too.

They were caring and tending to bereaved families, spending inordinate amounts of time stroking the brows of crying wives and elderly parents and cradling bereaved children in their arms. All sorts of miracles happened during these War years, little miracles like baskets of clean washing being folded and ironing done when there was no one around to do it…amazing really.

Waste of time in Mundis' opinion and certainly beneath his attention.

Other miracles occurred too, in the battlefields, men who were lost in the mists of no-man's-land being miraculously led back to their own battalion, men from either side - these higher beings did not seem to differentiate between Ally or Foe.

Dying men who were desperately trying to remember 'The Lord's Prayer' and even those who didn't even know there was a 'Lord's Prayer' would hear it whispered into their ears and instead of dying in fear and anguish, died peacefully, some with smiles on their lips.

Ah yes, these types of higher beings were very busy during these years. They would transport the English men back and forth from ports in England to the ports in Belgium. They would sit on the railings of the ships and roofs of trains, and would do a similar thing for the Germans.

They would march into the battlefields with their men, right alongside them, sometimes dressed in identical gear and sometimes perfectly visible. They would sing snatches of Hymns or popular songs to bolster failing spirits,

> *Pack up your troubles in your old kit bag*
> *And smile, smile, smile,*
> *While you've got a Lucifer to light your fag,*

Smile boys, that's the style,
What's the use of worrying, it never was worthwhile, so…
Pack up your troubles in your ol' kit bag
And smile, smile, smile.

The higher beings would smile knowingly at the word 'Lucifer' and think to themselves that they wish all he had ever done and was ever to do was to light a fag.

Sadly Lucifer had done much more than that, and this was precisely why they were all tramping through the mud of the French countryside instead of at home where they all belonged, doing whatever it was they all liked to do best.

The higher beings would think of the countless numbers of children who would never know the hugs of a father, and all the stories that would never be told, and all the armchairs that would forever remain empty and all the Christmases that would come and go without that one special person being there.

Not to mention all the mothers and fathers who felt that it was only yesterday that their brave boy had been born, and now he was in France fighting a war that was meant to end all wars.

Ah yes, they wished Lucifer had not done what he had, and that the earth was the way 'He who cannot be mentioned' had first intended it to be.

But 'He who cannot be mentioned' being the way HE is, gave us all free choice to follow Him or not to follow Him, both higher and lesser beings and this sadly was the result…tramping through mud across a landscape that used to be beautiful and was now a mess of trenches, tangles barbed wire and dead bodies.

Yes, everything would have been different but for Lucifer.

These precious higher beings would also stand watch as men grabbed a couple of hours sleep in those trenches. Shrouded as they were in their diamond dust coverings, they would be invisible to lesser beings' eyes.

Although sometimes those eyes, sad and yearning for home, would catch a glimpse of deep-set loving eyes that may have reminded them of other deep-set loving eyes back home. It was the sight of those eyes staring into theirs that would calm even the most terrified of souls, and they would sigh and turn over, and sleep soundly in hell holes festered with giant rats and filthy water.

And if sleep was not a miracle in those circumstances, then I do not know what is.

When their lesser being fell in battle they would go all the way back to England, Germany or wherever the lesser being came from to whisper the news into the ears of those who needed to hear, and then they would bring comfort and succour to broken hearts.

Yes, they were very busy during those years. And very sad too.

Mundis was busy too, well he planned to be. He had a nice routine going, up at seven-thirty, out at eleven, back for lunch. Oh yes, Mundis was busy too and never sad.

The only thing that made him feel a little on edge was the thought of a BEEP BEEP BEEP or the dreaded strains of 'We all live in a Yellow Submarine' issuing from his iPhone.

Sadly it was inevitable, but for now it was such a whirl – or was promising to be.

Post Script

But let us now leave the selfish little British Mundis, he does not need to be spoken about anymore. He is comfortable, his needs are met and his duty, as far as he is concerned, is done…for now.

Let us return to Palestinian Mundis and see how he is faring. Let us see if his needs are being met, let us see if he is comfortable, and let us see if he is doing his duty.

We shall watch with interest…

PART FIVE

"Thou, even thou, art Lord alone; thou hast made heaven, the heaven of heavens, with all their host the earth, and all things that are therein, the seas, and all that is therein, and thou preservest them all; and the host of heaven worshippeth thee."

Nehemiah 9:6

"The cowering prisoners will soon be set free; they will not die in their dungeon, nor will they lack bread."

Isaiah 51:14

1

THE FURTHER ADVENTURES OF PALESTINIAN MUNDIS

Beersheba in 1917 was certainly not looking anything like London in 1917, there was no 'Green Toad in the Hole Pub' for Mundis to while away the hours in, drinking straight brandy and eating whatever he felt like, no interesting sights to see or people to observe and certainly no fashions to comment on.

No, Beersheba in 1917 was extremely depressing and all Mundis got for his Cavalry charge efforts was a mouthful of sand and terrible backache, on account of the terrible landing when he fell off the Waler.

He slowly picked himself up and shook his head in wonder and disappointment.

What now… where to and who with? Mundis was in complete daze.

And being in a complete daze he did something that only Beings in complete dazes do. He texted Headquarters and asked for directions:

In middle of Beersheba with one onion and some drinking water. Any suggestions on where to next?

BEEP BEEP. Mundis read the text and could have kicked himself for being stupid enough to initiate the correspondence.

Names and numbers Veridis. Punch 'em through, we need 'em, Boss looking for someone to blame.

"Drat and double drat."

Mundis texted back, *Can't send names or numbers, no one here except me and very large higher being horses complete with very large higher being Australians.*

His iPhone remained silent for quite some time after that.

Mundis found a shady spot away from the fighting and proceeded to eat his onion and drink his water. He was leaning up against the wall of the mosque in the centre of town and from this spot he could see the Australians arriving and all the fighting that ensued. The Turks, poor chaps, were having a very bad time of it.

The huge higher being variety of Australians and their huge horses of the higher being variety were fighting alongside the lesser Australian Beings and doing a pretty good job. Mundis kept his eyes down; he wanted no eye contact thank you. These guys were on His Boss' turf and he really did not see what this war had to do with them.

Impudence, Mundis called it, sheer impudence. I mean to say, they don't belong here, they have their own turf. Somewhere way up there beyond the blue, Mundis had remembered hearing a song sung along those lines in a church he used to frequent.

This earth is not my home,
I'm just a passing through.
My home is way up there, somewhere beyond the bluuuuuee
The Angels beckon me through Heaven's open doooooor
And I don't feel at home on this earth anymooooore *

Good job, thought Mundis at the time, *'cause this earth is the Boss's turf and quite frankly we would rather you accepted the Angel's invitation and went somewhere up there, somewhere beyond the blue pronto-like, and that means each and every one of you boring churchgoing lesser beings.*[1]

Yes, Mundis had no idea why he was facing such opposition with regard to his assignment, really it seemed pretty straight forward to him:

1. Get names and numbers of green beings responsible for allowing Israel to come into play again,

2. Send names and numbers to Headquarters,

3. Green beings then punished,

4. And then Mundis gets to go home to Headquarters where he spends Eternity in peace and comfort surrounded by all he is happiest with and finds pleasure in.

---

1 Song sometimes attributed to Albert. E. Brumley 1905-1907. Pub.Radio Favourites 1937

Simple really… but somehow it just was not working out the way he wanted.

'He who cannot be mentioned and is best left alone' and who had His own domain somewhere up there beyond the blue - and should jolly well be happy with that - just kept getting involved.

Why? What could this earth and this silly little Nation of Israel possibly have that 'He who cannot be mentioned' wanted?

Why in the Boss' earth was Israel so important that the entire world was up in arms against it and wanted it dealt with?

And why come to think of it, did the Boss care in any case… huh? Couldn't he just leave well enough alone and be happy with what he did have…

Which to Mundis seemed like an awful lot.

Surely it could have nothing to do with all those lesser beings…?

Why would anyone want them; they had nothing.

NO power,

VERY little taste,

VERY limited brain capacity

and were so incredibly DULL… unless inhabited by one of us higher beings.

Mundis was at a complete loss.

2

Mundis made a pathetic picture. Sitting there in the shade of the mosque, surrounded by horrific carnage and death, he was no longer eating his onion and his water bottle had slipped from his hand as he watched the horror around him unfold.

One would think that he was beyond caring about what happened in the world of lesser beings and indeed he was, unless it personally affected him, and as far as he could gauge, this was personally affecting him.

He was stuck here in a place he didn't want to be, following orders that he didn't care about and fighting a war he didn't understand on any level…

Mundis had no idea how much he had in common with most of the young lesser Beings that were in Beersheba that day.

No matter, he had no choice. He could not request a transfer and he could not just disappear back to Switzerland; his head was too important to him and he knew too much about the Boss to think that his disobedience would go unpunished.

So he would stay exactly where he was and just go with the Australians when they finished fighting, wherever it was that they were going.

He lent his head back against the mosque, closed his eyes and tried to doze amidst the noise and the heat. Thoughts of his lovely apartment back home filled his mind. He smiled at the thought of the sun filtering through the trees and turning his room yellow-green; he thought of his books, his paintings and his comfortable chair with his bunny rug (green with yellow stripes); he thought of his drinks cabinet and his own personal Space Craft kept especially for specific missions.

He managed a slight smile when thinking about the Dihards and the fact that he could and would use that craft to visit them…they were soooo deliciously stupid, Edith especially.

T'was a good thing that he didn't know what British Mundis was up to, wandering through London and about to embark upon a particularly cushy time ensconced in the Red Boudoir of Number 10.

Yes, it was a very good thing that he didn't know any of that, it would have been too much for his selfish, egocentric nature to have coped with.

3

The other sort of higher beings were just as busy here as they were on the Western Front. Whispering comfort into the souls of injured and dying men, holding their hands till help arrived, and indeed in some cases materialising and actually being the help needed.

Wounded men would often wonder how they came in from remote areas in the battlefield to the hospital stations, and who indeed had brought them there.

Often no one could explain, apart from to say, "We don't know, but here you are, and here you will stay 'til we can mend what we can mend."

There were many such stories to be told, and many men in the years to come would lie in bed at night and wonder just who it was they should thank for their lives...

Some would remember and be thankful; for others, it would remain a lifelong mystery.

Mundis was not a creature who had ever felt shame. It was not part of his vocabulary or his nature, but now in this particular time in history, watching these higher beings stooping low to tend to the fallen...Mundis felt something unmistakably and uncharacteristically akin to shame.

He was not like British Mundis, surrounded by delicious distractions in every sense of the word.

There was nothing much to strive for in London if you had the means to partake of all it offered.

It is a fact of lesser being nature that when there is something to strive for, then the good in that nature comes to the fore and shines in the most adverse of circumstances, making something wonderful of something that has been previously nothing.

Palestine in 1917 was in the process of being made into something that had previously been nothing, therefore it was a place where one strived.

However in 1917, and indeed all through its existence, Palestine was not a place where one can lose oneself. There were no distractions in Palestine, it was brutally real and vibrant in an earthy sense, and it resounded with a different kind of beauty, raw and glaring, very much like Australia really.

It could also be said that part of its beauty was won through 'hard yakka', as the Australians would say.

In fact it was exactly the sort of country that the Australians could appreciate, and it was as though the blood that flowed through their veins and was shed on those battlefields seeped into a land that would bring forth mighty men of valour, who in the years to come would toil and fight to make Israel the land it is today, and indeed is still becoming.

And as I write this, I am very aware that we have not seen anything yet, as far as just how great Israel will one day become.

Still this is all in the future, and for now we are still in the dusty little town of Beersheba in 1917, with a little green higher fallen being, who for the first time in his existence is feeling the pangs of unexpected and unsought shame - an extraordinary sensation for a higher fallen being.

Mundis' heart was aching and his eyes were downcast as he watched as the higher beings tended to the dying and wounded and he was struck by his own uselessness.

And a knowledge that his presence was definitely not appreciated and only just tolerated.

Not that he had any real desire *to* help...that wasn't part of his makeup, he just felt small and insignificant as well as uncomfortable and therefore at a complete loss as to what to do.

He tried to look away and he tried to rearrange his sitting position. Embarrassment was not an emotion he had experienced before. He was quite simply undone, *again*.

Not that it lasted long.

It is a bit like the difference between genuine repentance and just being sorry for what you had done because it had simply brought about consequences you were not happy about.

Although it is fair to say that Mundis was not entirely sure what it was that he had done. I mean he was only doing exactly what he was made to do - his job, following the Boss' orders, something he had done since time begun - well it felt like he had done it since time began!

However badly he was feeling now, it was, sad to say, inevitable that the feelings of shame and uselessness would pass...and of course they did.

Mundis was again ready to get on with his assignment, which he assumed was to continue travelling with the Australians and getting any names and numbers that he could...not that he had much expectation in this area.

He still hadn't heard from the Transfer Department, but when in doubt just keep going the way you were told to go in the first place.

So there was nothing to do but wait, keep an eye on the Officers in charge and follow the Light Horse...

"Drat...another horse ride," he grumbled, and he was indeed quite right.

4

The wind was fierce and hot, it is called the Khamsin, and it blew all day and all night. Mundis wished the Transfer Department hadn't changed his outfit; he could have done with his long flowing robes and his Lawrence of Arabia headdress. He now understood why Lawrence wore it.

And it wasn't just to look chic, although the army boots were definitely a plus. The Jesus sandals would not have been an asset, too much sand between the toes.

The sand got in everything, under his shirt, through his pants, in his bag and even in his water, most unpleasant, and it made reading nigh impossible, I mean how was he supposed to really enjoy *Little Dorrit* with all this going on?

Wind, sand, blood, dying men, dead horses, dreadful smells, all most inconvenient and quite out of Mundis's comfort zone, not that he was concerned about the carnage, just the inconvenience of it - it made reading very difficult.

As you can see the feelings of shame had definitely evaporated, and Mundis was Mundis again, selfish, egocentric, opinionated, lazy and very green.

The call to mount up eventually came, and Mundis mounted.

He mounted the nearest beast he could find, and this time it was one belonging to an Officer, a large Waler called 'Just Bill'.

'Just Bill' was none too happy about transporting Mundis, (he shied and reared) but alas to no avail… Mundis hung on and stayed put.

The truth was that 'Just Bill' was a very sensible animal, and he could quite plainly see the other types of higher beings including Mundis, and consequently was more than aware of *just what* had landed on his back; and as a sensible and sensitive animal he was less than happy about it, but sadly, he, being a horse, was not in a position to pick and choose. He was lumbered with Mundis.

Mundis positioned himself behind the Officer, sitting astride and holding onto the Officer's belt, his bag conveniently strung across his body and his hat securely on his head at just the right angle. The band was under what passed as his chin and his other hand held it firm.

He had a self-satisfied nonchalant expression on his face that was truly sickening.

Mundis could always have hopped off and floated along with them, but sometimes floating was not all it was cracked up to be, and the dust would have been unbearable, and really it was just as easy to get a lift, even if it was on a horse.

Poor 'Just Bill', spare a thought for him, it truly was a degrading thing he was having to do, and his fellow Walers looked on with pity in their eyes.

They were very aware of the embarrassment that Mundis was causing their friend and comrade, and some wondered why on earth the other unfallen higher beings didn't deal with Mundis.

The truth was that the other unfallen type was also more than aware of Mundis' presence, but they had their instructions and in this case they were told to leave the fallen green being alone.

Although some of the higher beings remembered Mundis from eons past, when he, Mundis, had glittered in the courts of Heaven. When his mind had been fresh, and his wings new and firmly attached.

Then he had been resplendent in his greenness, which had sparkled with a thousand shards of diamonds and emeralds.

Mundis' conversation had been filled with praise and affirmation and his delight had been to serve, honour and obey 'He who cannot be mentioned', - He who, back then was mentioned all the time, and with love and adoration.

O yes, they remembered Mundis, with love and affection then, they remembered how they had delighted in his company and he in theirs. They had delighted in his quick mind and his readiness to make them laugh, in his hospitality and his friendship, and his great ability to make all feel special and loved.

Mundis' apartments in Heaven had been a focal point, a meeting place for discussing ideas and plans.

Although for some those discussions had ushered in a time when the seeds of rebellion had been sown, and the beginning of the end was birthed.

Yes, these higher beings remembered and were saddened to see just *how far* Mundis had fallen. I mean they knew, but sometimes, sadly, seeing is believing, and to see him, small and green, dressed in ridiculous army apparel, well, this was truly a *most* ignoble sight.

Some turned away, so ashamed of him they could not even bear to look at him.

T'was in a way better that Mundis couldn't remember his past; he too would have been mortified or immortified as the case was, had it been clearer.

'He who cannot be mentioned' had a purpose with respect to leaving Mundis right where he was, although He too, felt sorry for 'Just Bill', a noble and worthy animal, and He did 'Just Bill' the honour of whispering, just that into his ear.

'Just Bill's' ears pricked forward and he let out a happy prrrffffff, and indeed felt privileged, instead of ashamed. He tossed his head, and stamped his hoof and gave his comrades a 'It's *ok* guys, I can cope' look.

How affronted Mundis would have been had he known, he who thought he only followed orders from the Boss. Mundis was also naïve enough to think that the Boss's orders were all that *really* mattered, poor silly little green fallen higher being.

5

The call came and the battalion moved out. The battles were far from over and there was plenty of chasing Johnny Turk up the Philistia Plain toward Jerusalem.

Mundis bounced along, sometimes not even having to hold on to the Officer in front, although he frequently had to turn his head with the continual breaking of wind that was happening.

Honestly, and Beings complain about my smell, I do not know what this soldier had for breakfast, but I am certainly paying for it now.

Mundis was the sort of creature who didn't mind smelling himself, but was very critical of anyone else who offended *his* delicate nostrils.

Still he was rather proud of his ability to rise to the trot and sit into the canter, knees gripping the sides of the horse and back straight.

Oh yes, he fancied himself as quite the picture of modern warfare, hat at the correct angle, facial features a study of sheer determination. Truly he was beginning to feel he was an asset the ANZACS couldn't possibly do without.

He was beginning to forget that he was a small green being on a mission and that his job had nothing to do with chasing Johnny Turk back into the nether regions of the Northern Levant, and everything to do with getting names and numbers of the lax demons who had let their side down.

He had also forgotten that no lesser being ANZAC could see or hear him, and he was rather surprised when he would pipe up and ask what he thought was a sensible question and be totally ignored.

Mundis could have been excused for thinking he was the only higher being around.

The others, the unfallen type were there, but had hidden themselves in clouds of Diamond Dust and were invisible to any other fallen being, and of course lesser beings.

Mundis didn't know about this ploy and would have been most put out had he known. He always felt that the Boss' crowd had all the most up-dated technology and that the others, who should have stayed where they belonged, way up there beyond the blue, but wouldn't, were hopelessly outdated...

How wrong he was.

6

On they rode, caked in dirt, thirsty, hungry and tired, the ANZAC's were now riding with the British and the knowledge of this turned Mundis' thoughts to British Mundis, and he wondered just what his counterpart was up to.

The thought had crossed his mind to text him, and indeed he had tried,

How goes it… doin' it tough? I am – although I do feel as though I am pulling my weight.

(See, he had forgotten he was a green fallen higher being and was thinking he was an ANZAC).

He texted on,

In the saddle from morn till night, fierce fighting and much bloodshed, have sore bottom and a touch of dysentery, please text back and tell me your news?

A message had come in, and Palestinian Mundis was amazed to read that British Mundis had been doing exactly the same things!

My my, he's got a touch of dysentery too! And his bottom's sore, wow!

Then it dawned on him; the text had just come back to himself…

"Oh silly me," exclaimed Mundis, putting his hand to his head and shaking it in disbelief. He did manage a slight chuckle.

Headquarters being Headquarters must have changed their numbers, so the text had just come back to himself, and British Mundis' number was a mystery.

And sensibly it remained one.

Unbeknownst to Palestinian Mundis, British Mundis was having a ball. He and his fellow Downing Street inmates Adultery, Lust, Flirtation, Lies and Lush were continually on the town. West End shows were fabulous, they saw everything they could, they were continually dining out, spending weekends with the Aristocracy in the country and generally wearing themselves out with activity –

figuratively speaking of course, not that they *could* wear themselves out, being immortal and all.

They were totally unaware of the other types of fallen higher beings that had been introduced into the atmosphere because of the War. Beings such as Grief, Hardship, Pain, Fear, Anger, Poverty, Debilitation, Injury, Jealousy, Irreplaceable Loss and many others. Mundis and his crowd ignored these dreary chaps and concentrated on all that was pleasant and fun. They sometimes had to look hard for it, but no matter, that was half the game.

Downing Street was a hive of business, and most parts of it were completely accessible to Mundis and his associates. The only places that were off limits were Mrs. Lloyd George's apartments.

Mrs. Lloyd George was a Believer in 'Him who cannot be mentioned' and she was a pray-er.

Mundis believed in 'Him who cannot be mentioned' too, but the belief had quite different connotations for him.

Mundis and the 'fun gang' felt deathly ill whenever they saw her.

She would come down the stairs and surprise them (not that she could see them) and they would all keel over in a dead faint, draped wherever they fell. It was all *most* unbecoming and rather embarrassing.

The higher beings present would hide amused smiles and sail right on down behind Mrs. Lloyd George, trailing their diamond dust presence behind them.

Mrs. Lloyd George was blissfully unaware of the commotion she caused.

Oh my, yes. Mundis much preferred the company of Prime Minister Lloyd George's pretty young secretary, she was an absolute dish and anybody who was anybody wanted to get to know her; a firm favourite with the young Princes and indeed most of the Aristocracy, except perhaps the Queen, who was a firm favourite with Mrs. Lloyd George.

The young Secretary, as I have already intimated, was a very firm favourite with the Prime Minister.

But this was not meant to be about British Mundis, for now we are still travelling toward Jerusalem with Palestinian Mundis, and I can tell you he was not having quite the same time as his counterpart. If anyone had drawn the short straw it was him...

Although he was not entirely miserable, it was a bit of a 'Boys own adventure', especially if you were immortal.

Sshhh...I am really hoping Palestine Mundis never finds out about British Mundis' adventures. I cannot stand arguing and I am afraid there would be a real doozy if Palestinian Mundis discovered just what British Mundis was up to...

I am very relieved they cannot text each other...aren't you?

7

Let us now wholly concentrate on Palestinian Mundis for a while, and just what he was observing from the back of 'Just Bill' is a vital part of Israeli history.

Although we must remember that it had not been called Israel for many centuries, indeed it had been Palestine since the Roman Emperor Hadrian in 135 AD gave it that name.

And in calling it Palestine, they, the Romans, hoped to further insult the Jews by calling it after their age old enemies, the Philistines. The name Palestine is actually derived from the name Philistine.

Mundis, if he knew this, was not that interested, he was busy picking his teeth with the sharp end of one of the Ostrich feathers in the ANZAC's hat.

He hadn't brought a toothbrush and was feeling the deprivation.

'Just Bill' trotted on, tired and thirsty, but being the entirely devoted creature he was, he bore his Master with pride and faithfulness.

He bore Mundis with well disguised toleration. He savoured the words that had been spoken to him by 'He who cannot be Mentioned' like a tasty carrot all covered in sparkling dew on a spring morning...

"Ppprrrrrr," just the thought of those words kept him going.

'Just Bill's' heart was heavy and sad. He had seen many of his closest friends fall in battle and he missed their conversation and their company.

They had travelled many miles together and had shared many memories; some of them he had known from foalhood and indeed their deaths were a bitter blow to him.

Still they moved on, fighting where they had to, and generally pushing Johnny Turk further back to where he belonged. The casualties were great and the diamond clouded higher beings were busy doing their war work and carrying out their instructions.

They passed Jewish settlements where all the inhabitants came out to welcome the British/ANZAC forces. These villages were attractive, with red tiled roofs, whitewashed edifices and pretty gardens full of fruit trees and flower beds. The aroma of some of these late blooms was breathtakingly beautiful.

An oasis of colour in otherwise drab surroundings.

The cheering and excitement was tangible. Mundis kept hearing the word *Prophesy* and the word *Jerusalem* whispered in the same breath.

Perhaps it was the scent of the flowers, but suddenly, Mundis was sharply reminded of the vision he had seen in Basel, when Herzl had been addressing the First Zionist Convention.

Drat…but there right before his eyes was the veritable orchard that Mundis had seen back in Basel. Right there in front of him, orange trees, lemon trees and flowers of all descriptions, the aroma permeating the entire earth.

He tried to remember the year he had been in Basel…1897. And now it was 1917. Twenty years and look what had happened.

Mundis felt like throwing up. Why, he didn't really know but he just did. He just managed to swallow the bile that had risen up.

I mean, Mundis knew Israel was a nation again, he had known since 1948, but he was beginning to see that 'He who cannot be mentioned' was absolutely positively involved here, and no amount of higher fallen being activity could have stopped it, so why even bother trying to get names and numbers.

Truly the Boss was barking up the wrong tree here, but try telling him that…even if Mundis thought he could, he very quickly put it aside. Useless, the Boss had to have someone to blame, it was just the way he worked, and after eons of years in his service, Mundis knew better than to question.

And Mundis was learning that if 'He who cannot be mentioned and was best left alone' was involved, then Mundis had better not be, 'cause there was no winning for Mundis.

Still he had his orders…and even though no call had come through from Headquarters, he figured he would do his best in any case and keep on track, and try and get some names and numbers.

"I mean honestly, someone must have slipped up somewhere,

someone, that is, with a name and face and a number and a *head* that was going to roll…"

Although the way he said this to himself, was with a sort of false bravado.

He was really beyond thinking that he was ever going to pin Israel on anyone other than on … *Him who absolutely cannot be mentioned ever ever EVER!*

Mundis fingered his precious iPhone and savoured the thought of punching those names in, but with very little hope of really doing it.

Post Script

Amazing, what had happened in the twenty years since the first Zionist Conference in Basel.

Many Jewish settlers had returned to their ancient biblical homeland after an absence of nearly two thousand years.

Although this was not to say that Jews had *not* been living in Israel since the beginning of the Diaspora two thousand years before, they indeed had been. In fact, contrary to popular belief, there has always been a Jewish presence in Israel, since the days of the Exodus from Egypt.

However, now, there was a definite call in the Heavenlies to return home, and home they came.

'He who cannot be mentioned' had whistled for them, and dispatched His faithful higher being servants to assist.

And help them they did; they steadied weary feet, wiped away heartbroken tears and generally made the transition from Civilization to Frontier Life as easy as they could for their precious charges…

'He who cannot be mentioned' knew what was around the corner.

He knew the twentieth century was going to be one in which His chosen people would not fare well in Europe, *even* worse than they had fared in other centuries.

Indeed He was providing a safe haven for all those who would listen to His call…and that safe haven was their own Biblical home, Erezt Israel.

PART SIX

"I have posted watchmen on your walls, O Jerusalem; they will never be silent day or night. You who call on the LORD, give yourselves no rest, and give Him no rest till He establishes Jerusalem and makes her the Praise of the Earth...

Pass through, Pass through the gates!

Prepare the way for the people. Build up, build up the highway! Remove the stones. Raise a banner for the nations.

The Lord has made proclamation to the ends of the earth; "Say to the daughter of Zion, 'See, your Saviour comes! See His reward is with him'."

They will be called the Holy People, the redeemed of the LORD; and you will be called Sought After, the city no longer deserted."

Isaiah 62:6-7, 10-12

1

The talk in the old city of Jerusalem was one of doom and gloom. The green beings were predicting an exodus. There was much hanging upside down from available space and chewing this over, the facts were discussed, digested, spat out and discussed and then re-digested again.

This was certainly something of a shock after centuries of inhabiting the place. In fact it was something of a catastrophe; they were comfortable and familiar with their surroundings and had never even envisaged moving.

They belonged here, amidst the souks and the synagogues, amidst the smells and colours and general ambience that filled the place to overflowing. Truly it was and is one of the most vibrant places on the planet, and no higher or lesser being could ask for a more marvellous location to live, well, that is if they have to live here on earth.

Ahh, to be able to breathe in the very breath of the centre of the Universe…perfection indeed.

These oh so fortunate green beings knew their way around the rabbit warren that was the Old City like the back of their green and sometimes scaly hands. In fact in those days it was the only city, there was a scattering of tiny villages outside the walls, but the metropolis that is Jerusalem today, was still ninety plus years away.

They knew the families, and had known them for generations, they took a personal interest in all the different doings and goings on, and they generally just fitted in.

They were familiar with the Rabbi's prayers, the Mullah's cries and the Priest's routines. They certainly didn't disturb anyone, all was peaceful and friendly and no one could understand the need for change.

But rumour had it that the British were coming and the Turks would have to leave... and what this meant for the higher fallen beings of Jerusalem, well no one really knew.

Chances were they would have to move, and then perhaps be able to come back again after the initial shock and settling down period.

Chances were they would be replaced with another group of green beings, a sort of British contingent, and they, the original group, would have to go back from whence they came - but as that was over four hundred years ago it was sort of difficult to put into perspective.

Alas, most had forgotten from 'whence' it was they had come.

Although some remembered it was north of where they were now, somewhere hot, barren, hilly, where lesser beings wore long flowing robes and lived in whitewashed houses.

"Sounds exactly like where we are now, so why not stay..."

The general consensus was not to agree with the last statement, and concur very strongly with the first.

So, go they would.

Check out the new territory, maybe just north of the Galilee, then wait for the rabble to die down. Then they would move right back in again, introduce themselves to the British contingent and work out a Peace Plan and all would be hunky dory.

This was agreed upon as the most sensible idea.

"So pack lightly boys, we won't be away long, just long enough to let the dust settle, and then home again, home again...jiggity jog."

Yep, this is what they planned to do, but no hurry, it hadn't happened yet, and it still may not.

So being the lazy well fed demons they were, they just continued to hang about. Curled in the tops of market store roofs, asleep in the confessional booths of various Churches and stretched out along the top of the Western Wall.

Yep, no hurry, it may not happen, so why fuss.

2

B ut happen it did.
  And just as the Jerusalem green beings were gearing up for Christmas.

They were decorating the Christmas trees in the various churches, well they were *helping* to decorate the Christmas trees in the various Churches, (they were usually curled up asleep under the trees or buried beneath heaps of tinsel and other sparkly stuff).

They were also lighting the candles for Hanukah.

Truly it was a very inconvenient time to move.

In fact they had sort of forgotten about moving and were generally thinking along the lines of staying. They had heard some rumours since the first flurry, but as they had spent quite a bit of time asleep since the first flurry, then they had sort of missed out on the big important stuff.

Stuff like the 'British were almost here, and perhaps we really better leave'.

Now if Mundis had known this, he would have had a field day punching in the names and numbers of these lazy beings into his iPhone. Ah it would have been success at last, and he would then have been able to text Headquarters and say,

GOT 'EM, can I come home now please?

Mundis, however, was still sitting on 'Just Bill's' back. He really was a lazy little chap, he should have gotten off and wandered into Jerusalem ages ago and sought out the guys who were meant to be defending the so-called 'Holy City'.

However that thought had never really occurred to Mundis. In fact *he* had been asleep for much of the last stages of the journey. If his Officer had been fighting, he had not really been aware of it; the sleep he was in was a very deep sleep, in fact very like the sleep that had been put upon his colleagues in Jerusalem and their far-off colleagues at Number Ten in London.

Yes, *asleep,* his head up against the Officer's back and his hat askew and his mouth open, and, I am afraid to say, he was dribbling a bit and snoring very loudly; this was not a pretty sight. And if his Officer did leave the saddle to put his bayonet through a Turk, then Mundis just sort of slipped forward and continued sleeping.

When the Officer mounted 'Just Bill' again, he just sat on Mundis' head and no one was any the wiser, least of all Mundis. Inconveniences like that did not worry him.

The rare times he was awake, he complained (to no one in particular) about a very sore bottom and quite a head and back ache. He was also rather concerned about the touch of dysentery he had suffered, and whether or not it had damaged his large intestine, he wasn't sure, but he sincerely hoped not. He thought he would get it checked out as soon as he returned to Headquarters. They were very good at that sort of thing and although they were extraordinarily busy, they usually made room for him, being the Head Librarian and all. Mundis had no problem pulling strings.

The other sort of higher beings smiled as they saw him asleep or drinking whisky from his hip flask. This is exactly how he was meant to be, asleep. Mundis had no idea that they had anything to do with his constant tiredness and lack of energy.

These higher beings were getting ready to enter Jerusalem and rid it of anything to do with the Ottoman Empire. They were strapping on their armour, sharpening their swords and generally preparing themselves for a skirmish that would cleanse the place from enemy troops once and for all.

Their beautiful eyes were wide with excitement and their Angelic hearts beating rapidly. This was a day that had been anticipated for almost two thousand years and 'He who cannot be mentioned' was in charge here. *This was His city and He was calling the shots.*

The word in Heaven was THE TIME HAS COME.

This was to be the culmination of centuries of waiting. No-one in Heaven was silly enough to think it was going to be easy. They knew the years ahead would be fraught with hardship, fighting, endless discussions and many, many tears.

This was the natural progression since the days of Herzl's first Basel Conference in 1897 and all Heaven was rejoicing.

3

The shofar call, when it came, was loud and clear.

The host of higher beings on the ground around Jerusalem rose in one accord into the air, with wings wide and silver hair streaming. They descended upon the Holy City in a fury of brandished swords and a flurry of triumphant voices.

The startled green beings in Jerusalem rose from their sleep with no time to stretch or yawn. Falling over each other they ran for the closest exits into the desert, and for the purposes of this story, were never seen again.

The enemy host in the air was dealt a swift and deadly blow and they too were last seen flying high above the barren and rocky hills that surround His city.

On the Lesser Being level, the Turks pretty much did the same thing, although they ran through the streets saying to anyone who would listen, "We've got to go."

They too disappeared into the desert, eventually to be driven up to the North, which was indeed their original home.

Mundis, roused from his stupor by a shofar call which sounded vaguely familiar, peeped out from behind the Officer's back and was appalled to see the rear ends of countless numbers of green beings fleeing out of the Jaffa Gate and up the road in such a hurry as he had never before seen.

No use grabbing his iPhone and hoping to punch names and numbers in; he had missed it and again would have to explain to the Boss about his failure.

Mundis sank back into the saddle in shock and disappointment. His eyes lifted to the Heavenlies in a sense of hopelessness, and in doing so he caught a glimpse of the now plainly visible higher being host which was rising in triumph over the city of Jerusalem.

Swords held high above their heads and their voices praising and singing glory to 'He who cannot be mentioned', Who was sitting in magnificent splendour and amid tremendous excitement in the Heavenly City.

Mundis sat there speechless. There was nothing to say again, all was done and the future was before him. Mundis could see that there was no going home for him, no cosy apartment with his wonderful view and his faithful Hornback, no endless good books and lovely music, no watching the moon rise through the towering gum trees on a hot summer's night.

Mundis was now locked into crawling up through history in a futile effort of laying the blame on some unfortunate and elusive green being who would never materialise.

He let a real tear or two slip down his cheek and a real hiccup belch forth. Wiping his dripping nose on the back of the Officer's shirt, Mundis sniffed loudly.

In thinking this he was half right, but the future held quite a few surprises...and we shall see what they are in the next book.

BOOK TWO

INTRODUCTION

My first book about Mundis Veridis concentrated primarily on the beginning of the journey toward the rebirth of Israel, circa 1894 until 1917, and the opposition that one little green fallen being experienced.

So much so that he was unable to get even one name and number of even one fallen higher being whose lack of insight had allowed Israel's rebirth to happen.

He, as you will remember was aghast at this dismal state of affairs, and also, I think, embarrassed, although he did put on a sort of brave, if somewhat surprised, face.

This second book deals with the period of time between the two Great Wars, 1919 to 1939 and also during World War II and up to the time of the Declaration of the state of Israel in 1948.

Our hero is again the same small green being called Mundis.

He is still two Mundi, British Mundis and Palestinian Mundis, and he is still very green, very selfish and very fashion conscience.

About half way through the story we will see the introduction of a third Mundis; he will be known as German Mundis, and is also very green, very selfish and extremely fashion conscience.

In this book, however, they are all having an easier time.

All three Mundis beings are allowed to work hand in hand with their fallen Being cohorts, and are called to send the names and numbers of those who are responsible for making it difficult for Israel to exist.

The fortunate beings will then be given Prime Positions in the Boss' coming kingdom.

This is a much easier task, because as Mundis wisely observes… "everyone is making it difficult for Israel to exist", so hence all three of them are kept pretty busy sending names and numbers in to Headquarters.

Mim Lennon

PART ONE

"The days are coming," declares the Lord, "when men will no longer say, 'As surely as the Lord lives, who brought the Israelites up out of Egypt', but they will say, 'As surely as the Lord lives, who brought the Israelites up out of the land of the north and out of all the countries where He had banished them.'
For I will restore them to the land I gave to their forefathers."
Jeremiah 16:14-15

"For our struggle is not against flesh and blood, but against the rulers, against the authorities, against the powers of this dark world and against the spiritual forces of evil in the heavenly realms."
Ephesians 6:12

1

Palestinian Mundis

The call came to dismount.

Mundis dismounted.

And followed the Officer he had been riding behind for the last few weeks, into the parade line.

Mundis had become quite attached to him now, and did not really want to leave him; you know how it is when you have been travelling with someone for quite a long time, they sort of become very familiar (even their smell) in every sense of the word, and the future looks bleak without them.

Mundis did not feel the same way about 'Just Bill' - in fact I am ashamed to say that Mundis poked his tongue out at 'Just Bill' when he got off.

'Just Bill' stamped his hooves and tossed his head and gave a joyful whinny. He was far too mature and sensible to poke his tongue out, but he certainly felt like it and just restrained himself from reciprocating.

"Glad that's over," mumbled Mundis, "where to now?"

"FALL IN!"

And Mundis 'fell in'. Right in the front with the Officers, between his very own Officer and another, slightly smaller and more rotund one. They did look strange standing there, all three of them in a row, two tall Australians and one very short Mundis. It was a good thing the two Australians couldn't see him.

It was a good thing no one could see him.

However the other sort of higher beings *could* see him very well indeed They were again embarrassed by his presence, and the fact that he was so cock sure of his position, and his place with the ANZAC forces.

"Just who does he think he is?" they asked each other.

Mundis, had I think, forgotten that he was just a small green being on a mission, and had in fact got all mixed up with an identity problem, and was now not sure who he was.

He had in fact what I think is termed 'Stockholm Syndrome', even though the ANZACs hadn't kidnapped him (if anything it had been the other way around).

He was identifying with them, and had become very sympathetic to their cause; he was not entirely sure what their cause was, but he was right there with it and even had the uniform to match.

Not the bag though, he still had his Lawrence of Arabia bag slung across his body, complete with his water bottle and now dog-eared copy of Dickens' *Little Dorrit*.

In fact if anyone had taken the time to explain the ANZACs' cause, and what it was actually going to mean to him, personally, one day on a higher spiritual level, I know he would have been horrified.

But there was no one of that calibre around, at least no one of his sort of calibre, and even if there had been, they in all honesty (a dubious term when applied to a green being) really didn't understand what was going to happen in the end either...

(It really was something that only 'He who cannot be mentioned' understood completely and it was something He had shared with His forces, higher and lesser being and them only.

The Boss, had he been there at this point, would have picked Mundis up by his collar, and possibly thrown him into the middle of next week.

And this was something he was quite capable of doing.

The Boss would have understood the significance of the war in Palestine being won by the British, and he in his eternal wickedness would have been working overtime to throw spanner after spanner into the works.)

Or maybe it wasn't Stockholm Syndrome, maybe it was Jerusalem Syndrome which is sort of similar really. Or maybe Mundis just had a touch of the sun...

Or maybe having his head underneath the Officer's backside whilst he was asleep had squashed some brain cells - either way he was behaving in a most peculiar manner.

Or then again, perhaps it was the disappointment of not having a single name or number to send to Headquarters, and it had finally pushed him over the edge, and now he had decided that if he couldn't beat 'em, he'd join em.

Whatever…perhaps we shall never know just what he was thinking, or just where he was at.

The higher beings stationed on the ramparts of the Old City of Jerusalem were beginning to feel less embarrassed for him now, and were starting to see the funny side.

In fact some were beginning to roar with laughter at the mere sight of him falling in with his 'fellow soldiers'.

Others were literally holding each other up in hysterics, tears rolling down their golden cheeks, and their sides beginning to ache with mirth.

Perhaps it was a touch of hysteria on their part, they had just fought the Battle for Jerusalem and won.

But I don't think so.

He truly did look ridiculous; the expression on his face was priceless. Eyes ahead, shoulders and back straight and gun and hat at just the right angle. He had even polished his boots and got himself an extra long Ostrich feather.

Honestly, what a sight.

Happily for him, he had no idea that he was the cause of such jollity. His eyes were blinded to the magnificent higher beings above him, they were again shrouded in their diamond dust cloaks, and therefore completely invisible to the naked lesser, and fallen higher being eye.

Just as well really, he was so full of pride and so lacking in humour, especially when it concerned himself.

He would have had absolutely no concept of the joke at all.

Sadly he had lost all his sense of good honest fun, and his sense of the ridiculous, when he chose the wrong Master all those centuries ago.

Isn't that always the case, with people who take themselves too seriously? They are really *very* boring to be with, all religious in whatever it is they believe in and self inflated…very tedious.

Perhaps it is a deep down insecurity.

Mundis without realising it had *also* lost his absolute security centuries ago when he followed the wrong Master.

2

However for now, we shall leave him to stand with *his* ANZACs, and then when the time is right, to follow General Allenby, the leader in command of the British and ANZAC forces, as he walks through the Jaffa Gate into the Old City in order to make a formal declaration of Martial Law.

Allenby, like his men, had also dismounted, and in a sign of humility, had chosen to walk through the small door of the Jaffa Gate.

A door that had been shut for years, and was only opened especially for him on this occasion.

Mundis was to his right as the General walked in; he was standing as we know with the Australians and the New Zealanders, and on the other side were the men from England, Scotland, Wales and Ireland - all of whom had been involved in fighting against the Turks and the Germans in this Palestinian part of World War I.

This was a momentous time in history, and all present were aware of the solemnity of the occasion.

Mundis and the men formed a semi-circle opposite to Allenby, with their backs against the walls surrounding Christ Church. Allenby stood on the platform opposite Christ Church, and just in front of the citadel of David, the only authentic piece of building left since the time the Romans had ransacked the city two thousand years ago.

Here the Proclamation of Martial Law was read, in Arabic, Hebrew, English, French, Italian, Greek and Russian.

Mundis of course, understood every word in every language, and agreed wholeheartedly, nodding ever so slightly when appropriate.

Nobody else nodded, it was all a bit beyond them, except the English bits. The majority just wanted to go somewhere, relax, have a beer and take the weight of their feet.

PROCLAMATION

Of Martial Law in Jerusalem

To the inhabitants of Jerusalem and the people dwelling in its vicinity.

The defeat inflicted upon the Turks by the troops under my command has resulted in the occupation of your city by my forces. I therefore here and now proclaim it to be under Martial Law, under which form of administration it will remain so long as military considerations make it necessary.

However lest any of you should be alarmed by reason of your experience at the hands of the enemy who has retired, I hereby inform you that it is my desire that every person should pursue his lawful business without fear of interruption.

Furthermore, since your city is regarded with affection by the adherents of three of the greatest religions of mankind, and its soil has been consecrated by the prayers and pilgrimages of devout people of those three religions for many centuries, therefore do I make known to you that every sacred building, monument, holy spot, shrine, traditional site, endowment, pious bequest or customary place of prayer, of whatsoever form of the three religions, will be maintained and protected according to the existing customs and beliefs of those to whose faiths they are sacred.

General Allenby
Commander in Chief
Egyptian Expeditionary Forces
December 1917

The absolute outcome of this Proclamation was that Britain was in charge after four hundred years of Turkish Rule. And whilst in charge, they promised to respect the rights of the Religions in that city.

(A rash statement, for they had no idea what the future was to hold with relation to Religion in this city…how many tears, how much bloodshed).

'He who cannot be mentioned' knew and His heart went out to

His city and His people, but He understood it was a process, and one that in the end would be for His Glory and His Names' sake.

Johnny Turk was still in the process of being beaten, but his presence had already left Southern Palestine and Jerusalem, and he was being driven further north with the aid of fighter planes and men still out on patrol.

Mundis *did* feel proud - it was a heady thing to be part of the victorious army.

One wonders *when* reality was going to hit; it certainly wasn't happening now.

The higher beings had just managed to compose themselves, they had wished to listen to Allenby's declaration, as it was of the utmost importance to 'He who cannot be mentioned' and they certainly could not have arrived back in Heaven and said, "Sorry Sir, we were laughing so hard that we missed the whole thing."

Not that 'He who cannot be mentioned' could not see and hear the proceedings and declaration, but in this case He did expect *some decorum* from His forces.

And decorum He got.

His higher beings had lined the walls of the Old City around Christ Church and the citadel, while others had risen into the air and were peering down, their eyes shining with excitement and their hearts throbbing with love, with beautiful diamond dusted cloaks blowing in the wind and their armour just visible underneath. Some may have thought that even the Sun had crept closer to witness this spectacle.

Truly they hadn't been so excited since their Lord had been born just a few miles from this spot nearly two thousand years ago.

On that night they had filled the heavens with their praises and singing; on that night their beautiful eyes had been shining with love and their arms lifted in adoration...indeed,

"ALL HEAVEN DECLARED HIS GLORY" on THAT night.

3

Mundis continued to listen with interest - that is, until he could feel his iPhone vibrating in his back pocket.

Honestly, who can that be? Thank heavens I've put it on silent, t'would not be a good thing if the strains of 'We all live in a yellow submarine' were to shatter the proceedings of this important affair.

He really was a little confused, and more than a little out of touch with reality, as if anyone else in Jerusalem that day, could have heard his iPhone ringing.

S'pose I better get it… he had also forgotten ***just who*** it might be calling.

He slipped backwards out of the line and floated through the surrounding stone wall, into the grounds of Christ Church, the oldest Anglican Church in the Middle East and a bastion of Evangelical activities.

Mundis was not to know this, and even if he had, he would not have cared, he would have been delighted. He could usually find a way to water a good Evangelical message down, you know, a blackout, or an old lady fainting.

The possibilities were endless.

He was very good at disrupting Churches and had indeed won prizes for his outstanding services to duty:

CIRCA 20TH CENTURY PRIZE GIVING
1ST PRIZE FOR CHAOS IN LOCAL CHURCHES
Awarded to… M.Veridis.

THE LUCIFER PRIZE FOR DISHARMONY AND
GENERAL DISCORD
Awarded to… M.Veridis.

THE GENERAL PRIZE FOR APPALLING BEHAVIOUR IN

WORLD AFFAIRS
Awarded to... M.Veridis.

Mundis loved a really good chance to show his skills off, and he had the trophies to prove it, proudly displayed in his Trophy Cabinet back home.

Amazing pieces of Art.

The last prize I have mentioned, the one for 'Appalling Behaviour', stood at least one metre tall, and was a statue of the United Nations Building in solid gold with emerald encrusted vines wound all the way through and over it.

It was meant to signify confusion.

It worked very well, on the trophy and in reality.

In fact Mundis would have drinks parties complete with delicious canapés, and he would make the cabinet the focal point. He would make sure the conversation somehow got round to his prizes and he would then tell stories, and of course exaggerate the best bits.

Thankfully for the hardworking Vicar of Christ Church, there wasn't a service on today, everyone being out in the streets listening to what was happening and breathing in the atmosphere.

Mundis floated through the front doors and positioned himself just under the pulpit, sitting down with his back leaning up against the cool sandstone wall.

"Ahh, bliss!"

The peace of the church was soothing after the excitement outside, and Mundis was able to collect his thoughts and simply gather himself together.

T'was nice to sit down on something that didn't move, and it was nice to have no-one sitting immediately in front of you, making smells, and hopping off and killing people and other messy stuff.

Perhaps I am going to be able to function without my Officer...

Mundis checked the caller's ID and his heart sank.

Reality hit.

Big time.

And all his ANZAC delusions flew out the window, and Mundis remembered exactly who he was, and what he was meant to be doing.

He called back.

"Ah Veridis, any news, Veridis?"

"Ah no sir, ahh, only saw the backsides of the green beings as they fled Jerusalem, enemy forces got here first."

(I forgot to mention before, Mundis was horrified that none of the green beings he had seen leaving Jerusalem were wearing clothes. He was actually speechless; being very fashion conscious himself he could not quite get his head around their nakedness, and really felt they had let the Boss's side down badly. I mean, who cares that they had run, it was much worse that their sense of decorum was so sadly lacking, and they quite simply did not care how they looked.)

Mundis was amazed at his brazen honesty. Glory, but what had happened to him? No lie rose to his lips, he was aghast at his statement.

He'd clearly been with the Australians too long…and if anyone called a spade a spade, it was those lesser beings.

Again there was icy silence on the other end.

And then a *most* amazing thing happened.

"Veridis, we have changed tack, yes Veridis, you heard me, changed tack, I say…

"Instead of getting the names and numbers of the culprits responsible for not stopping Israel from coming into existence, we now need you to get us the names and numbers of all those responsible *for* making it difficult for Israel to exist.

We wish to reward them, and give them positions of GREAT IMPORTANCE IN MY COMING KINGDOM."

"Yes sir!" Mundis was standing now and saluting.

"Oh and Veridis, you may find a reward for yourself in all this too, yes Veridis. When I rule the world, you Veridis will be in charge back here in Headquarters, running your own skeleton staff. How do you like that idea Veridis?"

"Oh, very much sir, very much indeed, thank you sir, I'll do my best sir!"

"I Veridis will be in some capital, running *MY* world, *MY* way… perhaps Babylon, perhaps Rome, I haven't decided yet Veridis, but definitely eventually Jerusalem."

"Oh, yes sir, very good sir, as you say sir."

"Well goodbye Veridis, and keep your phone on...Oh, and one more thing Veridis, you are no longer *under* cover, you are able to hob nob and join your brothers in arms, you know Veridis like the three musketeers, one for all and all for one."

"Ooh, thank you Sir!"

And Mundis pressed the end button and flopped over in relief.

Amazing.

The Boss had seemed to accept that no one green being was to blame for Israel's existence, and that the real task now was to reward those who were making it *difficult* for her *to* exist...

Well that was no problem, the whole world seemed to be very good at that, yes the tide had turned, and Mundis envisaged punching names and numbers in all the time.

And to top it all off, Mundis one day would get to go home.

Home... the very word brought comfort to his heart and ease to his horse-bruised bottom.

Home, I'm going home! Don't know how many more sleeps, but who cares...

I AM GOING HOME!!

And he broke into a wonderful rendition of *When I rule the world* followed closely by *Homeward bound* - two of his very favourites, complete with dance steps and hand movements.

If the stained glass windows of Christ Church had been more than just stained glass windows, *well...*they would have looked down in wonder and amazement.

Postscript

Palestinian Mundis spent the next four years watching his cronies cause as much trouble as they possibly could in the British Military rule of Palestine.

At the end of 1921, Britain established the 'British Mandate' under the auspices of the League of Nations, the body set up after World War I in order to safeguard against another war.

Mundis during this time, was able to punch many names and numbers of green beings through to Headquarters, but only those he felt were due special rewards for outstanding service to the Boss and world.

He on the whole, was generally felt to be doing a great job.

Although his living quarters during this time left a little to be desired.

He frequented the souks and the alleyways that make up the Old City, and spent quite a bit of time in the Church of the Holy Sepulchre; he actually enjoyed this place and felt that the dome area had great potential - he wasn't sure for what, it was just a general feeling.

He loved to sit in the dark and watch the arguments that took place there. It was inhabited by many different factions of the Orthodox Church and no one could agree on anything.

Mundis did enjoy insidiously stirring the pot.

However it was not until the British High Commissioner arrived that Mundis had a permanent home in Jerusalem. This came as an absolute Boss-send to him. He was getting tired of the constant shifting, and really needed a place in order for him to become totally effective in the gathering of information and sending it on to Headquarters.

He felt a bit like one of those French Resistance workers in World War II, you know, setting up the radio equipment in the attic of a Parisian House, complete with antenna and short wave radio. He seriously contemplated getting a dark wig and flowered print dress, with some sensible shoes and bag to match.

Palestinian Mundis really did have a dramatic streak.

Herbert Samuel, a Jew, was the first British High Commissioner to Palestine. He was appointed in 1921 and was there to oversee the establishment of a Jewish homeland in Palestine, through immigration and the purchasing of land.

Samuel was also to keep watch on the rights of the Arabs in the land.

The commissioner moved into his apartments and Mundis moved right in with him - wonderful apartments from a Palestinian point of view. Definitely more on the British side than the Arabic, although it did have a slight sort of Byzantine feel. Mundis enjoyed that kind of décor, and made him feel right at home amongst the beautiful rugs, the hanging lamps and interesting ornaments.

Yes, Mundis did not at all mind a touch of Byzantine; he wished he could text British Mundis and compare notes, things like: "Where are you staying, I am at the British High Commissioner's, food okay, décor interesting, visitors fascinating, please text back your particulars, am dying to hear your news."

But to no avail, their numbers were different, and Palestinian Mundis was too nervous to ask Headquarters for the right number.

(He felt sure it would have been refused, and he was quite right, unnecessary communication between green beings on different missions in different countries was not encouraged.)

And as I have mentioned before, 'tis best that Palestinian Mundis, didn't know about British Mundis, as he, British Mundis, really had got the better end of the split.

Let us now spend a little bit of time catching up with British Mundis, we have left him for long enough and we need to see how he is faring, selfish little green being that he is.

4

B ritish Mundis was still ensconced at number 10 Downing Street and was enjoying a wonderful time, and in fact had not given Palestinian Mundis a thought since their original split. He had been having too much fun with his green friends Lust, Flirtation, Lush, Lies and Adultery.

I think he was definitely the most selfish of the Mundi pair, or maybe it was just that his circumstances were so different.

Although, you know how it is, when one person is having a ball, and the other is slogging it out…well there really isn't much common ground.

British Mundis, whilst having forgotten Palestinian Mundis, was not totally forgotten by the Boss, who, after quite a period of silence, remembered him, and made contact and gave orders similar to those he had given Palestinian Mundis…

"Get the names and numbers, Veridis, of all the green beings responsible for making Israel's existence on the face of this earth as uncomfortable as possible…we want to reward them."

He had also promised British Mundis the same carrot that he had promised Palestinian Mundis, that having Headquarters all to themselves, with a skeleton staff when he, the Boss, ruled the world.

And he was also able to come in from the cold and work with his cronies, out in the open.

The Boss didn't know that British Mundis had blown his cover months ago, and had been cavorting with his cronies for quite some time now.

(I can't wait to see what happens when these Mundi have to get together again, I suspect there will be a great deal of pushing and shoving, with one wanting to be on top of the other…so to speak.)

British Mundis had been so excited that, just like his desert counterpart, he did a rendition of *When I rule the world,* complete with dance steps and hand movements.

He didn't sing 'Homeward Bound'; he was not homesick, not the same way Palestinian Mundis was.

British Mundis had not been sitting on a horse and doin' it tough.

And he certainly didn't have an identity problem.

He had never thought he was an ANZAC or the British equivalent, nor did he have any desire to dress up as a French Resistance Worker; he was already dressed as the Kaiser Of Germany.

British Mundis was also excited, because nothing was said about him rejoining Palestinian Mundis, and this was a great relief.

Lloyd George was at this stage still in power, and at the very height of his popularity. He had won the war for the British and they loved him for it; in fact it was said by a leading Conservative "that he, Lloyd George, can be dictator for life".

British Mundis basked in Lloyd George's glory, the Number 10 address opened many doors for him, and he took great advantage of it.

He had followed Lloyd George to France for the Versailles Peace Conference talks, better known as the Treaty of Versailles in 1919. These talks concentrated on war reparations with relation to exactly what Germany should be paying in tribute to the Allied Powers.

As we know, this treaty was violated by Hitler, on almost every level, and has been said to be one of the main reasons for World War II. The economic sanctions placed on Germany were so heavy that one observer stated that she would not finish paying her dues until 2020.

Mundis was not the slightest bit interested in all this, and had decided *he* was on holiday, and did hardly any work at all. He took full advantage of his time in France.

He boated on the Seine, he enjoyed the Art Galleries, he perused the book shops on the Left Bank and even sat in on some lectures at the Sorbonne, the psychology ones being amongst his favourite.

Ahh yes, he had a wonderful time.

Catching the train down to Giverny to wander around Monet's garden was something he just loved. The unusual way the flowers had been planted, all clustered together, an absolute jumble of glorious colours.

He spent quite some time staying in the pretty pink house with the wonderful shutters, he was very well behaved and no one, but no one knew he was there.

Ahh bliss.

He was in Heaven (so to speak), his senses reeling with the delights, in fact he was so happy, he sang…

'Heaven, I'm in Heaven, and my heart beats so
That I can hardly speeeeeak,
And I seem to find the happiness I seek,
When we're out together dancing cheek to cheek…'

And with Lust, Flirtation, Lush, Lies and Adultery along, he certainly had plenty of beings to dance with.

And dance they did, up and down the paths, through the house and the garden, over the Japanese Bridge and back again.

Such fun, such frivolity.

The water garden was one of his favourite places, the pink, yellow and purple waterlilies, so beautiful, such a treat to behold. Although I must say, he did feel slightly homesick when he saw this, as memories of his own original Monet's back home in Headquarters came flooding back.

Not to mention the ones in the Transfer Department, it made him feel quite warm and fuzzy about them too, an amazing turn about, considering how he usually felt about those 'good for nothing scaly reptiles in cushy jobs'.

He wiped a sentimental tear from his eye and sniffed softly, it may be years before he saw 'Home' again.

Mundis during this time, was also able to observe Monet at work, he was actually painting one of the very Water Lily paintings that Mundis had at home in his very own apartment. Quite an experience really, to see something you now owned actually being created.

You know it is a great mistake to think that these higher fallen beings are not interested in beauty and culture and all the wonderful aspects of higher learning, it is a great mistake indeed. They worship the 'Created' and that was their downfall, they took their eyes off the

Creator.

Their dwellings here on earth are beautiful places, saturated in light, beauty and every convenience. Certainly not the dark evil, cob-webbed infested places that most people think of when thinking of fallen higher beings.

In any case we cannot wander through France with Mundis forever, although I would like too (well, not necessarily with him).

Sadly we need to come back to reality, and see what he actually did achieve with regard to work, limited as it was.

5

One can certainly attribute much of the tension between the British Foreign Office and the British Cabinet Office of the day, and the concerns about the running of Palestine, directly on Mundis and his friends (although lesser beings are quite capable of making a mess of things without their aid.)

These two differing bodies, the Foreign Office and the Cabinet Office, saw the administration of Palestine from two differing perspectives.

The Foreign Office was very conscience of the Arab population in Palestine, and did not want the creation of a Jewish state to upset them; the Cabinet Office wanted to continue to administer Palestine within the bounds of the Balfour Declaration.

Mundis and his cronies were frequently in on these meetings, hanging from the ceilings and draped around the backs of chairs, generally whispering confusing information into the hearts and minds of the various ministers involved.

Wonderful stuff and a tremendous amount of fun to be had.

British Mundis was able to send many names and numbers belonging to those green beings worthy of special awards into Headquarters.

Picture him, hanging upside down by his toes, from a light in the centre of the ceiling, whispering divisive utterances, and then punching in the names and numbers of those who were helping him.

There would be a veritable rush at the end of each session to see whose name had been sent to Headquarters. Oh yes, Mundis was very popular and everyone who was green toadied to him.

In fact he was so popular that other green beings took to following his fashion sense and copying his mannerisms. One should be careful when one sees that sort of thing going on; it is not healthy to be under the influence of anyone whose dress code you feel compelled to follow.

If it had not been for the work of the higher beings on the orders of 'He who cannot be mentioned', then I strongly doubt if Palestine would have remained a potential home for the Jews of the world for longer than five minutes.

His spectacular higher beings were in great demand. He kept them busier than they had been for years, and their tasks only rendered to make them more effective and more beautiful than they had ever been before.

They toadied to no one, simply obeying the orders of the Creator, and as a result each of the wonderful higher beings was a magnificent individual creation within themselves.

Their garments were made from a myriad of amazing colours, each with its own special identifying signature. They were breathtakingly beautiful, and when seen, shimmered like a thousand twinkling stars.

They spent countless hours in Palestine and in cities and towns around the world, but particularly in Europe. It was here that they gathered together the local Jewish population, and encouraged them to set up groups to learn about Palestine.

They also encouraged these groups to go to Zionist camps, in order to learn farming skills and outdoor life. These experiences paved the way for many Jews to arrive in Palestine with at least some idea of what to expect in the harsh conditions, lack of sophistication and culture - in short, a complete change from what they had been used to.

So many of the European Jews were academics, lawyers, artists, doctors and other highly skilled professions, truly the 'crème de la crème' of their respective societies. To imagine that these incredibly sophisticated lesser beings could possibly settle into Palestinian society without some sort of introduction was simply asking too much.

'He who cannot be mentioned' had set up these various camps and groups with the specific purpose to encourage them to leave Europe and quite simply go home. He had assigned His higher beings to minister to them, and to generally keep them free of all enemy opposition whilst the time was right.

Sadly though, the time was fast running out, and as many Jewish people as possible needed to leave whilst they still could.

Not that anyone actually saw these higher beings at their work, they were shrouded in their diamond dust cloaks, and were totally invisible to the naked eye. But lesser beings could testify to dreams they had concerning Palestine, and thoughts that popped unbidden into their minds, and the great and overwhelming desire they had to actually *go* there.

Something that their forbears had not had at all, although every year at Passover, they would have said, "next year in Jerusalem".

British Mundis and his cronies were aghast at this news and activity.

They could not understand that whilst their opposition was great, in the sense that many green beings, spent numerous hours whispering fear into the hearts of these European Jews, the overall desire to go to Palestine was *greater*.

Honestly, what was the attraction?

"Palestine?" British Mundis would grumble. "Don't they know it is a dreary place, full of sand, mosquitoes, swamps and flies and absolutely no culture at all?"

British Mundis had forgotten that in just a few years time, Europe especially would be a terrible place to live if you were a Jew.

(Remember both Mundi, whilst, highly intellectually gifted, were both emotional imbeciles, and totally disinterested in anyone but themselves).

And even if he did remember in a rare and rash moment, he certainly did not care.

Selfish little demon that he was.

The Boss, however, was very aware that the Jews should be kept out of Palestine, and as a result he overworked his forces almost to breaking point in a futile effort to keep the Jewish tide at bay.

6

Let us now return to Palestine and see what Palestinian Mundis is up to.

I heave a sigh of thankful relief that again they cannot contact each other. I can just imagine the terrible jealousy that would have erupted had Palestinian Mundis known that British Mundis had been watching Monet paint his Waterlilies. Not to mention actually being in the garden, and wandering through the various paths, smelling the divine scents and feasting his nasty little green/yellow eyes on the kaleidoscope of colours.

I feel quite weak at the thought of the argument that would have resulted. Ah yes, 'tis good that Palestinian Mundis thinks he is doing as well as he is, all settled nicely in the British High Commissioner's residence.

And that he knows nothing, thankfully, about British Mundis.

Palestinian Mundis was very busy in Palestine, punching in names and numbers all over the place in a frenzy of activity. (In fact, as we shall see, he was actually a little too busy.)

How relieved he was to be able to have something positive to send to Headquarters, instead of the miserable reports of the past, which as we know were absolutely devoid of any names at all.

Palestinian Mundis was also busy educating the 'new recruits of green beings', newly arrived in Jerusalem, in society. He was giving fashion tips, and generally speaking very strongly against nakedness, which he felt was a primeval condition, and one that did not best fit higher beings of any type.

The new British High Commissioner had turned into quite an ally; with a little bit of soft whispering from Mundis, he had made Haj Amin al Husseni, the Mufti Of Jerusalem.

Well, one can just imagine the fun that Mundis and his fellow Jerusalemites had with the Mufti - the upshot being, that this particular gentleman became a leading opponent to Jewish immigration, and was an ever-present source of encouragement with respect to riots and other forms of unrest.

Sadly, the Mufti's attitude did much to turn the British away from the original terms of the Balfour Declaration - although many of those British, stationed in the land, had never really taken the Balfour Declaration seriously in any case.

British Mundis and associates were pulling their combined weight quite effectively in London, they knew and understood the score, 'Keep Jews out of Palestine'. They played the game well - but more about them later.

Palestinian Mundis by now had realised that this was too big a job for him, and had set up an agency. It was called 'The No Jews for Palestine Agency'.

There was so much opposition going on with relation to the Jews settling in Palestine, and so much unpleasantness, and everyone was doing such a good job, that it was impossible to send all the names and numbers through to Headquarters.

Mundis set up a system, that went something like this: those who were 'eye-catchingly' good at their jobs received 10 points, those who did a good job but were more in the background, received 5 points, and those who were just down right lazy got 0.

A score of over 50 a day, meant that your name and number was sent through to Headquarters at the end of the week. You can just imagine the time that took. Especially as there was such fierce competition, and such pushing and shoving and general nastiness.

Well, quite frankly, it was just too much, and it left Mundis too little time to enjoy himself.

So, he set up another system, in the dome of the Church of the Holy Sepulchre, a sort of office set up.

Remember he'd had a sense that the Dome area had potential for some such purpose? He now knew why. The office was complete with office manager, on the spot name and number punchers who worked on a roster system, and whose job it was to peruse Jerusalem, and about a dozen secretaries to correlate the information and send it through.

He had computers for everyone, the most up-to-date models,

complete with high speed printers and photocopying machines.

Everyone, as you can imagine, was very well dressed.

Mundis had it all so very well organised, that he was able to take quite a few holidays.

7

...1937

Well, I did hear myself say something about Palestinian Mundis taking a holiday, did you hear that too?

Well personally, whilst not really on his side, I do feel he was probably quite entitled to one. He had by now been working in Jerusalem for all the 1920's and we are now somewhere in the mid 1930's, maybe a bit later, 1937, to be exact.

Well, it is true, he did take a holiday.... to Italy.

Yes, he left the office in the capable hands of another green being, who actually had many hands, not just two, in fact she had as many hands as Medusa had snakes for hair.

True again, but she was a pretty little thing and no one minded this oddity, in fact everyone had great respect for her, as she was able to achieve quite an amazing number of tasks in a very short space of time...not surprisingly, with that number of hands.

Palestinian Mundis felt quite happy leaving everything to her.

He did not, however, tell Headquarters that he was leaving Jerusalem, so therefore he had to get to Italy all by himself. This was not as easy as it is today, when you simply get on a flight at Tel Aviv and get off in Rome.

No, it was not an easy thing at all. The road to Tel Aviv was treacherous and the boat from Jaffa was not always reliable. Still he was determined to go, he hadn't had a holiday since Verbier and even he didn't know how long ago that was.

Mundis was in a bit of a frenzy, he had lost his backpack somewhere in transit (I think it was when he was coming into the Sinai, before he was recruited into the ANZACs) and had to actually carry luggage, a nasty sort of cardboard affair with his name painted on with white paint...

M. VERIDIS.
CHURCH OF THE HOLY SEPULCHRE,
JERUSALEM, PALESTINE

This was not an easy thing to carry, as it didn't even have wheels, but Mundis was not going to arrive in Italy without the right outfits.

After arranging his luggage, he then called the office together, and lied about where he was going.

"I have called you all here this morning to tell you that I will be away for the next three weeks. I am going on a business trip to see my brother, British Mundis, and cannot be contacted, so don't try."

Heads nodded - sometimes two heads on the same body, and in one case, three heads on the same body.

Mundis bowed slightly, said a quick goodbye, picked up his cardboard suitcase, and floated through the dome and into the atmosphere above Jerusalem.

He was heard to mumble something about wishing he had his jolly space craft, and where was it when you really needed it, huh?

Mundis took himself to the bus station in Jerusalem and boarded the next armoured bus going to Tel Aviv. The buses had to be armour-plated, because in those days there were so many Arab attacks against the Jews going to Tel Aviv and back again, that not to travel in an armour-plated bus was just too dangerous.

The Haganah, which had been formed in 1921, was the Jewish Defence Organisation, and could usually be relied on to protect these buses; the British sadly could not be relied upon. In fact the Haganah operated outside of their approval.

Mundis, always the being to take the most convenient way to anything, or indeed out of anything, had decided to take the bus. What did he care that he was working against the Jews and for the Arabs and with the British, he just wanted to get to Italy, and if this was the only way to go, bar floating there by himself, then this was the way he went.

He would have liked to just disperse his particles, but as we know, this meant telling Headquarters, and he certainly was not going to do that; a refusal often offends, and Mundis certainly did not want to be offended and to be told he couldn't go.

Mundis positioned himself up the back of the bus. He had put his case on the roof with the other luggage and was happily seated in between a Rabbi from Jerusalem and an Orthodox priest from his own home office.

Mundis' little legs stuck out in front of him and he pulled his beret over his eyes and slept all the way to Tel Aviv. Thankfully for him, there were no attacks and everyone was more than relieved to arrive. Travel in those days was definitely the luck of the draw.

Although had there been an attack, Mundis would have just floated the rest of the way, and left the dead and dying, dead and dying.

He was not someone who would have stayed around to help. Italy awaited, and with Italy came Rome, Florence and his favourite of all places, Venice.

8

The docks in Jaffa were busy with vessels. Mundis had hitched a ride there from the main bus station in Tel Aviv, and was now busy considering which boat to take to Italy.

There were actually three leaving in the next few days, but Mundis wished to be certain to choose the one with the most comfortable accommodation and preferably one that did not have too many lesser beings on board.

Sadly, he was not to be granted the whole wish, I mean the accommodation was adequate, but the number of people travelling was too many for his liking, and he was going to have to share the cabin.

He had chosen one with a British Officer. Mundis had seen this specimen of Britishness on the bus. Mundis liked the sound of his terribly British accent, although he was a little disappointed with his uniform. He was not as neat as Mundis would have liked and there was a distinct smell of onions about him, and visions of the Sinai and his one onion came rushing back.

But he was the best of a dubious bunch, and he had a spare bunk in his cabin. Mundis was not a green being who really enjoyed light fittings and so forth unless he really had to enjoy them.

The British officer was obviously going to Italy for a bit of rest and recuperation; yes, Mundis felt he could relate to this Lesser Being.

He was going for a bit of rest and recuperation too.

The cabin was light and airy, with bunk beds, a basin, a set of two drawers and a shared cupboard *and* a wonderful round port hole. The voyage took about four days, depending on conditions and Mundis felt that he would be quite comfortable in this set up.

Mundis chose the top bunk and unpacked his suitcase. The Officer was left with the bottom bunk, not that he seemed to mind, he simply didn't know he had had the decision taken out of his hands.

Mundis was lying peacefully on the bed, arms behind his head, watching the reflection of the sea on the ceiling and just about to drift off to sleep, when his room mate proceeded to kneel down and pray.

Mundis sat up, lent over and looked aghast at the man.

Honestly, but what does he think he is doing, kneeling there with his hands folded in prayer?

Horrified he began to listen.

"Heavenly Father, I ask that you would cleanse this cabin from any evil that has ever dwelt in here, and indeed is dwelling here, that you would make it fit for your purposes and your purposes only. I command all emissaries of the devil to leave henceforth and never return, and I pray this in the mighty name of your son, Yeshua."

With that prayer, two of the largest higher beings that Mundis had ever seen entered the room (without even knocking) and proceeded to pack up Mundis' belongings (without folding them) and then to grab Mundis most unceremoniously by the scruff of the neck and hoist him out of bed and into the corridor.

Where much to his amazement, he was left.

Mundis was astounded, and the only thing that occurred to him was that he was glad the Officer had not prayed that "any evil emissaries on this entire ship would be told to leave" because that would mean that Mundis and his luggage would have been left floating somewhere in the Mediterranean, and Mundis was not sure how well either he or his cardboard suitcase would float.

Mundis picked up his suitcase and wandered from cabin to cabin, trying to find one that had a completely free bunk. After that rather disappointing start to his holiday, he just did not feel like sharing with anyone, and he was not in the mood for light fittings or other demeaning places.

Nothing; everything was taken.

Mundis was left with either the corridor or the decks. It was a beautiful night, so he rather forlornly chose the latter.

Poor Mundis, picture him sitting there alone on the deck with his luggage, surrounded by ropes and funnels and air vents, and none too comfortable.

Never mind, he had a way of making the best of a bad situation and somehow he made himself comfortable and somehow he cheered himself up, although to say that he wasn't shaken and that his pride had not been hurt would not have been true.

He stretched himself out, put his stubby little arms behind his head, and gazed up at the stars above him. It was a beautiful night, with a slight breeze, but not too cold and the Mediterranean was as smooth as a mill pond.

Ahh bliss, he could enjoy this. His pride, as I have mentioned, was a little bit hurt, but he would get over it, although to be honest he had not experienced that sort of direct hit, so to speak, for many years.

It had, as I have also mentioned, left him perhaps a little bit shaken. I mean, when you think about it, he had been having a pretty smooth run. Sure he had not got any names and numbers when he was on his own, say during the battle of Beersheba, but that was quite some time ago now, and since then, since setting up the office in the Church dome, and really getting into some heavy work, well he had done okay, actually quite well he thought.

He had a wonderful reputation in Jerusalem, and indeed back in Headquarters, rumour had it that he was up for some new Award that the Boss had introduced as an encouragement for his forces out there on the front.

Names and numbers of green beings responsible for making it 'difficult for Israel' to exist had absolutely flooded in. Sure the Jews had kept arriving in Palestine, and there was certainly opposition from other higher beings, but on the whole he and the guys and gals were pulling their weight.

Yep, that episode with the British Officer had certainly left him shaken, but he would get over it, give him time, he is a tough little green being.

And Mundis had felt like some fresh air… so there!

Post Script

The years of the British Mandate in Palestine crawled on and were fraught with tensions between the Arabs, the British and the Jews.

Many British stationed in the land were actively opposed to a Jewish homeland, and others quite simply never took it seriously. Many also felt that the Arabs were not a people they wished to alienate, after all the Arabs had oil, and oil was something everyone needed.

However, there were, amidst all this tension, a few noble souls who understood the Scriptures and saw the hand of 'He who cannot be mentioned and is best left alone' in the whole process.

These noble souls worked with the Jews in an effort to bring the Zionist Ideal to a head, and thus see the Nation of Israel re-established.

One of these men was a British Officer named Orde Wingate. Somebody once made the comment that having dinner with this man was like having dinner with an Old Testament Prophet.

Wingate knew his Scriptures, having been brought up in the English School System and received as he put it, 'an injection of the Bible'. This had lain dormant for years and had only come to life when he reflected upon it in 1936 with respect to what was happening right in front of his very eyes in Palestine.

Wingate, having gained an understanding of Zionism, decided that he would help the Jew, who he now believed to have a claim to the land and who he also believed was not being fairly treated by the Arab.

And for all intents and purposes, Wingate did it well. The Jews in Palestine called him by his code name 'the Friend', or in Hebrew 'Hayedid'. At first this had been used sneeringly, as the Jews could not understand an Englishmen who was a Zionist, but as time wore on, it became a title of respect.

In Jerusalem today there is at least one Orde Wingate Street that I can remember travelling down, and I do not doubt that there are others.

Wingate taught the Jews to defend their settlements, he taught them to set out at night toward hostile Arab villages and catch those who were already on their way to attack the Jewish settlements, and to apprehend the Arabs before any damage was done.

In this he worked alongside the Haganah, and in working alongside the Haganah he was out of favour with many of his fellow British officers.

Mundis had already met Wingate, for he is the British Officer who knelt and prayed, and whose prayer was so effective that Mundis was immediately hoisted from the cabin.

In this next section, we shall briefly meet him again.

But before we do, I also need to mention that the restrictions placed on the Jews by the British with respect to immigration began to get even heavier than before.

In fact, so much so that by mid 1936 the Haganah set up an organisation called Aliyah Bet to find boats, hire those to crew them, and bring those who wanted to come to Palestine and settle without the British knowing.

T'was no easy feat, and one that meant being interned in Cyprus if they were caught; others simply drowned if the rusty old crates of ships they were in sank.

This was not a journey for the faint-hearted.

PART TWO

"But you, O Israel, my servant, Jacob, whom I have chosen, you descendants of Abraham my friend, I took you from the ends of the earth, from its farthest corners I called you.

I said, "You are my servant"; I have chosen you and have not rejected you. So do not fear, for I am with you; do not be dismayed, for I am your God. I will strengthen you and help you; I will uphold you with my righteous right hand."

Isaiah 41:8-10

1

...1937

Mundis was back home in Headquarters.

Home in his own bed, with the crisp clean cotton sheets ironed by his own Reptile. If he opened his eyes he would see the huge glass window in his bedroom, the one he never drew the curtains on.

Outside he would see the gum trees standing sentry, their black outlines against the grey starry night. He would see, if he looked closely, a thousand twinkling stars shining through those trees, and he would hear the waterfall plunging over the smooth rocks, way down into the pool below. He may also hear a lone cockatoo screeching as it flew home to its hole in a nearby tree.

Home, where his heart was, home where he had lived since almost the dawn of time...his home, his darling, darling home.

Mundis could smell it, the unusual smell of his Persian rugs and the potpourri he had in his ensuite, as well as the musty smell of his numerous first edition leather-bound books.

(Remember, Palestinian Mundis was always more of a homebody than British Mundis, strange considering that they are the same Mundis.)

Mundis stretched, sighed and turned over...and his nose hit an air vent on a horrid ship going to horrid Italy.

Drat!

His back ached, he was drenched in spray, the boat was pitching something dreadful, and he was a most unhappy green being.

He sat up and surveyed the miserable scene before him.

Honestly, that was one thing you could not count on when travelling by boat, and that was that everything would remain the same...

It didn't - it changed constantly, one moment peaceful and calm and the next, wet, blowy, and anything but calm.

This of course would not have been a problem had he been in bed in his own cabin…

Mundis quickly pushed that awful memory out of his mind; his pride was still stinging. He looked around cautiously, hoping not to catch sight of those most unpleasant higher beings that had so rudely hoicked him out of *his* cabin and who had made a horrid mess of his nice neatly packed suitcase.

He could see nothing and no one, and he breathed a sigh of relief. The night was very dark, the moon was not out and the sea as I have mentioned, was building up into something quite rough.

Mundis sat hunched up against the side of the boat, wet, hungry and cold. Fortunately he was travelling with a small bottle of whiskey, and this certainly helped. Wonderful sensation, the liquid warmed him from the inside out, and he immediately began to feel that perhaps he could cope with all that had befallen him.

Maybe Italy was not going to be too bad.

Mundis had been there before, but he could not really remember what he was doing, strange because he did feel that perhaps it involved War Work.

It was all a bit hazy, it should not have been, I mean Mundis' memory stretched back centuries before then…

What was I doing, when I was in Italy before?

Mundis was lost in thought, trying to piece together the scraps of memory that kept eluding him.

He did not notice a British Officer step up to the handrail of the deck and stare out to sea. He did not notice the huge higher beings that flanked him on either side, and he was certainly not aware that the Officer was praying and that the higher beings were singing High Praises to 'He who cannot be mentioned and is best left alone'.

And that whilst they did so, the sea around about was filled with a heavenly light and a myriad of higher beings that hovered and flew around a battered hulk of a ship that was almost overflowing with refugees from Germany.

Only the higher beings could see the ship and the light that surrounded it. The British Officer was lost in prayer, he knew it was out there somewhere, on its way to a lonely beach somewhere near

Tel Aviv, and that once it arrived it needed the cover of prayer not to be discovered by the British authorities in their Patrol boats or on land.

He knew that there would be a human chain of helping hands stretching out into the water from the beach, to bring these precious people to shore. He knew he needed to keep praying to bring them home...

Frightened, tired and cold people, who were under no allusion as to what the future held in Palestine. Hardship and a life so different from what they had always known, that it was all but incomprehensible, but who, even in their wildest dreams, could not have imagined the horror that awaited their friends and families back in Germany. Those trusting people who had not really believed that life could ever change and as a result, had not made the decision to leave whilst they could.

Mundis could not see or hear any of this, he was too busy chewing his fingernails and trying to work out what he had been doing years ago in Italy.

The higher beings smiled to themselves. Mundis was no match for them. They had successfully kept his thoughts so pre-occupied with himself that all the wonderful display of higher being power was completely lost on him.

2

Roma….1937

Mundis breathed deeply and savoured the moment. He had a Box Brownie with him and he had stopped a passing green being and asked him to take a snap of him in front of the Colosseum.

Mundis was not going to use his iPhone again and get located like he had been in Verbier all those eons ago. He arranged his hat, a good cream panama, just so on his head, straightened up his linen suit and smiled happily for the camera.

"Beautiful," well that was Mundis' response, not that he could see the photo. Box Brownies did not have a digital viewing screen, or a spit out automatic photo dispenser, but being the vain and egocentric green being that he was, he knew he cut a dashing figure in his new suit and hat.

He waved happily to passing green beings and went in search of lunch. So far so good, he had found a very nice Hotel just opposite the Pantheon and he had the entire top floor to himself.

The Pantheon was a wonderful old stomping ground of Mundis', built to honour all the gods of Ancient Rome, some of whom were amongst Mundis' closest friends.

Yes, there was no doubt about it, the Pantheon was a home away from home for Mundis. He could indeed have stayed there - it was a bit like being a member of a very up-market club in one city, you had reciprocal rights and could stay in similar clubs in other cities - but the plumbing was dreadful and the in-house service left a great deal to be desired.

Also it *had* been turned into a Church in the 7th century, and the services did get in the way of a good time - all that incense and bell ringing gave one a headache.

His luggage was unpacked and put away and his pride was in the process of being restored. He didn't have any fingernails left, and he couldn't quite believe that he *hadn't* remembered what he had been up to in Italy during World War II , as it had all come rushing back to him as soon as he had left the boat.

Although quite how he was going to marry what he had been then with what he was doing now, now that he was back in exactly the same timeframe, that he had been in then, if you follow me... well your guess is as good as mine!!!!

Just wait till you see what his job was then.

Not to worry about his fingernails, they would grow and perhaps he would be able to find a good manicurist of the green being type here in Roma.

Mundis never suspected that the higher beings had anything to do with his memory loss or confusion, he simply thought that the debacle in the cabin had perhaps left him a little more shaken than he had thought.

In any case he had not seen even a glimpse of the rude creatures since the unfortunate incident, and was beginning to think perhaps he had imagined it all - you know, stress of the job back in Jerusalem might be catching up with him.

It was a very big and important job he had...I mean how many beings do you know that have been put solely in charge of getting the names and numbers of the green beings in Jerusalem of all places, who are making it difficult for Israel to exist? A huge responsibility...

Lunch was a delightful affair - he had ordered a Spaghetti Marinara washed down with light white wine. He was joined by two very old friends who'd had no idea he was going to be in Italy, and indeed who he had not seen since the division of the Roman Empire in 395 AD, for they had been busy causing serious trouble in other parts of the world.

What a lot they had to catch up on, discussions like...

Was Theodosius right to have made two Empires out of the one?

What had gone wrong with respect to both the Western and the Eastern legs, and whose legs were they anyway?

And why had the Eastern leg lasted longer than the Western?

Was it because it had been wearing support hose?

That last question had them rolling on the floor in hysterics (Mundis was having such fun, he didn't care about his linen suit... he did have six of them, all exactly the same). He was laughing so hard, he had to cross his legs very tight to stop an accident...

"Such good times," Mundis mused. "What a life they had, what extraordinary opportunities. Indeed they had been part of some of the most momentous times in History, and they should all feel very privileged and just a little humbled."

(Perhaps for the first time ever the wine was having an effect?)

His two friends agreed wholeheartedly.

They parted with affectionate promises to catch up again, and a solemn promise not to let Headquarters know they had seen Mundis.

3

Mundis pulled his itinerary out and began to look at the list he had made of things to do.

He licked his pencil and began to go down the paper.

1. The Vatican… must do
2. The Sistine Chapel… must do.
3. The Spanish steps… must see
4. Vittorio Emmanuel Building (it had just been completed and was very impressive)… must see.
5. The Colosseum… not that important.

Mundis had spent quite a bit of time there in ages past and the memories were a little bit gruesome, he sort of couldn't put it all together with his nice linen suit and panama hat.

He had had his photo taken outside, maybe that would do. *I mean who is going to know if I really did go in or not?*

(And as we may suspect, he was quite capable of lying about it).

Yes, it is decided, no Colosseum, lunch at the Spanish steps, then a short stroll down to the Trevi Fountain to make a wish, and then home for an afternoon nap, perfect.

And off he set, panama at the right angle, umbrella in hand, shoes polished and linen suit looking just so. What an impressive sight, and how many green beings stopped to stare and comment!

Well, I am afraid if he thought he was going to be incognito, or at best just another green being, then he had another thought coming… He was a bit like a twentieth or twenty first century movie star who whinges about no privacy and then dresses up to the nines and makes himself as conspicuous as possible in the most public of places and then wonders why he doesn't have any…privacy.

"It's Veridis, you know Mundis Veridis, OOOOOOOH!"

"Oooohhhh, Mundis Veridis, yes, look, doesn't he cut a dashing figure!"

"Do you think he has put on a little weight?"

"Well I don't know, I only saw him the other day and he certainly hadn't then, perhaps all those official dinners?"

"Perhaps a little, but he is strikingly handsome!"

"Ooooh, and such a lovely shade of green!"

"Oh yes, shall we go and speak?"

"No, I am too shy, and he wouldn't remember me, we hardly met at all, but he did bow and kiss my hand…"

And so it went on, Mundis was recognised almost every where he went, and didn't he know it and didn't he just lap it up.

His wounded pride was being restored to perfection with every step he took.

Stupid Mundis, it was just a matter of time before the Boss found out and all Hell broke lose…so to speak.

And just a matter of time before he met himself coming backwards…but more about that later.

Italy, and especially Rome, really was not the smartest place for him to have come on holiday.

And if you are feeling a little confused by all this, don't worry, read on and all will be revealed.

4

Mundis was enjoying his time in Rome. It was only day two and he had already visited the Spanish Steps, the Trevi Fountain, the Vatican *and* the Sistine Chapel. He was not a being who really went into detail in these places, you know, a quick flit through and he had done it, ticked it off and was in the coffee shop stealing postcards and partaking of the delicacies.

Although he *had* spent a little more time lying on his back on the floor of the Sistine Chapel, just staring up at the creation above him...simply marvellous.

And when he got tired of lying there staring up at Michelangelo's masterpiece, he simply floated upwards and had a closer look, chipped a few bits of paint off as a keepsake, and then to give himself a giggle, floated back down with his umbrella open just like Mary Poppins.

Oh, he was a funny fellow...sort of. And one who was sailing very close to the wind, or living very close to the edge...either way describes Palestinian Mundis at this point in time very well indeed.

In any case, by now he was getting bored and it was time to move on...enough Vatican, enough St Peters and enough paintings.

He really was an Impressionist man, and all these cherubs and mother and baby pictures were beginning to get up his nose,

Honestly, just how many mother and baby pictures can you see... seen one, seen em all. Phheewww.

Next stop, the Vittorio Emmanuel Building, and a closer look at Mussolini.

Mundis' curiosity had gotten the better of him and he simply could not contain it any longer, he just had to have a peek at the great man.

Off he set, umbrella in hand and hat just so; it was quite a walk, but Mundis *had* overheard someone say,

"Hasn't he put on weight!"

And Mundis could not bear the thought of having put on anything.

So he walked and he walked and he walked, only stopping for coffee and cake twice along the way.

Ahh, there it was, rising up like a giant wedding cake in front of him. Mundis sighed.

The Vittorio Emmanuel Building - what memories, what times he had enjoyed and what speeches he had written and indeed spoken.

Right from just across the road and a little to his left...the Palazzo Venezia...*ahh, what a time*.

As I have mentioned he was a being who sailed close to the wind and yes, his curiosity was really up now, and he was sailing so close he was in great danger of capsizing...

Shall I or shan't I?
Can I or can't I?
Will I or won't I?
Dare I or don't I?

Oh, pooh and double pooh... I will, who will ever know, 'cept me and him.

And with that Mundis sailed right through the front door of the imposing Palazzo Venezia, and right up to the office of Benito Mussolini.

And there he sat, just as Mundis remembered him, writing his speeches, and there right next to him sat...

Yes, you guessed it...

MUNDIS VERIDIS, extraordinary green being, resplendent in his greenness and superbly dressed in an Italian Officer's uniform and writer of speeches 'par excellence'.

Palestinian Mundis coughed ever so slightly and Mussolini's Mundis looked up and scowled, his most ferocious one.

Palestinian Mundis had achieved what everyone said he would one day achieve...

He had met himself, coming backwards.

"Who and what are you?" Mussolini Mundis growled.

"I am quite simply, you!" Palestinian Mundis quipped, and

pirouetted and bowed with a flourish.

And with that Mussolini Mundis picked up his iPhone and started to call Headquarters.

Palestinian Mundis was amazed, but being the quick minded being that he was…he lunged at him, simply flying over the room, and knocking the phone out of his hand.

A terrible tumble and rumble under the furniture was the result of this deft move.

Kicking, biting, pulling, spitting, growling and much scratching ensued.

The noise was indescribably bad, swearing and cursing…ooh, but it makes my ears tingle just remembering it.

Really, for such an intelligent being Palestinian Mundis does leave me gasping, I mean don't we all do things that are ultimately not in our best interests - and invariably the one that suffers the most is undeniably oneself.

Well you would think after eons of living on and above this earth, he would have worked himself out a little better - Palestinian Mundis that is.

Mussolini Mundis, Palestinian Mundis and British Mundis were all the same Mundis and *all* deeply insecure beings, and they could not bear anyone upstaging themselves…even if it was one of them.

And this Palestinian Mundis or whoever he said he was, certainly was not going to take away from him, Mussolini Mundis, one of the best jobs he had ever had…

In command of all *and* renowned for making the trains run on time…what an achievement.

And what a mess.

Not that Benito Mussolini noticed, he just kept right on writing, although he was not moving as fast as before and was beginning to feel a little tired (thoughts of his mistress and tea time began to crowd in on him).

This sudden tiredness could have been because his chief speech writer was rolling under the desk with *himself* and making one horrible din, not that Mussolini could hear that either.

Well, this was a no-win situation, and had it not been for another green being (non-Mundis type) stepping into the room, well I don't like to think what the outcome might have been.

This other green being also had an iPhone and he - I am afraid to say, *did* call Headquarters…and without getting too completely mixed up, the upshot was that the Boss found out and Palestinian Mundis was called to task.

5

"Ahh Veridis, back and sideways from the future, I see."
     "Yes sir, ahh sorry sir, needed a holiday sir."
"MmmmmVeridis, I give the holiday calls, not you Veridis."
"Yes sir, sorry sir."
"And I, Veridis, book the tickets, confirm the reservations and generally keep a check on the whole thing."
"Yes sir, sorry sir, forgot sir…"
 What a liar Mundis was.
"Well now you are there Veridis, I have an assignment."
"Yes sir," said a very smelly and bruised Palestinian Mundis.
"You are already in Britain, another of you is in Italy, and the other is *meant* to be in Palestine, well now Veridis, you are to split and send another of you to Germany."
"Yes sir."
"Good Veridis, the Transfer Department *will* call and you *will* split and German Mundis *will* emerge and you Palestinian Mundis, *will* go back from whence you came!"
"Yes sir, very good sir."
And the line, as it has done so often before, went dead.
Palestinian Mundis stifled a disappointed sob, he probably did not even have time to go back and get his luggage; all his lovely things, his toiletries, the books he had bought, the sketches, ooohhh… drat and double drat.
Mussolini Mundis was back at his desk, looking very smug, and not even bothering to look up and say goodbye. He was simply dictating another speech, in between chewing the end of his pencil and cleaning his ears.
He was a complete mess, his uniform almost hanging off him and his face cut and bruised, but as he was the winner in this ordeal, the dishevelment only served to make him look more attractive, or so he felt.

Palestinian Mundis positively hated him.

The Transfer Department did call as promised, and Palestinian Mundis was told to get ready to split and then prepare for transfer back to Jerusalem.

Palestinian Mundis sat wearily down on the nearest chair.

Now he *really* was a mess, his beautiful linen suit was torn and grubby, his panama hat had a hole in it and his umbrella was broken, and his shoelaces were undone. He also had two black eyes and his nose had been bleeding, so you can imagine what that looked like on a grubby white linen suit.

Still he sat there, as he was told, and waited, sniffing now and again and dabbing at his nose with a handkerchief.

The split came.

German Mundis emerged, wearing a light grey trench coat over a black suit and Homburg hat. He bowed to Palestinian Mundis, clicked his heels together, 'sieg heiled' and sat down next to a grubby broken Palestinian Mundis to await his own transfer.

He did take a sideways glance at Palestinian Mundis, and turned away quickly; he was embarrassed to have emerged from such a scruffy being.

Palestinian Mundis stifled another sob, and disappeared back to the Church of the Holy Sepulchre in Jerusalem, which as we know is quite a long way from Rome.

He told terrible lies once he got there, he was certainly not going to tell his staff about his unfortunate experiences. But he did take things quietly for a few days, you know, breakfast in bed, a hot water bottle and a cold compress on his head and plenty of soluble aspirin.

His very capable assistant, the many handed little being was asked to keep running the Office for quite sometime. A job she was only to happy to do.

Mundis was just not quite up to the job, he was having recurring nightmares about having nowhere to sleep on ships and Mussolini not having his speeches finished.

A most inglorious end to what might have been a lovely holiday, but there is a lot of truth in the saying that 'curiosity killed the cat'.

Well, in this case, nothing could kill Mundis, but it certainly ruined what, as I have already said, may indeed have been a holiday to remember.

Now of course, it was a holiday best forgotten.

I have had one or two of those.. have you?

Post Script

So we have met German Mundis, and what a picture of Teutonic correctness he will prove to be. I doubt very much that you will see him flying close to the wind and emulating Palestinian Mundis' unfortunate Italian caper.

Although I wouldn't be surprised at anything these Mundi do, they have left me feeling very amazed and sometimes quite alarmed at their escapades.

In this next section we are going to revisit British Mundis and also German Mundis, who will both be involved in two very crucial pre-World War II events that will each have equally negative outcomes for Palestine and the Jews.

And strange to say, both these proceedings, Kristallnacht and the publishing of the White Paper occurred on the same day...the 9th of November 1938, with the former spilling over into the early morning hours of November 10th 1938.

Remember we have seen this before, with 'the Battle of Beersheba' and 'the Balfour Declaration' both occurring on October 18th 1917.

Sometimes when 'He who cannot be mentioned' really wants to make a point, He will say or do it twice. In this case these two negative occurrences with relation to the Jewish people and Palestine, seem to be a direct result of the Boss sensing that his time was indeed drawing to a close with the influx of Jews to Palestine and the gates having been opened, through Beersheba and the Balfour Declaration.

For those with ears to hear and eyes to see this is something worth being aware of. The Mundi of course did not have eyes to see or ears to hear, they were totally ignorant of the times in which they lived (any time in which they lived) from a spiritual point of view, and simply got on with following the Boss' orders and therefore causing as much hindrance as they possibly could.

PART THREE

"Therefore prophesy and say to them:
"This is what the sovereign LORD says: 'O my people, I am going
to open graves and bring you up from them; I will bring you back
to the land of Israel.
Then you my people will know that I am the Lord when I open your
graves and bring you up from them. I will put my Spirit in you and
you will live, and I will settle you in your own land. Then you will
know that I the Lord have spoken and I have done it declares the
Lord.'"
Ezekiel 37:12-14

"To the angel of the church in Pergamum write:
These are the words of Him who has the sharp double edge sword.
I know where you live - where Satan has his throne."
Revelation 2:12-13

1

...*1938*

T'was getting cold again and British Mundis having almost overcome his aversion to fires, was sitting in the drawing room of Number Ten with his feet up on the fender and drinking a very large brandy.

Wearing a pin-striped suit with a waistcoat and bow tie, he looked very dapper and very British. He had been working hard and had not dressed for dinner tonight, having come straight from the Office.

If he had dressed for dinner he would have been wearing white tie and tails and looking even more dapper. There is nothing like a white tie to really finish a being off...regardless of whether you are lesser or green.

The days of Lloyd George were long gone, but Mundis had seen no reason to leave Downing Street and indeed had permission from the Boss to stay. There would be much work to do in the days ahead collecting names and numbers, so why upset everything by moving out of Head Office.

British Mundis had set up a very similar sort of organisation to Palestinian Mundis, only this time it was right in the attic of Number Ten and just as well set up with equipment as in Jerusalem - you know, desks, computers, personnel and coffee rooms, all the most up-to-date equipment...twenty-first century up to date, not 1930's.

But time now for a break, the brandy was good and the conversation even better, some more friends had moved into Number 10 and one in particular was a very good friend of Mundis, his name was Appeasement.

Appeasement was a spineless little green being with a lisp, but Mundis didn't judge him on that, he was good at his job and reasonable company, *and* a good conversationalist, always very happy to agree with anything you said, *if* that makes for good conversation.

It was he who was keeping Mundis company by the fire this evening; they were discussing the days proceedings and congratulating themselves on a job well done in relation to the White Paper.

The notorious white paper had been published that day, the 9th of November, 1938 and it was not until May 1939 that it would be approved by the British Parliament, but both Mundis and Appeasement had no doubt that all would go smoothly.

Well Mundis knew all would go smoothly, as he was simply in the business of collecting the names and numbers of those who had done such a good job persuading the lesser beings into setting the White Paper up.

The White Paper was implemented by the British Government in an effort to appease the Arabs in Palestine by severely curtailing Jewish immigration, the aim being that when 'self-governing institutions' were introduced in Palestine in 1944 (six years after the introduction of the White Paper) the Arabs would have a majority and they would stop further Jewish immigration, and therefore there would never be a Jewish state.

The British in short were more interested in appeasing the Arabs than in securing a homeland for the Jews as per ordained in the Balfour Declaration.

This was a terrible thing to have happened to the Jews in Europe, who were desperate to leave and could see the writing on the wall in relation to Hitler and his attitude toward the Jewish race. Although as I have mentioned before, no one, but no one could have guessed just what Hitler meant to do to the Jews.

'He who cannot be mentioned and is best left alone' had his people were in place too...

They were the people in places of authority, who did what they could to help the Jews, and many Jews did get into Palestine without official certificates; they were known as illegals. Others were not so fortunate and were caught and interned and many were sent back to Europe where they died.

The Jews in Palestine, whilst horrified at Britain's decision, still chose to fight with the British against the Germans in the coming War. David Ben-Gurion announced that "the Jews of Palestine will fight the war as if there is no White Paper and will fight the White Paper as if there is no war."

In any case, we will return to Mundis and his friend Appeasement sitting comfortably by the fire and savouring the liquor and the day's proceedings...

"Ahh, good job ol' boy!"

"Thank you Mundif. I must say, I am exfaufted and will have to turn in foon, do make fure you put my name forward for promotion and/or an award of fome fort, I do wather feel I have deferved it."

"Absolutely Appeasement, you have gone way above and over the call of duty, and I have already submitted your name into Headquarters, I did it this afternoon when I was in the Office after the day's duties were done."

"Fplendid, Mundif ol chap. Nite nite..."

And with that Appeasement floated upstairs to the main bedroom and curled up on top of the tallboy; it was a bit dusty but he was an easygoing chap and didn't really care.

Mundis stayed behind and mused about the years that had gone by since he had first arrived at Number Ten. He had seen Lloyd George all the way up to Chamberlain and he had certainly had a lot of fun.

His job had not been as stressful as Palestinian Mundis, he had found the British Parliament on the whole to be very easy to work with in respect to anti-Jewish feelings, although he knew Winston Churchill's time was coming and that was going to mean a more pro-Jewish stance and therefore harder work for Mundis.

Not to worry, he would cope and have fun as he was doing it.

Ah, he *had* enjoyed some good holidays, shooting in Scotland, marvellous house parties, great company. He had seen the time of King George V and the abdication of Edward VIII, he had certainly liked Wallis Simpson and could not understand what all the fuss was about - he thought she would have made a jolly good Queen. Queen Wallis, very nice ring to it.

He had also seen the crowning of George VI and the birth of his children.

Yes, he had been busy and he was so very grateful that he had been sent to Britain and not Palestine, not that he really ever gave Palestinian Mundis a thought these days. Last time he had seen him he was wearing that ridiculous Lawrence of Arabia outfit and holding an onion somewhere in the Sinai in 1917.

British Mundis had conveniently forgotten that he had been wearing the same outfit and looked just as ridiculous.

We shall leave him now, frightful creature that he is, and we shall take a peek at German Mundis and follow his adventures for awhile.

Postscript

This is a fascinating and dreadful time in history and the Mundi are fascinating and dreadful creatures to share it with...so horribly content in their doings and so completely unaware of their wickedness.

To them it was all part of their job and following their Boss' orders.

I may add that they were completely unaware of why their Boss was waging his wicked war. They had fallen with him all those centuries ago simply because they had been bedazzled by his shining personality.

And because of this they had never really stopped to ask themselves important questions like...

"Just what *is it* that he stands for?" and

"Why does he think he can do a better job than 'He who cannot be mentioned and is best left alone'?" and

"Just who is he really... in any case?"

No, they had not asked themselves anything like that, they had simply followed blindly, blissfully unaware of the end that was looming closer and closer to them everyday.

Oh, silly Mundi.

2

...1938

German Mundis had been appalled when he first caught sight of Palestinian Mundis sitting forlornly on the chair in Benito Mussolini's office.

Who and what is he, surely nothing to do with me? Such a grubby and unkempt creature.

Wouldn't Palestinian Mundis be horrified to know that he had been thought of like that, he who was so particular about his appearance and so sensitive about what other people thought of him!

Thankfully German Mundis was not there long enough to speak to him.

If he had been, the conversation would have gone something like this...

"Excuse me, but have we met?"

Sniff, sob, sniff, extra big sob... from Palestinian Mundis.

"I do think you need to do something about your dress code, I am afraid you are letting the green being side down rather badly."

More sniffs and sobs from Palestinian Mundis.

"Well, you know it is no use crying about it Mien Freund, best to get yourself home and smarten up a bit."

And of course it would have all been spoken in German, and we know how incredibly precise the Germans can be.

And *that* could have been the cherry on top of the cake - the horrible fight that had just happened with Mussolini Mundis would have started again with German Mundis.

In fact Palestinian Mundis' eyes were just beginning to narrow and his fists were just beginning to clench and his blood was just beginning to boil...again.

So it was a very good thing that it was just a matter of seconds before German Mundis was whisked away and deposited in Berlin, complete with iPhone and a small bag of luggage.

It was night time and exactly the night of the 9th of November 1938. In fact it was just on midnight and German Mundis was a little annoyed that he had not been sent straight to an upmarket hotel, with an already turned down bed and a steaming mug of hot chocolate with a whisper of Brandy in it.

Instead he had been left standing on a deserted road somewhere in downtown fashionable Berlin. The Christmas decorations were up in the big department stores and the lights were twinkling, the first flurries of snow were falling and it was eerily peaceful. Even Mundis, who was actually not really into *'eerie'*, could sense the mood.

The Transfer Department had moved him forward in time. He hadn't realised this when he had left Italy, but it had soon become apparent, as the speed at which he was moving was faster than a sideways transfer, and he arrived just a little breathless and a teensy bit ahead of himself - by this I mean…

His head had actually gotten there first, and he was obliged to pick it up; it had rolled into a gutter and was staring up at him from under a snow drift. He picked it up quickly, fitted it into place and hoped no other green being had noticed.

His beautiful Homburg hat was nowhere to be seen, probably still drifting around somewhere in cyber space with all those deleted emails and so forth.

Although you know it jolly well serves him right if the green beings had noticed, his bad attitude back in Rome toward Palestinian Mundis would have served as a good lesson – 'treat others as you would like to be treated yourself'.

I guess this is probably asking too much, the Mundi seemed to have missed that lesson all those eons ago before the Fall. I suppose they were probably having rebellious thoughts somewhere else at the time.

In any case, Mundis was left to find a hotel all by himself and in this he was more than irritated.

Headquarters had omitted putting in a Baedeker Guide.

3

BEEP BEEP BEEP.
   If anything could break the eeriness of an empty street in Berlin two hours before Kristallnicht, it was the BEEP BEEP BEEP of an iPhone from the twenty-first century...

Happily there was no-one who could possibly have heard it except Mundis.

The message was from the dreaded Transfer department; it was detailed and read something like this...

Don't bother finding a comfortable hotel room, you are not in for a peaceful night. Get your iPhone ready and punch in the names and numbers of the green beings who are playing a prominent role in tonight's proceedings. There will be many of them and the Boss wishes to reward them with important positions in his coming kingdom.

After you have done this Veridis, you are to set up an Office in Berlin where you will do a similar thing...collecting names and numbers of green beings who are making it impossible for the Jews to survive. These green beings will also be rewarded with places of prominence in the Boss's coming kingdom.

You will find yourself very busy in the coming years Veridis. This era in History is disastrous for the Jewish race and you with your leadership skills, will be playing an important role in documenting this time.

The message ended and Mundis, whilst taking on board the Berlin Office part, decided to completely disregard the not-getting-a-hotel-room-and-working-through-the-night part.

Forget it... if the Boss thinks that I have had to emerge from my host being and then get transferred from one country to another and move ahead in time, literally losing mine in the process.... he has another thing coming.

And with that, the lazy little green being dressed immaculately in German dress of the day, decided to find the nearest department store and set himself up in the bedding department.

Okay, so I won't find a hotel, I'll obey that order, but I don't need to deprive myself of a good night's sleep!

Mundis drifted through the glass of the department store window, found the bed section and prepared to retire.

He unpacked and undressed, putting on a nice clean striped nightshirt with matching night cap. Availing himself of the men's room, he cleaned his light green pointy teeth, strolled out, fluffed up the pillow on the bed, crawled under the sheets and fell into a deep and dreamless sleep almost immediately. Mundis did not wake up until the following afternoon. When you think of the damage that was done in Berlin (and indeed in almost every city in Germany) with regard to synagogues and Jewish-owned businesses in the early hours of the morning of the 10th of November, 1938, then his ability to sleep and not hear the cries for help, the crashing glass and the looting that followed, is truly indicative of his selfish, lazy and all-round despicable nature.

Well, let's leave the selfish little being asleep, snoring blissfully and only waking up to turn over or perhaps go to the loo.

Kritstallnacht progressed very happily without him.

Kristallnacht was the direct result of the murder of Ernst Vom Rath, a German junior diplomat in Paris. The murder of Vom Rath was in turn the direct result of the actions of a young Jewish man called Herschel Grynszpan, whose family had been expelled from Germany for being of Polish Jewish descent on the night of the 18th of October, 1938.

Twelve thousand other Jews were expelled the same night, left on the border between Poland and Germany as penniless refugees with one suitcase, having left everything they had worked for during their entire lives back in Germany.

Grynszpan's family was just one of these families having been driven from their homes by the Gestapo. Grynszpan had received a hastily scribbled postcard from his sister describing the conditions they were living in and asking for help. He was so outraged by this that he took matters into his own hands and shot Vom Rath in the German Embassy in Paris.

This was just the excuse the Nazis were looking for to strike at the Jews, for no apparent reason other than that they were Jewish. The result was the 'Night of Broken Glass' or Kristallnacht.

No town or city in Germany was spared that night.

The Nazis however were driven by a force they had no control over; with their disrespect for the true Church and what she teaches, they had opened themselves up through pagan rituals to the dark forces of the Boss.

And the Boss simply hated the Jews.

Why did the Boss hate the Jews so much? The thought did sometimes cross Mundis' mind, but not often.

Mundis was blissfully asleep in his feather-down bed with his clean striped night shirt on and his cap, and even if he had been awake, he would not have had a clue as to why the Jews were signalled out for so much suffering. Nor did he care; he had a job to do, to follow the Boss' orders and all he really wanted was to go home and enjoy his beautiful apartment and read his books and sip his tea and drink his alcohol.

4

Mundis slept well and only awoke because he heard the voices of lesser beings in the shop discussing last night's atrocities, although sad to say they did not seem to think of them as atrocities, but rather as 'what the Jews had coming to them'.

Hitler's propaganda machine had worked well and many impressionable and very frightened people fell for it and indeed turned a blind eye to the perils of their neighbours, and in some cases, friends.

Not all though, there were certainly some who in the years to come hid their Jewish friends and sometimes complete Jewish strangers; they were known as 'Righteous Gentiles' or 'the Righteous amongst the Nations'.

Mundis of course was not a righteous Gentile but a very unrighteous green being who just followed orders, a real cog in the wheel, and as I have mentioned before, this is indeed tragic.

As it was certainly not why he was created.

So he awoke, stretched, belched, passed wind and scratched his bald head; not a pretty picture, his night shirt was all twisted and his cap had fallen off, but he had certainly had a good sleep.

He rubbed his eyes and crawled slowly out of bed on all fours. He looked like a frog getting down from a high place without hopping. He stretched again and went toward the bathroom, where after splashing his face in water and relieving himself, he began to think about the night ahead and finding a suitable place to set up an office.

His thoughts drifted back to that splendid office back in Jerusalem in the Dome of the Church of the Holy Sepulchre. A superb spot and such good staff surely they were a staff in a million, how on the Boss' earth could he possibly hope to procure a staff like that over here.

Mundis had forgotten his German History - if he could get good staff anywhere on a green being level it was certainly going to be in Germany between 1939 and 1945.

In any case he was yet to remember this, thoughtless little beast that he is.

For now he was simply immersed in finding suitable office space and the beings to staff it.

Mundis dressed with impeccable care, helping himself to a new Homburg hat to replace the one he had lost in transit. Ahh, what a picture he presented to the unseen world - wonderfully dressed, so very well appointed and so incredibly sure that he was following the right Boss.

He looked forward to the day when his Boss would be in charge (he didn't think about it too deeply but then again he didn't think about anything *too* deeply).

Sadly however the Boss would have to be under cover and his true glory would have to be hidden…but still amazingly in charge… and after so much time and so much waiting…yes…

"One day, soooome day…"

Mundis hummed this tune happily as he floated down the stairs and into a world that looked like the war had already started, but was in actual fact still months away in 1939.

What a mess - broken glass, broken furniture, broken lesser beings, both those being herded away like cattle and those herding them, although those being herded were actually less broken than those doing the herding.

The latter were miserable creatures incapable of thinking for themselves and incapable of therefore making a right decision regarding their captives, all fine upstanding members of the community, with no other fault than to be Jewish.

Mundis did not acknowledge the lesser beings, either the herded or those herding them; he was more interested in the incredible number of green beings just milling around.

Possible Office recruits… ah, bliss and double bliss.

The entire street was full of them, standing on street corners, hanging from lamp posts, blocking up doorways, sitting on steps and generally just lounging around. The whole place looked like

Headquarters after the Annual Prize Giving, you know the fun was over and everyone just loitering around savouring the atmosphere.

Not a lot of talking, everyone was too tired, but the general feeling was a job well done, and they all looked pretty satisfied.

5

Mundis found a suitable stage in the shape of a very expensive dining table that hadn't been looted yet; he climbed up, put two fingers to his lips and whistled. Immediately he had an audience and he began to speak in a beautiful cultured German voice - truly he was a being of extraordinary talents and charm.

I, however, will translate into English so as to avoid confusion.

"Honoured and respected green beings, I have been sent here by the Boss all the way back from the twenty-first century."

Murmurs of, "My, my, the twenty-first century, eh?" and "Glory, fashions obviously ain't changed!"

"Honoured Beings, I have reason to believe that time in the twenty-first century is drawing to a close and our Estimable and Glorious Boss will soon be inheriting his earth in the very near and foreseeable future!"

More murmurs, more feet shuffling and a few raised eyebrows.

"What O, think he got knocked on the 'ead last night?"

"Could be, though he looks a respectable sort of chap."

Mundis went on, "Yes, I am here to set up an office in order to take down the names and the numbers of those green beings who are responsible for making it difficult for Israel to come back onto the world scene."

Calls of, "Israel ain't on the world scene, what ya talking about… this is 1939, we got rid of her way back in 77 AD and then changed her name to Palestine!"

"Hey Mister, you *did* got knocked on the 'ead last night…"

"Yes, yes, I understand your point, but the fact is after this coming debacle known as World War II, Israel does indeed come onto the world scene. And I am here to get the names and numbers of those green beings who during this time, manage to make life impossible for the Jews, and therefore are securing for themselves a place in the Boss' coming kingdom when Israel will again be wiped *off* the world scene and he, our estimable and glorious Boss will rule the world!"

"If you follow me, well follow what I am saying…so to speak."

Well, there were more raised eyebrows and more mumbling, but the general consensus was,

"Okay, you sound like you might know what you is talkin' about,"

"We'll 'elp, we ain't doin' nuttin' else!"

"We done did, what we *done did* have to do, 'ere last night!"

Mundis went on with an air of arrogant confidence.

"Good, good, I now need a suitable office and I need you to find it for me, I am not as familiar with Berlin as I should be, indeed I have not been here since the days of the Germanic tribes and then I believe it was a swamp. It looks far more suitable now."

Mundis cast an approving eye around the district - he saw beyond the chaos of Kristallnacht and just focused on the potential.

Calls of ….

"Try the Reichstag, lot of space in the roof," and

"What about the Brandenburg Gate, chilly in Winter but quite pleasant in Summer."

"I know, I know," called a small and insistent voice, "the Pergamum Altar, it's in a mooooseeeeum."

"Perfect," said Mundis.

He knew it well, in fact the Boss had a seat there many eons ago when it was actually in Pergamum, that wonderful Hellenistic town in ancient Turkey; it was amazing that by chance it just happened to be here in Berlin.

Although by chance it was not.

The Boss had it moved there at the end of the nineteenth century, 1886 to be exact and indeed he and his most favoured generals often used the place to meet and discuss their diabolical plans. In this they had a lot of help, you know Zeus, the goddess Diana…they were all there, they came with the altar.

In fact to be precise 34 goddesses, 20 gods, 59 giants and 28 animals came with the altar.

They made the move quite easily. Turkey was not the place it used to be and they were very tired of the scenery, so they were more than happy with the change and Berlin was just fine, thank you very much.

They travelled quite easily, just merged into their respective statues and slept most of the way, only waking up when they got to Berlin to survey the scene and check out the town. It was certainly quite different from Turkey, but pleasant enough.

In fact, since the Battle of Beersheba and the Balfour Declaration in 1917, the Boss and his cronies had met at the Altar often. The possibility of Israel returning to the world stage was becoming a horrible likelihood and everything had to be done to stop it.

The Boss does not know the future; only 'He who cannot be mentioned and is best left alone' knows exactly what is happening.

And 'He who cannot be mentioned and is best left alone' had every intention of bringing Israel back into play.

And the Boss back in the twentieth century had every reason to be alarmed. In fact, he had not been so alarmed since the Resurrection nearly two thousand years before, and *that* had completely thrown him off guard.

Headquarters had not had an easy time of it then; the mood had been worse than black and the atmosphere thick with tension and unhappiness.

6

Mundis was totally disinterested in the horror and sorrows that surrounded him. He had a job to do and as always, no matter what country he was in, he did his best to carry out his orders.

It was this absolute obedience that had made him such a favourite with the Boss and even when he did divert from duty, like his Verbier escapade and the Italian holiday, he was amazingly forgiven and simply steered back onto the right path.

Well, when you think about it, he really did land some amazing positions…In England he was ensconced at Number 10, in Palestine he was in the Dome of the Church of the Holy Sepulchre and in Germany he was at the Pergamum Museum, on and around the very Altar where the Boss used to have his seat.

Yes, the horrid little green being was truly favoured in the eyes of the Boss and indeed most of Headquarters, although as always there were petty jealousies and back biting. But Mundis managed to deal with them, he had his ways, you know.

The office in the Museum was very well run and the names and numbers of green beings that were responsible for hounding and impounding the lesser beings just kept pouring in.

There was going to be an awful lot of green beings in prime positions in the Boss' coming kingdom.

Mundis would have to curtail things a bit, it was getting quite ridiculous, and Headquarters back/forward in Australia was positively overrun with names and numbers. Actually some green beings back in Australia were threatening a strike due to overwork.

So, Mundis organised a system similar to the one he had in Jerusalem, you remember, a point system, 10 points for outstanding Green Being work and so forth and the Green Being who got over 50 in a week was made special mention of. The only problem was that the score was too low and Mundis had to up it, so that only when a Green Being got over 5000 points was he mentioned.

This should give you some idea of just how bad things were in Germany in 1938 to 1945 in relation to the Jews and the threatened re-emergence of Israel on the world stage.

Kristallnacht was the culmination of at least half a dozen years of persecution for the Jews in Germany, but the real persecution was to begin during World War II. In fact there would be some who would say in the years afterward, that the War for Hitler was actually all about killing the Jews.

One should certainly not be surprised by this; the Boss himself inhabited Hitler during these years. In reality his was the soft and silky voice that the latter referred to. And what a voice, 'tis hardly surprising Hitler hated the Jews the way he did.

Six million Jews were killed in the Ghettos, and the Concentration Camps, the forced marches and firing squads, the latter, if they were lucky, for many were buried alive. In one town in Eastern Europe the ground moved over the bodies for at least twenty four hours after the shootings.

Such cruelty, such hatred and all because the Boss could not cope with the fact that Israel was possibly positioning herself to return. And how sad it was that he, the Boss found so many lesser beings that were willing to listen to a mad man named Hitler and who so willingly carried out his and the Boss' evil plans.

Well as far as the Boss was concerned, no Jews meant no Israel… and no Israel meant no worry for him.

Although the Boss was always worried about something; life was never simple in Headquarters, always stressed when he was around and always tense.

He really had no sense of fun at all.

Pity really, because before he had rebelled against 'He who cannot be mentioned and is best left alone', he had been one of the most beautifully 'fun' creatures in Heaven, along with his good and longstanding friend Mundis Veridis.

'He who cannot be mentioned and is best left alone' had his forces in place as well, and it was the same as during the first World War. Although sadly these beautiful higher beings cannot make any lesser being change their mind, once that mind is made up to do evil.

The higher beings can do nothing except help those who the evil is intended for.

And help they did, they walked into the Ghettos and onto the cattle trains, they comforted terrified lesser beings and held the dying in their arms, they marched into the Concentration Camps...

Auschwitz-Birkenau, Maidenek, Ravensbruck and Flossenburg, infamous names amongst a much larger infamous group of Camps. Green beings abounded here, inhabiting the bodies of lesser beings who were open to evil and all that it stood for.

'He who cannot be mentioned' sent his higher beings into these camps, here they walked into the Gas Chambers and held the dying in their arms and then shepherded their Spirits and Souls into a place of greater safety.

That was the beautiful part.

Rising above the dismal grey barracks of the Concentration Camps into the black starry night, their gorgeous diamond dust coverings were thrown back. Their wonderful kind faces were beautifully exposed and completely visible as they led their precious Jewish and non-Jewish charges home and into the open arms of 'He who cannot be mentioned' and in this case is certainly *not* 'best left alone'.

What a wonderful reunion.

How they loved seeing the reuniting of families and watching them settle into happy homes and familiar routines again, this time without the terrible fear and stress of War.

Yes this was a very happy time indeed, and was only marred because they had to make so many trips back to earth to do the same thing over and over again...

7

Mundis didn't know any of this and even if he had…what did he care?

Sixty-two million lesser beings were killed during World War II, and he had not noticed. His head was all wrapped up in names and numbers and getting the job done and when he did take a break it was to loot the homes of the lesser beings who were being taken away.

Yes, he got for himself some very nice art pieces during this time. He had 'em sent back to Headquarters with instructions to his private reptile where to hang them in his apartments - you know, where the light was going to reflect their beauty and more importantly where as many nasty little green beings as possible would see them.

The only problem was Hitler's hierarchy - they also had their eyes on the masterpieces, so Mundis had to make sure he and his henchmen got there first.

Some masterpieces have never been accounted for from those days…and now we know why.

The years dragged on and Destruction and Death were finally exhausted and slunk back into the pits from whence they came. They were lying in wait until the next time, biding the years and marking them carefully, only opening their slitted yellow eyes to check the time and then drowsily going back to sleep again. Although it was never a deep sleep, just a contented doze.

However in latter years, that being the twenty-first century, they are again beginning to open their eyes for longer stretches of time and indeed thrust their combined heads out of their caves for a better look at the time and the world they slunk away from all those years ago.

Mundis' work finished in Berlin, and he was indeed rewarded for a job well done. Now the question was, what does an out of work green being do after all the business is over?

Well pretty much what he did before; green beings in this part of lesser being History are never out of work for long, but you will have to read the next section to find out.

If Mundis thought anything about those days in Berlin - I mean if he had any opinion about what the Boss had been about with respect to rewarding green beings for persecuting the Jews, he would have had a vague sort of feeling that the Boss had overplayed his hand and that the death and destruction had been so great with respect to the Jews that somehow 'He who cannot be mentioned and is best left alone' would seek revenge.

Mundis was beginning to come to the sticky conclusion that maybe Israel was His revenge and that there was something very big and nasty up ahead. Also the Boss was going to have no control or say over the matter.

This all made Mundis feel rather sick in the tummy.

Ooh…how he longed for home and the peace and quiet of his own room, where the world outside could not bother him and the other green beings and reptiles inside were only there to serve…

"A Pims sir? A long one with dry ginger ale, ice and a cucumber?"

"Yes Hornback, put it there on my side table and I'll drink it as I listen to some more Wagner."

"Very good sir, and would sir like his bed turned down?"

"Yes, yes, Hornback, now you know the routine, don't bother me now."

"Very good sir."

Peace would reign again and the strains of the Ride of the Valkeryie would ring forth, and the Boss, if he was home, may come and join him and together they would look back over the centuries and at all the destruction and chaos they had managed to cause and they may perhaps smile and toast each other to a job well done.

But Mundis doubted it…the Boss was definitely a lot tenser than he had been once, and he wouldn't waste his precious time on a Pims and Wagner.

Pity, Mundis had so enjoyed the Boss' company once…*a long*

long long time ago.

Postscript

Mundis was right, the Boss *had* overplayed his hand and Israel was the result and the Jewish people *would* for the first time in two thousand years have their home, but not quite yet - there were more struggles to come and more work for Mundis and his associates to do.

This was not Britain's finest hour. Sadly, they for the most part capitulated to the demands of the Arab world, because the Arab world had one incredibly important asset - oil - and Britain needed it. The Balfour Declaration was something of the past and the displaced Jews of Europe languished in Displaced Persons Camps with a burning desire to return to Erezt Israel, which some managed largely through illegal means.

What terrible ordeals were suffered by the people of the 'Exodus' ships that were refused permission to land and stay in Palestine and were sent back to German Prison Camps, and what horrific lack of dignity and despair they were forced to undergo. But oh, what tremendous shows of courage they displayed as the majority escaped and made their way illegally back to Palestine on the Underground Sea Journey.

Truly the Modern Nation of Israel was founded among others by the graduates of Hitler's Concentration Camps and British Internment Camps in Cyprus.

PART FOUR

"On that Day I will raise up the tabernacle of David, which has fallen down, and repair damages; I will raise up its ruins, and rebuild it as in the days of old; I will bring back the captives of My people Israel; they shall build the waste cities and inhabit them; they shall plant vineyards and drink wine from them. I will plant them in their land, and no longer shall they be pulled up from the Land I have given them, says the Lord your God."
Amos 9:11, 14-15

"In that day it shall be said to Jerusalem, 'Fear thou not: and to Zion, let not thine hands be slack. The LORD thy God in the midst of thee is mighty; he will save, he will rejoice over thee with joy; he will rest in his love, he will joy over thee with singing'."
Zephaniah 3:16-17

"Thou believest that there is one God, thou doest well: the devils also believe and tremble."
James 2:19

1

...1945

So the War finished, millions died and Europe lay in ruins. People's lives were forever changed, places they had known had completely disappeared and more importantly people they had loved had been killed...and for what?

Europe was a graveyard and a place that most surviving Jews were desperate to leave. America was a favoured destination as were South Africa, South America, Australia, New Zealand and indeed Palestine.

Yes the war was over, and Pride, Greed, Envy, Lust, Sloth, Anger, Gluttony, Murder, Lies and the rest of the crew were out of a job. They sat around moping and looking at each other and getting bored. They would have liked to have gone home, but the Boss had plans and wanted to keep them at the ready and not too comfortable.

Yes, each above-mentioned hideous green being had finished his assigned work, the War Office at the Pergamum Altar had closed down, the computers, phones and desks and other paraphernalia were being put into storage and the atmosphere was one of depression.

They had worked hard, especially in Europe and now they found themselves hanging around street corners, blocking up doorways and sitting disconcertedly in stair wells smoking cigarettes and drinking.

German Mundis had finished too; his lot however was different, for *he* was being congratulated on a job exceedingly well done.

He was not hanging round in doorways, or smoking in stairwells.

He had been up to Hitler's 'Eagles Nest' in Bavaria, which was not destroyed and a very nice place to holiday. The air was so crisp and clear. Of course the Americans were there then, but Mundis didn't care, he didn't have sides.

He was a most fair-minded and biddable chap...almost ecumenical really.

He went hiking and bird-watching, dressed in all the correct gear, you know the Lederhosen and a Bavarian brown felt hat with the extra large ostrich feather and edelweiss pin. He even carried a stout walking stick and practiced his yodelling.

He had the sheep on the mountainsides totally confused.

He did, however, make mention to Headquarters via text regarding his troops back in Berlin and the fact that boredom was setting in.

He did not want a mutiny on his hands. The word came back from headquarters that there would be plenty of work for them to do and they just needed to be patient and the fun would start again.

So they waited.

And the work did come in, things like helping Nazi war criminals escape through Italy to South America or any other country they could get into.

Yes, amazing as it seems, many Nazis escaped to live perfectly normal lives as law abiding citizens and many green beings helped them do it. You know, distracting unsuspecting custom officials, setting up false passport systems. Yes, this was some of the ways Mundis's green beings were put to good use - some of the green beings - the others were told to bide their time and their turn would come again.

And come it did, for the Boss could see what was happening; the Jews who did not go to other parts of the world such as Australia, New Zealand and America all seemed to converge toward Palestine and this was the worst possible scenario.

All the work he did during the War to finish the Jews off was proving to be of no avail. Honestly, he had killed six million of them and they seemed to be reappearing before his eyes, emerging as it was from their graves and heading for the one place he did not want them to go.

And that one place was Palestine, the very place that 'He who cannot be mentioned and is best left alone' had given them all those centuries ago.

The Boss knew what could happen once they were back there, and the outcome for him personally was not a happy prospect. Although the Boss knew this, his minions didn't; they were under the impression that the Boss was on the same level as 'He who cannot be mentioned and is best left alone'.

Nothing could be further from the truth.

So in response to this dismal state of affairs he organised for all the green beings loitering around war torn Europe to regroup and head south to Palestine.

The official word went something like this...

"Regroup at the Pergamum altar and at the sound of the bugle, rise in one accord and fly south to Palestine."

German Mundis was at the head, dressed in British army fatigues; he was going to Palestine too and as it was still a British Mandate in 1945, he was therefore suitably dressed.

Although he was looking none too pleased. He had just heard the unwelcome news that once he arrived in Jerusalem and settled his troops he would have to re-merge with Palestinian Mundis.

How horrible! That badly dressed dirty green being, what on earth am I going to have in common with him? And worse still, I emerged from him to begin with so therefore he will be dominant... Well, I am not having it, I shall run away and join the circus.

There was not much chance of that, Mundis would have hated the circus and the Boss was keeping an eagle eye on him, so merging would be exactly what he would be doing.

The bugle call came and green beings en masse filled the air and headed south toward the Middle East like a great green cloud dark with poison, and that is a very apt description because that is exactly what they were...poisonous.

The Transfer Department had decided they were too big a task and they would have to get there under their own steam.

2

Have you ever heard the expression to 'meet oneself coming the other way'? Well, that is exactly what happened to German and Palestinian Mundis in a street not far from the Church of the Holy Sepulchre in Jerusalem.

German Mundis had arrived with all the other European green beings and they had all been assigned to various jobs, you know things like:

1. Stirring up trouble between Arabs and Jews.
2. Stirring up more trouble between Arabs and Jews.
3. Stirring up a lot more trouble between Arabs and Jews.

German Mundis had been in charge of this and organised his troops well; now the time had come for him to find Palestinian Mundis and merge.

He was a most unhappy green being, he had had such fun out on his own, doin' what he liked and enjoying his independence. He sort of felt like a teenage lesser beings that'd had the run of the house to themselves, and whose parents had come home and now the fun was over. The washing up needed to be done and the beer bottles put away...you know, you remember that feeling...maybe you don't, but I do.

Well off he went, dragging his feet and muttering dark words to himself, just strolling very slowly down the cobblestone streets.

And there from the other direction came Palestinian Mundis, not strolling but swaggering and looking absolutely delighted. He was dressed beautifully in a British Army Officers uniform, with not a wrinkle or a crease out of place.

"Hail fellow and well met!" Palestinian Mundis greeted German Mundis with exuberance and went on to add that wasn't it wonderful that they had met themselves coming the other way...ha ha.

German Mundis gritted his teeth and clenched his fists.

How he hated Palestinian Mundis.

"Come on ol' chap, we can make this easy or we can make it hard, why don't you just glide over here and slide into me…all easy and cosy like."

"Why don't you take a long hike up to Turkey and stay there," said rude and sulky German Mundis.

"Hmm, well you are being difficult, you will remember that it was you who emerged out of *me* German Mundis and I am the dominant Mundis and therefore you are obliged to merge back again."

"*YOU*, Palestinian Mundis are the dirtiest and most unappealing green being I have ever seen and I am appalled that I emerged out of you!"

German Mundis was oblivious to the fact that Palestinian Mundis was impeccably dressed and did not look anything like he looked last time.

"*I*, German Mundis, for your information was having a bad day *that* day and was uncharacteristically out of sorts, having just met myself in Mussolini's office."

This was said through gritted teeth and with a very nasty expression on his face.

German Mundis was furious, his hands were clenched, his teeth were barred and his smell was dreadful, and he didn't want to hear any of Palestinian Mundis's story.

Palestinian Mundis lunged at him, knocked him to the ground and swallowed him in one foul swoop.

He felt very bloated after that and made rather rude, smelly noises all the way back to the Church of the Holy Sepulchre; he did look rather strange though, dressed in British Army Officer apparel and goose stepping like a Nazi Storm Trooper.

And as far as I know, German Mundis has never been seen again, unlike Palestinian Mundis who we certainly haven't finished with.

3

...1946

Well for now we are going to revisit British Mundis, who has never in all this time left 10 Downing Street. Mundis was by now a fixture and as familiar with the place as you and I are with our own homes.

He had seen Winston Churchill come and go and he was now under the roof of Number 10 with Clement Attlee, literally under the roof. He was still ensconced in the office in the attic, although the Red Bedroom was where he spent most nights if he wasn't working.

Attlee was a steady moderate leader who led Britain after the war in a steady and moderate way. Mundis didn't mind him at all, although life was a little dull. Attlee was as Winston Churchill once said, "A sheep in sheep's clothing". He was also a man of very few words, 'laconic' was the way many described him, you got exactly what you saw, no hidden agendas - and this I am afraid, made life a little dull for Mundis who was if anything, a regular Party Being... and this did not mean Labor Party or Conservative, it just meant Party.

Mundis therefore requested a transfer, texting headquarters to let them know that he felt he should be put to better use somewhere closer to the action.

The text came back...

Cyprus, old Boy, Cyprus. Get ready for transfer.

Mundis was thrilled, and organised a quick going-away party in the main stateroom of Number 10. He managed to combine it with a dinner for the Heads of Commonwealth Countries, that way most of his closest friends/fiends would be attending.

Attlee had recently managed to change the name of the Empire into that of the Commonwealth. Just as well really, the Empire was fast disintegrating and the Commonwealth sounded much better than 'Defunct Empire'.

It was a White Tie dinner complete with brandy and cigars afterwards. Truly a lavish occasion, anybody who was anybody in the green world was there. They came with their hosts and some stayed on after they had left.

With fond farewells all round, Mundis could not believe he had been at Number 10 since The Balfour Declaration in 1918 and here it was 1946 - 28 years of fun and not a dull moment until Attlee.

Ah well...

"Wish me luck as you wave me goodbye, cheerio here I go on my way.."

Honestly, British Mundis sang about everything. For a creature who was involved in such mischief and misery he was an incredibly happy one, possibly because he never thought about the work he did; he just did it, following orders without questioning.

I guess there are 'none so blind as those who will not see'.

Mundis positioned himself dramatically on the front steps of Number 10, dressed once again in British army uniform circa 1946. He waved happily to the friends who had come to see him off and disappeared right before their very eyes, leaving his luggage on the steps, something he would be very annoyed about when he got to Cyprus.

The crowd around Number 10 dispersed, everyone was feeling a little low. Mundis had been so popular and such a reliable being if one was entertaining. He was just *always there,* the life of the party and such an expert on fashion and decorating...Number 10 was just not going to be the same without him.

Cleptis took Mundis' forgotten luggage home with him. He would organise to have it transferred later if Mundis was really lucky, if not, then Cleptis would be looking very chic at next season's dances.

4

O oh, but it was wonderful to be off on an adventure again.
Mundis could feel the wind beneath him and above him
and indeed right through him. His body had become completely
separated, his legs were over France - at least one was, the other was
still coming over the Channel - his arms were literally crossing, they
were winding around themselves and having a wonderful time over
Monte Carlo, and his torso and head were over the Mediterranean
headed for Cyprus...

And his luggage was in London with Cleptis, but he was yet to
discover that.

How he loved flying solo and how happy he was that he did not
have to sneak out of London, because that would have meant he
would have had to organise all travel himself in case the Boss found
out and put a stop to it.

All weekend House Parties and European Holidays for the last
28 years had been very undercover affairs. This time, however,
he was being legally transferred, and the Boss was fully aware of
everything, which meant Mundis did not have to live on the edge.

What a relief.

Although the Boss had always known exactly where Mundis
was and had turned a blind eye to it...Mundis really was a highly
favoured green being, for most beings would not have gotten away
with it.

Ooh, he could feel the wind, he could enjoy the scenery, he could
twist and turn and feel totally free.

A new life was about to start, new adventures about to happen
and new friends about to be made...although the latter was pretty
unlikely, Mundis had met every green being there was to meet; well
then, perhaps old friendships were about to be rekindled.

Ooh, what fun...he couldn't wait to see who he would meet! The
list was endless, he had so many fun acquaintances, green beings

whose company he always enjoyed and who were ever ready to have fun and create havoc.

Mundis had liked his friends in London but it was time for a change and he did so want to get back to a pleasant climate.

London could be so depressing, the climate was just awful and there were times that the attic in Number 10 leaked and that had been a real nuisance. Mundis was always stealing the MP's raincoats and draping them everywhere, not to mention their umbrellas. There were many puzzled MP'S who left Number 10 with lesser clothing and attachments than when they had arrived.

Just as well Mundis was leaving, he really needed a good jolt into reality, horrid little green snob that he had become, much, much worse than before.

5

...1948

Mundis descended slowly into Cyprus, circa early 1948. His body came together easily and he landed quite gently in the middle of a very run-down looking group of huts surrounded by barbed wire and watch towers.

Mundis stood there.

He looked around.

He looked up.

He looked down.

He walked around a hut.

He looked under the hut.

He looked on top of the hut.

He looked *in* the hut and was amazed to find it completely full of very Jewish-looking men all fast asleep. Mundis could tell they were Jewish by their prayer shawls and side curls.

Mundis texted headquarters:

You have made a mistake, you have sent me to Germany circa 1940 something. Am in Concentration Camp and not in Cyprus at all, thought I was flying over the Mediterranean but must have been mistaken. Please rectify.

Mundis discovered his luggage was missing so he texted about that too:

Am also missing luggage, please reconnect us, have some fav. outfits therein and do not want to lose them.

The text came back:

Cleptis has luggage.

Mundis replied:

Then I have lost it... what do you think Cleptis is short for?

The iPhone was silent.

Mundis found a step outside a barrack and sat there waiting

for his transfer. All the excitement he was feeling had left him and depression had set in.

He was recalling the Red Room back at Number 10. He remembered the comfort of dinner at eight every night and breakfast in the morning and the clean sheets and the friends he could dine out with and the banisters he loved to slide down and the light fittings he could hang from and the shops he could go to and the shows he could watch.

I AM A FOOL, thought Mundis.

And this was the first time in many centuries that he had even come close to thinking the truth about himself, because there is no doubt about it...a fool is exactly what he was.

His phone beeped and Mundis read the text:

Veridis you are not in Germany, you are in Cyprus and that is exactly where you will stay. The Jews who escaped from Hitler are making their way to Palestine and before they get there they are being interned in camps in Cyprus. We at Headquarters want the names and the numbers of the green beings who are making life difficult for them because they too will receive rewards in the Boss's coming Kingdom, very similar to your London work Veridis.

Mundis was appalled. Honestly, what had he done, this place was dreadful! He had not seen anything as bad since he left the Sinai all those years ago...

Ooh...how could he have longed for the excitement of a new life? His stupidity almost overwhelmed him; he put his head in his hands and shook it in disbelief.

It was the middle of the night in Cyprus and Mundis made a very sorry picture sitting there all alone with his head in his hands, no luggage, no food and no friends.

Anything less like what he had been used to was hard to imagine.

6

Morning dawned and Mundis who had fallen asleep on the step of the hut, found himself being trodden on by many Jewish feet as they wended their way to the meals hut for breakfast.

Mundis stirred and stretched and then, realising where he was, collapsed again in a disappointed heap.

But being the hungry little green being that he was, he recovered somewhat and decided to follow. Picture him traipsing after all these skeletons of people, the wraiths of Hitler's Germany as they line up for breakfast in a dilapidated hut...

Picture these same souls who six short years ago would have been having breakfast in their own apartments before going off to their respective professions and earning a good day's wage.

Now they were flotsam and jetsam of Germany's demonic episode and a more ragged and dispirited people it would have been hard to find. However they were hungry and grateful for what they were given to eat...it was certainly more than they had received from der Fuhrer.

Mundis lined up with them with a bowl and a spoon and was eagerly waiting to devour what he was about to receive - however when he had received it he was certainly not truly grateful.

Mundis was truly horrified and a great lump rose in his throat. He floated off to eat his gruel on a rafter up high in the corner of the hut, where he had considerable trouble balancing his plate and eating at the same time. His tears kept splashing into his bowl and making the gruel more salty than it already was.

No use thinking about bacon and eggs now, no use thinking about fresh orange juice and a hot cup of tea, and that pretty little housemaid that served it all...no use at all.

Mundis observed the room from his lofty position and was reminded of his time way back in Basel when he had attended

Herzl's Zionist Conference…for he was again the only green being in the room.

He sat there with his legs dangling…(not that they dangled very far, they were so short and stumpy), and looked and looked.

And to his amazement he really was alone, he was sure of it, just him and the Jewish men and some strange-looking people in blue shorts and white shirts manning the kitchen and the serving table and with such appallingly positive attitudes…

This was certainly not a Concentration Camp, no encouragement there.

These lesser beings in the blue shorts and white shirts were Palestinian Jews and had been sent to Cyprus to help the would-be immigrants to settle into Camp Life and to prepare them for life in Palestine. They were volunteers, and the life and soul of the detention camps, and certainly doing a much better job than the British would have done.

Mundis however was not alone, he just couldn't see them, but that did not mean that *they* were not there.

They were there…glorious higher beings dressed in glowing white and gold.

They had followed their precious Jewish souls all the way from war torn Europe. They had guided weary steps, smoothed ruffled brows and held wrinkled and skeletal hands. Now they hovered over their exhausted charges and gave wonderful unearthly encouragement that went straight into the souls and spirits of their lesser beings.

They were again encased in their diamond dusted cloaks and therefore completely invisible to Mundis and the lesser beings.

'He who cannot be mentioned and is best left alone' had sent them and He watched them and guided them and gave them instructions on how to best care for His precious children, each individual child, no matter what their age.

He watched Mundis too and was sad to think of what he once was, and what he had now become, and even sadder when He thought that for Mundis he could do nothing to stop what would one day happen in the future.

And indeed that future was coming closer everyday.

7

Mundis had to get out; there was no way he was going to stay in this green being forsaken place.

Sadly he would have to do it on his ownsome again. Memories of tracking down Herzl and then getting to Verbier and all his shooting trips in Scotland came to mind; yes he could do it, he'd done it before and he could do it again…disappear like a mist in the morning, never to be seen or heard from again.

"Whatever happened to that nice chap Mundis Veridis?"

"He disappeared like the mist in the morning, never been seen or heard from again."

Mundis felt quite sad just thinking about it. He was such a personable chap, such a fun being, others would miss him, in fact he would leave quite a hole, not that he knew anyone here, he was specifically thinking of his hundreds of friends back in London.

Was he ready to go through life like those pathetic ghosts he came across, all twisted up about stuff that had not gone right for them in their past life, whinging about who had 'done the wrong thing by 'em' and so on and so forth…and the complaint Mundis liked the best - "BUT no one told me". Even Mundis recognised that lie…most people had been given some sort of chance to hear the truth but many chose to ignore it because it did not fit in with their petty circumstances and lifestyle.

Now to be fair, Mundis was not entirely sure what the truth was himself, but he did know it existed and it had something to do with 'He who cannot be mentioned and is best left alone', and the eternal nuisances who had that very unpleasant blood smell about them.

Yes, it all made for rather uncomfortable type feelings, sort of trembly. Mundis would rather not go there…so he kept musing.

Was he ready to hang about in dismal surroundings hoping the Boss would not notice his absence?

Was he ready to forego Hornback and his wonderful apartment

back in Headquarters…

his paintings,

his books,

his armchair and bunny rug,

his carpets,

his view and *his* big comfortable bed with the clean cotton sheets.

No, *he* was not.

Therefore he would have to think again.

Mundis thought.

Picture him sitting on the end of a bunk bed in a hut in a detention camp in Cyprus surrounded by Jewish men reading the Torah and praying…he was even beginning to sway the same way they did, and in fact it was during this time that the idea came to him.

He would return to Palestine, find Palestinian Mundis and suggest that they work hand in hand. No merging into one, thank you very much, but working alongside each other in harmony and fellowship, shouldering each other's burdens and discussing each other's problems…

Yes, that is what he would do.

And he certainly didn't think about the fact that he had not given Palestinian Mundis a thought since 1917, not even a vague one - he had been having far too much fun for that, thank you very much.

But how to get there…now that was a problem.

The British were not being overly generous in relation to allowing the Jews into Palestine. British Mundis had seen to that back in Whitehall, and indeed had gotten the names and numbers of not a few green beings who had made sure that the Jews suffered greatly at the hands of the British…remember the White Paper and all that it stood for.

Well, he would just have to join the Jews in their clandestine ways of getting into Palestine.

Mundis was all for a bit of clandestine.

Yes, the thought appealed to him greatly. He would even get a clandestine outfit, a black cloak, a hat pulled down over his brow and a pair of black boots.

Mundis could do clandestine very well indeed. He put on his best clandestine face, the one with the serious narrowed eyes and the scowl and the lowered chin.

He glanced around the room. It was full of black cloak-like outfits and even a few hats that would do the job…none would be the wiser, although some would be the chillier, a bit of pilfering here and a bit of readjusting there and here he is…'Clandestine Mundis'.

Perhaps not as carefree and as easygoing as British Mundis, but necessity is the mother (or father) of invention, and Mundis could reinvent himself with absolute ease, yes, he could slip into any role and excel.

He truly was a most versatile green being, amazing really when you think about it - first he had been *just* Mundis and then he was Palestinian Mundis and British Mundis and then German Mundis. In each and every Mundi role he had proved his worth, followed orders, completed his work and taken his just rewards…warranted or unwarranted.

Interesting when you think about it - they were all the same Mundis, yes he was very versatile.

He certainly deserved more than just a mention at the next Demon and Alien Prize Giving.

Think about it…one green being getting all those prizes, amazing. He would hardly have time to sit down before collecting the next one.

Watching him receive them would just be like watching a green blur…

PART FIVE

"So the angel that communed with me said unto me, Cry thou saying, thus saith the Lord of Hosts: I am jealous for Jerusalem and for Zion with great jealousy.
And I am very displeased with the heathen that are at ease: for I was a little displeased, and they helped forward the affliction.
Therefore says the Lord; I am returned to Jerusalem with mercies: my house shall be built in it, saith the Lord of Hosts, and a line shall be stretched forth upon Jerusalem.
Cry yet, saying, thus saith the Lord of Hosts; My cities through prosperity shall be spread abroad; and the Lord shall yet comfort Zion, and shall yet chose Jerusalem."
Zechariah 1:14-17

"Therefore say to the house of Israel, 'Thus saith the Lord God: I do not this for your sakes O House of Israel, but for my holy name's sake'."
Ezekiel 36:22

"Dearly beloved, avenge not yourselves, but rather give place unto wrath: for it is written, VENGEANCE IS MINE; I WILL REPAY, saith the Lord."
Romans 12:20

"After that we who are still alive and are left will be caught up together with them in the clouds to meet the Lord in the air. And so we will be with the Lord forever."
1 Thessalonians 4:17

1

...1948

Well it was all much easier than expected. The British decided that 1,500 displaced people a month could enter Palestine, half from Cyprus and half from Europe. So all Mundis had to do was get on a boat and sail out legally but still incognito, you know 'clandestine-like'.

This he did.

He followed a group of Jewish small lesser beings up the gangplank of one of the oldest and most decrepit looking ships he had ever seen.

He was sure no-one noticed him - I mean he was the same height as the small lesser beings although he was not dressed like them and of course he was invisible, but not to the hundreds of diamond dusted higher beings who filled the air, praising and singing to 'Him who Cannot be Mentioned and is Best Left Alone'. Fortunately Mundis couldn't hear the singing - it would have made him feel quite trembly again and maybe even slightly nauseous.

Mundis' clothes weren't ragged and he had shoes on, sturdy strong ones and his tummy was quite full thank you and his heart was not broken. Mundis may have been the same size as the small lesser beings but that is where the similarity stopped. He had not seen every living relative he had killed in Germany...no, he was quite together emotionally, he just wanted to get out of this awful un-fun camp and find his brother Palestinian Mundis and help him make more trouble for these small lesser beings and their kind...

A most worthy cause - he was indeed a most worthy green being.

Mundis found a safe place on deck, the Captain's cabin, and proceeded to unpack the meagre belongings he had stolen for the voyage. Three glass bottles of water (the quota was one per lesser being), five loaves of bread and a bar of chocolate that some kind grown up lesser being had given one of the small lesser beings.

Mundis ate all the chocolate in the first five minutes.

The voyage was uneventful and the sea smooth and Mundis quite enjoyed it, even joining in some of the Zionist songs and dances and listening intently to a lecture on farming in Palestine. He took notes, although why I am not sure, as he certainly had no intention of farming in Palestine.

The decrepit hulk landed in Haifa early May 1948. The small lesser beings were sent to a kibbutz in the Galilee and Mundis caught a bus up to Jerusalem in order to find his brother.

Ex-British/Cypriot Mundis had found out where Palestinian Mundis lived, surreptiously you know, listening in on green being conversations in the dock, hovering over important looking green beings in the cafes…he was so sure they couldn't see him.

Silly Mundis, they knew he was there and so did the Boss, but everyone had been told to let him pass unhindered. The Boss had plans for ex-British /Cypriot Mundis and he did not want any interference from his minions, thank you very much.

So Mundis boarded a bus. It would take about four hours from Haifa, and he settled himself comfortably up the back and pulled his furry black Hassidic hat over his yellow green eyes and fell asleep with his head on the shoulder of an Orthodox Rabbi. They made quite a sweet picture, although only one of them was visible.

2

Central Bus Station in Jaffa Street Jerusalem; Mundis tumbled out with the rest of the passengers, grabbed his luggage and floated off toward the Church of the Holy Sepulchre.

Oh, what joy to see his dear and most beloved brother again, what a reunion awaited him. His little green heart beat rapidly and his little stumpy legs ran to catch up with it.

The Old City, how lovely it looked, the cobbled stones, the smell from the souks, the noise from the crowded alleyways, all just as he *couldn't remember* on account of how he had never been there. However Mundis was an expert at lying to himself and anyone else who cared to listen.

The Dome was in sight…home for the foreseeable future, home with his very own brother.

He floated into the Dome and slowly descended to the floor.

"Excuse me, but where may I find Palestinian Mundis?"

"He is in the office sir, and is expecting you," said a very pretty little many-handed green being.

Ex-British/Cypriot Mundis should have smelt a rat then, but being so wonderfully sure of himself…he didn't.

He was to regret it for a very very long time…Eternity in fact.

Ex-British/Cypriot Mundis paraded through the closed door, put his luggage down, held his stumpy little arms out and yelled,

" Bro… I'm hoooooooooooome!"

Palestinian Mundis stepped right through his desk with his arms out and his mouth open…and swallowed ex-British/Cypriot Mundis in one gulp.

Palestinian Mundis then went right back to work.

It was May 14th 1948 and the State of Israel was just about to be announced and he had an awful lot of green being monitoring to do.All over the Middle East, green beings were getting ready for War and Palestinian Mundis had to work out which ones were most deserving of prime positions in the Boss' coming kingdom.

And that, my friends, is the visible end of ex-British/Cypriot Mundis, although he certainly made his presence felt in Palestinian Mundis, who had, I am afraid to say, very bad indigestion for quite some time after.

3

...1947

For now, however, we need to travel back in time, just seven months.

"On November the 29th 1947, the United Nations General Assembly passed a resolution calling for the establishment of a Jewish State in Eretz Israel," announced David Ben Gurion.

The Boss was positively fuming...

But also already scheming to get the most out of the situation that he possibly could – for he had learnt that if something looked like it was inevitable he would manipulate it to best serve himself.

He worked on the policy that nothing was ever a lost cause...and as the years progressed and Israel remained, he saw the benefit as we well know of sending the Mundi back in time to get the names and numbers of the green beings who worked tirelessly with regard to making Israel's existence a struggle.

It was during this period that the Boss decided that his time had definitely come, and very soon *he would rule the world*.

I mean, he was already ruling the world, and had been for a very long time...so why not make it official...in an undercover sort of way...

Hence the endless list of green beings. He would need a lot of help - he was not a one Boss show.

So, before we finish our story t'would be a good idea to just take a glimpse at the state of the United Nations on the day the countries voted in favour of Eretz Israel.

What a day.

What a bun fight, every green being who was anyone was there.

Mussolini Mundis was present, wearing the latest in Italian fashions and escorting a very pretty little green Italian being who was hanging on to his arm very tightly. He did look smug; he was not actually representing Italy as Italy was not given a vote, but was merely there because it was the place to be.

But not the Boss, no, he wasn't there, he was way too strung out back at Headquarters, you know, pacing the floor, smoking cigar after cigar and drinking very strong coffees…just waiting for his iPhone to beep and announce what he felt was inevitable.

(You know not once did he see that he had overplayed his hand back in Europe with the Holocaust, and now he was desperately trying to forget 'He who cannot be mentioned and is best left alone's' words about vengeance being His.)

The Boss was under the illusion that the green beings at ground zero, being the United Nations Building were waiting in suspense for the vote to go through, if he could have seen them I don't think suspense is the word he would have used.

No, not at all.

They were playing cards with each other, drinking and smoking cigarettes, swapping ghoulish stories, and some were lying flat on their backs asleep right in the middle of the room, in fact the place looked like a bar at the height of the evening.

In sharp contrast to the seriousness of the lesser beings and the job they had to do.

You see the green beings did not know what the Boss knew - or suspected he knew - with respect to what exactly would happen to him and his cronies if Israel came into being again.

Oh no, they had no idea, they were just following orders again.

The general feeling being that "the Boss seems upset so we will do our best to keep him happy and make sure Israel doesn't come into play again." You know, that sort of general feeling.

But being the selfish little blighters they were, they had already forgotten the seriousness and were pursuing their own agendas… drinking, smoking, flirting, arguing and sleeping and certainly not keeping an eye on their respective lesser beings.

'He who cannot be mentioned and is best left alone' had much to do with this, he had sent his higher beings in and they were in definite control. They hovered around their respective lesser beings and generally kept a spirit of sanity in the room; they were not nervous, for they already knew the outcome.

'He who cannot be mentioned and is best left alone' had already told them. It was *His* time for Israel to come back onto the world stage and no fallen higher being could do anything to stop it.

Hence the atmosphere in Heaven was completely the opposite to the atmosphere back at Headquarters, where the air was thick with smoke and fear and apprehension.

The voting for the Partion of Palestine began. Each assigned green being got serious and scrambled to his feet and flew in the direction of his delegated Lesser Being.

However, 'He who cannot be mentioned and is best left alone' had already moved His forces into place. They stood behind each represented nation and looked into the hearts of those nations and saw what the outcomes would be.

They had been working with those nations for years in preparation for this day.

This was a battle that had already been won in the Heavenlies.

The Boss' troops did not stand behind their nations, they couldn't, they were absolutely petrified of the higher beings they saw that were already there. Hence, they ascended in a body and hung upside down from the ceiling and heckled as much as they dared, but not very loudly as the looks on the faces of the enemy were so stern and forbidding that they lost all heart…still they could not return to Headquarters and say they did nothing.

Thirty-three votes to thirteen and ten countries abstaining, the outcome being to replace the Palestinian Mandate with two States, one Jewish and one Arab.

'He who cannot be mentioned and is best left alone' smiled, Herzl's dream of fifty years ago had become a reality and Israel had been reborn.

Mussolini Mundis and his mates left by the roof and flew in unison straight back to Headquarters where they were given very short shift and a most undelicious dinner.

4

...1948

The official declaration of Independence for Israel came on the afternoon of the 14th of May 1948 and that day in Palestinian Mundis' calendar corresponded with his recall back to present day Headquarters.

Palestinian Mundis was sitting quietly at his desk with a nice cup of coffee and his constant companion, the delightful little many-handed green being. They were discussing the day's proceedings and talking about dinner that night - they were quite an item now days.

And suddenly the strains of 'We all live in a yellow submarine' shattered the peace.

Mundis' heart skipped a beat, it was many years since that phone had rung and he had almost forgotten what it sounded like.

He reached forward and picked it up gingerly.

"Veridis speaking."

"Ahh Mundis ol' chap, what a day Mundis, *what a day!!*"

The voice sounded years younger than it really was, there was an excitement and a lightness about it, most disturbing really.

"Mundis, your job is over, time to come home Veridis, back to Headquarters."

Mundis turned a pale shade of green and looked aghast, and reached for one of the many-handed green being's many hands.

"I beg your pardon sir, *I am home.*"

"Veridis, have you forgotten where you belong? You were sent back in time to track down the green beings that first of all didn't do their job to stop Israel's re-emergence and then to get the names and numbers of those who were making it difficult for Israel to exist. You are finished Veridis, a job for the most part well done."

"But sir...the state of Israel has only just been announced and I am sure there is plenty more for me to do here sir."

There was a lump forming in Mundis' throat and his eyes were watering up.

He looked longingly at the little green being with many hands.

"Bring her with you Veridis, I know all about her and I am sure we can find something for her to do."

"Oh thank you sir…"

"Oh and Veridis, something wonderful has happened, up here in the twenty-first century…all the eternal nuisances who smell of Blood have gone…"

"Vamoosssssed Veridis…gone!!!"

"Really sir, where have they gone?"

"Uuuummmm, I really don't know Veridis, and I really don't care, the way is open for me Veridis to rule my world the way I want to, and you Veridis will be in charge of Headquarters…how does that sound Mundis?"

"Oh very good sir, very good indeed!"

"Get ready for transfer now Veridis."

And the phone went dead.

Mundis took the many-handed little green being in his arms and told her the news and within minutes they had disappeared, leaving their fellow green beings in 1948 wondering what on earth had happened to them.

5

'The vamoosed' the Boss had spoken of is really called 'The Rapture' and that is what had happened. The mystical body of lesser beings on Earth who believed in and had a relationship with 'Him who cannot be mentioned and is best left alone' through His precious Son had been called home; in short, they had been Raptured.

The true Church had disappeared and left the unbelieving and unrepentant lesser beings behind, many of them still going to Church and in a complete daze as to what had happened.

And interestingly enough some of those raptured had never set foot in a church in their lives... they were amazed as they floated upwards toward their Lord... some had not even heard of the Rapture.

Oh I wish you could have seen it.

It was just beautiful, all these faithful lesser beings who had given their lives to 'Him who cannot be mentioned and is best left alone' suddenly changed in the twinkling of an eye, one moment dressed in their ordinary clothes, the next clad in Heavenly raiment shimmering in all the colours of the rainbow, the dominant colour best suiting their own precious personality.

They rose into Heaven to meet their Lord looking like a flower garden rising upwards.

The Boss back on Earth very kindly had many science fiction movies released so as to put the minds of the left behind lesser beings at rest... and indeed the talk did die down although there were millions who never stopped grieving loved ones who had disappeared. Imagine every lesser being under the age of thirteen was gone; think of all those empty bassinettes and cots and bunk beds.

The grieving in some cases never ever stopped, unless of course they met 'He who cannot be mentioned and is best left alone' and He through His representatives left on earth explained it all to them and brought peace and comfort to their aching souls.

Mundis and the little many-handed green being were married in a delightful ceremony back at Headquarters, just outside in the bush garden.

Medusa looked beautiful in a shimmery light green gown that set her skin off beautifully with wonderful poisonous wild flowers in her hair. She did, however, have trouble carrying the bouquet; she just couldn't decide which hand to use. Mundis in the end decided for her and carried it himself.

He of course looked absolutely splendid in a grey morning suit with a pale pink silk tie, stunning! He was smiling from ear to ear, the afternoon sun was making his little pointy green teeth sparkle brilliantly.

Amazing really, he had been alive for eons and this was the first time he had ever really fallen in love.

The Minister conducting the service was a very dignified Reptile, old and wise in his own eyes and he swears that when he asked Mundis if he took Medusa to be his lawfully wedded wife, he heard three "I do's."

One distinctly German one.

One very British one.

And one from Palestinian Mundis himself.

Postscript

'He who cannot be mentioned and is best left alone' was smiling far more broadly than Mundis.

His mystical church children, both Jews and Gentiles, were with Him in Heaven and His remaining Jewish children were either Home in Israel on Earth or would be soon and when they got there, the words, "Baruch haba b'shem Adonai " or "Blessed is He who comes in the name of the Lord" would almost be on their lips…

Yes, it was all coming together very nicely and exactly the way 'He who cannot be mentioned and is best left alone' had planned from the beginning.

The next seven years were not going to be easy for those left behind on Earth…and Mundis' newfound happiness was not to be everything he had ever dreamt of.

Was Mundis up to the challenge?

We shall see in the next book.

BOOK THREE

INTRODUCTION

This book about Mundis is set in the Seventieth week of Daniel… the time when the Lord is specifically dealing with the Nation of Israel.

The Mystical body of believers known as the 'true Church' has been raptured and is in heaven with the Lord attending the Marriage Supper of the Lamb and the Judgment seat of Christ.

The battle of Gog and Magog has happened and Israel is indeed cleaning up the mess and using the fallout from the nuclear explosions of energy for their own purposes.

'He who cannot be mentioned and is best left alone' has protected His Israel and vanquished His enemies until the next Battle, which will be Armageddon at the end of the Great Tribulation and just before the Second Coming of Christ.

The first three years on earth after the rapture are a time of great evangelism - the time of the two witnesses of Revelation 11:3 and the time of the 144,000 Jewish preachers, and multitudes of true salvations.

The Apostate Church will have great power during the first half of the Tribulation, which will help the Antichrist in his quest for total world domination.

This will last for three and a half years.

Then the Antichrist, who has previously made a covenant with Israel for Peace, will suddenly put a stop to all the temple worship and set himself up to be worshipped; this is the time of the 'Abomination of Desolation' referred to in Matthew 24:15-26.

Jesus prophesied here that all in Israel should flee to the mountains.

A third of his people escape to Bozrah otherwise known as Petra, while the two thirds who are left in Jerusalem perish or are taken captive at the hands of the Antichrist…

The Antichrist will also hunt down believers on a worldwide scale. He will be especially brutal toward the Jews because he knows that when they repent and call out "Baruch haba b'shem Adonai", then his time is finished and the Lord will return to Israel to rule and reign AND at their own invitation…

And I will pour upon the house of David, and upon the inhabitants of Jerusalem, the spirit of grace and of supplications, and they shall look upon me whom they have pierced, and they shall mourn for him as one mourns for his only son, and shall be in bitterness for him, as one that is in bitterness for his firstborn.
Zechariah 12:10

So hence this story takes us right up to the time of the Second Coming of Christ…

And on the fictional side, Mundis continues to be the best dressed higher fallen being in the Universe and a perfect match for the deliciously dreadful Medusa - although there are a few issues within their marriage…i.e. children or no children…Mundis is keen, Medusa is not.

I hear you saying they cannot have children?

Well, the gods of Olympus had children and they were very possibly the Nephilim, the result of the misconduct of Fallen Angels with the daughters of Men…Genesis 6.

My story alternates between heaven and earth and there are some surprises in store.

Go make yourself a nice cup of tea, put your feet up and enjoy.

Oh - if you are expecting a perfect description of what happens during the seventieth week of Daniel, otherwise known by some as the Tribulation, or the last three and a half years as 'The Great Tribulation'…then you will be disappointed.

I am a story teller, not a Biblical Scholar, but suffice to say that I have followed some of the major events as closely as I could and as best as I knew how.

Oh, and another thing...I believe animals are extremely intelligent and know far more about life than many lesser beings give them credit for...hence Samson the Wonder Dog and his part in this story...

And I also believe animals will be heaven....yes! Jesus comes back to earth on a white horse, and presumably He got on him in Heaven?

And I saw heaven opened, and behold a white horse; and He that sat upon him was called Faithful and True...
Revelation 19:11

So please go back and get that cup of tea.

Mim Lennon

PART ONE

Wherefore seeing we also are compassed about with so great a cloud of witnesses, let us lay aside every weight, and the sin which doth so easily beset us, and let us run with patience the race that is set before us.
Hebrews 12:1

The wolf also shall dwell with the lamb, and the leopard shall lie down with the kid; and the calf and the young lion and the fatling together: and a little child shall lead them.
Isaiah 11:6

Our Father which art in heaven,
Hallowed be thy name,
Thy Kingdom come, thy will be done,
On earth as it is in heaven,
Give us this day our Daily Bread,
And forgive us our debts,
As we forgive our debtors.
Lead us not into temptation, but deliver us from evil,
For thine is the Kingdom the Power and the Glory,
Forever and ever…AMEN.
Matthew 6:9-13

"And it shall come to pass at the same time when Gog shall come against the land of Israel," saith the Lord God, "that my fury shall come up in my face."
For in my jealousy and in the fire of my wrath have I spoken,
"Surely in that day there shall be a great shaking in the land of Israel."
Ezekiel 38:18-19

And it shall come to pass in that day, that I will give unto Gog a place there of graves in Israel, the valley of the passengers on the east of the sea: and it shall stop the noses of the passengers; there shall they bury Gog and all his multitude; and they shall call it the valley of Hammon Gog.
Ezekiel 39:11

Jesus said unto him, "Thomas because thou hast seen me, thou hast believed; blessed are they that have not seen, and yet have seen."
John 20:29

1

The best man Hornback made a spectacular speech; his memories about Mundis stretched back for centuries and therefore he had centuries to report on.

Fortunately for Medusa and the guests he curtailed it, although Mundis was disappointed, for there was nothing he liked better than hearing about himself.

He sat there throughout the dinner smiling from ear to ear and congratulating himself on how sensible he had been to have found such a worthy and capable wife.

Medusa was everything he had ever hoped for; he had known she was *the one* ever since that first time in the Church of the Holy Sepulchre when she had opened the door for him, typed a letter of introduction, made the coffee and cleaned the windows all without ever leaving her desk...

She had in short gotten the job as personal secretary and Mundis' heart all at the same time, although he was shy about admitting it then and consequently took his time.

He used to peek at her from behind his computer and marvel at the way she could rearrange her hair and put her makeup and earrings on *all* at the same time...

What a girl!

He had certainly been on the lookout for any possible rivals; there had been one concern in that department but Mundis had moved him to a remote area in South America where he was put in charge of mudslides, tropical storms and earthquakes.

The dancing began and as the music filled the spring night, the stars twinkled and the eucalyptus towered overhead. Mundis, wrapped in Medusa's many arms, swayed contentedly and hummed along to themes from many alien movies and other favourites.

His all-time favourite, *Don't fence me in,* was no longer his all-time favourite. He was well and truly ready to be fenced in, and hence *that* one was not sung or danced to or even mentioned.

In the background, small and large alien spacecraft could be seen entering and exiting the building. Mundis noticed them but was far too caught up in the wonder of the evening to give them much of a thought. This was truly an indication of Medusa's power over him, for there was nothing Mundis liked better than paying unsuspecting - or suspecting - lesser beings visits in his spacecraft.

He did think of the Dihards for one moment and giggled naughtily when he thought of the 'church' they had set up.

'Church for the Incorporation of the Mundi Philosophy'… IMP for short.

Mundis had paid them a fleeting visit in between returning home from Jerusalem and his wedding date. He was thrilled to see how it was thriving; all the members wore green skin-tight suits and discussed his latest teaching email which he sent out quarterly from Headquarters.

The monthly donations were growing. The Dihards kept a percentage and the rest of the money was sent to various organisations throughout the world that helped make life difficult for any Western type civilisation.

Although now with the Eternal Nuisances gone, those making it difficult for Western civilisation had largely done their job, so the money was used for holidays in the Bahamas and shopping in Paris and other exotic places.

The Dihard's property had been turned into a retreat for IMP purposes and the membership was growing daily. If Graeme was finding the lack of privacy a little testing, Edith was in her element, organising everything from lectures at home and abroad to book publishings, and wonderful morning teas with 'Mundis lemon tea cake' as the main treat.

That idiot Darlington Somerset from Oxford was often in residence.

The very Reverend Somerset would always be wearing his academic gown and drinking gin from a hip flask. He delighted in telling audiences about his experiences with Mundis; in fact he had written several books with some amazing titles, including,

Five good reasons why Jesus went to India after the Bungled Crucifixion;

Differences and Similarities between Mundis type Universities and ours;

Why much of the Church is Outdated and Missing.

The last book was very popular, due mainly to the fact that the Mystical Church was indeed missing. This therefore was seen as a very relevant topic, one that certainly sold the most copies and drew the most audiences at in-house lectures.

If Graeme's attitude didn't improve he would have to be dealt with…easy work, Mundis was not going to have any marriage break-ups in his church. He didn't really have to worry; Medusa was very skilled at that kind of thing…all those hands.

And Mundis knew just the lesser being to take over as husband to the indomitable Edith, a short quiet man at least 15 years younger but very good looking.

Edith had already noticed him and spent quite a bit of time with him sending all the emails out, at least that is what she said they were doing. Mundis was inclined to believe her; the man in question was such an insipid specimen that the thought of him doing anything else was almost inconceivable.

Perhaps getting Graeme dealt with may just be a good idea, he would whisper the suggestion to Medusa tonight and perhaps include it in their Honeymoon.

"Ahh, bliss," sighed Mundis as he was swept up into a very fast fox trot. "I am a clever fellow and a jolly lucky one too."

The Boss could not attend the wedding but had sent his personal best wishes via his iPhone, and an autographed photograph of himself in full military uniform delivered by one of his lackeys.

Mundis and Medusa had put it in a prime position in their apartment; Mundis had even moved a Monet for it, although chances were the Monet would be moved back and the Boss may end up in the pantry.

The Boss really was not looking his best these days, certainly not the magnificent creature that Mundis had idolised in heaven all those eons ago, when his brilliance had captivated a third of the higher beings and initiated a war that to this very day still raged.

Yes, sadly the Boss was definitely looking the worse for wear; centuries of hard slog was beginning to take its toll and he was far too thin, and his skin was beginning to hang in folds around his face and torso.

He was well passed his prime and the rarefied and rejuvenated air of heaven was not as accessible to him anymore, in fact very soon he would be banished to earth permanently.

Although this was not how he tells it…his story is that the earth was now his and that 'He who cannot be mentioned and is best left alone' had conceded defeat and retreated back to heaven with His eternal nuisances, thus giving he, the Boss, the earth as his very own.

The Boss was awfully fond of saying things like, "I will exalt my throne above the stars of 'He who cannot be mentioned and is best left alone', and, "I will be like the most High".

And of course all higher fallen beings/green beings believed him; he was awfully persuasive.

And sadly the mugginess of earth *did* have a stultifying effect on body, spirit and soul…it induced the aging process, whereas heaven completely stops it.

The Boss could hardly complain, he had no one to blame but himself for the mugginess of earth's atmosphere.

Before the fall of man in Genesis – and, I might add, at the Boss' suggestion - earth had been anything but muggy; it had been delightful, perfect in every way.

But there was no use reminding the Boss about this, he had a very selective memory, and nothing was ever his fault.

2

Graeme Dihard was the most miserable man on earth. His haven, his paradise, his escape from the world was overrun with ridiculous Mundis Veridis lookalikes and lemon tea cake.

Even his rose garden had been hijacked and was being redesigned into the shape of a spacecraft, and some of the disgruntled dozen were now trying to propagate a new yellow rose called 'Mundis Musings'.

Edith was the worst; she had lost a considerable amount of weight - although Graeme couldn't imagine why after making all those Mundis Lemon tea cakes - but nonetheless she looked fabulous, especially in her tight luminous Mundis suit.

Fabulous she might look, but fabulous she was not, chasing unashamedly after that wimp fifteen years her junior and winning no less.

The wimp was putty in her hands.

Graeme unfortunately recognised himself twenty-five years ago...*putty in her hands,* and he had remained putty up until a few months ago when the disappearances occurred and his grandchildren had been taken.

His children and their spouses were living with them on the property now and all trying for more babies. That was another problem, he really didn't want to live with his children anymore and he certainly didn't want to think of them trying to have babies, and under his roof.

He had done his work, he had brought them up and now he needed peace. When he thought about it, each and every one of them was Edith's child and really nothing to do with him at all. He had tried to have a say in their upbringing but had been overruled at every turn. All he was good for was paying their bills and looking after their children - fortunately he had enjoyed the latter part.

He had loved his grandchildren, and he didn't want to love any new ones.

Their tricycles, two wheelers and sandpit equipment made his heart bleed and he could not bear to look at their pictures.

Edith didn't seem to mind much, she had, in her words, 'moved on' and Graeme had to do likewise; their grandchildren were safe, they had been taken to another planet to begin the repopulation of that world and Graeme would see them again.

Mundis, that font of all information had said so...

He had sat with his legs neatly crossed on the sofa and expounded on interplanetary life and all the benefits the children would have: wonderful schooling, great living conditions, healthy food and marvellous galactic beings to look after them...and yes, there would be plenty of time for play and holidays.

Graeme was not so sure about all this, it gave him a sort of sickly feeling in his stomach and heart as he listened, and at one stage he actually got up and left the room.

This did not go unnoticed by Mundis.

Yes, Graeme concluded that he may see his grandchildren again but he had a sinking feeling that it would not be as Mundis said. He personally had some tough decisions to make and some serious repenting to do.

The words of that fanatical preacher at the New Gospel Church they had left all those months ago were beginning to make sense. Graeme was quite sure now that the man was not a fanatic but a good preacher who had tried to warn all his flock about the coming rapture and tribulation, but sadly Edith and Graeme had not listened.

It was becoming very clear to Graeme that neither he nor Edith had ever really known the Lord. Oh, they had known about Him, but they had not known Him and in reality, neither of them were saved; but as neither of them up until this point in time knew that they weren't saved, then it was not much of a problem to them...if you get my meaning.

Although Graeme's redemption was nigh and with that the entire universe was about to change for him.

The rapture of the Church, the Tribulation, the Second Coming of Christ, the Millennium Reign and the new heaven and earth were all beginning to take shape in Graeme's mind. Come to think of it, not once was Mundis mentioned in the Bible...unless of course he was related to the fall of Satan and a third of the angels.

Graeme was beginning to feel that this was the case, but where to go to find out? Everyone he knew that would have known had been taken during the rapture.

Graeme was the most miserable man on earth.

Fortunately the most miserable man on earth had kept a Bible.

He had in one of his many sheds, a money safe built into the floor. It was covered up by a dirty oil-stained rug and no one, not even the indomitable Edith, knew about it.

Had Edith known, they would have had a 'Mundis burn the Bible ceremony' as all Bibles had been deemed outdated and irrelevant.

"I mean who has seen the Lord? Not I," said Edith, "but I have seen Mundis and I totally believe in him."

Edith had not read the Scripture in John 20.29 "Blessed are those who have not seen and yet have believed."

Graeme was beginning to spend a considerable amount of time in this shed. Edith didn't care, she was spending a considerable amount of time with 'Mr 40 years old and counting backwards'.

Graeme read Ezekiel 36 and 37 about the rebirth of Israel and the valley of dry bones. He now understood the significance of the dry bones; they represented the house of Israel coming back to the land, the lack of breath in the bones speaking of the lack of spiritual life in the house of Israel.

So they will come back to the land in unbelief before Messiah returns a second time and then they themselves will have invited him back, as it says in Zechariah 12.10:

"And I will pour out my spirit on the house of David and the inhabitants of Jerusalem a spirit of grace and supplication. They will look on me, the one they have pierced, and they will mourn for him as one mourns for an only child, and grieve bitterly for him as one grieves for a firstborn son."

Graeme was amazed as he understood especially the significance of the Holocaust and the people coming out of their graves... amazing, how many years ago did Ezekiel prophesy this and yet it happened just in the last seventy years, within living memory.

Graeme shook his head in wonder and could not understand how he could have been so silly as to not have listened before. It was all very well blaming Edith but in all honesty he could not. Every man or woman has to make his own decision concerning the truth of the Bible and Graeme had chosen not to listen; he was too busy sulking and missing his upfront and important position in the church.

He fell to his knees in repentance and asked the Lord into his life in a way that he never dreamt of doing before, all the while shedding bitter tears of remorse.

When he arose sometime later it was as a humbler and redeemed man.

Graeme read about the rapture in I Corinthians 15 and also I Thessalonians 4. He went back and read Ezekiel chapter 38 about the war of Gog and Magog, which he felt had already occurred.

Israel even now was cleaning up the debris and the dead; it was all beginning to make perfect and horrifying sense.

Graeme spent hours in that shed. He was never missed and he did not miss anyone outside it; he simply drank in as much Scripture as he could and spent time in prayer and repentance. It was a time of sweet fellowship with the Lord. Graeme's heart was healing and he was becoming the man he was created to be.

Samson the Wonder Dog, his ever faithful companion, prayed along with him and when he wasn't praying his doggy prayers he was asleep and snoring loudly.

Graeme, in spending such time alone with His Lord, became very sure he had to leave Edith and the madness that surrounded her. There was no talking sense *with* her or *to* her, for she was utterly convinced that Mundis was the answer to the world's problems and she for one was not going to miss out.

But how to get away?

He was meant to be in charge of this ridiculous retreat and to uphold the Mundis banner high.

True, there really was a Mundis banner, complete with a picture of his horrid green Mundis face and spacecraft in the background.

Graeme also had a feeling he was a marked man; if he stayed

he would be done away with, and Edith and 'Mr 40 years old and counting backwards' would inherit his land and house and all he had ever worked for.

He didn't get the feeling that Edith would kill him, but he certainly sensed the evil in Mundis and suspected that he was quite capable of murder...how right he was.

Every time Graeme picked his Bible up the feeling of urgency increased. He was sure 'He who cannot be mentioned and is best left alone' was telling him to leave, not that Graeme called him by that name. To Graeme he was simply the Lord, and He was fast becoming the best friend that Graeme had ever had.

3

The wedding was over. Mundis had carried Medusa over the threshold of their apartment and even now was simply staring into her beautiful black eyes and stroking her lustrous hair. It was true bliss and Mundis was the happiest green being on earth.

He was home and the apartment he had so often thought about was just as he had remembered, although he had had to make some adjustments. Medusa needed a dressing room and her own ensuite - she was an independent girl and had lived alone for many, many centuries and was not really good at sharing.

That was fine with Mundis - he liked his privacy too.

What an amazing day, the day they had found each other…how had Mundis managed after all these eons to get so lucky?

Fate, they decided, had been smiling on them and had them just in the right place at the right time.

Mundis of course had heard about Medusa for years, but mainly because she was the lady who had snakes for hair. Mundis was relieved that she had gotten rid of the snakes and opted for hands instead - a far better choice and much more useful - and the hair she had chosen was so beautiful, long and black with a hint of golden green through it.

"The honeymoon sweetheart, where shall we go, the Boss has given us at least a month."

Medusa smiled up at him and whispered, "Australia, my darling, why don't we go and get rid of that nuisance Graeme you told me about?"

"Ahh, Medusa, my thoughts exactly. Yes Australia, home, right where we are now, what a lovely idea and then we can spend some time travelling up the coast and enjoying the scenery."

"Marvellous, shall we let Edith know we are coming?"

"No my darling, we shall do the deed and then appear after about a week to comfort the stricken, although I doubt very much that too many will be stricken."

"Perfect," sighed Medusa and snuggled in and fell fast asleep.

It had been a very busy day and indeed a very busy few months. The lead-up to the wedding was hectic and the events in the world had not helped; every green being who was anyone had been away in Israel fighting against 'He who cannot be mentioned and is best left alone'.

Honestly it had made wedding preparations very difficult, but no matter, everything had come together and Mundis and Medusa were legally married and all was well with the Boss' world.

The Boss was such a stickler for legalism.

They even had a piece of their wedding cake under their pillow - it had been a monstrous green affair with marvellous black roses on every layer - and Medusa insisted on putting it there for luck.

Mundis lay there and stared up into the heavenlies, through the tall grey gum trees to the twinkling stars beyond. He listened to the gentle fall of the waterfall and the croaking of the frogs below and the occasional screech of a cockatoo flying home…

"Ahh, bliss," and with Medusa's head on his shoulder, he too fell asleep, snoring softly and smiling.

Mundis and Medusa Veridis. What an amazing couple. Let's leave them there to sleep in Mundis' beautiful four-poster bed, surrounded by amazing paintings and all Mundis' trophies.

Although Medusa had a few of her own, but she was yet to move them in.

4

How to leave without causing a fuss?

There could be no showdown with Edith; there was never any point in having a showdown with her as she always won. She had this uncanny knack of twisting everything around and somehow Graeme always came out the worst.

No, there was no point in arguing with her.

He would have to pray about it and work it out; he felt sure that the Lord was telling him to leave, but where to go and how to do it?

And he certainly couldn't leave wearing this ridiculous suit that Edith had them all wearing. 'Mr 40 years old and counting backwards' looked okay in his; Graeme on the other hand looked absurd, he was overweight and bald and this did not lend itself to wearing skintight luminous green suits. Although Edith had assured him he looked fine, sadly he knew she was lying and the only reason she wanted him to wear it was because if he didn't, it may look like she did not have everything under control.

Graeme had heard her and Mr 40 giggling about his suit one night in the office, and it was all he could do to stop himself getting his gun and blasting a hole through Mr 40's chest.

He had prayed and the peace of the Lord had descended and Graeme went to bed and dreamt of his grandchildren playing in fields of daffodils and waving happily to him.

Still, that was last week, and this week Graeme had to work out how to leave. Fortunately he had saved some of his old clothes and was able to get them into the back of his truck without anyone noticing, folded up in an old hessian bag buried beneath a power saw he used to cut firewood.

Now to think of a plausible excuse to get into town.

He needed to fool Edith into thinking he was just making a routine trip in and would be coming back directly. He needed to catch her off guard when she was in a very good mood, perhaps after the weekly Mundis email reading; she was always relaxed after that.

He needed to get some money and his Bible. Happily he had plenty of money and had been secreting it away as the months went on - you know a percentage for the Dihards and a percentage for IMP and another percentage for Graeme. He felt sure the Lord would understand and allow him to take it...

He was wrong.

When he went to get it, he felt that strong check in his spirit. The Lord did not want Mundis' Money; Graeme would have to use what he had in the bank and in doing so he would have to withdraw it, something Edith would be onto immediately.

He relented, he would be obedient to the Lord and only take what was untainted and his money.

Now how and when to leave...

5

Graeme's grandchildren *were* playing in fields of daffodils and learning more about heaven than other generations had ever learnt, mainly due to the fact that they were there.

Not for one moment did they miss their parents or their grandmother. They did, however, miss their grandpa and they would often look over the banisters of heaven and cheer him on and pray that he would be safe and make the correct decisions; they were indeed part of the great cloud of witnesses that Hebrews 12 talks about.

'He who cannot be mentioned and is best left alone' heard their prayers and sent the help that Graeme needed to escape his impossible situation and find the friends he was going to need to survive the next six and a half years.

Heaven was a glorious place. The children were supremely happy, school was not a tiresome and frightening experience but a delicious dip into every possible experience...this was onsite learning, travel at the tip of your fingers, wonderful food and expert care.

They matured more in a week than they would have had they spent years at earthly schools or universities.

As there was no danger in heaven, they were allowed to wander wherever they wanted to and to play with whichever animal came across their path.

Graeme's oldest grandchild Sarah had a full-grown male lion for a pet, which slept each night on the end of her very large bed. Needless to say there was not much room for Sarah, but that was not a problem, she just scrunched her legs up and cuddled down into her pillows.

Occasionally this magnificent beast would stretch out full length beside her and put one paw over her body just to keep her warm and extra safe.

Sarah did not miss earth at all.

6

B ack on earth, Israel was cleaning up after the Battle of Gog and Magog, the battle described in Ezekiel 38 and 39.

The Nations of Russia, Iran, Libya and Sudan as well as others had attacked her, and 'He who cannot be mentioned and is best left alone' had miraculously come to her rescue. This was something that the green beings involved were so distraught about that the counselling couches back at Headquarters were never empty and the number of little white pills prescribed was monumental.

The green beings just did not believe the kick back they received. They had experienced defeat before, but only after a lot of damage had been done; this time they got swiped in the first innings. Needless to say there were a lot of very drugged green beings loitering around Headquarters, drinking coffee and lining up for the physiatrist's couch.

The Boss was not impressed with any of this and told them in no uncertain terms to pull themselves together. Some had literally fallen apart; there were green limbs and torsos everywhere.

In any case the Boss was claiming the victory was his, not openly but through the man of the moment who was fast becoming a front-runner on the world stage, the man the Bible calls the Antichrist.

Graeme in the meantime couldn't care less about what was happening in Israel; all he cared about was escaping from his own home alive.

And this he had done.

Right now he was driving down the road that led into town with a breaking heart. Having left his second best friend, Samson the Wonder Dog behind, he was crying unashamedly and cursing Edith and Mundis and anyone else who came to mind.

He felt he could not possibly take him, how would he look after a dog on the run - he wasn't even sure how he would look after himself.

Graeme was just about to learn an awful lot about the Lord.

He had also ditched his ridiculous skintight Mundis suit, peeling it off at the first available opportunity and stuffing it into a hole in a tree. He was now feeling far more comfortable dressed once again in jeans, striped shirt and riding boots, with Driza-bone coat and an old working hat. The only other things he'd managed to take was a small backpack with a bottle of water and a loaf of bread; he could not risk anything else for Edith the Indomitable would notice.

It was late afternoon and he had used the excuse that he needed petrol for the mower and would be back in an hour or two. This meant he had approximately an hour and a half to get rid of the ute, and leave the area as fast as he could.

Steady, ol chap, steady. Graeme was talking to himself the same way he had talked to Sarah when he had taught her to ride a two-wheeler bike…

"Steady Sarah, steady, I've got you…don't be afraid."

Little did he know that Sarah hanging over the banisters of heaven was saying pretty much the same to him…

"Steady Granpa, steady, the Lord's got you and we are praying."

Graeme felt a sense of peace and he looked up and thanked the Lord. A clear picture of what he needed to do was forming in his mind and just the sense of direction he was getting made him feel that perhaps he was going to make it.

He pulled up outside the bank and used his debit card to withdraw all the cash he could from his private account. He would have to withdraw some more along the way, it was a nuisance but there was a limit to what you can take out.

So far so good, cash in hand, ticket already bought…now what to do with the ute.

Graeme looked around and spotted a caravan park. Right, he would drive it in there and park it and go.

The train was leaving in ten minutes. There was one last thing to do; walking to the end of the pier, he took the battery and the sim card out of his phone and dropped all three separately into the bay. He did not want Edith calling him.

In fact he never wanted to hear her voice again.

Wow. After twenty-six years of bondage he was a free man. Never would he have to lay eyes on his wife again - never would he have to listen to her voice explaining IMP philosophy and giving out the recipe for Mundis Lemon Tea Cake...

Honestly, what had he been under and why had he never noticed what sort of person she was before?

Probably because he had been utterly bewitched by her personality and persuasive ways - never did he see that personality as being seductive and her persuasive ways as being controlling. Edith had used her affections as a tool to get her own way, and when she didn't get her own way she withheld her affections. Graeme had been a pawn in her hands...until his grandchildren had disappeared and his heart had broken and he had cried out to His Lord for the first time in his life.

Strange, but it was through such pain that Graeme had come into a place of real faith, something that could not have happened otherwise. Everything had always been too easy and he had always been such putty in her hands.

It was as a free man that he boarded that train to Sydney. He settled into the carriage and fell fast asleep and dreamt of stairways to heaven, two wheeler bicycles and fields of daffodils.

PART TWO

*If any man builds on this foundation using gold, silver, costly
stones, wood, hay, stubble.
Every man's work shall be made manifest; for the day shall declare
it, because it shall be revealed by fire; and the fire shall try every
man's work of what sort it is.
If any man's work abide which he hath built thereupon, he shall
receive a reward.
If any man's work shall be burned, he shall suffer loss; but he himself shall be saved; yet so as by fire.*
I Corinthians 3:12-15

*Are not all angels ministering spirits sent to serve those who will
inherit salvation?*
Hebrews 1:14

*And I will give unto thee, and to thy seed after thee, the land
wherein thou art a stranger, all the land of Canaan, for an everlasting possession; and I will be their God.*
Genesis 17:8

*Thus saith the Lord, which giveth the sun for a light by day, and the
ordinances of the moon and of the stars for a light by night, which
divideth the sea when the waves thereof roar; the Lord of hosts is
his name:
"If those ordinances depart from before me," saith the Lord, "then
the seed of Israel also shall cease from being a nation before me
forever."*
Jeremiah 31:35-36

1

Mundis and Medusa Veridis were just packing the last of their cases and getting them ready for Hornback to put into the spacecraft, although they were a little concerned because Medusa's luggage was made out of genuine crocodile skin and she was not sure that the crocodile hadn't been a relation of Hornback's.

Medusa didn't want to upset him.

Mundis, being the gentleman he was, told her not to worry; he would put her cases in himself and that way Hornback would not know the difference.

Sadly Hornback had already worked this out, and had booked himself into the in-house medical centre for counselling. He had decided not to say anything to Mundis and Medusa as he didn't want to upset them…

Honestly it was a real comedy of errors.

Mundis and Medusa were doing their honeymoon as aliens and not higher fallen beings, (not that they called *themselves* higher fallen beings) they had decided that there needed to be more 'Mundis-type Retreat Centres', and not just in Australia.

Israel perhaps?

Rumour has it that Israel was the most popular place on the planet for UFO's…

Israel it is then, they would deal with Graeme later.

Mundis and Medusa settled themselves in the spacecraft, buckled up and waved goodbye to Hornback.

They lifted off into the starry night and headed for Israel, where they planned to land on the border between Lebanon and Israel in no man's land and totally confuse the border patrols on either side.

They had not gone too far before Mundis decided to check on the situation in Australia with Edith and Graeme. He had a *niggly* feeling about them and was wondering if perhaps he had been too hasty about deciding on Israel when Australia *had* been their first choice.

Mundis brought up his 'Mundis Retreat Australian Style' Facebook page and was aghast to see that Graeme was missing and had been for at least a few days - and Edith was now running the property with 'Mr 40 years old and counting backwards'.

Only a few days, and the high standards of the Boss had already been compromised.

The page sported a very small blog about Graeme having done a bunk and a large picture of 'Mr Insipid 40 and counting backwards' with his arm around a stricken but inwardly glowing Edith and a caption that read:

KEEPING UP THE HIGH STANDARDS OF IMP IN A TRYING TIME.

Mundis fumed; this had all been done without his help.

He had no trouble with Edith and 'Mr 40 and counting backwards' being together but it should have been done his way…

Mundis explained the situation to Medusa; they were a team now and planned to do everything together.

Mundis skillfully turned the craft in a semicircle and headed for the Australian seaside town. Fortunately they had only just reached the Indian Ocean coastline and didn't have far to go back.

They made sure every light on the craft was visible and then flew very low over the habitable areas, although this was no easy feat over central Australia, due to the fact that there are not too many habitable areas.

However they did manage a mention in a few Local papers…

LOW FLYING UFO SEEN OVER CENTRAL AUSTRALIAN CATTLE STATIONS…

If the inhabitants of the cattle station had been looking very closely they would have seen Medusa painting her toenails whilst Mundis was driving, a very domesticated scene - they were a close and loving couple, it was like they had always known each other.

Mundis and Medusa landed at the Dihard property just after nightfall and waited for dinnertime, not that they wanted to join in, they were very invisible.

Samson the Wonder Dog knew they were there, he could smell 'em and he guessed at what they might be up to.

Samson was not a stupid dog and as he didn't like any of the inmates, he kept mum about the whole thing.

Didn't even raise a whimper.

The Veridis' played cards on the top of the kitchen dresser and when the time was just right they sprinkled each and every dessert plate with invisible poison icing sugar…just the right topping for Mundis Lemon tea cake and just the right way to finish off every gullible Mundis retreat inmate.

He and Medusa had no trouble doing this together; in fact from the light fitting in the centre of the ceiling it was easy. Medusa could get to every plate without even stretching, Mundis gave her the poison and she with those incredible hands just did the job.

What a girl and what a lucky chap Mundis was…

Edith, 'Mr 40 year old and counting backwards' and all the inmates of 'Mundis' Retreat Australian Style' died pretty much instantly, and certainly before anyone could get to their mobiles.

Mundis and Medusa had hidden all mobiles in the woodpile, a fact that really puzzled the police when they did their investigation.

Graeme was a widower without even knowing it.

The Australian Police had no answers other than to suspect a mass suicide bid, perhaps carried out because of the loss of their leader and mentor Graeme, which just goes to show how much they didn't know.

Either way the case was closed and the bodies buried. The police at a later date did discover Graeme's whereabouts and he was exonerated from any suspicion, which was a very good thing as Graeme was to need that farm later on in the story.

The departed souls however, were kept in Hades awaiting the Great White Throne Judgment which by earthly standards was quite a long way away…a thousand-plus years to be precise.

They really didn't have a lot to look forward to really, as after the Great White Throne Judgment, they would eventually discover their names were *not* written in the Book of Life and their next stop was to be the Lake of Fire…but as yet they knew none of this, so we won't tell them, no use making a miserable time even worse.

Edith was aghast, she had had no intention of waking up dead, it simply was not part of her plan and she did not hesitate to tell any who would listen.

Strange to say there were not many who *would* listen, in fact Edith found herself pretty much isolated in Hades. It seems that everyone's eyes had been opened to just what sort of person she really had been and no one particularly wanted to stand close.

They were all too busy trying to convince themselves that they had been good people who would surely pass the test and be ushered into heaven.

Although sadly no one really believed it, they all had that sinking feeling that there was one very important ingredient that they had known about all their lives and decided to ignore…

His name was Jesus and his ultimate sacrifice on the cross to pay the price for their sins was not something you could ignore, had you been fortunate enough to be told.

Each and every one of these people HAD been told and had ignored it…deeming it unimportant and really not worth their attention.

Mundis, having done his job, simply hopped back into his spacecraft and flew off to Israel with his arm around Medusa's shoulder…he had a honeymoon to go to.

Samson the Wonder Dog chewed through his leash and escaped. He had known instinctively about the poison and did not want to wake up dead after eating Mundis Lemon teacake.

Samson had never liked Mundis and more or less told Graeme so from the beginning, in fact Samson knew exactly where Mundis hailed from.

Graeme however had been a bit slow.

In any case as I write, Samson the Wonder Dog is hot on Graeme's tail; he is following the scent of one of Graeme's smelly socks.

We leave him bounding down the road toward the train station where he will board the 20.10, changing once in Melbourne en route to Sydney.

He knows the way - he is not a stupid dog.

2

Sarah didn't think it was possible to be unhappy in heaven and was surprised that she was.

The Wedding Supper of the Lamb was about to begin and during this celebration the rewards for service to the King of Kings and the Lord of Lords would be given out.

Sarah quite honestly did not want to go.

Sarah was seven-years-old and she could not think of one thing she had done that the Lord had told her to do and she had done; in her way of thinking He had not told her to do anything.

Sarah decided that she simply would not go. She would hide here at home and play with the animals; nobody would miss her, there were millions going and one less seven-year-old really would not matter.

Although how to hide? There were higher beings everywhere preparing for the feast and decorating the tents - well, Sarah thought they were tents.

The tents were a beautiful sight, gold and silver with the most wonderful flowers growing inside them...these tents had no walls, just roofs.

Sarah did not realise that it was really one huge canopy called a chuppah, and this chuppah had been there for eons, as the vines that were holding the canopy up were thicker than a strong man's waist.

From where Sarah was standing she could see the whole valley below her was filled with this 'tent' and the valley extended for as far as her eyes could see...way off in the distance she could see mountains with snow-covered tops and perhaps a waterfall, although she could not be sure.

Sarah turned away sadly and went in search of her lion. They would curl up and sleep and play quietly, no one would know, and if she got hungry, well that was no problem in heaven, for there were amazing fruit trees everywhere and plenty of water to drink, truly she would be just fine…rather that than be embarrassed to be the only person not getting a prize.

That had happened once before at school back on earth, she had forgotten to do her homework when she was five and did not receive a sticker like the rest of the class; it was mortifyingly terrible and she had cried all the way home.

Sarah was absolutely not going to go through that again.

3

Samson the Wonder Dog arrived at Central Station in Sydney well rested, fed and watered, for the Lord had looked after him beautifully.

Samson had not doubted Him.

Now all he had to do was follow the higher being in front of him who was holding one of Graeme's smelly socks. The higher being knew where Graeme was, the sock was just for effect, although why he needed the sock, Samson was not sure; it was a very smelly one.

Off they set, up into Oxford Street and almost to Centennial Park and then a left turn down Queen Street and another left into Moncur and then into the heart of Paddington, where it was just a matter of time before he found the right street.

Samson followed trustingly behind.

All the houses looked the same. The higher being strode on looking for numbers...

Ahh here it was, green door, white paintwork, exactly the same as every other house.

But for one thing. Samson the Wonder Dog could smell Graeme, not his one dirty sock that was being held by the higher being, but Graeme himself.

He sat on the front door step and barked and barked.

The door flew open and Samson the Wonder Dog bounded into the arms of a large beaming man who was crying and praising God through his tears. The higher being holding the one smelly sock smiled happily and floated back into heaven where he went to find Sarah and tell her the happy story.

Samson the Wonder Dog picked up the one smelly sock in his teeth and presented it to Graeme who was totally bemused. That sock was one of a pair that had been in his locked shed, stuffed into an old pair of soccer boots that he had not worn for years. It even a name tag sewn in it,

G. DIHARD.

4

The higher being in charge of the smelly sock returned to heaven to help serve at the wedding supper of the Lamb. The Bride and Groom had been joined together in holy matrimony and the supper was well underway.

The higher being of smelly sock fame was serving on Sarah's table, having requested it especially. The only problem was that Sarah was not there…

He looked under the table.

He looked under the next table.

He looked behind the vines and in between the flowers.

But he could not find Sarah.

Feeling a gentle tap on his shoulder, he turned and there stood the Bridegroom.

"She is back home, hiding on the terrace with Lejon, she thinks she will not be receiving any prizes. Please go and tell her there is something very special waiting for her, but she must be brave enough to come and receive it. Lejon can come too."

The higher being of the smelly sock bowed and left for Sarah's home. It was not far, nothing was far in heaven and yet it was larger than the entire universe.

It was springtime in heaven and the flowers were blooming and the breeze was gentle and the birds were nesting. Truly the walk to Sarah's house was magnificent. The higher being, whose name incidentally was Angelo, never tired of heaven and found going to earth on assignments rather tiresome - the air down there was so muggy and dirty, whereas in heaven it was crystal clear and *so* good for you.

Angelo was tall with light brown shoulder length hair and he wore a pale blue t-shirt and a pair of jeans, no shoes; it was not necessary, there were no stones on the roads in heaven.

His face shone like the morning sun and his eyes were dark blue and sparkled like light on water, he looked about 18 but in reality was older than our planet and every other planet.

He knew Sarah well, for he was the higher being assigned to keep her from harm. He had met her in heaven before she came to earth and he had guarded her during her short time on earth.

He was familiar with all her ways and he vividly remembered the scene in the classroom. The teacher who hadn't given her the sticker, was not present at the Wedding Supper; Angelo did not know where she was and I am afraid to say did not care, Sarah was his responsibility and he took it very seriously.

Sarah's house was a large grey stone mansion built right on the water, not the sea as there are no seas in heaven, but there is water… and therein lies the difference.

Sarah shared the house with her younger brother and sister and two very small cousins, looked after by higher beings who lived with them and cared for them just as they had done so on earth except that this time they were visible.

Graeme's room was ready too; in fact he had an entire wing of the house to himself. His favourite books were there and also a few of his favourite sports matches on DVD.

Truly heaven was everything one could possibly hope for.

The Lord had known all along that Graeme would choose Him and that Edith wouldn't want to know Him, Edith always knew best about everything, there was no telling her anything…ever.

Sadly Edith had been a very spoilt child who nobody had ever stood up to. She had gotten her own way from the moment she was born and even in Hades was still trying.

Although it was turning out to be more difficult than anything she could have imagined…everyone just kept driiifffffting away.

Hades was a very impermanent place.

Sarah's house was surrounded by a delightful garden with tall fir trees lining the front yard and a huge stretch of water out the back. In fact the terrace literally backed right onto the water, which glistened and lapped right up to the edge. It was truly beautiful, and on a clear day you could see the most magnificent cliffs in the distance.

The terrace had white garden furniture on it and was bathed in sunlight, never too strong, always just right.

Angelo walked round the back of the house and softly called her name...

"Saaaraah..."

5

Mundis and Medusa arrived in Monaco, and booked into the casino in Monte Carlo.

They had flown all night since their Australian interlude and had made sure they got there as fast as they could, no flying low and causing exciting UFO sightings, they were in a hurry to really start their honeymoon.

Invisible fallen higher green beings had their own entrance and reception desk. They simply shared the rooms with lesser beings and as the former were invisible they all fitted in very well.

Although invariably there were complaints about the mini bar, which seemed to run out even when the lesser beings weren't using it.

Mundis and Medusa had decided to bypass Israel.

The Boss had just taken up residence in Jerusalem and Mundis really wanted a honeymoon; chances were that the Boss would forget all about his promise to Mundis about a month off and haul him back into work.

Mundis was in real honeymoon mode, dressed in a pair of cream pants, pink shirt with sailing shoes and no socks, plus a very smart Panama hat and his Armanis.

Mundis didn't want to get sunburnt, he peeled.

Medusa was wearing black leggings, a frilly linen smocked dress, her hair was done up in a loose bun with whispy bits all round her face and she was teetering around in a pair of very high platform shoes.

She looked very pretty, her eyes were sparkling and her skin was the most beautiful shade of pale green.

Medusa also wore a hat, a beautiful white one with a very large brim, which she had no trouble keeping on with all those hands.

They had both enjoyed disposing of Edith and Mundis' devoted followers. It had added a real spark to the honeymoon, and they were just going over the world map to see where and whom they could get next.

Perhaps some of those who had recently discovered what they thought was the truth about 'He who cannot be mentioned and is best left alone', they might be fun to kill...but Mundis sensed it would have to be a real undercover job, they perhaps may not fall for a visible alien.

Persecution has a way of sharpening the senses and they would not take to Mundis at all, see through him in an instant, actually both see through him and smell him out. So either way, visible alien or invisible green being, he would be beaten before he even started.

In any case we will tell that part of the story as it emerges; for now let's just enjoy Monte Carlo with the Veridis' - such a lovely couple, such charming company and so well travelled.

They had booked into the Presidential suite in the Casino and were enjoying the view, having ordered cocktails on the verandah followed by dinner in the restaurant just above the main chandelier and then a night on the tables.

Medusa was just deciding what gown to wear and how her hair should be done. They had left the spacecraft on the roof, which was fairly empty at the moment because most green beings were pretty much occupied at work, it being the Boss' world and all.

In fact Mundis and Medusa were one of the very few who were on holiday.

"I think the black sequined dress with my hair worn down?"

"Whatever you wear Medusa will be wonderful, surprise me..." sighed Mundis, who was enjoying every moment of his holiday.

Remember he had been very busy for the last twenty-eight years. 1894 to 1948 and been absolutely action packed and just thinking about it made him tired.

Although he had almost forgotten about his Verbier stint and his Italian debacle; *they* had been holidays, the former definitely better than the latter.

Mundis had tried to squash the memory of Mussolini Mundis and his very rude treatment of himself...honestly, could Mussolini

Mundis not see the joke?

No matter, he had been lonely then, he hadn't realised it...but now he would never be lonely again.

He watched his lovely wife brushing her hair with a brush in each and every hand, no wonder her hair shone the way it did...

He was a lucky chap.

The evening was perfect, the dinner superb and the gambling such fun. Mundis managed to rig every table and Medusa and he left with the entire winnings for the evening.

The casino was put on lock down because no one could work out where the money had gone.

They were just enjoying a nightcap and a romantic interlude when Mundis' iPhone rang. Mundis had changed the ring tone to 'Come fly with me, let's fly, let's fly away...'

He almost missed the call; he had heard 'We all live in a Yellow Submarine' for so many centuries and had forgotten he changed it.

"Mundis speaking."

"Veridis," the smooth voice hissed, "the honeymoon is over, hot tail it back here now, I need you and Medusa in Jerusalem and then in a week to New York. We have also heard that there is possible opposition coming from the enemy."

"But Sir, this is my honeymoon and I thought you told me that the enemy had given you the world and retreated into heaven with the Eternal Nuisances, and that everything was under your control now."

"Veridis, I am not in the mood to answer any questions or queries, get back to Jerusalem now."

Mundis took a deep breath and said...

"One more question sir, I thought you said Headquarters was mine and that Medusa and I could run that and leave you to run the rest of the world from Jerusalem?"

"Move it, Mundisssss."

Mundis moved it, explained the situation to Medusa, packed their bags and went back to Jerusalem.

There was no winning when the Boss was in that mood.

Fortunately Medusa worked for the same company and understood completely.

6

Graeme and Samson the Wonder Dog sat in a state of glorious mutual admiration.

Samson was singing a song he had made up for his recent journey. He had sung it all the way from South Australia to Sydney...

Samson the Wonder Dog, diddly dee diddly deeeeeee,
KILLER of rabbits,
FRIEND of Graeme,
Didn't like EDITH,
Thank you for PRAYIN,
Samson the Wonder dog, diddly dee.

Graeme on the sofa and Samson resting his head on his lap, singing softly and staring up at him every now and again with his large brown eyes and wagging his happy Samson tail...

Now this was true bliss...back at Edith's establishment no dog was allowed past the back door. Samson had never been inside before so this was a wonderful experience and not at all like he had imagined.

He had thought that indoors was just like outdoors but smaller, you know dirt and grass on the ground, a few bones and a number of parked cars, trees, flowers and a small dam or two, maybe even some chickens and a few mice.

Indoors was much nicer, soft sofas, comfy beds, indoor bowls with food and water, although the food only appeared at certain times of the day; no worries, at least he didn't have to catch it.

After Graeme had left, Edith had not fed him and sometimes she had kicked him. Samson had become very good at catching rabbits and tearing them from limb to limb - sad but true, a dog does have to eat - and then when he had arrived home once to show her one of his catches, she had very nastily tied him up and told him he could starve.

That was the last straw, he chewed and chewed at his lead and left just as Edith and the others were eating their Mundis Lemon Tea cake with the surprise invisible icing sugar on top.

The higher being of the smelly sock had found him just as he was running down the drive and had kindly offered to come with him to Sydney. He knew pretty much exactly where Graeme was and the two of them could find him together.

And that is exactly what had happened, and here he was living happily with Graeme and a very nice lady called Vanessa who was sad but bearing up bravely and who, wonder upon wonders, did not mind dogs, especially ones called Samson.

Vanessa was a distant cousin of Graeme's and had been a nominal believer at the time of the rapture.

Vanessa was an advertising executive and she used to have a nice husband called Tim who had worked from home; she also used to have two young children, Josh aged six and Lucas, seven.

Tim was a believer and had not wanted his children in daycare centres. In fact he had insisted that he give up work and care for their children as he felt this is what the Lord wanted and he would honour that.

Vanessa didn't argue, she had a very high paying job and a very good degree behind her, she didn't really care *what* the Lord wanted…in short she really didn't know Him like Tim did, although she loved Tim and her children and was happy to be the working mum with the stay-at-home dad.

It was a happy marriage even though they were not together in their faith, although Tim had thought they had been once.

He was wrong.

Vanessa had fallen in love with the handsome youth leader at St David's Church and had played the game well; he being rather over-awed with this slightly older and strikingly good looking young woman had responded and the rest is history.

They had not been unhappy; on the contrary they had been very happy. Tim took the children to Sunday School while Vanessa stayed in bed having worked all week. Tim also took the children to school and after-school activities, and juggled his work around their lives.

It all worked surprisingly well - the children were happy, Tim was happy and Vanessa was happy...until the rapture.

That was the day in which everything in Vanessa's life changed dramatically.

She had woken up as usual and had noticed that Tim was not in bed. She didn't worry, she jumped up and put on her running gear and headed for the door, glancing quickly in at the children as she passed - they were not there either.

She ran downstairs expecting to see them having an early breakfast but was met with silence. The kitchen was empty, the family room was empty and the car was parked in the street; worse still, there was Tim's mobile and back pack, just where he had left them the night before.

Vanessa's heart had begun to pound. She raced back up to their bedrooms and noticed for the first time that their pyjamas were in their beds, just as they would be had they been sleeping in them.

Josh's were all cuddled up and Lucas' were sprawled across the bed.

Vanessa checked her bed and there was Tim's t-shirt and his boxers - exactly in the position they would have been had he still been in them.

Vanessa knew what had happened.

Tim had believed in the rapture. He had also believed in the importance of Israel with respect to end time events and had spoken about it. He had been an enigma at St David's, no one else had taken him seriously; they had liked him, it was impossible not to like Tim, he was a man with no guile, but they had still not taken him seriously...

Nor had his wife.

Especially when he suggested that all the fuss in the world about Israel was directly due to Satan not wanting the Jews back in the land, that once they returned Satan's fear of God's vengeance toward him with respect to his rebellion at the beginning of the age would be realised...he knew there was a dungeon waiting for him and an eventual lake of fire as explained in Revelation 20.

Tim maintained that Satan knew his time was short and therefore if he could wipe Israel off the map he could buy himself some more time; if he *couldn't* wipe Israel off the map then he would instead set himself up to rule it and gain control that way.

"Why," some curious listeners would say, "does God want the Jews back in the land, and what has it do with Satan? Is Satan really real?"

Tim knew exactly what it felt like to be up against a brick wall, but he knew he was in the right Church. God had placed him there years ago and he would stay until God moved him on or took him home, whatever came first.

Tim would pray silently and then begin his mini sermon.

He would begin by pointing out that salvation came through the Jews. Jesus was Jewish, of the line of King David, born of the seed of woman, fully God and fully man. Tim would often quote Tolstoy:

"How odd of God to choose the Jews, but odder still are those who choose a Jewish God and scorn the Jews."

He would then go on to explain from Scripture that God had given the land of Israel to the Jews way back when Abraham left his home in Ur of the Chal'dees:

And the Lord said unto Abram, after that Lot was separated from him: "Lift up now thine eyes, and look from the place where thou art northward, and southward, and eastward, and westward: for all the land which thou seest, to thee will I give it, and to thy seed forever".
Genesis 13:14-15

In the same day the Lord made a covenant with Abram, saying, unto thy seed have I given this land, from the river of Egypt, unto the great river, the river Euphrates.
Genesis 15:18

God had also promised the people a deliverer, a Messiah who would come and save them from their sins, one who would be far greater than Moses:

For unto us a child is born, unto us a son is given; and the government shall be upon his shoulders; and his name shall be called Wonderful, Counsellor, the mighty God, the everlasting Father, the Prince of Peace.

Isaiah 9:6

He would go on to say that in the fullness of time Messiah was born in a manger in Bethlehem, but the people did not recognise Him for who He was, - some of course did, but the nation as a whole did not.

The Jews as a nation were beholden to God for their land and had to obey Him by following very strict laws. Messiah came not to abolish the Laws but to fulfil them and to set up His Kingdom on earth. Sadly they missed it, and after the Crucifixion of Messiah the land was taken from them a mere 70 years later.

The Romans sacked Jerusalem and the Diaspora began and lasted up until the late 1800s when the Jews began trickling back into Palestine, as it was then called.

Tim would continue; God has now done in this day and age what He had promised in His Word He would do, and that was to restore the Jews to their land. Out of the ashes of the Holocaust, Israel has been reborn and Satan knows that the Ancient Prophecy spoken about him in Genesis - *And I will put enmity between you and the woman, and between your offspring and hers; he will crush your head and you will strike his heel* - will be fulfilled when the Jewish people call out to Jesus and invite Him back to be their Messiah.

This would happen during a time of great persecution against the Jews in the land of Israel, a time known as the Time of Jacob's Trouble, and it would be during this time that they would:

... look upon me the one they have pierced and they shall mourn for Him as one mourns for an only son.

Zechariah 12:12

...and personally invite Him back to rule and reign:

*"baruch haba b'shem Adonai"...Blessed is he who comes in
the name of the Lord.*
Luke 13:35

And then and only then will Jesus return and the Millennium
begin. Satan will be chained for a thousand years and only be let out
at the end for a short time to truly show that God really is in control;
and then and only then would he be thrown into the Lake of Fire.

It was all too much of a fairy tale for the people at St David's
and they really didn't much care; they had the children to educate,
the house to pay off, the lawn to mow and the dog to walk...life was
busy,

And who in all honesty had time to complicate it with Israel.

Tim, whilst without guile was also stubborn and would insist that
God was a covenant-keeping God and He had given that land to the
Jews forever...

*And I will establish my covenant between me and thee and thy
seed after me in thy generations for an everlasting covenant, to be
a God unto thee and thy seed after thee.*

*And I will give unto thee and to thy seed after thee the land
wherein thou art a stranger, all the land of Canaan, for an
everlasting possession; and I will be their God.*
Genesis 17:7-8

And then he would quote Isaiah 11:11-12 in a last ditch attempt
to explain that it is God who has brought them back to the land:

*And it shall come to pass in that day, that the Lord shall set his
hand again the second time to recover the remnant of his people,
which shall be left from Assyria, and from Egypt, and from Path-
ros, and from Cush, and from E'lam, and from Shi-nar and from
Ha-math and from the islands of the sea.*

*And he shall set up an ensign for the nations, and shall
assemble the outcasts of Israel, and gather together the dispersed
of Judah from the four corners of the earth.*

No one could accuse Tim of not trying.

His words unfortunately fell for the most part on deaf ears and those who sort of listened soon got caught up in the world again and the Church roster - you know Lemon Tea Cake, Bible studies and all that stuff...

Tim would sigh and tell the Lord that he had tried and would keep trying to minister to them, but for the most part he could see that the Church in the greater part of the Western World was asleep and had no idea of the times in which they lived...

They were, as far removed as the church was in the book of Acts as they could be, and neither remembered from whence they had come nor had any idea of where they were going.

They were afloat in a *sea* of church fairs and conventions, in many cases so like the world that it was almost impossible to tell where one began and the other ended.

Still the Gospel was preached and there were salvations and testimonies, and for that Tim gave thanks.

When Tim and his Minister met in heaven after the rapture, there was never an 'I told you so' from Tim, just a smile and a hug and a quiet apology from the Minister, who was hoping he could repent for replacement theology in heaven and wondering at the same time if it was still an issue...

Vanessa had put Tim's belief down to too many American Christian novels and too many online courses, and had teased him and got on with life. Tim had smiled good-naturedly and teased her back, telling her that he would grab her round the waist and take her with him. They had laughed together and all had gone smoothly until now.

Tim had understood Vanessa well and knew that it was only going to be the Lord who changed her heart toward Him. Tim had done everything he knew to do, from fasting and praying to seriously talking to her. Nothing changed, but that did not mean he did not love her; he certainly did, and went right on praying, praising and waiting.

Every night Vanessa would come to bed and step over Tim as he laid full length on the floor interceding for everyone he knew to intercede for. It had been a nightly ritual for as long as they had been married and one that Vanessa accepted with good grace.

But now it was all over, Tim her knight in shining armour, had been taken and the children with him.

Vanessa switched on the television and sat there watching the early morning news with stories of the disappearances of millions of people from around the globe.

Vanessa put her head in her hands and sobbed, surprisingly not just for herself but for every person in the world who was facing the pain she was facing now.

She did not know it, but this was her first step in the gift of intercession.

Tim's prayers were being answered, maybe not the way he had expected and hoped for but answered nonetheless.

PART THREE

And he shall confirm the covenant with many for one week; and in the midst of the week he shall cause the sacrifice and the oblation to cease, and for the overspreading of abominations he shall make it desolate, even until the consummation, and that determined shall be poured upon the desolate…
Daniel 9:27

When ye therefore shall see the ABOMINATION OF DESOLATION, spoken of by Daniel the prophet, stand in the holy place,
Then let them which be in Judea flee into the Mountains…
Matthew 24:15-16

1

The newly appointed World Leader was magnificent; he was being egged on by the Boss who was standing directly beside him.

Although very soon he would be standing right in the middle of him, t'was only a matter of time.

At the moment the Boss was still engaged in a fierce battle in heaven and was not available to be totally present on the earth just yet.

But soon, very soon…and every green being was holding their breath waiting for that day.

Mundis had seen him encourage any number of world leaders throughout History…

Antiochus Ephinanes,

Attila the Hun,

Genghis Khan,

Tsars of Russia,

Kings of England,

Hitler, Stalin…but this particular time excelled them all.

He prompted with such reason, reassuring people after the disappearances, settling things with Israel after the war inflicted on them by various Middle Eastern nations.

He truly was oil personified on troubled waters…for now.

Mundis and Medusa had front row seats in the United Nations, not that anyone could see them. They were perched on the laps of the representatives from the United States of America and Germany.

Both Mundis and Medusa felt highly favoured and it certainly beat hanging from the light fittings.

Perhaps the Boss was making up for calling them back from their honeymoon, but I strongly doubt it - he had probably forgotten they were even meant to be on one. Things were so frantic in the world;

one little green being honeymoon was neither here nor there, even if it was the honeymoon of one of his oldest friends in the entire universe.

Medusa was looking stunning in a pale pink twinset with pearls, her hair done up in a magnificent beehive. The green being behind her had to resort to the light fitting otherwise he would not see a thing. Mundis was dressed to kill, figuratively speaking, in a dark grey suit with a pink and white striped shirt with a darker pink tie; they really were a perfect match.

Medusa blew the Boss a kiss and swears that he winked back, but could not really be sure.

Mundis did not think so, gearing up to running the world was not conducive to winking, but personally I feel Mundis may have been feeling a trifle threatened even at the mere suggestion of a wink.

They had arrived back in Jerusalem and had been there for a week before being called to New York. Whilst they had been in Jerusalem they had set up their office not in their old stomping ground in the Old City, but at the King David Hotel opposite the YMCA. Again they took the Presidential suite with views over the Old City, and again Medusa would assume the role of Mundis' PA.

She was certainly not going to give *that* job to anyone else.

They smiled and remembered those days back in the 1940's; although in reality it was only a matter of weeks ago in 'Mundis time', it was over sixty years in real time.

Medusa was amazed at the fashions in Jerusalem. Honestly, when she was here last, women had not been wearing jeans and t-shirts although the shoes were still similar, very high platforms, and she was thrilled she had a few pairs with her. The traffic, though, was appalling, so she was very pleased they had their spacecraft and did not have to use public transport.

Hornback was with them and was feeling much better. The councilor had deduced (with the help of DNA testing) that Medusa's crocodile skin luggage was not related to him and therefore he had not breached any family honour by associating with those who had such scant respect for reptiles.

He was feeling very relaxed and looking forward to serving sir and madam in Jerusalem.

2

"*Saaaarah… Saaaarah!*"

Angelo stood on the verandah and looked out across the water, trying to pretend that he could not see Sarah hiding underneath the large teak table. Of course she was impossible to miss as Lejon was under there with her and most of him was sticking out.

Angelo tried not to laugh.

Sarah crawled out and Lejon followed.

"Sarah, the Lord is waiting for you, he understands about the sticker episode when you were five and He wants you to know that He is not handing out stickers but crowns and prizes and there is one for you, but you have to be brave enough to come and get it."

Sarah brushed away a few tears and put her hand on Lejon's mane.

"Can Lejon come too?"

"Certainly, he can lie beside you, and even go up and receive the prize with you."

"Okay, we will come then."

"You may want to change into the pretty white party dress that is laid out on your bed and put on the pink sandals. Lejon will just have to be happy in his lion skin."

Sarah ran up to change as Lejon and Angelo waited for her on the verandah. Angelo smiled, he had followed his Masters orders and had cared faithfully for Sarah and was thrilled that the rapture had happened when it had. He had dreaded that she would grow up and forget about Heaven and the Lord. She had never mentioned either whilst on earth, but Angelo could see when he looked into her eyes that she believed, and he never wanted her to lose that belief.

He had also seen that in the family she had been born into there was every chance that she would lose her simple belief; they were a self-centred, tough lot and Angelo was none too fond of them.

Their own higher beings were worn out with trying to turn them back to the Lord, although rumour had it that Graeme had returned and even now was making extraordinarily fast progress.

His higher being was ecstatic.

Whereas Edith's higher being had come back to heaven defeated and a little depressed. The Lord however had not held it against him, for there is nothing in heaven or in earth that can change a lesser being's mind once that mind is made up to go its own way.

Sarah returned; she had forgotten to brush her hair and wash her face so she was sent back to do both *and* to clean her teeth. She returned again and Angelo clapped and Lejon purred, for she made a very pretty picture, perfectly completed when Angelo tied the beautiful pink velvet ribbon around her hair.

Off they set, Sarah riding on Lejon's back and Angelo walking alongside.

Angelo told her the happy smelly sock story about Samson the Wonder Dog and Graeme. Sarah loved it and wanted to hear it more than once; she was particularly interested in how Samson had gone to the loo when he was on the train. Angelo explained that there were various corners of that train that would never quite smell the same again.

Sarah and Angelo laughed out loud when they thought of that.

Happily the air in heaven smelt quite different. It was crystal clear and smelt of spring as the birds sang, the wild flowers bloomed and the small field creatures got on with life.

The small creatures had never lived anywhere but heaven and could not really understand the excitement about the rapture and the Wedding Supper of the Lamb. All seemed like a lot of hard work and a terrible fuss when there were much more important things to do like finding food and having babies.

And don't ask me why heaven is not overrun with small creatures. I simply do not know the answer, but will ask when I get there.

3

Vanessa's life had changed - she was no longer a wife and mother and had not been for at least two years. She was now the sole owner of a terrace house in Paddington, Sydney that was the centre of an underground church network.

Graeme and Samson were not her only tenants. A very nice Jewish man called Aaron was another; fortunately he liked dogs, because if Graeme was away Samson slept on his bed. Samson preferred men, and was still processing women since his experience with Edith. He was warming to Vanessa and one day he would surprise her by choosing her bed, but not just yet...

For now he guarded the house, entertained the higher beings who visited and made up songs to sing to himself.

Vanessa's heart still ached but the Lord had healed and brought comfort in ways she would not have imagined. She still found it difficult to look into the children's room but as it was Graeme's now and as the door was mostly closed she could walk past and almost forget, safe in the knowledge that she would see them all again one day soon.

The fact that Graeme too was grieving the loss of his grandchildren gave them a common bond and point of contact that brought comfort to them both; they could share stories and laugh and cry all at the same time.

Aaron had arrived in her life very shortly after Graeme and Samson and she could now thank the Lord that she was truly not alone. She was becoming quite a different person to the one she had been, now taking Tim's place on the floor and interceding for all her Lord put on her heart.

Sometimes she thought she could still smell traces of Tim but perhaps it was just her imagination... or perhaps it was the higher being standing over her and bringing her small bits of comfort, not smelly sock comfort but that 'special smell that reminds us of special people's comfort.

Vanessa understood far more about higher beings now than she used to and once she almost felt she had seen one. She had thought he was standing over Graeme as he slept on the downstairs sofa and he was smiling at Samson who was grinning back and wagging his tail.

Aaron had arrived from Israel after the rapture, when persecution started to break out against Israel.

Aaron had been saved along with 144,000 other Jewish men and was from one of the twelve tribes of Israel. He was an invaluable member of the household and many would come from all over Sydney to hear him preach and to be prayed for; in fact it was like the first days of the church in the book of Acts...

And the Lord added to their number daily those who were being saved.
Acts 2:47

It was amazing really, friends of Vanessa's who had never shown any interest in Christianity before were now clamouring for information.

There were those from St David's who had only gone to church at Christmas and Easter time and those from her work who had known Tim was a believer and had disappeared and wanted to know why Vanessa seemed to be holding up the way she was. Many of them had lost children in the rapture too and they felt safe to cry with Vanessa and grieve; she in turn could then share where her strength came from.

These were heady days and dangerous ones. The Lord was sending His Seal, Trumpet and Bowl Judgments on the world and it was only going to get worse. These days were certainly not for the fainthearted, and had not the Lord shortened the days, none would have survived...

If those days had not been cut short, no one would survive, but for the sake of the elect those days will be shortened.
Matthew 24:22

4

Three years had now passed since the rapture and the treaty the Boss (disguised as the world leader or Antichrist in Biblical terms) had made with Israel was broken and he was now demanding the entire world worship him.

The Antichrist was now completely indwelt by the Boss, and he the Boss, was in his element.

He was in the process of setting himself up as world leader in the newly built Temple in Jerusalem and Mundis and Medusa had been given front row seats again...

They had spent the last three years in Jerusalem, much to Mundis' disgust. He wanted to go home and start a family in Headquarters and he felt that children would be better there away from all the fuss that centred around Jerusalem, especially now that there was so much opposition from 'He who cannot be mentioned and is best left alone'.

The so-called Judgments 'He who cannot be mentioned and was best left alone' had sent and *was* sending were a terrible nuisance and did not lend themselves to the Boss' cause at all.

Not that Mundis felt nervous about all this opposition, he firmly believed that this earth was the Boss' and the opposition was just putting on a good show and would soon get tired of it and retreat further into heaven.

Well, that is what Mundis wanted to believe.

He was a family green being now with the responsibility of a wife and possible children. He had put his frivolous and empty-headed ways behind him and he really did not want to bring children into a world that 'He who cannot be mentioned and is best left alone' kept interfering in.

It would be fair to say that he *did* spend quite a bit of time pushing back memories from his past yet very recent assignments...

The episode with Dreyfus in prison and the many shafts of light that cascaded around him; the room in Basel when Herzl spoke and the fact that there were no other green beings there beside Mundis - and he had been dressed so nicely in his dinner suit and had absolutely no one to show off to.

Mundis could not decide which was worse…the fact that he was the only green being there and that 'He who cannot be mentioned and is best left alone' was so obviously in charge, or that he had no one to impress with his fine clothes.

Then there were the sights he had seen with respect to the Battle of Beersheba, those huge Walers with those huge higher beings on them that galloped along with the lesser beings on their much smaller Walers. And then there were the higher beings on the ship to Italy, the ones that had so rudely hoisted him out of his cabin, and then the United Nations vote for Israel and the number of higher beings that were in the auditorium then.

Yes, Mundis spent quite a bit of time trying to suppress those memories…

It is a good thing that British Mundis could not put his two cents worth in, as he had some stories to tell too…the bound up green beings during the Balfour Declaration at Number 10 and the lack of any green being presence in the displaced persons' camp in Cyprus.

German Mundis would not have had much to add, he had pretty much had carte blanche in Berlin during his period of service.

Medusa agreed about babies and Headquarters, but only half heartedly; she really did not want anyone taking her place as Mundis' PA, even part time, and besides, having children was really going to spoil her figure. Medusa had such a stunning figure and memories of her mother came flooding back, her mother had played Ursula the Sea Witch in Walt Disney's *Little Mermaid*.

Medusa, whilst proud of her mother, did not think much of her figure and history does have a way of repeating itself…genetics and all.

No, Medusa would stall the babies for as long as she could, life was far too much fun and she had waited such a long time for Mundis and did not want to share him with anyone, thank you very much.

Her biggest problem at the moment was what to wear to the inauguration of the Boss as world leader tomorrow. Should she go as Grecian princess, Egyptian queen or American movie star? Anyone would do, they were all gorgeous.

Mundis had chosen his outfit, he was going as Ben Hur and would arrive in a space chariot without horses...well I guess that settled it for Medusa, she would go as a Roman princess, and ride in the chariot with him.

Not for a moment was she letting him out of her sight, he was just too good a catch and far too attractive. She just loved the way his green skin sparkled in the sun and gave off that wonderful odour when he was upset.

Obviously neither Mundis nor Medusa had really grasped the story around Ben Hur, you know the deeper points...but then again neither of them were deeper Beings.

Incredibly intellectually brilliant, but not deep.

5

As Sarah and Angelo approached they could hear a low buzzing that gradually became louder, the happy chatter of a multitude of people who were involved in a Wedding Supper that had been planned for centuries and even now was underway.

Imagine that…going to a wedding that was planned before you or any of your ancestors were even born.

This was a very well planned wedding.

Angelo and Sarah crested the brow of a hill and looked down. Sarah gasped in awe, for there in front of her was a valley that seemed to be just one enormous silver and gold tent that stretched as far as she could see in every direction.

The smell of flowers that rose up to greet them was simply beautiful. Neither Angelo or Sarah could move; the beauty and the ambience was overwhelming.

Lejon was not shy, he headed on down the hill with his tail twitching in happiness, smiling a happy lion smile and shaking his glorious mane. He could see the Bridegroom in the distance, and the Bridegroom was Lejon's favourite person in *all* heaven.

"Ah Lejon, welcome friend and have you brought her?"

Lejon stopped and rubbed his wonderful mane up against the Bridegroom's thigh. The Bridegroom laughed and ruffled the beautiful soft tresses and then caressed Lejon's velvety back as Lejon purred and purred.

Lejon then turned and looked in the direction of the hill and seemed to beckon Sarah with his eyes.

Sarah was transfixed. It seemed her legs did not want to move and her stomach had risen to her mouth and her heart had dropped to her sandals. Angelo took her by the hand and led her through the tables to the Bridegroom, who stopped and kissed her forehead.

"Welcome my Princess, thank you for finding your courage and coming to our Wedding Party."

"Yes, sir."

Sarah was looking at His hands and feet; they had holes in them and for some reason those holes brought a lump to her throat and an ache to her heart. She was not sure why they were there and why no one had put a bandage on them.

The Bridegroom knew her heart and her thoughts like He knows all our hearts and thoughts and gently stroked her head.

"Now, Angelo will take you to the table and there you will wait to receive your prize - and Sarah, *it is* something better than a sticker."

Sarah's eyes opened wide and she smiled and curtsied. Sarah had never curtsied in her life but it came naturally and was indeed very prettily done.

"Yes, sir."

Sarah turned to go and then much to her own surprise she turned back and threw her arms around the Bridegroom's waist and hugged him. Memories long buried came flooding back and tears came to her eyes and she looked up and whispered, "I remember You and I remember what You did for me, thank you…"

The Bridegroom hugged her back and bent down and whispered back, *"I remember you too little one, I have never forgotten you and thank you for thanking me."*

Angelo again took her by the hand and gently led her to her table, where she was seated with her little brother and sister and even smaller cousins who were being held by their own special higher beings.

She was also seated with a great-grandmother she had never met and quite a lot of great aunts and uncles who all seemed very pleased to see her. Not one of them looked any older than her own parents had been and Sarah seemed to remember her mother saying she was 21, every birthday.

Angelo himself waited on her and Lejon settled himself under the table with his head just below Sarah's dangling legs.

Sarah sighed happily and picked up a peanut butter sandwich on delicious white bread, her very favourite type of supper.

The air in heaven is so pure and so inundated with Goodness and

Wisdom and Knowledge that nothing is ever boring. Sarah sat there transfixed with an expression of sheer delight and wonder on her face, and she never got bored and was never sleepy.

Her younger brother and sister were the same; although very young in an earthly sense, they sat totally absorbed in the proceedings in a way that even adults in our world would have found beyond themselves.

The babies at the table slept and woke up and gurgled and ate and slept and woke up again and generally behaved just the way babies always behave but without the ill temper that is consistent with the fall of man...

6

Graeme stood on the hill that overlooked his farm and gloried in the perfection of the morning. The frost was thawing and every blade of grass sparkled.

The fog that enveloped the house was beginning to lift and Graeme could see its green tin roof and the garden that surrounded it…home, *his* home. He had not realised how much he loved it and how hard it had been to actually leave it, although at the time it was imperative that he did.

Graeme could tell that it was going to be the most beautiful day with clear blue skies at just the right temperature.

Wonderful April weather.

How marvellous to be home. He wandered down the hill and climbed through the fence that led to the stables. He had redesigned every stable into a self-contained unit complete with ensuite and tiny kitchen, no easy feat and quite expensive, but he and some local builders had managed it and Graeme had been pleased with the end result.

He walked through the courtyard and noticed the roses were very overgrown and had not been pruned for quite a while - he would see to that as soon as there was time.

He went to open the kitchen door and was surprised to find it was locked. No problem, he simply floated through and continued walking through to the dining room.

He was also surprised to see the table partially covered with crockery and glasses, all with a very heavy layer of dust.

Graeme leaned forward to inspect the table - there seemed to be something written in the dust…

Psalm 107 verses 6 and 7.

With that he awoke.

Graeme was sweating and his heart was beating rapidly. He immediately reached for his Bible and looked up Psalm 107 and the relevant verses:

Then they cried out to the Lord in their trouble,
And he delivered them from their distress.
He led them by a straight way
To a city where they could settle.

An answer to prayer...

"Thank you Lord, thank you. I sense that now is the right time to return to the farm and that you *will* lead and provide."

Graeme knew that Edith and the others had died and he fortunately was not implicated in the murders, having left the farm at least a week before they had occurred. Graeme was seen by many credible people in Sydney and his story believed by the police.

He had not returned previously because there was too much work to do in Sydney. He and Vanessa and Aaron had been running a teaching centre in Paddington for almost four years; this however was about to change and Graeme had been praying about what direction to take next.

The situation in the world was dreadful and a city, even though it was a marvellous place to witness and teach in, was not safe.

The Lord had been releasing the Seal, Trumpet and Bowl Judgments and life was anything but tranquil. The plagues and wars were terrible and the suffering almost inconceivable but through it all the harvest had been plentiful and in this they rejoiced.

The Lord had been faithful and their number had been protected, but for how much longer, no one knew.

Life, however, was about to take a decided turn for the worst.

The One World leader was now insisting that every person take the Mark of the Beast. This meant that money would no longer exist and that everyone would be asked to have a mark on their hand or forehead in order to buy or sell.

Graeme and Vanessa and the others knew that by taking that

mark they would forfeit their right to heaven for eternity.

And by not taking it they would die, probably by beheading.

Even now the centres for this type of death were being prepared in sports stadiums and under airport terminals, in fact in the latter case they had been prepared a long time ago…even before the rapture.

It was time to leave the city and the Lord had told Graeme that He would take them by a straight way.

Graeme held Samson the Wonder Dog close and told him of their impending journey.

Samson smiled. He already knew; the higher being of the smelly sock fame was in the room and had told him personally not ten minutes before Graeme had woken up.

PART FOUR

Alas! For the day is great, so that none is like it: it is even the time of Jacob's trouble; but he shall be saved out of it.
For it shall come to pass in that day, saith the Lord of Hosts, that I will break his yoke from off thy neck, and will burst thy bonds, and strangers shall no more serve themselves of him:
But they shall serve the Lord their God, and David their king whom I will raise up unto them.
Therefore fear thou not, O my servant Jacob, saith the Lord; neither be dismayed, O Israel: for lo I will save thee from afar, and thy seed from the land of their captivity; and Jacob shall return, and shall be in rest, and be quiet and none shall make him afraid.
For I am with thee, saith the Lord, to save thee : though I make a full end of all the nations whither I have scattered thee, yet I will not make a full end of thee: but I will correct thee in measure, and will not leave thee altogether unpunished.
Jeremiah 30:7-11

For then there shall be great tribulation, such as was not seen since the beginning of the world to this time, no, nor ever shall be.
Matthew 24:21

And the woman fled into the wilderness, where she hath a place prepared of God, that they should feed her there a thousand three hundred and threescore days.
Revelation 12:6

And he saith unto me, "Write, blessed are they which are called unto the marriage supper of the Lamb." And he saith unto me, "These are the true sayings of God."
Revelation 19:9

1

Mundis dreamt about his apartment in Headquarters. He dreamt about the towering eucalyptus that he could see outside of his windows, he dreamt about his Monets and his trophy cabinet and his armchair, he wondered how the alterations were going with respect to Medusa's ensuite and he thought longingly of the extensions he would have built when the babies arrived.

He would sit on the balcony overlooking the Old City in Jerusalem and wish he was home and ache for the soft green light of the bush instead of the harsh white light of Jerusalem in mid-summer.

"No matter, not much use longing for something you could not have," Mundis would sigh and take another sip of his Pims and Dry Ginger and a nibble of the strawberry that floated in it.

Medusa was off having her hair done at 'Aliens and Green Beings Coiffures' and wouldn't be back for a while.

Mundis was beginning to suspect that Medusa really did not want children, because if she had, nothing in the heavenlies or on earth would have stopped her. Medusa could have wound even the Boss around all those little fingers of hers, but the Boss had disappointingly decreed that there was to be no breeding at this point in history, it was an all-hands-on-deck time and not one for pleasing themselves.

Mundis had noticed the look of relief that had flooded Medusa's face.

Mundis sighed again and tried not to think of rope swings hanging from trees and cubby houses in branches and small flying saucers for training purposes, you know, very little ones with leading ropes and trainer wheels.

His heart just ached for children.

Perhaps he would talk to her again and if he promised to get plenty of help and not expect her to do all the work…perhaps they could set up a nursery in the King David Hotel.

And then try and cajole the Boss into thinking along the same lines.

Mmm, now that may work, there was certainly plenty room here and he was sure Hornback had some relatives who would make very good nannies and nursery maids.

Yes, he would broach the subject again tonight after a very romantic dinner. He would make sure to comment on her hair and her nails and to whisper plenty of sweet nothings into her marvellous green ears, making sure not to get his pointy green teeth stuck in her filigree lattice-worked mother of pearl earrings.

Mundis relaxed and ordered another Pims.

Hornback shuffled away to get it.

Hornback enjoyed Jerusalem, it was not far from Egypt and he had plenty of relatives along the Nile and on his annual holiday he could be found conversing with them along the banks of the river.

Hornback in a deck chair with Panama hat, cigarette and gin and tonic, and crocodile relatives and friends sliding up on the bank whiling away the hours…

And oh boy, how those reptiles could talk, hours and hours of stories stretching back through time for centuries and centuries.

Yes, Hornback thoroughly enjoyed the Middle East. He loved the souks and the alleyways and the history.

Hornback was a great reader and had brought many of his books with him from Headquarters, and when not catering to Mundis' every need he could often be found stretched out on the roof of the King David reading and chuckling to himself.

He was at this point in time, re-reading Rudyard Kipling's *Just So Stories*. He particularly loved *How the Elephant Got his trunk* and he would tell anyone who would listen that he felt the crocodile in the story was indeed a relative of his and could still be found along the banks of the great 'grey green greasy Limpopo River all set about with fever trees'.

Hornback was also an expert storyteller and he did a great impression of the Elephant Child in the above-mentioned story. If you have not read it, get a copy; it is well worth a read.

Hornback was also waiting for children, not his own, but Mundis' children. He felt sure they would be absolutely adorable, all green and sparkly and soft and damp and he desperately craved a small green being audience for his story telling - he felt his true gifts were with small green beings.

He was a little concerned about *perhaps* wanting to eat them but would cope with that temptation when it came. Madam, he felt would not be as forgiving as Mundis, who absolutely adored Hornback.

Hornback liked Medusa but she was not the warm fuzzy creature he had wanted for his Master.

No, she was anything but warm and fuzzy. He had never seen anyone with such a temper and an ability to throw things *and* all at the same time…she was awe inspiring and Mundis and Hornback could often be found cowering behind the sofa together clutching their drinks and waiting for the furor to subside.

Lately they had taken to leaving the decanters, the ice bucket, the dry ginger ale and the tonic behind the sofa…in case they needed refills.

Still his master was happy and they were very much in love and on the whole life was good and never dull.

The all-hands-on-deck time in history was pumping up to be something quite spectacular.

Hornback was so enthralled he was taking notes and filming scenes he found particularly interesting. He could often be seen by the other reptilian creatures and green beings, who of course were all totally invisible to lesser being eyes, ambling around Jerusalem with his satchel over his shoulder containing his camcorder and Blackberry, wearing his favourite Hawaiian shirt, his dark glasses and his little peaked tourist cap to keep the sun off his delicate reptile skin.

He had quite overlooked the fact that his name was Hornback for a reason.

2

Sarah was amazed. She had never dreamt that she would receive a real life trophy award, and of Samson the Wonder Dog too.

Yes, it was a solid gold statuette of Samson sitting next to his dinner bowl smiling. Sarah had put it right next to her bedside table where she could look at it before going to bed at night and when she woke up in the morning.

Sarah had forgotten the time when she had fed Samson.

He had been banished to his kennel by Grandma Edith who was very cross because Samson had bitten Mundis' toe and had left a hole in his space boot.

Mundis had brushed it off, but Sarah had seen the wicked glint in his eyes and had followed Grandma Edith and Samson outside and had heard Grandma Edith say that he was not having dinner that night.

Samson was tied up next to his kennel and Grandma Edith had even tipped his water out.

Sarah had not agreed with this behaviour but had the sense to keep quiet about it and when Edith had gone back inside, Sarah had fed Samson and given him water and had sat by him and patted him until he fell asleep.

Samson loved Sarah and Sarah loved Samson.

Sarah did not love Grandma Edith or Mundis and could not understand why everyone made such a fuss about Mundis. To Sarah he was just a small green man who had a bad, bad feeling about him, sort of like one of the teachers at school who no one liked…but Mundis was ten hundred thousand times worse.

Sarah was rather good at numbers.

Sarah had tried to tell Grandpa how she felt about Mundis, but Grandpa only listened to Grandma and whilst he loved Sarah he simply told her she was just a child and Grandma and Grandpa knew best and Mundis was a very special visitor from outer space who was teaching them about things that will happen in the future and they must listen to him.

Sarah had sighed and had gone outside to play, but once she heard Mundis talking to another green being and she distinctly heard him say that Edith and Graeme were two of the stupidest lesser beings he had ever met and that this whole exercise was great fun because they were so silly, and Mundis and the other little green man had then rolled about on the ground laughing and holding their horrible little green tummies.

Sarah did not think that was very respectful or kind of Mundis to say, especially as Grandma and Grandpa went of their way to make him feel so special. Sarah had decided she would tell Grandpa, but she never got the chance as the next thing she knew she was in heaven and Angelo was looking after her and she was living with her little brother and sister and her tiny cousins in the large grey stone house near the water's edge.

In fact she was having such a lovely time in heaven, finding shells by the water's edge, paddling in the rock pools and playing with Lejon that she never really gave the horrible Mundis another thought. Although she did pray for Grandpa, as he definitely needed help and Angelo would take her to the banisters of heaven regularly so that she could peer down to earth and cheer Grandpa on.

There had been other prizes given at the Marriage Supper of the Lamb and Sarah had loved watching the presentations…magnificent Crowns had been presented, the Victors' Crown, for those who had withstood temptation, the Soul Winners' Crown for those who had told people about Jesus, the Crown of Righteousness for those who watched and waited for the Lord's returning and delighted in doing so, the Crown of Glory for those who looked after the flock of God and then the final Crown, the Martyrs' Crown for those who died for Jesus.

Sarah did not mind not receiving a crown; she was just thrilled to be given her statue of Samson and hear the kind words of the Bridegroom and the applause of the others at the tables.

She had curtsied politely and smiled up happily at the Bridegroom, who had hugged her again and bowed to her curtsy.

There were some however, who received nothing, the works they had done had not been in obedience to the Bridegroom but rather had just been 'good works', and were burnt up in a large bonfire in a valley to the side of the Chuppa.

Sarah noticed people looking very sad but at the same time relieved to simply be there at all…it was no light thing to be included in the Wedding Supper of the Lamb.

3

The excitement was intense, the flames reached to the heavens and Samson could not contain his joy. He ran round and round the bonfire barking and jumping and leaping for the sheer fun of it.

How good it was to be home, how good it was to sniff his kennel and to know that he did not have to sleep in it anymore but rather snuggle up to Graeme right under the covers.

Yes, Samson was one delighted dog.

The burning ceremony included every piece of Mundis memorabilia that Graeme, Vanessa and Aaron and the others could lay their hands on.

There were boxes of the stuff - Mundis coffee mugs, Mundis snow globes, Mundis t-shirts, Mundis toy spacecrafts, books about Mundis, written by Mundis, edited by Mundis and printed by Mundis.

There were Mundis teaching DVDs with Mundis walking about a large stage dressed in his space suit and digressing on "Why the Bible is a waste of time and should not be read", and Mundis teaching CDs and interviews with Mundis on both DVD and CD… Mundis answering questions about the future and giving his opinion on world events, always impeccably dressed in his green space suit.

But the best part of all was the actual burning of the ridiculous Mundis space suits with the Mundis hologram on the chest. Vanessa and the others laughed till they cried when they saw them.

There were also a few of the ridiculous Darlington Somerset books too, and they were thrown in as well, much to Graeme's delight. The very Reverend Somerset was almost on par with Mundis in Graeme's eyes.

It took a week before the place was cleansed of Mundis, and another week before it felt right to name the property and place the name on the mantelpiece in the sitting room…

"KEBAR KEBAR"

Four-year-old James had been singing the name for about a week in his high singsong voice.

Graeme had walked with the little fellow over the paddocks and smiled as he listened to him.

Kebar Kebar Kebar Kebar….

At some point in time Graeme had realised that God was speaking through this child and giving them the new name of the property.

It was such an obscure name; no one really knew where it had come from.

Graeme did some research and discovered there was a Kebar river in Ezekiel 1:1 where the Jewish exiles would meet to lament their exile.

The Jews had been forced out of Israel because of their disobedience and for them it was a time of mourning. Ezekiel the Prophet had been sent by God to speak to them and tell them to repent and to encourage them that one day they would be returned to their land, Israel.

For Graeme and the others, 'Kebar' was another type of refuge, a refuge from the Antichrist and his destructive forces.

The parallel in history is that it is in Ezekiel that God promises to restore the Jewish people to Israel, and indeed Graeme could see this is exactly what was taking place today.

Graeme also discovered that it was not only in Ezekiel that God promised to restore the Jews to Israel but also in Leviticus, Deuteronomy, Nehemiah, the Psalms, Isaiah and Jeremiah, Hosea, Micah, Zephaniah and Zechariah, but Graeme's favourite was in the book of Amos:

"Behold the days come", saith the Lord, "that the plowman shall overtake the reaper, and the treader of grapes him that sows the seed; and the mountains shall drop sweet wine, and the hills shall melt.
And I will bring again the captives of my people Israel, and they shall build the waste cities, and inhabit them; and they shall plant vineyards, and drink the wine thereof; and they shall also make

gardens and eat the fruit of them.
And I will plant them upon their land, and they shall no more be
pulled up out of their land which I have given them, saith the Lord
thy God."
Amos 9:13-15

Graeme was home and his home was not only his refuge but also a refuge for all he had brought with him from Sydney. He now no longer idolised it but humbly accepted that it was a gift from God and one that he was grateful for.

There were twelve people in all, three couples with three children between them including James, Aaron their Jewish teacher, Vanessa, Graeme and one Wonder Dog called Samson.

Graeme felt sure there were more people to come and indeed he had the room for them. He praised God that he had made those stables into living quarters all that time ago; no matter that they had been for Mundis' disciples, the Lord had known and now they were for His disciples.

There had been no reason to tell anyone in the nearest town that he was home, the property belonged outright to Graeme and was fairly self-sufficient. There were four dams on the property and two huge water tanks, and the rainfall was good as they were quite near the coast.

For food they relied on the kangaroo and the rabbit population, although what they would do when the ammunition for the rifle ran out was a bridge they had yet to cross.

Perhaps Samson would have to hone his rabbiting skills for the sake of the whole community.

The vegetables were still in the garden although many had gone to seed; still others could be saved and there seemed to be enough and for this they thanked God.

The property was well hidden and the nearest neighbours were miles away and not able to see into the property at all, so all in all it truly was a haven, a light place in a dark world.

4

S trange that anyone should find the time of 'Jacobs Trouble' to be something they would want to record on DVD.

It was very strange indeed...Not according to Hornback though, he was in his element.

Armageddon, the time when the entire world gathers against Israel in order to wipe her out, and indeed two thirds of the Jewish people in Israel are killed according to Zechariah 13.8-9:

And it shall come to pass, that in all the lands saith the Lord, two parts therein shall be cut off and die; but the third shall be left therein.
And I will bring the third part through the fire, and will refine them as silver is refined, and will try them as gold is tried, they shall call on my name, and I will hear them: I will say it is my people, and they shall say "The Lord is my God."

Armageddon was brewing, the nations were gathering and the IDF (Israeli Defence Force) were calling for those who wanted to leave to go now...to the Rose Red City of Petra.

Hornback had been recording it all and giving lectures at night. Entitled, appropriately enough, *An Evening with Hornback*, the evenings comprised a short lecture given by Hornback wearing his black horn-rimmed glasses and using his laptop to display pictures and short explanations. The functions were very well attended, refreshments were served midway and books and DVDs were sold.

There was even a very accomplished orchestra that played during the breaks; The Reptiles played hits from the last few centuries. They really got going with the *Crocodile Rock* but Hornback curtailed this as it tended to take the emphasis off the lectures.

There was time for discussion afterwards and this mainly centred around:

1. How the world will look with the Boss really in charge.
2. Would the main capital be in Jerusalem or Babylon or Rome?
3. The dispersion of green beings and what cities they will be stationed in, according to preferences...you know 1st preference, 2nd preference and so forth.

The evenings always went over schedule, as everyone was fascinated to think of a world without the Jews and with the Boss absolutely in charge. Who knows...he may even be visible to the lesser beings, and that meant that all the other green beings/fallen higher beings would be visible too!

No more sneaking round, no more masquerading as aliens, but at last lording it over these jumped up lesser beings, or at least those who have survived the so-called End of the World...

Ahh, what fun was to be had!

There was quite a heated discussion concerning what to do about the millions of spacecraft that they had amassed. The general consensus was to keep them as they were such a useful mode of transport and therefore too good to be disposed of.

Who knows...maybe they could interest the lesser being population in them and start a trend...'Forget your BMW - get a space craft!'

The possibilities were endless and the excitement palpable.

Hornback was a very persuasive speaker and nobody doubted for a minute that what he was saying would not come to pass.

Of course Hornback was in for some terrible surprises - but no use telling him or even debating with him. Hornback does not debate well, he gets all hot and bothered and tends to eat his opponents, and this makes for a very unfair and messy experience.

Well let's leave him lecturing and answering questions. Truly he is in his element, and what an opportunity for someone who up until now, has really just been Mundis' valet.

Indeed there is no accounting for hidden talents. I mean look at Hitler, he used to hang wallpaper.

5

The ammunition had run out and the rabbit population was beginning to double in size. Samson did his best but sometimes he forgot he had a job to do and ate the rabbits himself.

The Lord was faithful and vegetables grew and mushrooms were plentiful; one learnt to be very grateful for vegetables and mushrooms and to not complain.

Graeme, however, found the responsibility of so many people to weigh heavily on his mind; he should have given it all to the Lord on a regular basis...but sometimes he quite simply forgot.

One morning he had decided to go and check his rabbit traps earlier than usual, and left the house without telling anyone. He and Samson walked through the paddocks and up to the hill behind the house, and into the bush that stretched to the boundary of the property.

The bush went for quite a distance, and Graeme enjoyed the walk. The wild flowers were in bloom and the little water holes were full.

Kangaroos stopped nibbling the grass to look at him and slowly bounded away on his approach. Graeme loved the way their strong legs carried them through the undergrowth, over logs and through the trees all with such ease and grace. He thanked God for the roos and the joy they gave him. Sadly though, Graeme had not sought the Lord on this particular venture.

He walked further than he should have and found himself right at the end of the property and face to face with an armed soldier from the Global Peace Patrol.

The soldier had parked his armoured vehicle on the dirt road and had just finished relieving himself beside a tree.

He was wearing a suit very similar to the one Graeme had worn when he was part of IMP. It was pale green with the Global Peace Logo on his chest.

In fact when Graeme first saw him, his first thought had been, "But I thought all Mundis' IMP people had been killed. Who is this and where has he been hiding?"

It all happened very quickly. Graeme was asked if he had his identity chip in place and if he swore allegiance to the Global World Leader.

His answers were "no" and "no."

Graeme was quite simply shot on the spot, and I am afraid the Global Peace Patrol guard shot Samson too. Samson did not swear allegiance or have a chip either, although it was most unfair, as he was not even asked.

Had he been asked he would have said "no" and "no" too.

The guard left Graeme and Samson's bodies where they fell and drove off. He had other things to attend to besides burying dissenters.

Fortunately he was not interested in finding out if there were other dissenters; he had fallen in love with a local girl and he was quite simply too misty eyed to care about anything but her.

Those back at the farm eventually found the bodies lying where they had fallen, although Samson had managed to crawl to where Graeme lay and to rest his head on Graeme's hand.

They were buried together with honour and much sadness.

Everyone thanked God for Graeme who had indeed become the leader and the mentor that God had always meant him to be.

He and Samson were both loved and missed.

Aaron comforted the sad little group with the promise that it would not be long before they all saw each other again and what a mighty reunion that would be.

6

The Battle that the Bible calls Armageddon was in its initial stages. The nations were gearing up in the Valley of Jezreel for the final countdown against Israel, and the Jews within the city who wanted to leave were preparing to do just that.

They were loading up their cars and preparing their families for the drive to Petra, explaining to the elderly and the young that if they wanted to survive this coming war they needed to be in a place of safety.

Hornback, when onto a good thing, did not give up easily; he managed to negotiate with Mundis and Medusa to take his annual leave earlier than planned. He wanted to follow the Jews fleeing Jerusalem into the rose red city of Petra or Bozrah - whichever you wish to call it - and continue documenting.

Both Mundis and Medusa agreed. They had employed one of Hornback's cousins to fill in. Clawdia was a smaller reptile and very solicitous toward Medusa, who was at last pregnant and not feeling at all well.

(Mundis was ecstatic and had the nursery already set up and the bottles ready.)

In fact Clawdia would remain even after Hornback returned as Medusa had a sneaking suspicion that he really hadn't beaten his cannibalistic tendencies. And Medusa jolly well was not going to do this pregnancy thing again...it was horrible and really played havoc with both her work and social life.

Mundis of course wanted four children, but he would have to think again. Memories of her mother kept filtering back and *her* figure was indeed a mess.

Hornback prepared himself for the journey. He had a small back pack with some dried provisions and some warm clothes, - his Gortex anorak and his walking boots and a very warm sleeping bag, plus of course his laptop and his digital camcorder and Blackberry.

Hornback had some idea of what Petra looked like and it did not look comfortable, still he would go and document and enjoy the messy end when the Boss and army swept in and annihilated this rebellious Jewish nation once and for all.

Hornback had decided to travel to Petra in a large four wheel Volvo. The family in question did not have eight children like the usual Orthodox clans but were a smaller family with only two children and an elderly grandmother. Hornback could squash in the middle and as he would be invisible he really would not be a problem at all.

The Central Bus Station in Jerusalem was the main meeting point and it was chaos. Black-clothed people and baby strollers and luggage and talking and goodbying and crying...in short it was pandemonium.

Cars would leave before buses and were therefore parked along the roadside in preparation for the exodus.

Hornback found his lift and positioned himself comfortably in the middle. The youngest child was placed in her car seat right through him. She giggled when she saw him and said "croc, croc, croc" a few times and turned to pat his elongated face.

Her parents looked at her in surprise and could not work out where the "croc" was. They gave her a bottle with some sleeping mixture in it and prayed she would sleep for the journey, which she duly did, but only after laying her head on Hornback's neck and stroking one of his clawlike feet.

Hornback was enchanted and decided he would not allow her to be killed; he would adopt her and bring her back to Jerusalem to live and reign with him and the Boss...and he would not eat her.

NO, NO, NO!!!

If necessary he would go back to the counselling clinic at Headquarters and get some very serious counselling re eating other beings' children...it must be in his family tree somewhere along the line and therefore it was an issue that needed to be dealt with.

He took her little starfish like hand in his and patted it and sang one of his reptile lullabies to her:

"Go to sleep little lizard, go to sleeeeep,
Go to sleeeep little lizard…go to sleeeeep.
I won't eat you little lizard…. not even your ear…..
I won't eat you little lizard…..you need have noooo fear…" *

His Hebrew was not perfect, he was not the scholar Mundis was, but the effect was good and the child slept.

(*Sung to Brahms lullaby)

PART FIVE

Let not your heart be troubled: ye believe in God, believe also in me.
In My Father's house are many mansions: If it were not so I would have told you. I go to prepare a place for you.
And if I go to prepare a place for you, I will come again, and receive you unto myself; that where I am, there ye may be also.
John 14:1-4

And one of the elders answered, saying unto me, "What are these that are arrayed in white robes and whence came they?"
And I said unto him, "Sir, thou knowst." And he said to me, "These are they which came out of great tribulation, and have washed their robes, and made them white in the blood of the lamb."
Revelation 7:13-14

Verily, verily, I say unto you, he that entereth not by the door into the sheepfold, but climbeth up some other way, the same is a thief and a robber.
But he that entereth in by the door is the shepherd of the sheep.
John 10:1-2

1

There was a soft breeze blowing and the paper on the easel kept lifting up. Sarah bent down to find the blue tak so as to fasten the paper to the board.

She straightened up and surveyed her handiwork.

Not bad, she decided, she would show it to the Master tomorrow; not the Master, her beloved Lord, but her painting Master, who, whilst he had lived on earth had been an amazing artist who had been born in Europe in the late 1800s.

He had been rather unstable in his life but he had loved the Lord and sought to serve him, not always in an orthodox way but nevertheless with a willing heart, one that had also led him astray on more than one occasion.

Heaven was the very best place for this artist.

Earth had been too full of torment and the enemy's tactics had been used relentlessly against him and he, having been born when and where he had been, had absolutely no idea how to combat the onslaught.

Sarah was nearly thirteen and half now, she was tall and slim and her blonde hair was shoulder length, certainly not the little girl she had been at the rapture.

The last six and half years since that momentous event had been wonderful. Sarah had learnt so much, her mind had been exposed to the most amazing teachings and her senses stimulated beyond anything our world can imagine.

Every day was an adventure and every moment an act of worship. If she ever remembered her life on earth it was as one remembers a dream and not necessarily a good one.

Sarah however had not forgotten Graeme and she prayed for him often as she leant over the banisters of heaven and encouraged him to keep going. She did not know he had been shot; she had not been told, for her True Master wanted to surprise her.

Sarah bit her bottom lip in an effort to concentrate. She was mixing some blue and yellow pigment and needed to get just the right shade of green for the stems of the water iris she was painting.

The irises stood in a fishpond at the edge of the verandah and were magnificent, their purple and yellow flowers proudly reaching to the sky as if to say, "On earth we are beautiful, but here in heaven we are eternally magnificent."

She reached down again, lost in thought to pat Lejon who was licking her foot.

Lejon's head had grown smaller; in fact it felt like he had shrunk. Sarah looked at him and gasped.

It was not Lejon but a small staffie dog with a red coat and soft brown eyes. Sarah let out a cry…

"Samson…oh my Samson, my Wonder Dog!!!"

Samson smiled up at her and bounded into her arms.

Graeme watched from the sunroom that led onto the verandah and smiled as the tears rolled down his cheeks.

"Isn't she beautiful, Angelo?"

"She is," replied the tall higher being. "And she is clever too. Come Graeme, it is time to let her know you are here. "

"Sarah, Sarah!"

Sarah turned and there standing in the winter sunlight was a much younger Grandpa, not as she had last seen him in that ridiculous Mundis suit, but in his jeans, his riding boots and his striped shirt and holding his Akubra hat.

Sarah burst into tears, dropped poor Samson who didn't mind and ran, throwing herself into his arms.

"Oh Grandpa, oh it is you, oh, how and when, oh Grandpa…"

Nothing was said for quite some time, just a lot of hugging and crying.

Angelo looked on and a golden tear rolled down his cheek, and he thought to himself for the thousandth time, *how wonderful to be a lesser being and experience the love and the pain they go through…*

Angelo did not really envy them; he simply marvelled at them and wondered how it must feel to experience all that emotion.

Angelo just experienced total adoration for the Father, Son and Holy Spirit and indeed that was enough.

But sometimes he did wonder…

2

The higher beings sent to earth to accompany the flight into Petra were excited.

They had a sense unlike anything they had ever experienced before…a wonderful light feeling in their hearts; this was the end - or nearly the end - and soon justice would reign and sorrow and sighing would flee away.

Oh, joy! This really was it!

The higher beings knew the Scriptures, they knew the flight to Petra was one of the last things that happened before the return of Christ, they knew that very soon the Jewish lesser beings on their way to Petra would call to the Lord once they got there…

"Baruch haba B'shem Adonai" or in English, "Blessed is he who comes in the name of the Lord" - Luke 13:35

Oh Joy of Joys…they would call out and ask Christ to return, and He would come back on His White Horse a second time, and this time as conquering King and not a suffering servant…Oh, praise the Lord…

And on His White Horse no less, the one that He had been grooming especially for this day, ever since the fall of the lesser being Adam and his wife Eve.

That White Horse was the most magnificent beast.

All of the higher beings in heaven longed to see him, he however was not known to them, but only to the Lord.

This horse had been grazing in the most beautiful paddocks, roaming the hills and drinking of the streams of heaven, but not alone, always with his brothers and sisters who were also white…so no one in heaven except the Father and the Son actually knew which horse was *the one*.

Oh, what a day! What a day was coming when He, their Lord appeared out of heaven on *His* horse.

However they could not get ahead of themselves, there was still work to do and do it they must, even if they did forget occasionally and fly higher than normal and do a few loop the loops in absolute elation...What a sight they made, wonderful huge circles of light dancing above the buses and cars on their way to Petra.

Hornback was in for a surprise.

He had been spotted by one of the higher beings.

He had been spotted riding in the Volvo happily asleep with a lesser Being baby's head on his neck.

The higher being was not impressed and reached down and grabbed Hornback by the scruff of his Hawaiian shirt and quite simply hoicked him out of the car and deposited him on the side of the road where the dust from hundreds of buses and cars covered him.

Hornback was furious and not a little perplexed. He had not experienced that sort of opposition for a very long time and it was a rude reminder that perhaps the Boss was not quite as comfortable and as stable in his kingship as Hornback had thought.

Not to be outdone, Hornback quite simply disappeared into the undercarriage luggage locker of the Egged bus from Jerusalem and sulked. His Hawaiian shirt had been ripped and his pride had been severely wounded and he had left his backpack and his computer in the Volvo.

And he was missing that adorable baby lesser being who had so trustingly held his hand...he would find her and rescue her from those disgusting higher and lesser beings as soon as they arrived in Petra. And he would NOT eat her...*no, no, no.*

The adorable baby lesser being had woken up when Hornback had been hoicked out of the car and was now howling for the 'Croc'.

The higher being responsible for the hoicking was now sitting in Hornback's place making peek–a-boo faces, and the howling was soon replaced by giggles of delight.

Her parents and grandmother were all a little perplexed and wondered if perhaps they had given her a little too much sleep mixture.

Petra was getting closer. They had passed the checkpoint between

Israel and Jordan and had been amazed to see that there had been no border patrol guards and no passport checks. They had simply driven through what before had been a very lengthy process, and not one for the faint hearted.

The higher beings had dealt with the border guards and they were all fast asleep in the checkpoint offices, curled up on the floor and sleeping as they had not slept since they were babies.

On and on the convoy travelled, up the Kings Highway into Jordan and to the rose red city of Petra.

Here the cars and buses had to be abandoned and they had to walk in through the Siq, the narrow eastern entrance to the ancient capital of the Nabataeans and the place that the Lord had chosen for them, a place of safety and refuge.

3

V anessa and the others struggled on without Graeme and Samson. They really did miss them terribly.

Graeme had been such a source of strength in relation to food and water and how everything on the farm worked. Others were now taking his place but were not as well versed in traps and pumps and generators as he was. These city boys were more at home with computers, printers, Blackberrys, iPhones and iPads.

Vanessa manned the vegetable garden, fed the chooks and collected the eggs with the children. She also tended the rose garden and the graves of Graeme and Samson; the roses she had planted there were still small as the sad event had only happened a couple of months back.

Graeme in the six and half years she had known him, had become her very closest friend and confidant. They had not fallen in love but they had loved each other with a deep spiritual commitment and had they not been living at the end of the age, they probably would have married.

Vanessa was pleased they hadn't…to have lost two husbands would have been too hard, Second Coming or no Second Coming.

She brushed away her tears and watered the roses on the graves and in her concentrated state of mind she did not hear the truck that had pulled up outside the house.

She did however hear the loudspeaker and the rude voice coming through it.

"All inside and in the immediate vicinity assemble out here now!"

The small group led by Aaron and Vanessa came together and warily watched these strangely dressed men in their pale green latex suits.

Little James, who was now ten called out, "But we burnt all those Mundis suits when we got here, who are these people and why are they wearing them?"

Vanessa took him by the hand and said, "Hush, hush."

The men in the latex suits asked the group the same questions that the lone Global Peace Patrol guard had asked Graeme.

"Do you swear allegiance to the World leader and have you received the microchip that entails you to buy and sell?"

Everyone but the babies answered, "no" and "no".

The automatic rifles discharged their ammunition and before, where there had stood an alive and vibrant community, there now lay dead bodies covered in blood.

The Global Peace Patrol were neat men and they simply doused the area with petrol and set it alight and climbed back into their truck and drove home.

They all had a wedding to go to, the man who had shot Graeme and Samson was getting married that very afternoon and it was looking like it was going to be a great party.

The farm lay empty as smoke billowed upwards, and the chooks wondered who would feed them tonight.

4

Hornback was in a real pickle. He had been hoisted out of the car and then had to sit all squashed up in the luggage section of the Egged Bus. He had a sore tail; a crick in his neck and one of his teeth had been knocked loose by a falling peace of luggage.

He was not a happy reptile and the confidence and pride he had known back in Jerusalem when he had been hosting his *Evenings with Hornback* had well and truly evaporated.

He was now in the dubious position of being hoisted right out of this 'Green Being Forsaken place', whatever it was called - Petra, Bozrah, Rose Red Something - it was all the same to him.

There was not a coffee shop in sight and the lack of green beings and reptiles was truly appalling…there were not any, not even one.

Hornback was all alone and he longed for Jerusalem and the warmth and comfort of his own room at the King David. He would not even mind being in on one of Medusa's many tantrums.

He had crept out of the luggage compartment and was determined to stay very close to the walls of the Siq, where he felt he blended in. This was a lie; he did not blend in at all. In fact his loud red and yellow Hawaiian shirt made him stand out like a sore thumb, but he was far too proud to take it off, even if it was ripped.

Of course he was invisible to the other lesser beings, who couldn't see him at all unless they were under the age of two - they and every other higher being in the place, fallen or otherwise.

Hornback edged along the wall of the Siq, keeping his eyes down and his body as close to the wall as he could manage.

Of course every higher being in the area could see him, but they decided he was only one, so why bother. They would keep an eye on him; he would not be allowed to put one foot so much as out of place.

Let him document all he wanted to, he could then spend the next thousand years playing it to himself in prison...

Hornback had no idea he was going to be spending the next thousand years in prison, no idea at all. He thought he was going to be living it up in Jerusalem with Mundis and Medusa and the babies, under the benevolent eyes of the Boss.

He would have been horrified to know the truth and even more horrified to actually see the truth. His future accommodation would be nothing like he was used to - Five Star Hotels, Headquarters with all its comforts. No, the prison or dungeon he was headed for was a dreary dank place with dreadful plumbing...and worse still there was a good chance he would be sharing a room with a lot of other reptiles. Outside every door there would be a huge higher being and that higher being would be there on a roster basis with other higher beings for a thousand years, and would not be very communicative.

In any case he does not know any of this as yet, so let's just watch what he does in Petra surrounded by refugees from Jerusalem and the bordering areas.

5

James was the first to speak.

"Hey! Where did those men in the green suits go? And hey, where are we in any case?"

The small group from 'Kebar Kebar' stood in the midst of a green field surrounded by red poppies and beautiful blue cornflowers, as well as other flowers that were not recognised but were nonetheless breathtakingly lovely. The scent of those flowers was like nothing anyone had ever smelt before, amazing beyond words, intoxicatingly glorious without being overpowering.

They joined hands and wandered toward what looked like a garden wall.

It was a low sandstone wall that encompassed a sweet smelling garden with a fountain in the middle. James pushed the gate open and went in, the others following.

No one said anything, for the peace and the beauty of the place made speaking unnecessary. They all sat down on the soft grass and listened to the birds and the fountain splashing into the pool.

They could have sat there for minutes or for days. No one really knew how long it had been before they heard the gate open, and a voice full of warmth and love say...

"Welcome my Brothers and Sisters, welcome and well done, blessed are they that have come out of the Tribulation and have washed their robes in the Blood of the Lamb."

Everyone turned at once and stood to their feet, instinctively bowing low with great respect.

Aaron was the first to find his voice.

"Thank you sir, thank you for waiting for us and please sir, forgive us all for not recognising you before the rapture, all us adults that is sir, the children you know, were born after the disappearances."

The Lord threw back his head and laughed - a great happy laugh.

"That is all finished with, you are Home now and there is no condemnation for those in Me."

The small group ran as one and knelt by the scarred feet of the Master, kissing His scarred hands and stroking his wounded side, and crying tears of pure joy.

Tears of Joy are allowed in heaven…

"Come my children, come and see what I have prepared for you since the beginning of time."

And everyone rose and followed their true Master and LORD out of the Garden and further into heaven.

And thus began their new life, bigger and better than anything they had ever experienced before. The love that filled their hearts for Him and for one another and for everything that their eyes looked upon was truly miraculous, and the peace that flooded their souls was beyond our earthly comprehension, so much so that I can say no more about heaven in this book…

You will just have to wait and see for yourself when you get there.

PART SIX

Who is this that cometh from Edom, with dyed garments from Bozrah, this that is glorious in his apparel, travelling in the greatness of his strength? I that speak in righteousness, mighty to save.
Isaiah 63:1

And I will pour upon the House of David, and upon the inhabitants of Jerusalem, the spirit of grace and supplication: and they shall look upon me whom they have pierced, and they shall mourn for him, as one mourneth for his only son, and shall be in bitterness for him, as one that is in bitterness for his firstborn.
Zechariah 12:10

1

Well Hornback was having a *terrible* time.

He had not brought a tent with him and was having to share the Treasury Building in Petra with at least five Orthodox families.

The inside of the Treasury Building is not very big, that movie *Raiders of the Lost Ark* gave a false impression and Hornback had a good mind to complain to someone. However at this point in history it did not seem like a sensible idea…he had a sneaking suspicion that complaining to *anyone* was a thing of the past, and this did not make him feel warm and cosy inside.

Hornback secured a spot for himself out of the wind and curled up for a good sleep. Sadly it was not to be; the Orthodox have a lot of children, mostly under two, and a whole pack of them descended on him and wanted to play. Their parents were mystified…

"Croc, Croc!"

"Pull Croc's tail!"

"Eat his feet and poke his eyes!"

Hornback snarled and gritted his teeth. This deterred them for a little while but not for long; they would crawl away and sit and watch him and then just as he got back to sleep they would pounce and start again…

"Croc!"

"Love Croc, funny Croc."

"Keep Croc…eat him up!"

Poor Hornback, nothing he did would deter them. He would just have to wait until they went to sleep.

He got his cigarettes out and lit one and wiled away the time smoking and reading and being crawled over…although the babies found the crawling part disappointing as they just sunk into him. He was no fun to crawl over, he had no substance…well not for them, he didn't.

Eventually it was bedtime and the mothers came and collected their offspring and settled them down for the night. Hebrew lullabies filled the room and every baby drifted off to sleep.

Peace descended on the Treasury Building, the fires flickered on the walls and the whole inside took on an unearthly type of beauty. It was as though the whole place was rejoicing for what was happening; the walls of the cave and the floor and the very air that had lain undisturbed for so long and even now was witnessing what it had indeed been created for…the time of 'Jacob's Trouble' and the time of Israel's repentance.

Hornback watched and an uneasy sort of feeling descended on him and an ache began to form in his heart…he had no idea why.

But then to Hornback's dismay one of the Rabbis in the group opened a Bible and started to read from Isaiah 53;

Who hath believed our report? And to whom is the arm of the Lord revealed?

For he shall grow up before him as a tender plant, and as a root out of dry ground, he hath no form or comeliness; and when we shall see him, there is no beauty that we should desire him.

He is despised and rejected of men; a man of sorrows and acquainted with grief; and we hid as it were our faces from him; he was despised and we esteemed him not.

Surely he hath borne our griefs, and carried our sorrow; yet we did esteem him stricken, smitten of God and afflicted.

But he was wounded for our transgressions, he was bruised for our iniquities: the chastisement of our peace was upon him; and with his stripes we are healed.

All we like sheep have gone astray; we have turned everyone to his own way; and the Lord hath laid on him the iniquity of us all.

He was oppressed, and he was afflicted, yet he opened not his mouth: he is brought as a lamb to the slaughter, and as a sheep before her shearers is dumb, so he openeth not his mouth.

He was taken from prison and from judgment: and who shall declare his generation? For he was cut out of the land of the living: for the transgressions of my people was he stricken.

And he made his grave with the wicked, and with the rich in his death; because he had done no violence, neither was any deceit in his mouth.

Yet it pleased the Lord to bruise him; he hath put him to grief: when thou shalt make his soul an offering for sin, he shall see his seed, he shall prolong his days, and the pleasure of the Lord shall prosper in his hand.

He shall see the travail of his soul, and shall be satisfied: by his knowledge shall my righteous servant justify many; for he shall bear their iniquities.

Therefore will I divide him a portion with the great, and he shall divide the spoil with the strong; because he hath poured out his soul unto death: and he was numbered with the transgressors; and he bare the sin of many, and made intercession for the transgressors.

The Rabbi then, to Hornback's complete horror, began to expound upon this passage and to ask his cave-dwelling congregation who they thought the passage was talking about.

The Rabbi asked the group if they thought it was interesting that the passage talks of *All we like sheep have gone astray*. He made mention of the fact that here they were in an ancient sheep pen, Petra, and would anyone like to comment on the analogy?

Hornback reached for another cigarette and his hip flask. This was not shaping up to be the documentary he had hoped for... perhaps he should leave this dwelling and go look for his adorable baby lesser being and camp with *her* family.

Hornback decided to make the move; the conversation was becoming ridiculous, something along the lines of some guy called Yeshua coming back and saving them from the Boss and his army...

Worse still, this dude had been here before and he was born in a manger in Bethlehem and Israel didn't recognise him the first time and because of this they crucified him on a Cross...

And it got worse...once this Yeshua chap returned he would rescue the Jews, lock the Boss and his minions in a dungeon and set up the Millennial Kingdom for a thousand years and then at the end of the thousand years the Boss and the minions (that would mean Mundis, Medusa, Hornback, Clawdia and everyone else they knew) would be released for one final battle where they would again be overthrown and sent to the Lake of Fire for eternity!

This made Hornback feel really sick…he wondered if the Lake of Fire was a sort of an allegorical tropical paradise with five star resorts - or THE REAL THING?

Well, if this Yeshua dude is coming back, thought a badly shaken Hornback, perhaps he will be mighty angry with them and not feel like rescuing them at all, perhaps he will wipe the Jews out and the Boss won't have to. I certainly know how I would feel if anyone did that to me, honestly what rubbish.

And with that Hornback packed up his kit and made a move for the door. The babies were all sleeping so he was able to leave without causing any fuss.

Outside the night air was cold and Hornback immediately regretted his decision. He looked hopefully for another cave or tent in which to spend the night but was greeted with hundreds of closed flaps on hundreds of tents and when he did poke his head in, it was to see wall to wall lesser beings asleep or in the process of getting to sleep….

Hornback did not feel like being that close.

One lesser being baby did see him and instead of laughing and greeting him with joy, the child let out a roar and woke up everyone in all the adjacent tents.

Poor Hornback, he was not having a good night; the higher beings on the rocks surrounding Petra looked down on him with amusement and wisely decided to leave him alone.

"Who knows, he may hear the truth down there, not that it will do him any good, his fate was sealed when he followed the Enemy all those eons ago."

They were not to know that he had already heard the truth but had rejected it as absolute rubbish.

2

Jerusalem was encircled, the armies of the world were poised for action and Mundis was placating his pregnant wife because he was unable to procure any bananas. He tried singing that popular song, *Yes we have no bananas, we have no bananas today...*, but *Medusa was not laughing*.

She had already had one screaming fit with respect to the lack of bananas and was just gearing up for another.

Mundis was beginning to understand why none of Medusa's previous relationships had lasted; she really was very difficult...

Mundis made himself another Gin and tonic and sent a text to Hornback.

How goes it ol' friend, am missing you here. Medusa behaving very badly and situation in Jerusalem dreadful with armies all about and horrible higher beings thinking they have the upper hand - huh! We know the truth, the Boss wins - text back and tell me your news.

Mundis sighed and looked out the window. The night sky was lit by the most magnificent moon and it was easy to see the armies that encroached upon Jerusalem. All was peaceful for now but tomorrow would see a different story. Mundis had been in Jerusalem before in a time of war; it had never really disturbed his plans and he had no reason to believe this was going to be any different.

He firmly believed that very soon the Boss would be in total control and there would be no more interference from 'He who cannot be mentioned and is best left alone'.

Mundis would take Medusa back to live in Headquarters and he, Mundis would be in charge and all would be peaceful and serene and he would build that swing and that cubby house and life would be just the way he had always imagined...ah Bliss, ah double Bliss.

Mundis was just enjoying his daydream when he heard a crash from the bedroom. He got up wearily and floated in to find that

Medusa had thrown the baby cradle through the mirror and was standing on the bed threatening to skin Clawdia alive and make shoes out of her hide.

Mundis decided then and there to find those bananas.

3

"Okay, I give up" and with that Hornback did an about face and returned to the Treasury Building where, much to his horror, he found two of the hugest higher beings he had ever seen guarding the entrance.

Hornback did not even try to get in. The looks on their faces spelt certain banishment for any reptile silly enough to even attempt an entry. Hornback was beginning to have serious doubts about this; he was beginning to think that perhaps it was not going to be as cut and dried as he had thought and hoped.

Just then his iPhone beeped and Mundis' text came through. Hornback read it and did not even have the heart to reply; Mundis was having enough of a hard time with Medusa without Hornback coming in with his Isaiah 53 story and the bit about this dude called Yeshua.

No, Hornback would suffer this one out and hope against all hope that what he'd heard about the Jews being rescued and a Millennium Kingdom being established on the earth was all rubbish.

He withdrew to a safer place behind a rock, put on his Gortex anorak, lay down, curled up with head on his backpack and went to sleep, and did not wake up until the next morning when someone blew a shofar and called the people to prayer.

Hornback groaned and tried to roll over and go back to sleep, but was rudely hoicked to his feet by a very tough looking higher being who said in a most unpleasant manner, "Document this, reptile, and give it to your Boss…this is something he needs to see *and* hear."

Hornback was horrified; he had not been ordered around like this *ever*.

Still he was in no position to argue - he was surrounded by some of the fiercest looking higher beings he had ever seen.

Gold, they were, and silver, and some the most amazing green, similar to Mundis but a thousand times more vibrant, with diamond encrusted wings and headdresses…Hornback was mesmerised by their beauty and their directness; these were not the sort of beings you negotiated with.

He was handed his very own computer and digital camcorder and told to start recording, and even escorted to a higher point from where he could see all the valley encompassing Petra.

Acres of tents filled his vision, and thousands of people gathered beneath him. The meeting was conducted by the chief Orthodox Rabbi of Jerusalem and went as follows…

"My People, we are here in the valley of Bozrah, the very same one spoken of in Isaiah 63.

My people, it is my belief we are at the very End of the Age and we need to repent. We need to call upon our God as we have never called on Him before. We need to call on Him as Daniel called upon Him in Chapter 9 and the Lord heard Daniel and granted him a vision.

O my people, we need more than a vision; we need to call to Yeshua and invite Him to come back to Israel. We need to seek his forgiveness for not recognising Him before and to mourn before Him as one mourns for an only son…as it says will we do in Zechariah 12:10.

My people, join with me as we call upon Yeshua…baruch haba b'shem Adonai."

And with that a cloud of grief descended upon the gathering as men, women and children grouped together in families and greater families and as a body fell to the ground and wept for Yeshua.

Yeshua - who they and their ancestors had dismissed so many centuries before.

Hornback recorded all this; even though his claws were shaking and the sweat was dripping from his brow, he recorded all that he could and then he saved and stored it in his device.

When he was allowed to finish, he fell on all fours and wept for himself and the foolishness of his own heart and the Eternity that now stretched before him, devoid of all beauty and comfort and light.

4

"Yes we have no bananas, we have no bananas todaaaaayyyy…"
Mundis was so relived to get away from the screaming Medusa that he was singing at the top of his voice. He was flying through the streets of a seemingly deserted Jerusalem in his smallest invisible alien craft looking for bananas; not an easy feat as the city had been in a state of siege for weeks now and bananas had not been a high priority on anyone's list.

Perhaps he should forget Jerusalem and fly to Cyprus, now they may have bananas…

Good thinking, Mundis, said Mundis to himself. He lifted the controls and the craft gained altitude and rose far above the city of Jerusalem and the armies of the world.

Mundis was not worried about leaving Medusa alone; she was one capable lady and the Boss was there and all his forces and Medusa could not have been in better hands.

Mundis could not see the mighty army of heaven encamped further back and above the armies of the world. Mundis could not see them at all; they were again shrouded in their diamond dust cloaks awaiting the call from 'He who cannot be mentioned and is best left alone'.

In anticipation of the call they had waited for since the fall of Man in the Garden of Eden, the call that would end this age and begin the next.

There was a marvellous feeling of excitement in the forces of heaven.

Mundis sensed none of this, he was too busy singing and thinking about bananas…

"Yes, we have no bananas, we have no bananas today…"

Perhaps he and Medusa's baby was going to be a yellow being instead of a green being?

He laughed out loud at the thought of having a yellow banana-like baby.

5

Hornback didn't see what happened next but when he opened his eyes he was no longer on a cliff overlooking Petra but he was back outside the King David Hotel in Jerusalem opposite the YMCA building and standing in a deserted street.

He was clutching his digital camcorder and his computer and he was still wearing his Gortex anorak with his Hawaiian shirt under it, and the tears were still on his cheeks and his hands were still shaking.

He stumbled into the reception area and took the lift up to the Presidential suite; too shaky to float...in his state he may end up anywhere.

He even knocked on the door and was ushered into the room by a tearful and exhausted Clawdia who was wearing every item of clothing she owned in case Medusa fulfilled her promise and skinned her for shoes.

Hornback sank into the nearest sofa, and clutching his computer and digital camcorder to his chest, fell fast asleep.

Clawdia had the good sense to leave him alone and retire to her own room. Medusa was at last asleep and everything was as peaceful as it could possibly be, so we shall leave them there because what happens next is going to be anything but peaceful, or for that matter, comfortable.

6

They were grieving and mourning, just as He had told them they would when He had spoken to them through Zechariah the Prophet.

He came to earth so softly and so gently that on one heard. He would not come that way when He returned to Jerusalem, but Jerusalem was still in the future, the very, very, very near future, but the future nonetheless.

He was amongst them and they did not realise. He stood in their midst and no one saw. His garments were stained with Blood, His Blood.

He had walked into Petra, strode actually in great strength, but they were so overcome with grief and sorrow that it was not until He was in the midst of them that they noticed.

Slowly they became aware of His presence.

A holy awe filled Petra and a deep silence enveloped the people. One by one they knelt in adoration, much like the shepherds and the Magi who came to worship Him at His birth in Bethlehem.

He spread His arms out wide and smiled at His people and spoke soft words to them. He was not angry, just so, so happy to be back with them…and even happier to think that they were back with Him, as He had always known they would be…

and yet,

and yet,

it had been such a long time coming.

PART SEVEN

And I saw heaven opened, and behold a white horse; and he that sat there upon him was called Faithful and True, and in righteousness he doth judge and make war.

His eyes were as a flame of fire, and on his head were many crowns; and he had a name written, but no man knew but he himself.

And he was clothed with a vesture dipped in blood: and his name is called the word of God.

And the armies which were in heaven followed him upon white horses, clothed in fine linen, white and clean.

And out of His mouth goeth a sharp sword, and with it he should smite the nations: and he shall rule them with a rod of iron: and he treadeth the winepress of the fierceness and wrath of Almighty God.

And he hath on his vesture and on his thigh a name written,
KING OF KINGS AND LORD OF LORDS.

Revelation 19:11-16

1

Cyprus was good for the bananas.

Mundis had parked his craft on the roof of a Supermarket; descended through the roof, hovered above the banana section and taken every banana in the tray…he had brought a very big bag with him.

It was after midnight and the store was deserted so the sudden disappearance of the bananas was not a major drama.

He then floated back up through the roof where he deposited all his stolen goods on the back seat, even into the expectant baby green being capsule, and prepared to go home.

On second thoughts, why not find a bar and grab a drink before going home…

I mean, home really was not that much fun at the moment, screaming wife, terrified Clawdia and no Hornback…yep, he would go get a drink.

Mundis found a seedy bar in downtown Limassol, where he proceeded to down one Gin and Tonic after another…not that it had any effect, just sort of relaxed him up a bit and got him in the mood for some serious green being eyeing.

The place was fit to bursting, lesser beings, green beings, a few reptiles, all in the mood for a good night out.

Mundis, however, much to his surprise, sensed that he just did not have it in him anymore. He was a married green being and it seemed that Medusa for all her impossible ways, really was the one for him and therefore he would go home and take the bananas with him.

He was just lifting off the seat and preparing to go through the ceiling when he overheard a most curious remark.

"Hornback returned to Jerusalem and he has a recording of what has been happening in Petra. He can't show it, he is too upset, just sits on the sofa and mumbles and cries and clutches his digital camcorder and computer. Clawdia is trying to reach him but he won't speak to anyone."

Mundis did a double take and stared hard at the reptile speaking... who didn't notice him and just ordered another drink.

Mundis' heart skipped a beat and he left very speedily...straight through the ceiling in record time.

2

I t was pitch black as Mundis in his little craft, lifted up into the atmosphere. The smell of bananas was overpowering but Mundis was not thinking about bananas, he was thinking about the reptile at the bar's words about Hornback.

"Hornback is in Jerusalem and has a recording of what has been happening in Petra…"

So, thought Mundis, *what has been happening in Petra? And why was it so bad that Hornback, couldn't talk about it?*

Mundis trusted Hornback.

Hornback, since Mundis' marriage to Medusa, had become a closer friend than ever before. He and Hornback had spent quite a few nights behind the sofa with the decanters of drink whilst Medusa yelled and screamed and threw things about…

Yes, Hornback was now much more than just his valet reptile - he was his close friend and confidant.

Mundis took the little craft up to full speed and sped across the sky toward Israel.

There was not a star in the sky and the moon was nowhere to be seen and there were no clouds either. Mundis was feeling decidedly shaken, in fact he had not felt this bad since…well he couldn't remember when he had felt like this before. In fact he was not sure if he had ever felt like this…ever.

He briefly wondered where the stars were and the moon for that matter, but was in such inner turmoil that all he could think of was getting back to Jerusalem and finding out what was going on.

Mundis had never read the Bible. He had burnt a few in his time but no, he had never read it…hence he did not know the Scripture,

Immediately after the tribulation of those days shall the sun be darkened, and the moon shall not give her light, and the stars shall

fall from heaven, and the powers of the heavens shall be shaken.
Matthew 24:29

If he had known that scripture he then would have been familiar with the second line of that verse...

And then shall appear the sign of the Son of man in heaven: and then shall all the tribes of the earth mourn, and they shall see the Son of man coming in the clouds of heaven with power and great glory.
Matthew 24:30

Well, it is just as well Mundis didn't know that because if he had, he certainly would not have been streaking across the very black sky in his little space craft, but hiding under a rock or in a cave where all the other unrepentant lesser beings and lost higher fallen beings were going to be...very soon.

Mundis was passing over the Mediterranean Sea now; he leaned over to look down and could see nothing, but was surprised at what he was hearing...

A roaring noise, never in his memory - which one had to remember spans centuries of earthly history - never had he heard the sea make that extraordinary noise! The only sound he could remotely liken it to was one of those huge dinosaurs that Mundis remembered, a huge dinosaur in tremendous pain and agony...it was an awful sound.

Again if Mundis had known the Scriptures he would have had more cause to be concerned....

And there shall be signs in the sun, and in the moon and in the stars; and upon the earth the distress of nations, the seas and the waves roaring
Luke 21:25

Mundis flew on. Time passed.

His eyes fell on the digital time on the control panel in his craft. It was 5.15 in the morning...

Mundis gasped and wondered where the sun was. The earth

below him was black and the heavens above him even blacker. It was freezing cold and Mundis wished he had brought an anorak with him, and his warm woolly hat with his sheepskin gloves.

He reached forward and put the heating on; it made some difference but not much. His toes were beginning to freeze and that was through his new very expensive Italian leather shoes and his pure wool merino socks.

It was so black that Mundis had to navigate using his GPS system. He could not see familiar landmarks; he could not see anything.

Mundis began to panic, and the smell he exuded completely overpowered the bananas. He reached for his iPhone and punched in Hornback's number…no answer.

He tried Medusa; he was really panicking now…no answer.

He tried the Boss…now this was a real step in courage - if you rang the Boss the chances were you would be given countless assignments to perform and with this is mind…well, you just did not ring the Boss - he rang you.

Mundis in desperation punched the Boss' number in, and received this reply:

"The number you have called has been disconnected… 6666666666"

3

The craft's GPS system told Mundis that he was approximately over The King David Hotel. Mundis prepared to land.

The craft descended and descended and descended...and landed on a pile of rubble that used to be The King David Hotel.

Mundis emerged, and was immediately handcuffed to a horribly fierce and most aggressive higher being who rudely announced that if Mundis kept his eyes open he was about to see the most amazing fireworks display he had ever seen.

Mundis was speechless. Every ounce of 'joie de vivre' left him, and as the earth was black and the heavens were black, so the true state of Mundis' spirit was revealed - black.

He was helpless, incarcerated by a being twenty times his size. Mundis had forgotten that once he used to be exactly the same size and indeed was just as fierce and as zealous for his Lord; but since he had rebelled and turned the other way and followed the wrong Boss, in doing so his spirit and his stature had shrunk.

Maybe I mentioned this before, but no matter, it deserves to be mentioned again, for this is what happens to all beings, higher or lesser if they rebel against He *"...which made heaven, and earth, the sea, and all that therein is: which keepeth true forever."* Psalm 146:6

We shrink, and become less than what we are meant to be.

Mundis and the gargantuan higher being stood there and stared up into the heavens.

Mundis could hear cries for help, he could hear groaning and sobbing, but he could not see a thing except the huge being that had captured him and that was only because he was right on top of him.

Suddenly the sky lit up with a flash of the brightest lightening Mundis had ever seen, splitting the sky from east to west. Mundis could see now, he could see destruction everywhere - countless green beings and reptiles in the hands of huge higher beings, lesser beings cowering under the rubble and crying for mercy, chaos everywhere.

And then his eyes lifted to the heavens and he saw heaven open and there in front of all the earth was He who had been sent to earth by 'He who cannot be mentioned and is best left alone'. He was seated on a horse, a white horse and behind were all the armies of heaven…

And I saw heaven opened, and behold a white horse; and he that sat upon him was called Faithful and True, and in righteousness he doth judge and make war. Revelation 19:11

Mundis sank to his knees and wept for all he was about to lose and indeed had already lost. He was not repentant, that was a gift that had been denied him since the fall of man and the decision he had made to rebel.

He was just very, very sorry for himself and terrified of what the future held.

4

"Hallelujah! Hallelujah! Hallelujah!
For the Lord God omnipotent reigneth…
The kingdom of this world
Is become the kingdom of our Lord,
And of his Christ;
And he shall reign for ever and ever…
King of Kings! And Lord of Lords!
Hallelujah…"

As you can imagine, Mundis was not singing this song…
But every higher being on the earth was and every lesser being who had accepted the Son of Man's death on the cross for their sins was joining in…even if they thought they didn't know the words, they found to their absolute amazement that they did. The words just seemed to flow from their spirits and rise into the heavens, and all with such incredible power and majesty.

Everything was visible now; the light from Yeshua lit up the entire earth.

Mundis could see very plainly what was about to take place… and it filled him with added terror and horror.

A huge higher being had descended from heaven holding a key and a great chain.

He gave a great shout and every higher being with a captive reptile or green being proceeded toward what is known as the Abyss…they came from all over the earth.

Mundis' legs trembled as he was propelled on. The Abyss was opened and Mundis could see stairs going down into deep darkness, down and down and down, winding like a great python curled around the bowels of the earth.

Mundis could see the Boss being pushed in first. How small and undignified he looked; Mundis could not believe he was the same being who had controlled all the world…or so he had thought. And then every other green being and reptile that Mundis had ever known in all the ages he had lived, followed, it was a dreary and dreadful descent.

Soon it was Mundis' turn to descend into the Abyss. He stumbled forward and scraped the leather of the toe of one his new Italian shoes. He cursed and wondered if there were shops and galleries where he was headed so as to get scuff polish, and for one brief moment he also pondered on the décor down there, but then thought again.

He began his descent and had the sudden realisation that what was happening to him now was exactly what he had known deep, deep, deep down would happen to him all along. He *had* rebelled and followed the Boss.

He was a created being and had been all along, but he had been created by 'He who cannot be mentioned and is best left alone' and not by the Boss…he had just allowed the Boss to mess with what was already a perfect creation and the end result was to be eternal damnation.

Again this is not to say he was repentant, just very, very sorry for himself, and as usual Mundis was foremost on his own mind…yes even before Medusa and the baby and Hornback.

Polonius' advice to his son Laertes in Shakespeare's 'Hamlet' could have quite as easily been given to Mundis… *"To* thine own self be true."

Mundis was exceedingly true to his own selfish self.

EPILOGUE

And the Lord shall make thee the head, and not the tail; and thou shall be above only, and thou shall not be beneath; if thou hearken unto the commandments of the Lord thy God, which I commanded thee this day, to observe and to do them.
Deuteronomy 28:13

The millennium had begun and the time of Jacob's Trouble was over. The Jewish Nation of Israel was at last to be the head and not the tail and all the earth would rejoice in her greatness.

Yeshua ruled from Jerusalem and all was peaceful, although there was an awful lot of cleaning up to do.

However...can you believe this...there will be those in the millennium who will rebel against God...AGAIN.

These rebellious lesser beings will be some of the children of the believers who go through into the millennium from the tribulation. Their parents obviously will not have been martyred during this time; they will have survived the horrors and will have been protected by a gracious and forgiving God...although thousands would have died around them, both believers and unbelievers.

Satan and his hordes will be let out of the Abyss after a thousand years so as to join with these rebellious lesser beings and fight against God.

Personally I cannot think of anything sillier than fighting against God.

And why would God let Satan out even for a short time?

Because He has to show once and for all that He is in charge and there is no room for rebellion on His earth against Him.

This time the war will be very short indeed. Satan and his demons and the lesser beings who rebelled, will be completely overthrown and cast into the Lake of Fire.

This is the time when all Mundis' fears about fire and lakes will come to fruition.

He *will* be reunited with Edith, but this will be one meeting neither will enjoy…

And whoever was not found in the book of life was cast into the Lake of Fire.
Revelation 20:15